Leonard Lamensdorf

Kane's
WORLD

a novel by
LEONARD
LAMENSDORF

SIMON AND SCHUSTER
New York

First printing

Library of Congress Catalog Card Number: 68–21309
Designed by Richard Karwoski
Manufactured in the United States of America
By H. Wolff, New York

To Joyce

Kane's
WORLD

1

I did not look at Miss Fritch when I handed her the memos—I knew she would be frowning at my scribbled notes. Miss Fritch preferred to have me dictate my correspondence, but I couldn't overcome my old lawyer's habit of writing things down on long yellow legal foolscap.

The phone rang. Miss Fritch reached for it, but I was quicker.

"Mr. Ellison?"

"Right."

"It's McNeill, Mr. Ellison. Western Machine is supposed to move into their space today, but the partitions aren't finished and we were wondering whether—"

"Isn't this something you can work out yourself?"

"Well, I suppose so—"

"Then do it."

I handed the phone to Miss Fritch, who placed it on the receiver with a look that was almost approving.

"All right, Miss Fritch, I'll dictate a few letters." I knew that would please her, and after all, the letters had to be written.

But the phone was ringing again.

"It's Mr. Hanson," the switchboard operator told me. "From the bank."

"Hello, Vern."

"Good morning, Eddie. Listen, Carrelli is in for a payout— almost three million dollars. Is it all right to put it through?"

"I believe I signed the approval, Vern."

"You did. But the way things have been going with Carrelli, I just wanted to be certain you hadn't changed your mind."

"I think Carrelli is on his best behavior now."

"I hope you're right."

"Don't worry, Vern, we're watching every move he makes."

"Good, Eddie. Very good. Well, thanks. That's all I wanted to know."

I dictated a few letters to Miss Fritch, then dismissed her. She gathered up my memos and marched from the room. The finished papers, perfectly typed, would be back on my desk long before I wanted to see them again.

Once again the phone rang. Instead of answering it, I flicked up the key on my intercom. "Hold my calls," I said. I almost added, "I'm busy," but that wasn't necessary. No explanations were necessary here. No explanations were expected. Not at Kane Enterprises.

I had the whole machine well tuned and working smoothly. Everything and everybody. It was a good feeling, but a strange one. All these people taking my orders, all this money changing hands at my direction.

It was a joke. I think Norman would have appreciated it. I can fool them, Norman, but not you. You knew me too well.

I looked around the room while I thought of Norman Kane. I tried to imagine how he would feel if he were sitting across from me, watching me command his empire.

What an empire! Paper, piles of it: notes, stocks, debentures, contracts, leases, mortgages. The whole bit—but mostly Norman. Norman was the empire. Norman built it. Without him it's only land and buildings, surrounded by screaming partners, mumbling lawyers, squirming accountants and gloomy bankers. Norman made it a kingdom.

I had a vision of Norman then—not the brilliant financier, but the boy I went to college with—a fuzzy-haired, sloppy kid, toting a laughably large briefcase. I heard him too, quoting Montaigne in West Side accents that were weirdly inappropriate, but remarkably compelling—saw him hitting a tennis ball as if his racket were a fly swatter, but getting the ball over the net somehow. On the other side, a pretty girl was laughing at him—Frieda. But in a second, she was running after the ball. Her form was beautiful, but Norman kept her running.

I looked down at my legal pad. Unconsciously, I had been scribbling random numbers—2 . . . 0 . . . 6 . . . "206" . . . Not random, after all: the address of Norman's first La Salle street office building. And there he was again—older, now, neater. But still exuberant. Clapping his hands with pleasure, exulting aloud the minute we finished signing the papers that made the building his. Well, not his alone. Norman had his syndicates of investors, at first small, then large, then relatively small again. Finally just a few men, each investing up to a million dollars or more. But Norman ran the show. From the time he bought his first small store building until he built Lake Shore Plaza, Norman was in control. Completely. He could not have lived any other way.

Well, then, what would Norman think? I had to admit I didn't know. I was his lawyer. He claimed I was his friend. Perhaps. Usually he confided in me, but not always. Even when he did, he was already thinking of something else, so that his words were often jumbled, the sentences composed of bits and pieces of what he was supposed to be explaining and other fragments from what he was really thinking.

Anyway, here I was, in Norman's office, working at Norman's desk. My own office was at the other end of the Loop: Hardwick, Burns, Ellison and Dean, attorneys-at-law. Thirty senior and junior partners and thirty-five associates. One of the oldest and most distinguished firms in the city. I was a senior partner.

I smiled, thinking of my partners. They had never been

very happy about my representing Norman Kane. No one had dared to say anything to me directly, but their disapproval was evident. What did a firm that represented Standard Oil, U.S. Steel and United Airlines need with Norman Kane?

Perhaps they didn't need him. I did. I was never quite sure why, but there was something about him—something special. He annoyed me many times. More than once I seriously considered telling him to take his business elsewhere. That would have pleased my partners. Maybe that's why I didn't do it. Norman provided the one little corner of my life that Hardwick, Burns, Ellison and Dean didn't own.

Still, when everything crashed for Norman, I realized I couldn't handle things from my own office. I told my law partners that someone else would have to take over my practice while I settled Norman's affairs. They weren't too happy about that. But they were relieved when I said I was moving temporarily to Norman's office in the Cormack Tower. At least they would be spared the presence of Norman's volatile partners on their own premises.

Each morning on my way to work I crossed La Salle Street; Norman's street. Past two of his buildings, and then on to the Cormack Tower. Norman tried to buy it many times, but the family wouldn't sell. He had to be content to lease his office there.

Up in the elevators to the forty-third floor. Then walk up to the forty-fourth. Norman's floor—his alone. A penthouse built on top of the Cormack Tower to Norman's design. It was annoying to have to walk up the final floor, but still it was unique.

I had been there for months, but each day when I walked in, everything seemed as it had always been. The elegant reception room, the beautiful receptionist smiling impersonally, then on along the carpeted corridors, past the rows of desks, a few smiles, the others intent upon their tasks. An illusion: Norman is still alive. When I enter his office, he'll be there, bounding up from the huge desk to greet me, unconsciously smoothing the hair over his bald spot, stretching up to his full five feet seven, shoulders back, smiling wryly.

Miss Fritch greeting me soberly, as always. Trim, prim,

homely, but a nice figure. Quite a difference from the beauties in the outer office. Norman's handpicked harem— most of them smart, but all of them good-looking. Norman liked to be surrounded by good-looking women. There were rumors. Norman loved the rumors. Whether he loved the women, I may never know. He implied that he did, but Norman was great at innuendo.

Fritchie up on her feet and opening the door for me. Then inside. But no Norman. A magnificent stage, but no magician. Not even Norman can make himself reappear.

Still, the room is impressive. Forty feet long and forty feet wide. Six sets of French windows in the room, eight feet high, two in each of three walls. Often I walked straight ahead to the most distant pair, pushed them open and walked out on the balcony. It was broad and surrounded by an ornate balustrade. Even the balcony was fully equipped: chairs, a table, small trees planted in round concrete pots, even a telephone and an intercom. I scanned the skyline as Norman must have done. I could see as far north as Milwaukee, as far south as Gary. Perhaps it was an illusion. One thing was certain. From this spot I could see a dozen buildings Norman had built. Millions of square feet of offices and apartments. All rather new, all gleaming in the sun. But still no Norman.

I walked back into the office, closed the French windows behind me and took my unaccustomed place at Norman's desk.

———◆———

Norman sat here, in this chair, the day Ernest Barry brought him his biggest deal. Barry arrived without an appointment, which Norman found annoying. Impulsive action was for Norman Kane, not for other people. But he knew Barry wouldn't appear—just like that—unless something was up. Something big. Norman's blood raced at the thought. Big deals, even screwy ones, fascinated him. He was attuned to big numbers. Even when he had grown accustomed to gigantic transactions, the phrase "a million dollars" mumbled in an adjoining booth in a restaurant was enough to alert his senses.

Norman kept Barry waiting while he called Miss Fritch into his office. "Did he say what he wanted?"

"No, Mr. Kane."

Norman sat staring at her while he tried to puzzle it out. The Cormack Tower? No, the Cormacks never worked with brokers. A dozen other possibilities flickered through his mind and he rejected them all. It had to be something special.

Miss Fritch stood before his desk, waiting, her pale-green stenographer's pad held to her breast. Another idea, totally unrelated to Ernest Barry, skipped into a corner of Norman's brain. He glanced from Miss Fritch to the couch and back again. That voluptuous body under the plain, bland face.

Suddenly Norman was angry. "Oh, goddamn it, send Barry in." He was still fuming when Ernest Barry entered the room, but not too preoccupied to flip up the key on his intercom. Miss Fritch, in the outer office, realized at once that she was expected to transcribe the meeting.

The sight of Ernest Barry served only to deepen Norman's unhappiness. Barry was tall, slender and distinguished, with wavy hair, graying at the sideburns, and bright blue eyes. His mellifluous voice was yet another irritant.

"Norman, how splendid to see you again," he intoned.

Norman did not rise. Why match his five feet seven inches against the other man's six feet two? Barry seemed not to notice. He walked to the desk and reached across it to grasp Norman's hand. At this range, Norman was subjected to the broker's masculine cologne. Flinching, he barely noticed the crisp grip that crushed his fingers.

"Sit down, Barry. How are you?"

"Fine, Norman, just fine. Happy to see you looking so well." Somehow this innocuous compliment almost unnerved Norman Kane.

"You're looking well yourself, Ernie—" Norman knew Barry hated this nickname—"but then you always do."

"Why, thank you, old boy."

"Sure. One big deal a year and you can spend the rest of your time sunning at Palm Beach."

"Oh, come now. Still angry about the Lamson Building?"

"Damn right. You should have brought that deal to me."

"How could I, Norman? You know I had to offer it to Lamson's grandson."

"Balls! Lamson's been dead for fifteen years. If he wanted his grandson to have the building, why didn't he give it to him?"

"Norman, the boy was only nineteen when the old man died."

"Oh, hell, we've had this same discussion a hundred times."

"Look, Norman, I couldn't deliver that deal, but don't forget I'm the guy who brought you 206 South La Salle."

Norman literally snorted. "Sure, you're the guy who brought me 206 South La Salle—after every other investor in town turned it down. And who made it work, me or you? Who found the cancellation clause in all those old leases that let me renegotiate the terms? Who got the new long-term financing and the short-term bank loan? Who, Ernie? Me or you?"

"You, of course, Norman."

"That's what I love about brokers. All you do is drop a deal on a guy's doorstep and you earn a fat commission. Meanwhile I'm spitting blood to make it work."

Barry laughed evenly, twinkling his blue eyes and flashing Chiclet-toned teeth. "OK, Norman. All brokers are parasites. Right? Do you want to hear what this parasite is selling, or not?"

Norman was silent.

"Seriously, Norman, I do have a deal for you."

"Bring it to Lamson's grandson."

"Too big. This one takes your touch."

"Balls."

"I'm not conning you." Barry stood up suddenly. "Come over here, Norman, let me show you something." The broker stepped to the French windows at the east end of the room and pushed them open.

"It's windy out there," Norman said.

Barry laughed. "Damned if I know why you built this balcony. I'll bet you never use it." He walked to the stone balustrade. Norman advanced only as far as the threshold. It was a few inches higher than the balcony and it narrowed his height disadvantage. The balcony was windswept, and although the breeze did not dislodge Barry's silvery locks, Norman was certain it would ruffle his own thinning hair, perhaps even reveal the bald spot his barber had carefully covered that morning. Despite his irritation, he remembered to flick the "on" button of the balcony intercom, hoping the wind would not swallow Barry's words.

Barry gestured impatiently. "Come here, Norman. You can't see a damn thing from that doorway."

Norman sighed and walked to Barry's side. Sure enough, the wind spun his hair into his eyes. Grimacing, he tried to smooth it down over his bald spot, but the persistent breeze defeated him.

"Over there, Norman, beyond the Palmolive Building— east of the Drake where the drive curves sharply, that's 191- 231 East Lake Shore Drive. You can buy the entire parcel right through to Walton Street."

Norman leaned forward involuntarily, even forgetting his wildly whipping hair. "That's the Kincaid property."

"Right."

"But the estate's been in the courts for years. You can't get clear title."

"Wrong."

"Wrong?"

"You heard me. My friend Charlie Ross at Laffler, Ross and White tells me the heirs have agreed to a settlement. And the settlement requires a sale of the property."

"Are you sure?"

"Look, Norman, I'm not here to waste your time or mine. Ross phoned me this morning and I came right over to see you. If you hadn't kept me waiting in your reception room, I could have told you an hour ago."

"Who knows?"

"Knows what?"

"About the settlement?"

"The lawyers and the heirs. Norman, the timing is perfect. They just decided to sell. If you jump right in waving a certi- fied check, you'll walk away with the property."

"How much do they want?"

"They haven't set a price. You'll have to come up with an

14

offer—make it all cash, Norman, don't screw around. Those characters don't know from options, purchase-money mortgages and crap like that." (Norman noted that when he was excited, Ernest Barry talked more State Street than Harvard Yard.)

"What do you think, Ernie? What would you offer?"

The broker hesitated. "Down at 1010 Lake Shore they paid seven million dollars for a piece not half as good or half as big. I think you'll have to offer fifteen million to take it."

"In cash? Are you out of your fucking mind? Where do you think I can get fifteen million bucks cold cash?"

Barry smiled. "I'm just a humble broker; you're the financier."

"Who else knows about this?"

"You asked me that, Norman." Barry frowned. "I swear I haven't told a soul."

"Not even your partner?"

"Are you mad? I haven't told anyone."

"What do you want, Ernie?"

"A piece of the action."

"How big?"

"You tell me, Norman."

"No, you tell me."

"Five per cent of the equity."

Norman laughed.

"Why not?"

"Look, Ernie, to make this deal pay, I'll have to build at least two thousand apartments. That's ten thousand rooms at five thousand dollars a room which comes to fifty million—plus the land. Sixty-five million, Ernie. You want five per cent of that?"

"You're exaggerating, Norman. You won't build that many units and you won't spend that much money."

"How much will it cost?"

"Maybe forty million."

"I repeat my question."

"Just five per cent of the equity, Norman. You won't have forty million cash in the deal."

Listen, shmuck, Norman thought, *if I can help it I won't have a dime in the deal.* But it was stupid to argue with Barry

15

now. Norman smiled and said, "We'll work things out if and when I get the property."

Barry hesitated. "All right, Norman, you know I trust you."

"Bullshit," said Norman. "But I ain't gonna screw you. It don't pay. Now leave me alone, Ernie. I got to figure this one out."

"I'll make an appointment for you with the owners."

"Do you know the Kincaids?"

"I've been introduced to them."

"Then forget it. Anyway, I don't need an introduction. I need an angle." Norman turned and re-entered his office. He stood at his desk, unconsciously smoothing his hair while his mind raced. He moved to pick up his phone, and was shocked to see Ernest Barry in his line of vision. He recoiled and almost stumbled over his own chair.

Barry was laughing. "Norman, you forgot all about me."

"Don't be ridiculous," Norman protested. Then he was angry. "Listen, Barry, you want me to make this deal, give me room to breathe. You delivered your message, now let me get to work."

Barry flushed at the abrupt dismissal. Still, he knew there were few men with the resources and temperament for this deal, and despite his coarseness, Norman Kane was probably the most competent among them. Barry had hoped to reach a firm understanding regarding his compensation, but that seemed impossible now. Kane would chisel him but not cut him out altogether. Not if he wanted to continue doing business in Chicago.

"You're still standing there, pal."

Barry flushed again. He, too, had drifted into a reverie. "Sorry, Norman. I'm on my way. Let me know if I can help."

Norman nodded absently. "Thanks," he mumbled, eager to have Barry out of the room. "Thanks for bringing me the news."

The instant the broker was gone, Norman grabbed the telephone. It was already ringing. "Goddamn it," he screamed into the phone, "give me a line!"

Miss Fritch's voice did not waver. "Alan Hughes is calling from New York."

"Goddamn it," Norman roared even louder. But now a new thought was struggling with the old: What did Hughes want? He seldom called, and when he did, it was usually important.

Norman sighed deeply at the perversity of things and people. "Put Hughes on," he said in a subdued voice.

Hughes' voice was almost a duplicate of Ernest Barry's: cool, modulated and controlled. Norman had not noticed the resemblance before, perhaps because he had never spoken to the two men in such rapid sequence.

"Good morning, Norman. Alan Hughes in New York."

Of course, you idiot, Norman thought, *you've already been announced.*

"How are you, Norman?"

"Splendid, just splendid. And you?" The exchange of pleasantries was exasperating but essential.

"Fine, Norman, and happy to hear you sound so cheerful. Tell me, have you heard from Ernest Barry lately?"

"Aha!" said Norman.

"What?"

"Nothing, Alan. Nothing at all. What about Barry?"

"I simply asked whether you've heard from him."

"Why the sudden interest in Barry? I didn't know you were friends."

Hughes' voice betrayed no irritation. "I'm not interested in Ernest Barry. I'm interested in you."

"Oh?"

"Barry called this morning with a proposition he wants me to submit to Leventhal and Company. I asked him why he didn't talk to you, since you're in Chicago. Barry said you were too busy, but the more I thought about it, the more convinced I became that the deal exactly suited you. I decided to call you first on the outside chance you might be interested."

"Very kind of you, Alan." Norman knew Hughes was bluffing; Leventhal couldn't possibly handle the deal.

"Not at all, Norman. It seems like a natural."

"What seems like a natural?"

"The Kincaid property on Lake Shore Drive."

"What about it?"

"It's for sale, Norman."

"Really? Since when? I understand the estate will be in the courts for years."

"No. It's all being settled right now. The heirs want to sell."

"Does Barry have an exclusive?"

There was a pause. "I don't think so, but I don't believe anyone else knows about it yet. Barry wants a quick answer from Leventhal."

"What did you tell him?"

"I said I'd let him know."

"Good. Terrific. Call him tomorrow and say your people are interested."

"My people?"

"He doesn't have to know I'm your people."

"I suppose not." Hughes sounded dubious.

"You have nothing to lose, Alan. We both know Leventhal can't handle it, and I can. You keep Barry on the hook while I buy the property. He likes to think he has two pigeons."

"Two? Who's the other one?"

"Me."

"I don't get it."

"Barry walked out of here five minutes ago."

"But he promised not to submit this to anyone else until he heard from me."

"That's Barry."

"I see."

"So you keep him hooked, understand? As long as you can."

"I don't think this is quite proper, Norman."

"Cut the crap, Alan. You never intended to submit the deal to Leventhal."

"No, but—"

"Don't get pious. Stick with me and you may earn half a commission. Otherwise, you're out in the cold."

There was no sigh on the other end of the line, but Norman heard one anyway.

"All right, Norman. I'll do my best, but you better protect me."

"I'll call you in a few days." Norman hung up before Hughes could reply.

"That bastard," Norman muttered, "that dirty bastard." *Which one?* an inner voice asked him. "Both," Norman said, and laughed aloud.

Now he could proceed with a clear conscience. Norman assumed that most men were no better than whores, but there was always a chance that a few might prove to be exceptions. He was relieved when a man established his duplicity beyond a reasonable doubt.

Still, punishing Barry and Hughes was secondary. First, Norman Kane had to figure out how to make the deal. He sat alone in his office, while precious minutes ticked away. What was the angle? How could he approach the Kincaids? Who should talk to them?

That was it: "Who." "Who" was more important than "how" or "what." Everyone knew that. It was elementary.

Norman would not dare approach the Kincaids directly, even though he could probably buy and sell the lot of them (Norman liked to tell himself that about everybody, even when he had good reason to doubt it). The Kincaids were what Norman called "old-line Chicagoans." They might snub him, and that he could not bear. Besides, it was the wrong way to make the deal. The Kincaids would never sell *him* the property for less than fifteen million dollars. He would have to pay the price for his questionable background (northwest side, middle class, public schools and University of Chicago) and his flamboyant business reputation.

Who was the right man? The man who could offer thirteen million dollars or even less, without being thrown out. Norman would pay the full price if he had to. But with those damn third-generation millionaires, you never knew for sure. They didn't say yes and they didn't say no. Sometimes they even sold their property to other people at a lower price— provided the other people were the "right people."

Of course, Norman had no personal knowledge of such a transaction, but he had heard stories, and they sounded logical to him. That is, they sounded illogical, which was what Norman believed one should logically expect from other people.

He quickly reviewed the names and characteristics of all of

his associates, sadly rejecting them one by one. Then he remembered Vern Hanson.

"That's it," he shouted, rising to his feet. "Vern Hanson. Why not Vern Hanson?" Norman often shouted his conclusions aloud, if only to savor them. And this conclusion, Norman thought, was sheer genius.

Once again—this time triumphantly—he reached for the telephone.

I waited for Norman in front of the bank, wondering why he had invited me to join him at lunch with Hanson. In a moment, Norman arrived and was slapping my back, urging me inside, ignoring my request for enlightenment.

We passed beneath the imposing Ionic colonnade, through the polished brass doors, and stepped onto the vast main banking floor.

Norman nodded to several men. Everyone at Chicago National seemed to know him. He was remarkably at ease in these austere surroundings.

We crossed the beige terrazzo floor, heading for the green-carpeted oasis where the officers performed their mysterious rites. Most of them were spare-framed and gray-haired, almost all sat erect behind their polished desks. In one corner, behind a low partition, was the office of Vernon Hanson.

Norman took my arm and pulled me to a halt. "Look at that," he said. "Vern's with a customer. He's staring right through the man. Doesn't move, doesn't smile. Just nods his head once in a while."

"What's wrong with that?"

"What's wrong? Boy, you'd never make a modern banker, either. You're watching Hanson display his greatest weakness —small talk. He hasn't got any."

I shook my head.

"Eddie, don't you understand? That's unforgivable. Hanson's supposed to be a salesman. He's supposed to romance every customer."

"He doesn't look as if he's trying." Hanson was tapping a

pencil on his desk now, staring down at it somberly.

Norman whispered again. "Used to drive me nuts, that tapping. You think he's not listening, but he is. Only he ignores the bullshit. You talk for an hour, you think you're conning him, and then he asks one or two key questions and blows up your whole presentation."

"But you said that's all wrong."

"Yeah, it's all wrong, but he's still the sharpest guy in this bank."

It was hard to believe. Hanson appeared so unpretentious, with his thick hands and thick neck, smooth, almost bland, face, and metal-framed glasses. Yet he was the head of his department, one of the half-dozen top operating officers in the bank.

"You can't kid him, Eddie, and he won't kid you. No B.S. about loan committees and bank policy. If your deal's no good, Hanson tells you right out. No two-week wait and a chickenshit letter. 'No deal,' he says, and that's it."

"When was the last time he told you 'No deal'?"

Norman smiled. "Never. And he better not start now. Come on, let's move over where he can see us."

Hanson noticed us, almost smiled, rose from his chair, said something to his customer, shook his hand and led him out of the office. The man seemed bewildered. Once he was gone, Hanson approached us.

"You rescued me, Norman. Next time, come a little earlier. How are you, Eddie? Norman didn't say you were coming."

"I forgot, Vern. I should have remembered you need two weeks' notice to get a table for three in the dining room."

Norman's jibe had no effect on Hanson. He gave Norman a fatherly pat on the shoulder and then escorted us to the elevator.

I watched Norman as we entered the low-ceilinged, heavily paneled room. In this sanctuary the leading executives of the bank entertained their most important customers. Norman was proud to be there. He nodded pleasantly to many men, not all of whom knew him, or so it seemed to me.

As soon as we ordered lunch, Hanson asked bluntly, "What's up, Norman?"

"The Kincaid property on Lake Shore Drive."

Both Hanson and I looked at Norman blankly.

"I'm gonna buy it, fellas, that's what's up."

"Oh no, not more apartment buildings." The words escaped me before I had time to think.

Hanson nodded in apparent agreement, but Norman ignored him and directed his response to me. "What's wrong with apartment buildings?"

"Look, Norman, you already own ten of them on Lake Shore Drive. It took three years to dig you out of the last deal, and if you hadn't sold four of your worst buildings to that New York syndicate, you would have been ruined."

Norman frowned. "That's a great thing to tell your client in front of his banker."

"As if Vern didn't know. Who the hell loaned you the million dollars that kept you going until the deal was closed?" Before he could answer, I plunged ahead. "No more apartments, Norman, I can't stand the strain."

Norman hesitated, glanced at Vern Hanson (who was tapping his fork), then smiled.

"That's what I like about you, Eddie, your imagination. Most lawyers see things in black and white—but you, you see Technicolor."

"What's this got to do with my imagination, Norman? I'm not the one who dreams up these apartment-house deals."

"Like I said, your imagination overwhelms me. If I say La Salle Street, you think office buildings; if I say State Street, you think department stores; and if I mention Lake Shore Drive—automatically it's apartments."

"I don't get you, Norman."

"Wrong. You do get me. I don't want to build any more apartments."

"Then what's this about the Kincaid property?"

If we had not been sitting in the bank dining room, I think Norman would have exploded. "Listen, Eddie, you're the guy who's putting apartment houses on the Kincaid property. Not me."

I was stunned. I looked at Vern Hanson, but could not tell how Norman's remark had affected him. "That's the prettiest place on the Drive," I said. "There have been apartments there for fifty years."

"They're coming down, Eddie, and we're not going to put them back."

"Then what will you build, Norman?"

He hesitated, waiting until he had our full attention, then leaned across the table to whisper his surprise to us: "Six of the biggest, tallest, most elegant office buildings you've ever seen."

Vern Hanson laid his fork across his plate. "Are you serious?" he asked.

Norman smiled and nodded.

"You can't do it," I told him. "The property isn't zoned commercial."

"I'll get it rezoned."

I started to protest, but I realized Norman was the one man in Chicago who might be able to get that property rezoned.

Hanson went back to eating his lunch. I stared at Norman. He waited for a moment, then began again.

"Hold on to your fork, Vern, that's just part of the story. Only three of my buildings are going south of the Drive; the others will be built on the north side."

Vern Hanson blinked. I laughed aloud. "You must be kidding," I said. "That's a public beach over there."

"The hell it is. The beach belongs to the Kincaid estate— or part of it does. The rest goes with the Simmons property."

Norman sat there grinning, while I stuttered stupidly. "I forgot," I said. I may even have blushed.

"You forgot? Not you, Eddie. You're the guy who drew the contracts when I bought the Simmons property. Think back. All that lake-front real estate is divided between the Simmons Corporation and the Kincaid family estate, right?" Norman looked at me, but he was talking to Hanson. "Now tell me, Eddie. What happened when you ordered a title policy on the Simmons property?"

I recited dutifully, *"The riparian rights are covered by easements in perpetuity. Neither the owners of the Simmons property nor the Kincaid estate can build on the lake side of the Drive without the consent of the other party."* I realized

23

that this was why Norman had invited me to lunch. But now his attention turned to Vern Hanson.

"You see, Vern, that's how it works. For fifty years nobody did anything because Simmons hated Kincaid and Kincaid was jealous of Simmons. Everybody else forgets. The city widens the Drive and builds a beach on the other side. They act like it's public property. But once a year for fifty years Simmons and Kincaid send men out onto the beach to put up a fence and block it off for a few days, which keeps the city from getting title to it. Well, it's sort of a joke. The public goes on using the beach and people like Eddie forget all about it. But the fact is that anyone who owns both pieces of property can build on both sides of the Drive."

Norman was triumphant. Hanson conceded him a small smile. "That's splendid, Norman, but nobody's ever built office buildings on that part of Lake Shore Drive."

"Can you think of a better place? La Salle Street is too narrow, dingy and decrepit. Even this bank needs a face lifting. Wacker Drive is a real-estate promoter's joke. It sits with its stinking rear end leaning over the river. They spend millions building ugly buildings on it and they're wrong—goddamn wrong. This is the age of glamour, Vern, and the suckers are getting the smelly, dirty Chicago River."

"But, Norman," I said, "there are still open spots on Michigan Avenue, let alone the Drive."

"Don't kid yourself, Michigan Avenue is coming, but it still hasn't got one tenth the glamour of Lake Shore Drive. In this town, Lake Shore Drive is the only address worth having."

"Maybe. But you're far removed from the established financial and office districts."

"That's the beauty of the whole thing. You take these prestige-conscious bastards from New York and offer them a spot on Lake Shore Drive overlooking beautiful Lake Michigan—the best address and the finest buildings in town. You give them a district that's almost residential, with some of the finest shops in the city next door on North Michigan Avenue. You can't miss."

For a while no one spoke. Vern Hanson went back to tapping his fork. Norman looked at each of us in turn, expectantly. I wasn't sure what he wanted, but I thought I'd better say something.

"When did you accomplish all this, Norman?"

"Accomplish what?"

"Buy the Kincaid property?"

"Are you kidding? I haven't even talked to the owners yet. Ernest Barry just told me about the property yesterday. But by the end of the week, word will be all over town."

"Does it matter? How many developers are big enough to handle a deal this size?"

"One besides me is one too many. That's why I have to find the best way to get to the heirs."

Vern Hanson smiled. "Why is that a problem? Who else but you wants to buy the property?"

"Vern, people all over the United States have been watching the Kincaid property for years."

"Aren't you the guy who always tells me you'll never get into a bidding contest?"

"That's right, and I still feel that way. I know what the land is worth better than anyone else, and I have a better idea for using it than anyone else. But I need an angle."

"What have you in mind?"

"There must be an inside track, Vern, and I think you can help me find it."

Hanson looked surprised. "I don't see how."

"You know the Kincaid family, even if they do bank down the street."

"Of course I know the Kincaids. Everybody knows the Kincaids. In fact, I'm friendly with a couple of them, but I still don't see how that will help you."

"Maybe yes, maybe no. The Kincaids must have a weak point somewhere."

Hanson smiled. "They've got plenty of weak points. Not one of them has done a decent day's work since old Timothy Kincaid died thirty years ago. Hell, they've owned the property you want to buy for fifty years. All they do is let it deteriorate, while they quarrel among themselves."

"Yes, but now they've stopped quarreling."

25

Hanson looked sharply at Norman. "You've got a point there."

Norman leaned across the table. "Of course I have. After years of bickering, the Kincaids have suddenly agreed to sell the finest piece of real estate they own. Now what brought that about?"

Hanson went back to his food. "Damned if I know."

"Yes, but Vern, that's what we have to find out. Somebody forced this move. Which Kincaid has enough initiative to push a sale?"

"I don't know, Norman. The Kincaids I talk to are all older men. Their only interest in life is an occasional round of golf."

"I don't think it is one of the older Kincaids; it must be a younger man. Which young Kincaid has guts?"

Hanson slowly shook his head. "Like I said, Norman, damned if I know."

The meeting with Hanson disappointed Norman. He had hoped, perhaps unreasonably, that Hanson would instantly offer him the key that would open the door to the Kincaids. Of course, there was still hope. Norman's simple request for help was enough to move Hanson to the limits of propriety.

Anyway, Norman did not stop to brood. He left me outside the bank and hurried away to keep an appointment on the South Side.

Norman drove his own car along a street which had once been called Grand Boulevard but now was named South Parkway. Oh, yes, there was a parkway in the middle, but it was ill-kept, littered with garbage and debris. The few residences which still faced it were crumbling hulks whose ornate stonework hinted pathetically at departed elegance. However, a fantastic transformation was taking place. Most of the buildings had been razed, and the ground lay raw for miles in every direction. What remained was a stratum of rock and gravel and ancient brick; a harsh manmade desert. On every side, tall buildings of concrete, steel and masonry were rising. The architecture was not impressive—some men claimed these were the slums of the future—but the towers were new and modern and offered almost infinite improvement in the standards of living of their inhabitants.

Norman found the neighborhood frightening. He drove rapidly with his car windows closed. On street corners here and there he noticed small groups of Negroes idling away the spring afternoon. They eyed him with slight curiosity; long Cadillacs driven by white men (and even black men) were not uncommon here. Still, Norman was afraid to lock eyes with anyone. He didn't want to "start anything."

Leaving the Parkway, Norman angled up one street and down another, through the monochrome rubble and high-rise landscape, until he located the ancient gray stone residence he was seeking. Norman parked his car at the curb, carefully avoiding broken glass and chipped bricks. He could not shake off the vague feeling that he was a target.

Norman took the steps up to the old rough stone porch as quickly as he could. Finding no buzzer, he rapped on the door. It seemed quite a long time before a bent little old man, bald, but wearing an amazing fringe of white hair, answered the door.

"Dr. Friedrichs?"

The old man nodded, and the white fringe floated up and down, echoing his gesture.

"I'm Norman Kane."

"Oh, yes, Mr. Kane. Come in." The old man pushed open the screen door. Norman stepped around it and entered the house.

Dr. Friedrichs conducted him along a dimly lit corridor into a surprisingly bright and cheerful room. Norman blinked; and then felt as if his blink flicked away the vision of the slum world and presented him with a new film, in strange contrast to the previous one.

The walls and ceiling were white; there was no rug on the black floor. One entire wall was lined with white shelves filled with books of varying ages, sizes and colors. A long drafting board hung from the opposite wall and above it, pinned at random, were dozens of prints and sketches, all of startling design.

In the center of the room, a huge, square glass coffee table

27

rose above three thin, black metal legs. It was difficult to believe that the thick slab of glass could float on these slender supports. Around the table stood a number of chairs, no two alike, each molded into a curve of its own. None of them looked solid.

"Sit down, Mr. Kane, sit down," murmured the old man in slow and guttural accents. Norman perched gingerly on one steel-and-leather contraption which appeared more stable than the rest. It yielded at first contact and then seemed to receive him. In a moment he found he could sit back with comfort and apparently solid support.

"That always amuses me, Mr. Kane. These chairs and this table are left over from various exhibits I have given around the world. They do not match, but they give me the history of what I have done. Almost no one believes they will support a human form, and I confess that I myself was doubtful when the craftsmen first constructed them. Nevertheless, they have carried far larger men than you for great lengths of time and during somewhat violent discussions."

The old man sat down on a chair across from Norman and lifted his feet, heavily shod, onto the glass table. It did not appear to be an affectation, but rather a matter of comfort for him.

"Do you know who I am, Dr. Friedrichs?"

The old man shook his head.

"Perhaps that is best. I am a real-estate developer. I own properties all over the country, but most of the largest ones are in Chicago. You may know my buildings. For example, I developed the Apartment Quadrangle at 57th and the lake."

"Lanceman," said the old man quietly. "Lanceman was the architect. Absolutely horrible. Ugly."

Norman wasn't affronted. "I agree, Doctor. And yet the apartments are all rented."

The old man shrugged.

"And I built the apartment houses at 1118, 1230, 1460 and 1544 Lake Shore Drive."

"Ericson and Ericson," said the old man almost sadly. "They look as if they were all built from one set of plans."

"They were."

"And a bad set at that."

"Not too bad, Doctor. The air conditioning works, the elevators work, and the windows don't leak."

"But the foundations sank at 1460."

"You heard about that. Well, I can't blame Ericson and Ericson. The structural engineer made a serious error. We're lucky we didn't suffer a total collapse. A little underpinning, a few more pilings, and we saved the building."

"Hardly worth it."

"Not to you, sir, but to me. Otherwise, I would have gone bankrupt."

"Very well then, Mr. Kane, you are a commercial builder, and apparently a successful one. What now?"

Norman was reluctant to come to the point. "I know your work, Doctor. As a matter of fact, I've studied it for many years. Last summer I went to Germany, and in Stuttgart I visited the public school you designed. Unfortunately, one of the wings was destroyed during the war, but the rest of the building still stands, and I must say that it is one of the most attractive and ingenious school buildings I have ever seen."

"Yes, but the windows leak." Norman detected a twinkle in the old man's eyes.

Norman smiled. "I visited other cities in West Germany. In Frankfurt I particularly admired your office building. I've never seen a photograph of it in any architectural magazine, which surprises me, because your design antedates the Lever House in New York. I took some photographs of my own, Dr. Friedrichs; perhaps you'd like to see them."

The old man hesitated. "Well, yes, I would like to see them."

Norman reached into his jacket pocket, brought forth a slim envelope, and passed it to the old man. Dr. Friedrichs' fingers trembled. He pulled the flap open and spilled the photographs onto the glass tabletop. For a moment he seemed to forget Norman Kane. He picked up the photographs and peered at them closely. Then he walked to the window, raising the photographs to the light. Finally he carried them to his drafting board and studied them under a magnifying glass. At last, reluctantly, he returned the pictures to Norman Kane.

"Who took these photographs?"

"As I said, I took them myself."

"They are excellent."

"Please, do me the honor of accepting them, Doctor."

"You're very generous."

"It's nothing. I still have the negatives. If you would like to have some large prints, I will be happy to have them made for you."

For a moment, Friedrichs seemed to wrestle with himself. "Ah, no," he said. "That is not necessary. Thank you very much for these."

"I also admire the auditorium you designed for the Fielding Institute here in Chicago."

"Thank you."

"That was seven years ago. Since then, the Institute has built a new medical center and a science building. To my surprise, they were designed by other architects."

This statement seemed to pierce the old man's armor. Norman pressed his advantage. "In my opinion, their work is atrocious. I don't believe that such a conglomeration of architecture is the proper design for an educational institution. I recall the setting you had planned for the auditorium. Oh, yes, there it is." Norman rose from his chair and walked quickly to the architect's drawing board. Pinned to the wall above it was a sketch which showed the auditorium standing in a plaza framed by structures which echoed its design.

"Yes," said Norman, "the campus would have been beautiful. Unfortunately it doesn't look like that now. At one end there is a tall pseudo-Gothic structure, at the other a Romanesque pile. Together they have almost destroyed the lines of your auditorium."

"It seems, Mr. Kane, that you are a student of architecture." The words were obviously chosen carefully.

"Hardly, sir. A dilettante and admirer, but basically just a developer. I am aware of my limitations. I fully recognize that the buildings I have built are not the best architecture." Norman hesitated for only a moment. He felt a compulsion to explain himself, which he realized was foolish, childish—even dangerous. But he could not restrain himself.

"I started as a bookkeeper, Doctor. A crummy bookkeeper in a crummy pants factory. On the side I worked for a charitable organization" (he could not bring himself to tell Friedrichs that it was a Jewish charity). "After a few years I got friendly with some of the men I solicited for funds. One of them gave me a chance to buy in on a small store building with apartments above it. That was how I got started. I was in real estate. I began putting investors and deals together. Little deals. Then a little bigger deals. I did well, very well. I quit my job at the pants factory and worked full time on my real estate."

Friedrichs was studying him coolly. Norman could not tell what effect, if any, this history was having on him.

"But there was something wrong. Something missing. I was making a lot of money, but there was still something missing. I thought about it for a long time before I figured it out. The answer was simple. I was a secondhand dealer. Even the man who owned the pants factory was better than I was. He took raw materials and made them into something new and useful. All I was doing was trading buildings other men had built.

"I started building my own buildings. My first construction project was an apartment house on the South Side. It was something I had created—every inch of it—from the concrete footings to the stone coping on the parapet. It didn't look like much. But what did that matter? Here was a building I had built. Something that never existed before.

"I went on from there, building stores and apartment houses, as fast as I could. I hired the same commercial architects everyone else did—the guys you could trust because they kept the cost down. It didn't matter to me whether the buildings were good-looking or not. All that mattered was whether they paid off. And they did."

Norman hesitated for a moment. He had not intended to reveal this much of himself to Friedrichs. Still, what difference did it make?

Norman returned to the table, sat down on the chair, pressed his hands on the glass and leaned toward Dr. Friedrichs. "One thing I know. My buildings would have rented as well, and perhaps better, had they been beautifully designed, instead of being hooked together by men who were more contractors than architects."

"Why did you hire them, then?"

"Because they were more contractors than architects."

The old man laughed aloud. "At least you're honest, Mr. Kane. You may have a taste for better architecture, but you haven't let it stand in the way of your financial success."

Norman brooded for a moment. "What you say is true, Dr. Friedrichs. But just because I employed inferior architects before doesn't mean that I must be wed to them forever."

"They are not easy to escape, Mr. Kane. They are everywhere."

"Almost everywhere. Still, good design and economy are not necessarily contradictory. I think, sir, that given the opportunity, you could combine the two."

The old man did not reply.

"In any event, I wanted to meet you. I am planning projects which will be larger and more important than any I have attempted before. One in particular will be so spectacular that the design of it must be absolutely perfect, or the result will be a blot on this city. And there are enough of those, sir. I myself have perpetrated a few. But this time, Doctor—this time I can't afford mediocre architecture. In this case poor design might be an economic catastrophe."

The old man nodded, perhaps in spite of himself. It was the first time that he acknowledged agreement with anything Norman Kane had said.

Norman noted the nod and decided to end the interview.

"Thank you for seeing me, Doctor. I'm happy to have been able to bring you the photographs. I trust we will meet again, and I hope you will show me through your auditorium and perhaps analyze its structure for me. I would also appreciate the chance to look through the portfolios, if you have them, of buildings you built in Europe."

"I look forward to that, Mr. Kane."

Norman rose. "Again, many thanks for your time." He reached out and shook the old man's hand, waved him off when Friedrichs seemed about to lead him out of the apartment, and hurried from the bright room through the darkened hall and out the door. He ran down the steps, across the walk and entered the sanctuary of his air-conditioned Cadillac.

But the same faces floated up and down the streets, staring at him, some curiously and others incuriously. The car motor roared reassuringly to life under his touch, and it was only a matter of minutes before he had escaped from the gray rubble-strewn desert, the staring faces, and Dr. Friedrichs.

Hanson surprised Norman by calling him at home that evening.

"You've got a sixth sense, Norman; I don't know why I ever doubt you. I took the afternoon off today and went to the Club to play golf. Three other men in the clubhouse asked me to make a foursome. One was Samuel Kincaid. You know Sam, oldest living member of the clan, but the so-and-so still plays to a twelve handicap. Anyway, after nine holes the others went on, and Sam and I stopped to have a drink. Well, we sat in the clubhouse for a while, and I mentioned the Kincaid Lake Shore Drive property. Sure enough, the old boy came clean."

"Came clean?"

"Right. Sam told me he personally thought the family ought to hold onto it until they all died. But, being so far up in years, he isn't going to interfere. As you guessed, one of the younger men has been pestering them to sell."

"Who?"

"Will you let me tell the story?"

"Of course, Vern."

"Well, as I said, one of the younger boys has been badgering the family for two or three years. They finally gave in and told him to sell the property if he could. But he insisted on having an agreement from the whole family. So you see, Norman, you don't have to deal with a dozen Kincaids. The heirs all signed an instrument giving young Kincaid a six-months option."

"Fantastic."

"You're telling me."

"Who's the guy, Vern?"

"Delbert Kincaid."

"Delbert? Who the hell is Delbert?"

Vern Hanson's dry laugh crackled across the line. "Tell you the truth, I never heard his name before. Sam says he's forty years old and hasn't worked a day in his life. Until now he's been perfectly content to play polo, clip coupons and travel around the world."

"What stirred him up?"

"Sam thinks it may be his wife. She's supposed to be a pretty restless type. But then, old Sam thinks anybody under seventy is restless. Anyway, young Kincaid must have something in mind. Of course, he owns more than fifteen per cent of the property in his own name; just selling it would bring him a hell of a lot of cash."

"Do you think he may be fronting for some developer?"

"I don't know, but Sam says he's kind of a loner; hasn't many friends in the business world."

"Vern, you're marvelous. Say, you don't happen to know where this guy lives?"

"I looked it up: 1826 Shore Acres Road in Kenilworth."

"It figures."

"It figures?"

"Never mind. That's great. His name is Delbert Kincaid and he lives on Shore Acres Road in Kenilworth. By God, I'm going to try and see him this weekend."

Norman decided to mix himself a drink. He walked behind the bar, took out a bottle of Scotch, filled a tall glass with ice, and poured the liquor almost to the brim. He laughed at himself. *What am I doing? I poured that like a Coke.* But Norman did not empty the glass. He sat at the bar while the ice melted and crackled, and he hummed to himself.

Where the hell is Frieda? he wondered irritably. Then he remembered that his wife was busy at some charitable function. *Damn it.*

Norman watched through the tall windows of his apartment as the sun followed its downward course, whitening the great skyline. The low slanting light caught his paintings. He pulled the heavy drapes along the west window to protect them, then flicked a switch lighting the canvases from the ceiling. Norman adjusted the rheostat to exactly the degree of illumination he wanted and again perched on a stool in front of the bar.

Norman loved his paintings. They were nearly as precious to him as his buildings, though he never said so. It would not have been in keeping with his image as a tough, no-nonsense businessman. But the fact was that he had been an avid collector since his college days. Then he had treasured cheap prints and inexpensive lithographs. Now he could afford fine oils. But the feeling was the same.

Norman wrote off his frequent visits to Europe as business trips. The truth was that he never came home with a deal, but he often returned with works of art. The Signac, for example. Norman had found it in Paris years before, in an old shop in the Rue de Seine. The dealer had seemed unaware of its worth, but Norman had haggled with him, nevertheless. Finally, after much discussion, he had bought it for a fraction of its value. Then he had felt uncertain. Was it genuine? He took the first available flight to New York and hurried to the Metropolitan, where a curator had verified its authenticity.

Norman studied the painting—Signac's favorite subject: ships and sea. It was a watercolor, and Norman preferred Signac's watercolors to his oils. He liked the architectural strength of the firm, dynamic dark lines outlining the sails, the hulls of the boats and the shore. The wash melted from sky to land to sea. The work shimmered with life and power. Its colors were delicate but clean, and the tightly controlled, powerful lines held the composition together.

But whom could Norman tell that to? As far as he was concerned—no one. It was a pleasure that must remain personal. He glanced about the room, enjoying the million-faceted shimmer of a Paris street scene by Pissarro, the cool pastel charm of a Degas dancer, the exuberant, earthy glow of a young girl by Renoir. Or was it Renoir? The man at the Art Institute had assured him it was. Norman privately doubted it, but he loved the painting all the same.

It's a damn fine collection, he thought. *Who would expect a West Side punk to own a Corot landscape, a sketch by David, a Van Gogh watercolor, and all the rest of this?* He looked about him with deep satisfaction. *And all bought right, too.* He smiled at himself. A true collector shouldn't think like that.

His eyes moved from the paintings to the city and back to the paintings again. *My God,* he thought, *I'm almost content. Isn't that wild? Here I am cooking up a crazy, dangerous deal and I am almost content. Well, I've got to drive that out of my soul.* He did not permit himself to look directly at the niche on Lake Shore Drive in which he planned to place his six buildings.

Norman forced his eyes downward—thirty-five floors—to the park below. It was spring, and the short grass was like a worn carpet with its brown backing showing through. His eyes moved along the grass to the onyx platform on which an appropriately golden-hued Alexander Hamilton stood braced against a black marble shaft, staring with perpetual disapproval at a naked, muscular statue of Goethe across the road. To the east, unseen breezes rumpled the lake, sending spidery wavelets skittering shoreward. In the harbor the yacht moorings were empty, and the pilings looked like the abandoned relics of some race of stilt-house dwellers. Norman's gaze turned west to a calm lagoon, shaped like a hand mirror, with its handle pointing downtown. Floating leaves mottled one end of the otherwise smooth surface, so that it seemed as if the silver had flaked and peeled away. He barely noticed the cars. From this height they were distinguishable only by color. Otherwise, their flow seemed continuous. They moved on invisible wheels set on invisible tracks, merging, dividing— neon strips that flashed up and down the margins of the park.

Buildings were more interesting: to the west, the brown-and-gray pattern of the low city. Homes and apartments laced in regular, irregular patterns. Three- and six-flat buildings. Nine- and twelve-story buildings. Shabby brick fronts ornamented in stone or terra cotta. The sides were dull masonry framed in duller cement. Rows of frumpy women in old corsets with dirty make-up. *I used to live out there,* he thought. *I wonder where.* He studied the patterns, but he could not guess which street was Armitage. *I'm lost. I could never find my way back.*

Norman studied the ranks of flat roofs. A few were surrounded by elaborate balustrades framing promenades where no one ever walked. Dirty skylights glinted dully in the sun. The porches were maintenance gray, the chimneys stained black, the windows dull, whether open or closed, draped, blinded, curtained or heavy-lidded with shades.

Norman raised his head to confront a glass-and-aluminum monster at the far end of the park. He smiled at the small flat head with its rows of slit black eyes. The monster stood on short spindle legs, lacking only arms with which to shoulder itself away from its seedy, ancient neighbors.

Who built these buildings? Who leaned that split-beam Tudor fraud against its equally fraudulent Gothic neighbor? And the trees—the untrimmed beards of these ancient retainers, their dark bristle scraping against the dirty walls. Why don't the trees give up?

Finally Norman permitted himself a look at the high city. His eyes moved from the absurd corncobs of Marina City to the Prudential Building—up close, a cheese-grater; from here, a huge conning tower floating above an unseen sea. He smiled at the gay, fragile Wrigley Building and the squat, stodgy Merchandise Mart.

The sun touched the slender spire of Lincoln Tower and the polished brass of the Carbide Building. It was dark now on the east faces of Miës van der Rohe's black cages. Even the gracefully pleated Palmolive Building looked dull against the sky.

Norman shook his head. The newer buildings were all flat and rectilinear, designed by Erector-set architects. Some were glass and steel, some glass and marble, some glass and brick, but all as imaginative as the chain sprockets on a bicycle.

Finally, as the ultimate prize, Norman permitted himself to stare at *the* place on Lake Shore Drive. His property. He narrowed his eyes and tried to imagine his six buildings—right there. It was impossible. He had studied this view for twenty years and watched it change, oh so gradually, across the years. The idea that he would superimpose his buildings on this land had stirred his soul; yet he could not visualize them now. The buildings were strips of paper that he tried to paste against the skyline. But they peeled away before his eyes, and the skyline remained as it had been before.

I hope this is not some kind of pre-vision. He began to

shudder. *I hope I'm really going to be able to do it.* He slammed his hand down on the bar, and the Scotch spilled on his pants.

Goddamn it, he thought. *Where the hell is Frieda?* He dabbed a towel ineffectively at his pants leg while his anger grew. She had said she was going to Donna Kohler's apartment. Norman stalked to the telephone, stiff-legged and uncomfortable from the seeping Scotch.

"May I speak to Mrs. Kane, please." He felt a pang of fear. What if she was not there? But the feminine voice at the other end said, "Just a minute."

Norman nursed his anger as he waited.

"Hello?"

"Frieda? Is that you?"

"Norman?"

"What the hell do you think you're doing over there?"

"I told you this morning, dear. We're working on the annual dinner dance."

"You told me nothing of the kind. You're not fooling me, Frieda. I know you're not alone."

There was a moment's hesitation. "Of course not, Norman. There are ten other women over here."

"And who else, Frieda? Who else?"

"Please, Norman. Not again."

"Who else, Frieda? Just tell me."

"No one, Norman. Just the girls."

He forced a bitter laugh. "You expect me to believe that? I know better, Frieda. Why do you keep lying to me?"

"Please, Norman. This is silly. I'll talk to you when I get home."

"I don't care. You understand, Frieda? I know all about it, but I don't give a damn. You hear? I don't give a damn." He slammed down the phone.

Norman's heart was pounding. But somehow he felt better. He walked to the windows. Suddenly he could see the six buildings. Perhaps it was the fading light, perhaps the liquor. But now for the first time, the six buildings graced the skyline. Six spires, clean, spartan, elegant. He felt like crying. *My God, one lousy drink and I feel like crying.* He laughed at himself, but he could not discourage his own sentimentality. *Imagine me, Norman Kane, six buildings, six million square feet right there.* Now he could see them more clearly than ever.

Norman woke with a start, frightened and confused. His head ached horribly, and he felt stabs of pain in his body. *God,* he thought, *where am I? Where am I?* Suddenly it became clear. He was on the couch in his own living room. The lights were still lit over his paintings, but there was no other light in the room. He had fallen asleep where he sat. He looked down and saw several empty Scotch glasses on the coffee table. *What an idiot. I even forgot to eat dinner. No wonder my head aches and my stomach hurts.* His next thought staggered him. Was Frieda home?

Norman stood up, and it brought fresh pain. He still wore his jacket, shirt and pants, though he had kicked his shoes off. His clothes were rumpled and he felt sticky and dirty. He was certain that he smelled. Norman felt his face—unshaven. He shuddered at his own condition as he staggered into the bedroom.

Frieda was there, sleeping peacefully. Norman had the urge to waken her. *Imagine letting me sleep on that couch.* He suddenly felt too weak and hungry to be properly angry. He shook his head, turned and tottered toward the kitchen.

When he turned on the ceiling light in the kitchen, the fluorescent glare pricked yet another point of pain in his brain. The refrigerator was filled with food. He could have anything he wanted, but it was too difficult to make a choice. *What should I eat? Better not be too heavy: something that will lie in my stomach. Maybe a bowl of cereal.* He took a carton of milk from the refrigerator and some cereal from a cabinet and poured the two into a bowl. He chewed thoughtfully, almost as if the cereal were a steak. The food felt good in his throat and stomach and he drank down another glass of milk while he ate. When he finished, he was still hungry. Inside the breadbox he found a bag of sweet rolls. He squeezed them one at a time until he found one that was still soft, and he munched on it.

Norman stumbled from the kitchen to the bathroom and flicked the light switch. Again the glare caught him. *Agh, terrible,* he thought. He splashed water on his face, pulled off his shirt and pants and left them in a heap on the floor. He did not brush his teeth; it was too much effort. He staggered into the bedroom, pulled the spread off his own bed and fell across it.

He glanced across at Frieda, sleeping only a few feet away. The sight annoyed him. "Sure," he said. "You can sleep. Like a baby you can sleep."

Frieda stirred. Norman raised his voice. "How you do it I don't know. The kind of life you live, you'd think you'd never be able to sleep."

"What, Norman?" Frieda was half awake now.

"Nothing. Absolutely nothing. Just leave me sleeping on the couch. What do you care?"

"I tried to wake you up, but I couldn't."

"Sure."

She was fully awake now. "Really, Norman. You must have been drunk. You were very surly, even half asleep. I couldn't budge you."

Now he was furious. He rolled off the bed, ripped the covers off his wife and screamed at her. "Stop lying, you bitch. You were with him again."

Frieda stared up at him, both appalled and fascinated. "Who, Norman?"

"How should I know?" he yelled. If he had not been black with rage, she would have laughed.

They posed like that, frozen, for a moment. Then Norman tore himself away. He was even more tired and irritable than before. "You'll see," he muttered. "You won't get away with it." Once more he fell across his bed. He waited for Frieda to speak again, but she was silent.

Then he thought of Delbert Kincaid, and annoyingly his blood began to race again. Frieda was forgotten. *I've got to see that boy. I've got to see him just as soon as I can. Oh, the hell with it. I've got to get a few hours sleep.* But he could not get Kincaid out of his mind. *Round. Got to be round and short and fat. Any Kincaid I ever saw was round and short and fat and bald. Well, guys like that are sometimes easy to handle and sometimes hard.*

Without realizing it he sat up in bed. *What am I doing? I should be going to sleep.* His head began to ache again. He forced himself to rise from his bed and walked to his dresser. Inside there was a bottle of tranquilizers. He shook out a couple, then realized he would have to get water from the bathroom. Once again he was subjected to that flashing fluorescent torture. As soon as he found a glass, he turned off the light, poured the water in by touch alone and swallowed the tranquilizers.

That should do it. He stumbled back into the bedroom, past Frieda, who lay silent, awake. He ignored her. Still, he did not sleep. Visions of Delbert Kincaid danced in his head. Every vision was a different man, sometimes tall, sometimes short, sometimes lean, sometimes fat. *Delbert Kincaid. What the hell kind of a name is that?* Once again Norman discovered that despite himself he was sitting up in bed. *Oh hell,* he thought. *Used to be I would have a cigarette, but now, goddamn it, I don't smoke any more. I've got to sleep.* He lay down again.

He could not find a comfortable position. Each new thought made him twist and move about. He did not want to lie on his side facing Frieda. He did not want to think about her. But somehow, time and again, he found himself looking toward her. The room was dark, but now his eyes were accustomed to it.

Norman peered through the darkness, studying his wife. She lay on her back, her body outlined hazily by the thin covers. One arm was stretched over her head in a gesture Norman found both strange and graceful. *She never looks bad,* he thought, *even when she's not trying.* Her hair was down, of course. She seldom wore it that way, except at bedtime or when he demanded it. Now, even at a distance, his fingers tingled with the texture of Frieda's long, fine blond hair. The room was too dark for details, but Norman could imagine her eyes, deep blue-green, dominating her face despite the high cheekbones, the delicate tone of her fair skin. Those eyes. Sometimes aflame with passion—or anger. Always alive, piercing his brain, measuring his worth, judging his true value. Most important, her hair was down. Norman always felt better when Frieda's hair swung loose and free. When she wore it upswept she seemed unbearably regal to him. Distant. Disdainful. Arrogant. Somehow he couldn't get close to her when she looked like that.

As he watched, Frieda stirred, and her hand came down in a smooth arc to her side. Norman smiled. *Just like she was serving*. He rolled onto his back and thought about his wife. She still played tennis—and well. He had given up the game years before. No time. But Frieda still played with the same easy grace and precision he remembered from their college days. That was when he had first seen her—on a tennis court. And that was what had made Norman take up the game. He wanted to meet that tall, slim, high-breasted beauty who stroked the ball so smoothly, but with such devastating power.

It hadn't worked. Not then, anyway. Norman managed to play a few sets with Frieda, but he never was able to date her. She intimidated him. Each day she arrived on campus in a chauffeur-driven limousine. Each day, after classes, the chauffeur picked her up in front of the Commons. He had tried to imagine the kind of world she lived in, this elegant princess who arrived and departed each day in her shining coach.

Norman was humbly grateful that Frieda deigned to play tennis with him. It took him months to reach even that equivocal level of bliss. But when the game ended, she was whisked away. Norman was left with his sweaty tennis clothes and meaningless victories.

She never complimented him on his game, no matter how well he played. She seemed not so much to disdain him as to be uninterested. Still, he was well aware what a shabby figure he cut. He saw himself through her eyes and found himself wanting. Homely, short and poor. Smart, maybe, but poor.

It came as a great shock to Norman when he learned that Frieda was Jewish. He should have known. Her surname was a common Jewish one. But somehow he never connected the name with this blond princess until he was directly informed of her heritage.

He felt deceived. Then he thought this might be a hopeful sign. But he soon concluded that this connection was too tenuous to rely on.

Later, at a fund-raising affair for a Jewish charity, Norman met Frieda's father. Another shock. The man looked like him. A little man, with quick eyes and quick hands, even the trace of an accent.

Deceived again, Norman thought. The only difference between her forebears and his was money. At least, that was what he told himself. For a moment he felt a surge of hope. If he could make it big, he could have her. Yes, all it would take would be plenty of dough. Then he was not so sure. He doubted that Frieda was looking for someone who resembled her father—probably just the opposite.

He soon found he was right. She had run off with Charlie Clark, a handsome if unstable man. And a Gentile in the bargain. It was shattering for Norman, but only for a while. He was going to make that big buck, and someday he was going to find Frieda again. That thing with Clark couldn't last.

What a beauty she had been. She was great now—magnificent. Still, whenever he was away from her, whenever he tried to visualize her, the first image that came to him was of Frieda as a girl. On a tennis court, with her hair swinging down. He lay motionless, remembering her. Cool and beautiful. And distant. Norman turned his head to look at her. She was still beautiful. Still slim and finely drawn. For a moment, in the darkness, she seemed a girl again.

And then he wanted her. Badly. Just as he had so many years ago. The wanting coursed through him. He brought his knees up and stared at her intently. He wet his lips before he spoke.

"Frieda?"

No response.

Norman slipped from his bed and edged toward his wife. Finally he stood beside her bed. He bent his head close to hers.

"Frieda?"

She was asleep. Or she was pretending to be asleep, which was worse. If so, he had humiliated himself again.

Norman was angry; frustrated and angry. He tried to laugh at himself, but he couldn't. The vision and the desire were still with him. Why did it have to be this way? The constant battles. The distance between them, only closing now and then at unexpected moments. At times when he was not prepared. Ridiculous.

Norman lay down on his own bed, even more agitated than before. It was a long time before he finally dozed off.

In a few moments (it seemed) Norman was awake again. He looked quickly at his watch and saw that it was 7:30 A.M. "Goddamn it to hell," he said aloud, and jumped up. "I'm going to see that bastard today. Yes sir, I'm going to see that bastard today." If Frieda heard him she gave no sign. He walked into the bathroom and turned the water on in the tub. *I'll take a hot bath and a shave and I'll feel a lot better.*

Norman paced himself through his typical morning ritual, bathing and shaving and the rest, assiduously combing his hair so that it covered his bald spot, checking his face with his hands and a mirror to make sure that there was no stubble anywhere. By the time he finished, he felt relaxed for the first time in many hours. He laughed. *That's pretty good. Now that you're ready to go out, I'll bet you're relaxed enough to go back to sleep.* "Oh, yeah," he said aloud, "that's pretty good."

Norman left without breakfast and without saying goodbye to Frieda. That quarrel would wait. He took the automatic service elevator down to the garage. He walked along in the darkened basement beneath the low ceiling, annoyed by the breeze from the ventilators redistributing the foul air. *All garages stink,* he thought. He assessed the cars in the garage: Cadillac, Lincoln, Lincoln, Cadillac, Cadillac, Cadillac. It took him a while to find his own—there were so many similar to it. He jumped into his car, started the motor, maneuvered it out of the narrow slot and drove it out of the garage. The attendant stared in amazement. He had never seen Kane take out his own car.

It was a beautiful day, one of those calm, clear days that delude Chicagoans into forgetting how miserable their climate really is. The temperature was in the 60's and climbing slowly. There was very little breeze, just enough to stir the leaves now and then. The haze that usually covered the city, even on the clearest of days, had lifted, and the buildings, the trees and the lake stood out in bold relief.

I'll take Sheridan, he thought, *to hell with the expressway.* Norman drove at a leisurely pace along Chicago's lakefront, carefully following the sharp curves, occasionally scanning the beaches, which were already graced by a few sun worshipers. The road was busy, but the cars did not move as quickly as on weekdays. He turned off his air conditioning and pressed the buttons lowering his car windows. He felt like an outdoorsman.

"Well, it's the day for it. If I can't ride with the windows down today, I should have them sealed shut." The breeze riffled his hair—for once he did not mind. *Who cares?* he thought. *Who gives a damn?* He found that he had unconsciously pressed down on the accelerator.

Now the drive arched through the park, crossing one stone bridge after another, piercing a manicured jungle where Norman never walked. The roadway turned left in a sweeping curve past huge new apartment buildings, then north again into Sheridan Road. Once flanked with mansions (among them the home of the pants manufacturer who had employed Norman as his bookkeeper), today Sheridan Road was lined with tall apartment towers.

Norman passed through a dying commercial district and then once again between apartment buildings in Rogers Park. These were older structures, the vestiges of once respectable neighborhoods. After a while, the road swung to the lake again, passing a cemetery on his left, its tombstones so ancient, ugly and oddly shaped, that they did not make him think of death. On his right was the lake, very calm this morning, playfully touching the pale shore. In a minute, the road left the lake and wandered into Evanston. Strips of park and beach came up from time to time at Norman's right. Most of the homes were older ones with large lots. The houses no longer seemed as elegant as in former years, but they were substantial, and the tall trees, thick-bodied and full-leaved, radiated strength and permanence. *All be gone one day. All be apartments. Every inch of it. Oh, well, I doubt I'll be here to see it. I doubt that I'm the man to do it.*

Norman slowed his car until the drivers following him began to blow their horns and pull around him. He was the focus of attention, which did not please him. Norman turned off onto one of the side roads.

It's probably easier this way, anyway. He followed the street to the end and there, to his surprise, he found Shore Acres Road. *Now what was the number? 1800? 1850? Oh, yeah, now I remember. 1826.* Driving slowly he followed the house numbers.

The homes on both sides were massively built. Most were forty or fifty years old. A few were strikingly modern. *There can't be a house here worth less than a hundred thousand dollars.*

The settings were as impressive as the homes; trees grew very thickly and the lawns and gardens were beautifully kept. The homes on the lake side were particularly elegant. In comparison, the fine houses on Sheridan Road in Evanston seemed almost ragged.

Finally he found 1826. A semicircular driveway led from Shore Acres Road to a house set back at least one hundred and fifty feet from the street. Magnificent flowerbeds framed a huge two-story central structure with rambling wings. The style was New England rather than North Shore. The house was built of red brick painted white, and the paint had been permitted to weather away, leaving a cool pink-and-white surface. Shutters framed the windows, and the entry was Cape Cod ornate.

Must be eighteen, maybe twenty rooms in that house, and the lot is the biggest on the street. Well, it figures. Once again the vision of a plump, pale Delbert Kincaid danced in his head.

As Norman turned into the driveway, he noticed that the garage doors were open. Three cars sat in the garage. One was a Lincoln at least five years old. The others were a battered station wagon—a Ford—and a small Corvair.

It figures. These really rich goyim never drive new cars. He shook his head. At that moment Norman felt sickeningly out of place. His long Cadillac was a huge black stain on the graveled driveway, an insult to the restrained façade of the Kincaid house. He turned off the motor and discovered that the street was perfectly quiet. No, not perfectly—in the distance he could hear the lake languidly lapping the shore.

Fearful that someone might be watching, Norman permitted himself but a single glance in the mirror and a quick flick of his hands to straighten his hair before he got out of his car. *I wish I'd made an appointment.* But it was too late. As Norman stood indecisively in the driveway, an indistinct male figure appeared behind the screened entrance door.

"Hi," said a voice, which apparently issued from the doorway.

"Hello," Norman said. He walked up the steps.

The screening was very thick and the glare reflected from the pink-white walls made it difficult for him to see the figure.

"I'm Norman Kane."

The screen door pushed open. "Hi, I'm Del Kincaid. What can I do for you?"

Norman had schooled himself to control his reactions, but the sight of Delbert Kincaid was almost too much. The man was tall, very tall, perhaps six foot two or three, and quite lean. He was a bit hunched in the shoulders, but his shoulders were broad and the short-sleeved shirt revealed his muscular arms. Kincaid's face was long and narrow, with straight brows, a thin nose, thin lips and white teeth. A brush hair cut completed his boyish appearance. Norman was totally disarmed.

The man smiled again. "I said, what can I do for you?"

"Oh, I'm sorry. You'll have to forgive me. I know this is a stupid thing to say, but I was expecting a much older man."

Kincaid chuckled and Norman flushed.

"Don't be embarrassed," Kincaid said. "I'm positively fascinated by a guy who pulls into my driveway in a forty-foot

47

Cadillac and tells me how young I look. What did you say your name was?"

Norman instantly regained control. "Kane. K-a-n-e. Norman Kane. I'd like to talk to you about a business matter. I should have called you for an appointment, but I thought I'd take a chance and come out here."

"Well, now I'm more fascinated than ever. Come on in, Mr. Kane." Kincaid swung the screen door open so that Norman could enter the house. "Let's go into the family room; it's brighter there."

Norman followed Kincaid through the dark, cool house. His eyes were not accustomed to the darkness and it was difficult for him to gain any clear impressions of the rooms except that they were large and filled with comfortable-looking furniture. He could tell the furniture was not new and the carpets, though deep, were somewhat worn. *It figures*, he thought, *it figures*.

Kincaid led him into a large room which contrasted sharply with the rest of the house. The stone walls followed no discernibly regular shape whatever, and most of them were glazed with louvered windows that opened onto the garden. The floor was paved with smooth, random-shaped stone blocks, and there was a large stone fireplace at one end. Deep, comfortable chairs were scattered about and colorful cushions were piled here and there on the floor.

"Somehow or other we always end up in the family room. It saves wear and tear on the rest of the house. But then, we don't seem to use the rest of the house, so I wonder what we're saving it for."

Norman forced a chuckle. In the distance he could hear children laughing, and now he could see that the windows faced a large swimming pool, itself irregular in shape.

Norman stared in amazement. There must have been twenty or more children, of varying ages and sexes, leaping about, in or out of the water, splashing and screaming.

"Maybe this isn't the best place to talk. Ever since we put in the pool, this has been the favorite spot in the neighborhood. I've got four kids of my own, and each one has at least six friends out there."

"Delightful," said Norman. "I don't mind the noise at all.

All those cheerful young voices are a pleasant sound on a spring day." Kincaid raised an eyebrow but said nothing. Both men stood for a moment watching the children. Then Norman's eyes lifted beyond the pool. He could see that the garden continued for several hundred feet ending at a low stone wall, beyond which must be the beach and the lake.

"Damned if I know why they need the pool. They can swim in the lake any time they want to. Of course, on cool days when the lake kicks up, a heated pool is a nice thing to have. In the winter we put up partitions and enclose it. Anyway, my kids talked me into it, and they certainly seem to enjoy it.

"Sit down, Mr. Kane. That's the most comfortable chair in the house. Tell me what brings you here."

Norman sat erect in the plush armchair—that is, as erect as the yielding down pillows permitted. Kincaid, meanwhile, eased himself onto the couch opposite. He stretched out, leaned on one elbow and looked inquisitively at Norman. His shoes (not shoes—sneakers over bare feet) rested on the couch, but he seemed unmindful of it. Kincaid radiated an aura of good health and contentment which Norman found faintly repulsive.

"Perhaps I should start by telling you a little bit about myself, Mr. Kincaid."

Kincaid rolled over on his back and assumed a knees-up posture. "Let me see," he said. "You own 206 South La Salle, the Acme Tower, and at least six apartment houses on Lake Shore Drive. I think you have property in San Francisco and Los Angeles, plus other real estate in Dallas, Denver, St. Louis and, oh, yes, one major office building in Cleveland." Then he rolled back on his side and grinned at Norman. "Right?"

"Right."

"You see, you don't have to tell me who you are or what you've done. I know all that." He paused. "What do you want to do?"

Norman smiled and relaxed for the first time. He was far more pleased than surprised to learn that Kincaid knew so much about him. And he was doubly pleased that the man came at him so directly.

"I want to buy the Kincaid Lake Shore Drive land."

"So do I."

"But you already own it."

"No, just 15.76 per cent. I want the whole thing."

"I don't blame you, but that will take a great deal of money. Surely your family doesn't intend to give you the property."

"It will take a lot of money, but 15.76 per cent less for me than anyone else."

"A good point. Tell me, Mr. Kincaid, what do you plan to do with the property?"

"We shall see. What do you plan to do with it?"

Norman did not hesitate. "I'm going to combine it with the Simmons property I already own—merging the estates so I can build on both sides of the Drive. Then I'll tear down the Simmons and Kincaid buildings and put up six new buildings, with a million square feet in each. Six office towers, all glass and steel, designed by Karl Friedrichs. Fidelity Standard Life Insurance Company of Illinois will give me the permanent mortgage funds, and the Chicago National Bank will provide the interim financing. Two or three phone calls and I should be able to line up tenants for at least two million square feet of space. The rest I'll rent as I go along."

"Interesting. I'm happy to hear you have the whole thing worked out."

"That's my business. I put up money and buy land. I build buildings and I lease them. What's your business, Mr. Kincaid?"

Kincaid smiled. "What you mean is you don't think I could put this kind of deal together."

"I'm not challenging you, I'd be crazy to do that. But you see, I've been thinking and planning what to do with that property for a long time. I bought the Simmons property seven years ago. It yields a very small return, but I knew all about the restrictions in the Simmons and Kincaid deeds, and I figured that so long as the property paid its way, I might as well buy it. While I own it, nobody can build north of the Drive without my consent. If I get the Kincaid property, I'll be in the driver's seat."

Kincaid rolled over on his back again, his knees hunched

up, his eyes staring at the ceiling. "It seems like you have something I want and I have something you want."

"You're right. We've got a lot in common."

Kincaid appraised Norman with a vaguely disdainful look. "We have nothing in common except that we both want the same property. Of course, I can build without the Simmons property. There's room for a couple of million square feet on our real estate."

"Sure, but you can't build north of the Drive, which means you can't develop this project the way it should be developed. I don't know about you, but I don't like to do things halfway. Tell me, Mr. Kincaid, have you ever done anything important just the way you wanted to?"

This was a dangerous tack and Norman knew it.

Kincaid hesitated. "You have something there. The best solution would be to use both properties. Listen, Kane, I'll buy you out. Put a price on the Simmons property and I'll buy it."

Norman laughed. "No, I wouldn't be happy. I'm not the kind of guy who likes to see the right thing done by somebody else. I want to do it myself. I think I'll hold on to the Simmons property. Who knows? You may buy the Kincaid real estate from your family, and then again you may not. Or you may get control of it and still not be able to develop the property. I may get it a year from today, or maybe in five years. I can wait."

"I'll be damned if I'll sell it to you."

"Why not?"

"Where does that leave me? I don't need the money. I want to develop the property."

Norman rose from his seat and walked over to the couch. He stood above Kincaid and looked down at him. "Let me make a crazy suggestion: we'll buy it together and develop it together."

Kincaid sat up suddenly and even in a sitting posture he was almost as tall as Norman. Kincaid frowned. "Develop it *together?* You can't be serious."

Norman felt his cheeks burning. "Why not? I've been in deals with bigger, richer and smarter men than you."

Kincaid studied him with a pleased expression. "I see that you do have a soft spot." He stood up and began to walk nervously about the room, his shoulders hunched, hands jammed into his pockets, sneakers slapping against the stone floor. Finally he stopped, turned and stared intently at Norman. "Fifty-fifty."

"Bullshit."

Kincaid's face fell. "Well, what then?"

"Look, Kincaid, let's level with each other. You have an option on the property and you can probably buy it if you want to. But after that, what use are you to me? You're no developer. You've never planned a project or leased a building."

The tall man seemed to shrink. "I'm not stupid. I learn fast."

"By the time you learn, I'll have six million feet rented and six buildings built."

"Well, what then? What percentage?"

"Ten per cent."

"Ten per cent? For God's sake, I own more than fifteen per cent now."

"You own fifteen per cent of nothing. I'm offering you ten per cent of something. You see that I get the property at the right price, and I'll give you ten per cent of my interest. You got a good name, you look good and you talk good. Maybe we can do things together. In the meantime you can be part of the biggest development that ever hit this town."

"But ten per cent."

"I'm being generous. You can't possibly earn that ten per cent. You'll get your fifteen per cent of the sales price, and you'll still have ten per cent of my interest in the completed project."

"I'm entitled to more than that just for getting you the property."

"Oh, hell, if that's what you want, I'll pay you a brokerage fee."

Kincaid flushed again and seemed to shrink even more. Norman relished the moment.

"Ten per cent is not enough."

"Mr. Kincaid, I'm not here to negotiate with you. I came to meet you. You asked what I wanted and I told you. You asked me what you could get and I told you. If it's not enough, I'm sorry. No deal. You play with the property yourself. You try and build a hundred-million-dollar project on your own. Oh, they know your name in this town, but I can show you places in New York where the Astors and the Rockefellers fell on their faces and they've got more money and a better name than yours."

Delbert Kincaid stood uncertainly for a moment. Then he smiled, and when he did, to Norman's surprise he regained his former size. *My God,* Norman thought. *He puffs up and down like a balloon.*

"OK. It's crazy. It's absolutely crazy, but you've got a deal." He took three strides across the room and shook Norman's hand. Norman permitted himself a small smile, mostly to mask his feeling of triumph.

"What now, Kane?"

"First I need all the available information on the property. Then we figure out how to make certain we exercise your option properly. By the way, now that we're partners, how about telling me the option price?"

"Twelve million dollars."

Norman smiled.

"Why does that amuse you?"

"I just like big numbers." Then Norman abruptly changed the subject. "Why don't you come to my office one day next week, Kincaid? Bring the agreements and we'll review them together."

"Fine. Of course, I won't say anything to anyone—will you?"

Norman smiled again. "Look, you and I just shook hands on a big deal. We could spend the next six months trying to draw agreements to keep us honest. Let's just trust each other to keep our mouths shut and work this out." Norman put out his hand again to shake Kincaid's hand and end the interview.

Kincaid seemed reluctant to close their discussion. "Can't I offer you a drink or something?"

"I don't think I have time."

"Of course you have, Mr. Kane." The voice was not Delbert Kincaid's. Norman turned; he was in for his second shock of the morning.

"Mr. Kane, this is my wife, Tina."

Later, recalling his first meeting with Tina Kincaid, Norman imagined she had made so shattering an impression that he had stumbled backwards. If Del Kincaid had surprised him, Tina astounded him. Like her husband, she seemed remarkably youthful. But Delbert Kincaid was tall and blond, and Tina was small, very round, and raven-haired.

"I would shake your hand," she said, stepping forward, "but as you can see, I'm dripping wet." Of course, Norman could see. Evidently Tina Kincaid had just come out of the pool, for her black hair hung about her face in long damp strands. *There are few women,* he thought, *who can wear their hair like that and still be beautiful.*

She wore a bikini, though perhaps "wore" was not the right word. Rather, it rode upon her body. Whatever its original color, the bikini was now darkened by the water and the two thin strips were mere black strings across her body. She was, as she had said, dripping wet. Drops of water ran from her hair down her shoulders and across her breasts. Norman was stunned. She looked like a girl of twenty, a magnificent, voluptuous little creature, all brown and black except where the inadequate bikini bared luscious lines of milky flesh.

Norman noted all this in a second. Despite his surprise, he mustered a cavalier smile and took her hand. "Who would pass up the opportunity to shake hands with a water sprite?" The touch of her hand, cool and wet, was yet another shock; he made a conscious effort to keep from tightening his grip. "I thought that only children were in the pool today."

"Really?" Tina Kincaid glanced down at herself appraisingly.

Norman laughed aloud. "No one would mistake you for a child, Mrs. Kincaid."

She smiled up at him. "My name is Tina." Their eyes held

briefly, then she turned to her husband. "What's going on, Delbert? What are you two men conjuring up?"

Kincaid shook his head. "We're not conjuring anything, Tina. Kane and I have made a business deal."

"Fine. Why don't you both come out to the patio, and I'll fix us a drink to celebrate."

Without waiting for a response, Tina turned and walked out onto the patio. Norman and her husband followed. The tiny G-string riding on Tina's hips was a marker focusing Norman's eyes. His hands tingled with the imagined feel of tautly swaying flesh. Only the bright sunlight broke the spell.

"Over here," said Del Kincaid. "Let me show you the place." Norman followed Kincaid, who led him through intricately casual gardens, down a winding path, through a copse of thin-barked willows to the beach. The sand was white and very smooth. A few feet away, the blue lake tugged ceaselessly at the shore.

"It's beautiful here," Norman said. "I've always wanted to live on the lake myself."

"We have a lot of fun. Of course, it can get pretty rough in the winter, but even then, the snow and ice piled up along the shore look rather interesting. We try to keep the kids from going out on it."

Kincaid continued describing the property as he led Norman across the beach and then back along yet another path through other gardens, and past a charming guesthouse. Norman tried to concentrate on Kincaid's description of his grounds but he could not shake off the vision of Tina Kincaid.

Finally, they strolled back to the patio. Two chairs were pulled up to an umbrella-shaded table. Alongside, Tina Kincaid stretched on a chaise, drying herself in the sun. "I've made three Tom Collins," she said, her eyes closed. "I hope that will be satisfactory.

"Fine," Norman said and sank into one of the aluminum-and-plastic chairs, happy to be out of the sun. He kept his eyes on Del Kincaid as much as possible, but time and again his glance found the lovely girl reclining beside him. Even when she was lying on her back, the bikini rode high on her firm breasts, and the pressure of the chaise did not spread her hips. He could see her legs better now and they were amazingly supple, unmarked and in perfect proportion to the rest of her. *She must be in her early thirties at least,* Norman thought, *and yet her skin is as clear and firm as a girl's.*

Again and again his eyes returned to her body, following the length and shape of it with a pleasure he could scarcely contain. Once, after staring at her breasts, his eyes flicked to her face and he saw that Tina Kincaid held one hand to her forehead shading the sun, while she looked at him coolly and directly. He was embarrassed, but Tina smiled and closed her eyes.

There is something there, Norman thought. He realized he should cut short the meeting. He had accomplished everything he wanted, and Kincaid was obviously growing uncomfortable. Norman finished his drink and stood up.

"Thanks for your hospitality. It was certainly a pleasure meeting both of you. I hope we'll be seeing a lot of each other in the future."

Tina Kincaid turned on her side and leaned on one arm, just as her husband had done in the family room. But the results were somewhat different. This new position served to accentuate even more the roundness of her hips and breasts, increasing Norman's agitation. He wrenched his eyes away and put out his hand to Del Kincaid. "Your home is beautiful and your grounds are magnificent. It was awfully good of you to see me without an appointment. I'll meet you at my office in a few days and we can go over the details."

"Fine, Norman. Just fine. I'm delighted you came."

Norman turned and nodded goodbye to Tina Kincaid, who looked abstracted now. She nodded back but did not smile. Norman followed Del Kincaid around the side of the house and to his own car. They shook hands again. Norman started the motor and pulled away. When he had first arrived, he had driven into the driveway quite slowly, shuddering a bit as the gravel crunched beneath his car. Now he heard the gravel spin out from under his wheels with a feeling of triumph and great anticipation.

Goddamn it, I've got to stay away from that broad. Then he laughed. *What am I thinking about? I'm fifteen years older than she is, and not so pretty in the bargain.* Norman slapped his forehead with the heel of his hand. *What do I want? Kincaid's property or his wife?*

"You know, that son of a bitch always keeps us waiting." August Lentman slammed his hand on the conference table, pushed his chair back and walked to the window.

"You're sure right there. Every time we have a meeting, the same thing happens. Kane comes in an hour late while we sit around here and twiddle our thumbs." Harper Rhodes joined Lentman at the window.

Now the others rose from the table and began to wander about the room muttering to each other or to the group in general.

I sat alone at the end of the conference table, my yellow pad and briefcase lined up before me, pencil on the pad, parallel to the green lines. Phil Winsley sat down beside me. He tried to talk in a confidential tone but was unsuccessful. His voice, hoarse, powerful, filled the office. The others stopped to listen.

"Come on now, Eddie. What's cooking this time? Why don't you let us in on it?"

I shook my head. "Phil, I'm sorry Norman is late, but I'm surely not the man to tell you what he has on his mind."

Phil Winsley smiled at me. "OK. If that's the way you want it. I suppose we can wait. We've been waiting for this guy for years now. What's a few minutes more?" He, too, rose and walked to the windows.

I sat back and looked from man to man. August Lentman, Harper Rhodes, Phil Winsley, Stanley Klein, Joseph Woodward, George Lillis. "The boys." The ultimate distillation from a mixture of thousands of investors. The real millionaires. Lentman and Winsley were from Chicago; Rhodes, Klein and Woodward from New York; George Lillis from Los Angeles. Where Norman found them, I do not know. Why they stayed with him was easy to understand.

Physically the men were very different: One handsome

(Lillis), one very ugly (Winsley), one quite tall (Rhodes), one short (Lentman), one fat (Woodward), one lean (Klein). Their personalities and interests varied greatly as well. Yet I doubt that in Norman's mind they had any individual identity whatsoever. To him they were a group. He never said "Let's call Lentman"; I never remember him telling me "Don't do it that way because Klein won't like it." Just "Call the boys," or "Tell the boys." They were a composite—an instrument Norman wielded for his own ends.

Eventually the door banged open and Norman hurried in. He did not greet the men individually, he shook no hands. He waved a casual greeting to all, then motioned them to sit down at the table.

"Pleased you could come, boys. Very pleased. There's a deal coming up, the biggest deal I've ever had, and you're going to be part of it." The boys exchanged looks. "I know I can trust you, but this deal takes even more delicate treatment than anything we've worked on before. Wait a minute, I'll show you what I'm talking about." Norman left his seat, walked to the French windows and pushed them open. Fortunately the wind was almost calm, and Norman stepped confidently onto the sunny balcony.

"Out here, boys. Stand along the rail. You see the Palmolive building over there? Beyond it is the Drake, and east of that is the Simmons property, which I own. Just east are several small apartment buildings, twelve stories high; some face the lake, the others face Walton. You can't see them very well because of the buildings in between, but you know the property. Say, Phil, doesn't your brother live at 211 East Lake Shore?"

Winsley nodded.

"Well, that's one of the buildings I'm talking about, part of the Kincaid estate."

I watched the faces of the men as they leaned across the railing and peered northeast toward the property Norman was describing. Each face betrayed irritation as each man tried to visualize something which was out of sight.

"The Kincaid family has owned those buildings for fifty years, but not any more, because I'm going to buy them."

"Buy them?" said Lentman. "Why the hell do you want to buy them? Nobody wants those old apartments any more."

Norman responded to Lentman with the same patience he had shown Hanson. "I'm not interested in apartments. We still have three or four buildings of our own that aren't fully rented. I'm going to tear down those apartment houses and build office buildings."

"Office buildings!" There were exclamations from several voices. "That isn't commercial real estate; it's zoned for apartments."

Norman waved his arms. "Just a minute. This is the biggest deal that ever hit this town. If you're not interested, forget it. I have someone who'll put up all the money. But you guys have been pretty decent up till now so I thought I'd give you first crack at it. Of course, if you don't want to hear any more, just say so."

The men moved restlessly on the balcony, but no one spoke.

"Besides, you're probably going to be unhappy when I bring in some new partners." Norman waited.

Finally Stanley Klein asked, "Who, Norman?"

"Delbert Kincaid, for one."

"Kincaid? Why?"

"Because he's the guy who's got the option to buy the family property. I need him and he needs me. I suppose I'll have to convince him he needs you, too."

The men did not respond to Norman's provocation.

"Here's the deal. I've got Kincaid sewed up, so I know I can buy the property. I've been East and lined up several major tenants. I talked to Fidelity Standard and they'll give me the money. But I haven't told you the best part. I'm going to put together the Kincaid and Simmons properties and then we can build on the north side of the drive."

"The north side? That's a beach."

"Yeah? Only part of it. Some is in the lake. But it's gonna be my beach and my piece of the lake. It isn't city property like you think. Once we put the Simmons and Kincaid properties together we can fill in the land and build on it."

Again the men were silent.

"Kind of surprised you, huh? Well, visualize this if you can: six buildings, three on each side of the drive. A million square feet in each building. Six million square feet altogether. Just look at that location. If there's a better spot in the city of Chicago, you tell me where it is."

"Six million feet." It was Joe Woodward. "My God, Norman, I don't think they've built six million square feet of office space in this town since World War Two. How do you expect to rent it?"

Norman spoke angrily. "Don't you listen? I've rented nearly a million feet with just a few phone calls."

Woodward tried another tack. "How much equity will it take, Norman?"

"Let's talk about that inside." Norman herded the men through the French doors and back to the conference table.

"First we'll look at it overall. Six million square feet. About thirty dollars a foot. A hundred and eighty million dollars."

There were general exclamations. The boys had not responded well thus far. Norman was both angry and frightened.

"Plus another eight million for the Simmons property—at my cost, and that doesn't include the Kincaid land."

"How much for the Kincaid land?"

"Twelve million dollars."

"Two hundred million total," said Rhodes. "How much is that per square foot?"

"Goddamn it, I'll give you projections, estimates and comparisons later. Right now I'm trying to give you the general picture. It's gonna cost two hundred million dollars, give or take a few million."

There were a few chuckles at this remark, but not hearty ones.

"What do you want from us, Norman?"

"The money."

"Not two hundred million dollars."

"Of course not. I'll borrow about a hundred and sixty million from Fidelity Standard, which means the deal will take forty million in cash."

"You don't expect us to put up forty million dollars."

"Listen, fellas," Norman said, "this deal will net close to ten million dollars a year."

The boys were obviously impressed.

"That sounds great," Winsley said, "but you know damn well we're not going to invest forty million dollars in one deal."

"All right. But I do expect you to put up at least twenty million. I'll bring in the other twenty."

This seemed to confuse them. "How do you plan to split up the equity?" Lillis asked.

"I hadn't thought of that," Norman lied. "I'll need five per cent for various pimps, brokers and the like. Then I need ten per cent for Kincaid. That's his price for delivering the property. That leaves eighty-five. I want thirty myself for putting the deal together, which leaves fifty-five."

"Wait a minute," said August Lentman. "Are you trying to say that we should put up half of the total cash for twenty-seven and a half per cent of the equity?"

"Not exactly, Augie. If you prefer, you can put up forty million for fifty-five per cent of the deal."

"Ridiculous," shouted Phil Winsley, rising to his feet. "You offered us bad deals before, Norman, but nothing as lousy as this." No one else spoke, so Winsley felt compelled to keep talking. "We generally put up all the money for two-thirds of the deal. Now you want us to put up half for only twenty-seven and a half per cent. I think it stinks."

"So stay out of the deal." Norman's words were braver than he felt. But Winsley was impressed.

"That ain't fair, Norman. We're entitled to negotiate. You can't just say take it or leave it."

"Why not? It's my deal."

"Except," Joe Woodward said quietly, "you don't have the money."

Norman smiled at Woodward. "Joe, I'll have no difficulty putting up the front money. Even Kincaid would help. But then he'd want more of the action. Oh, I can get the money. In fact, I can get it all in one place."

"Forty million dollars?" snorted Harper Rhodes. "Ridiculous."

Kane ignored Rhodes and stared at Winsley, who was still

standing at the table. "Are you going or coming, Phil?"

Winsley noted the expressionless faces of the other men. He sat down slowly. "I don't know whether I'm in or out, Norman, but I'll listen, I'll listen."

"Well, that's an improvement."

Woodward spoke mildly. "Don't you think we're entitled to more complete information before we invest our twenty million dollars? After all, we're not a charitable institution, Norman."

"Of course. My staff is preparing projections now. I'm sure this deal will bring us all a handsome profit over a period of years. As usual, I won't take any of the profits until you get your money back. And to impress you even more, this time I'm willing to buy into your part of the deal—for cash. That is, if you'll let me."

The men were obviously surprised. George Lillis stared up at the high ceiling. "It's not that we don't trust you, Norman. We've shot craps with you for quite a while. You've made about eleven straight passes, and we wonder whether you can make twelve."

"This isn't shooting craps. This is business. This is lay it on the line, build it, work it out and make it pay."

"Yes, I know," Lillis continued. "We've each put a million dollars or more in various deals of yours and we've done very well. Including you, Norman. But now you're asking us for more cash than ever before. Let's say you put up two million. That still leaves eighteen to come from the six of us. Three million apiece, which is a hell of a lot more than we have invested in any other deal. And this time we won't have control, Norman."

"What's fifty-five per cent of the deal if not control?"

"Remember, Norman, we're only taking twenty-seven and a half per cent."

"That's up to you. If you want, you can have fifty-five per cent, and that's control."

"Who's the other partner?"

"General Stone."

All of the men leaned forward. "You mean General Stone wants a piece of this deal?"

"Not a piece—the whole thing. I've had one hell of a time persuading him to take you boys in as partners."

"Listen," said Stanley Klein, "not even General Stone writes out forty-million-dollar checks every day."

"I don't know where Stone gets his money and I don't care. He told me he'd take the whole deal, and that sounds pretty good to me. One investor to deal with instead of a committee. But I told Stone you fellas are my regular partners. I said the boys are always in my deals. He was reluctant but he finally agreed. Now, if you don't want in, I'll just tell Stone you're not interested."

"He's a tough cookie."

"Yeah, he's a tough cookie, but he has enough faith in this deal to put forty million dollars on the line. Now, boys, either you're in or you're out."

"You'll show us the projections before we go ahead," Woodward said.

"You know I always give you all the information you need. But right now I want your commitment. Are you in or out?"

The men looked at each other. "I'm in," said Harper Rhodes. "Me too," said Stanley Klein. One by one the others nodded their assent.

"Fine. We've got a deal. All right. Don't talk to anybody, like I said. Don't even talk to each other. And for God's sake, don't discuss this with General Stone. If he thinks he's gonna have to deal with six other guys besides me, we'll lose him altogether."

Chairs scraped on the parquet floor. There was a general exchange of handshakes, and in a few minutes the men were gone. I remained seated at one end of the table. Norman sank into a chair at the other. For several minutes we were both silent.

"I thought you were beyond that, Norman."

"Beyond what?"

"I still remember when you started out in this game: going to one man and telling him you had an agreement with somebody else. Running to the mortgage lender and pretending you had tenants. Telling tenants you had a mortgage. I remember those days, and although I was often deeply concerned, I have to admit there was probably no other way to get started. But I thought you were beyond that now."

"Eddie, this is a two-hundred-million-dollar deal."

"But, Norman, at this point you have absolutely nothing pinned down. Was that story about Kincaid true?"

"Yep. Met him Saturday morning. We'll work out the details later this week."

"Then you don't have a firm deal?"

"Eddie, this thing is moving too fast; I have to take a few chances."

"Why? Why do you have to take chances? After reaching this point in your life, after overcoming a thousand obstacles —any one of which might have ruined you—why take on a deal so big it could easily crush you?"

"Stop that kind of talk, Eddie. Pretty soon you'll have me doubting myself."

"That will be the day."

"It's true, Eddie, you're making me nervous."

"You don't even have the property zoned properly."

"That's tomorrow's job."

"Maybe your new partner, General Stone, can help you."

"Him I haven't even talked to yet."

"Now you're joking."

"No, I'm serious. How the hell do you think I sold the boys on coming up with twenty million bucks? I had to convince them somebody else would put twenty million in too, even if it was a guy like Stone."

"How do you know he'll take your deal?"

"Stone has been flirting with me for fifteen years. Every time I start a new project he sends his pigeons over to ask if I want him for a partner. Every time I get into trouble, he offers to lend me money. But I keep remembering that this guy has taken over more bankrupt projects than any other man in Chicago. I tell you he's slobbering to get at me."

"Is he slobbering twenty million dollars' worth?"

"That we shall see. But first, I think I'll talk to McGarrity."

Norman suggested a luncheon meeting at his club, but Dan McGarrity turned him down; he did not affect casual luncheons in private clubs. When Norman called, McGarrity said, "Come on up to the office, old buddy. We'll have lunch some other time."

McGarrity's office was located on the near South Side of Chicago in a district still predominantly Irish and Polish but now surrounded by Negro neighborhoods. McGarrity was too shrewd to move his office downtown; he knew it was best to stay "back of the yards," among "his people," and near the Mayor.

The Mayor, John Conlin, had always lived in this ancient neighborhood, in a house that was bright and clean and in excellent repair, but over forty years old. The Mayor's children attended public schools and went to church every Sunday. Had one of his sons gotten into serious trouble, the Mayor would have taken him behind the house and whipped the boy himself.

I went to school with John Conlin. Not grade or high school or even college—to law school, at the University of Chicago. In those days he was quite a polished speaker. Even during his early political career, as an alderman and city clerk, the Mayor was known for his command of language. But once he decided he wanted the top municipal office, John Conlin lapsed back into the tones and diction of his youth.

His public loved it. They forgave him for attending a private college and law school. In fact, John Conlin never mentioned his college education or his law degree. He lived among his people and he spoke their language. Who could fault him for that? Surely not Norman Kane, who used the same tactics himself when the occasion demanded it. As far as Mayor Conlin was concerned, the situation always demanded it, regardless of whether he spoke to a local ward committeeman or a visiting foreign dignitary.

John Conlin surrounded himself with a strange assortment of professionals. Some were high-minded civic types, aloof from the day-to-day political clashes of the city. Others were like Dan McGarrity, crude but effective street fighters. Together these men, working officially and otherwise, carried out the Mayor's programs.

Some of them had grown rich. Chicago is a big city with a big budget, and it is perhaps inevitable that a few men will treat the city's business—the city's revenue—as their own. Not the Mayor. Money did not seem to interest him; he was content with power.

For Dan McGarrity, that was not enough. He performed the tasks the Mayor assigned to him with commendable efficiency. He enjoyed the power and prestige that his association with the Mayor gave him—but only as a means to an end. What the Mayor apparently did not know was that McGarrity also ruled a private realm. In that world, McGarrity was the prince of the fixers, the manipulators. If you wanted to get something done in Chicago, you were told to see Dan McGarrity or Jack Kinzman or Billy Golubiewski. McGarrity's name was usually mentioned first. Dan McGarrity no longer dirtied his hands, but he knew where to find men willing to remove their gloves, and he knew how to control them.

McGarrity did not feel it was necessary to inform the Mayor of these incidental activities. After all, the job had to be done, and why should he bother busy Johnny Conlin with such trivial matters? McGarrity righteously considered himself to be the insulation between the Mayor and the sometimes noxious political climate of Chicago.

I knew about this, as all Chicagoans claimed to know about it, and I was shocked by it, as all Chicagoans claimed to be shocked. But it did not shock Norman Kane.

"Look, you get yourself stuck in some town that's filled with do-gooders and honest guys, or small-time crooks and inexperienced grafters, and you're in trouble. You can't get anything done. You may want to build the finest project the town has ever seen, but they don't know how to handle it. Some rich guy who's been bribing the tax assessor for thirty years gives you a bum rap and this poor little assessor ain't going to do anything for you. He's going to shove it so far up your ass you won't be able to move.

"In Chicago it's different. You pay, but the price is based on the product. The price will be reasonable because you're dealing with good businessmen. Of course, you gotta have a mayor who's personally honest. A man who wants the power but not the dough, see? That's what makes it possible for a guy like McGarrity to operate. He can use his position with the Mayor to get things done. Of course, he expects you to pay him for turning the trick. But not too much. Otherwise you might get upset. Complain to the Mayor. And that's the end of the line for McGarrity. So he has to set a fair price. That's the beauty of Chicago. You can always get things done if you're willing to pay the price."

"You astound me, Norman. How can you approve of anything so dishonest?"

"Yeah, it's dishonest, but it's predictable, and a businessman's key to success is predictability. I don't give a damn how smart you are or how well you plan things—if you're faced with politicians who can't be trusted or who don't know what's best for their city, you're in big trouble."

"How can you depend on politicians to do the right thing?"

"You can't. But look at the record. In Chicago the crooks have accomplished as much as all the honest administrations in all the other cities of America put together. You don't hear of buildings collapsing or neighborhoods being ruined. No, it all works pretty well. I don't know how they do it but they do it, and frankly I don't mind the system at all."

That was Norman's viewpoint. And now he sat across the desk from Dan McGarrity, about to find out if the system was still operating smoothly.

McGarrity's office was on the second floor of an ancient building. There was no elevator. The halls were lined with a wainscot of aging orange-toned oak. The windows in McGarrity's office looked as if they had never been washed, and the freckled green shades were rolled halfway down. A dark-green carpet matched the shades, but it was too small for the room, and it exposed an unfinished wood floor that squeaked when you stepped on it. The place stank—not of graft or corruption, just of old age.

"You know, Dan, you might open a window in here once in a while."

McGarrity laughed. "I like it this way, Normie. I'm happy with these familiar old smells. There are some new ones floating down the streets these days that I'd just as soon keep out." He turned his head toward the window, and when Norman followed his gesture, he could see the line of tall City Housing Authority buildings. Both men knew they were filled with Negroes.

"Well, Norm, buddy, how goes it? Apartment buildings doing well?"

"Just fine, Dan."

"We didn't skin you too hard on the taxes?"

"No. Exactly what you said they'd be. I have no gripe."

"Fine, we like to keep you builders happy. That's the way we get all this beautiful new development in Chicago. Got to keep it coming, Norm. It's the lifeblood of the city." He said everything in a hearty, sincere manner. At times he was so overpowering that even Norman had to lower his eyes.

"Well, what's in the works for you now? Going to buy City Hall and convert it into a tenement?"

"Why not? You fellas bought all the tenements and turned them into City Hall."

The big Irishman laughed appreciatively. "That's what I like about you, Normie. We understand each other."

Norman nodded. He always felt at ease with McGarrity. "I've got a new deal cooking, Dan. A very special one. You'll have to keep it under your hat until we get it off the ground."

"No problem. Nothing you say to me ever goes farther than this office." Even McGarrity smiled when he said it.

"Of course, Dan." And with that, Norman began to outline to McGarrity his plans to merge the Simmons and Kincaid properties and to construct office buildings on both sides of Lake Shore Drive. During Norman's explanation McGarrity showed no emotion whatever.

"That's it, Dan. Of course, the area's zoned residential and we'll have to get it changed to permit the construction of highrise office buildings."

"There'll be a lot of opposition, Norman."

"From who?"

"Well, I doubt it will be popular, and you know the Mayor

is always worried about whether things are popular or not, particularly in an election year. Most of the people who will object are not people the Mayor is particularly concerned about. These Michigan Avenue and Lake Shore Drive folks contribute to the old man's campaign chest, but they don't control many votes. Still, it won't be a popular thing."

"I don't get you, Dan."

"Well, Norman, you're going to take a part of Chicago that people have gotten used to and you're going to build buildings on it of a kind they're *not* used to. You're going to take part of their beach and their lake, fill it in and build tall buildings. Now I know the property doesn't belong to the city, but *they* don't, and the newspapers are sure to confuse the issue. That I promise you."

"We've been through it all before, Dan. After a while it dies down, and besides, this project is good for the city."

"I don't doubt it a bit. Worth a lot more to us than all those fancy cooperative apartments. Probably bring a lot of jobs to Chicago."

"Exactly."

"Still, it won't be popular. You know the battle we've been having about the air rights over the train tracks in the Loop. We keep getting a lot of bad publicity over that."

"Oh, yes. But they built the Prudential Building and the Outer Drive East apartments, and there are other projects planned. Nobody seems unhappy now."

"All true, Norman. But the fact remains it's not really popular with the people. They keep driving up and down the Outer Drive and saying, 'Look what they're doing to our city. Never used to be any buildings here and now they're ruining it.' "

"Dan, you're closer to the people than I am, but I don't think many people are bothered by high-rise structures in the Loop."

"You'd be surprised, Norman. You'd truly be surprised. I myself am amazed at how angry people can get over these things. Now you take that Harrison-Halsted thing, that problem we had with the University of Illinois. Now there's a project that surely is good for the city. A large branch of the

University, built in a very sensible location. Why, it was a dying neighborhood. Yet look at all the bad publicity we got. The Mayor has reached the stage in his career where he's very sensitive about these things. I tell you, Norman, it won't be easy."

Norman said nothing. Something did not ring true, but he could not figure out what it was. If McGarrity wanted money, he had only to say so. Their relationship was beyond the stage where price could not be discussed.

On the other hand, Norman did not dare accuse McGarrity of not leveling with him. Men like McGarrity believed in the honor of reliable miscreants. They would tell you what they wanted, and they would tell you what you would get for it. If you weren't satisfied—if you decided to fight—well, that was up to you. However, if you could afford to let them have what they wanted, there was seldom any difficulty. But you must never accuse them of being dishonest. Therefore Norman sat quietly staring out the window at rows of apartment buildings. Tall, ugly, each an exact replica of its faceless neighbor.

"Tell me, Norman," McGarrity resumed, "who'll be in this with you?" He walked to the window and looked out across the barren city landscape.

"The usual group: Lentman, Rhodes, Klein, Woodward and the others. The boys."

"Oh, yes, the same fellows who invested in your apartment houses, right?"

"That's right. Plus young Del Kincaid."

"Anyone else?"

"I don't know. It's going to take a lot of money, Dan—two hundred million dollars." McGarrity showed no surprise, but then why should he? The city's own budget totaled hundreds of millions of dollars annually, and McGarrity controlled a good part of it.

"Just wondering, Norman. Just wondering. I'm sure your partners are all good men. Even Kincaid won't hurt you. Highly respected name in this town. And his family's given a lot to the Mayor's campaign fund in the past. No, just wondering, Norman."

"What about the rezoning, Dan?"

"I'll have to give it some thought. For the time being, I

won't even approach the Mayor. This is a funny deal, and if we hit Johnny the wrong way he may nix us, right off the bat. I'd like to see it go through, for your sake and mine and the city's as well."

"Dan, I trust your judgment. When you figure it out, let me know."

McGarrity remained at the window.

"By golly, there must be a thousand of them on the streets today. I remember when the old boy didn't have more than two or three."

Norman could not imagine what McGarrity was talking about. Again he looked out the window. Below them, waiting at a stop light, was one of the familiar green-and-white trucks of the Stone Warehouse Company.

"Yes," said McGarrity, "the General's come a long way. You can't drive three blocks in this town without seeing a Stone truck. Right, Norman?"

"I see what you mean."

"As you said, Norman, there's a right way and a wrong way. Somehow I feel that you'll come up with the right way."

Norman put out his hand. "Thanks, Dan. You've given me one hell of an idea."

"An idea? By George, I didn't realize I'd given you any ideas. I was afraid I pretty much got you down on this thing."

"No, there's something about talking to you, Dan. I always get a kick out of it and I always learn something. Thanks again, pal. I'll be talking to you real soon."

"Good luck there, Norman. Glad to be able to help."

Norman fairly ran down the stairs. So that was it. McGarrity was fronting for the old man. Marvelous. The story he had fed the boys was almost true. General Stone wanted to be in his deal.

Then he began to worry. He hesitated for a moment on the landing. How did Stone know? And how had word gotten so quickly to Dan McGarrity? Well, that mystery would have to be unraveled. In the meantime, the important thing was that Stone wanted a piece of the action.

Suddenly Norman felt elated. He took the remaining steps down from McGarrity's office two at a time. *My God,* he thought, *I haven't done that since I was in college.*

71

2

Norman's elation did not last. In size and scope, Lake Shore Plaza surpassed all the deals he had ever developed before. And to put it together he would have to extract twenty million dollars from General Mervin Lee Stone. The prospect was worse than sobering; it was almost depressing.

At first, Norman suggested I accompany him to General Stone's office. I was surprised. I considered it unlikely that many legal questions would arise at this first confrontation. It didn't occur to me that Norman might be frightened. All I could think of was that bringing a lawyer to a first conference might tend to distort the dialogue, and I mentioned this to him.

"You really get me," he replied. "Every time I tell you about one of my meetings you say, 'I wish I could have been there.' Now I invite you along and you tell me you're afraid you might kill the deal."

On the day set for the meeting I kept my schedule open,

but I did not call Norman. He seldom forgot details. If Norman wanted me to attend, he would call in plenty of time. The hours passed. I worked on other matters, jumping a little at each ring of my telephone and watching the clock until it grew so late that I knew Norman had either canceled his appointment or gone without me.

He called at 6 P.M., just as I was ready to call it a day.

"What are you doing, Eddie?"

"Going home."

"Why don't you stay downtown? I want to talk to you."

"Well, I don't know, Norman."

"Come on, Eddie. Something exciting happened. I got to tell somebody. Come over to the club and have a drink with me."

There was an element of mystery mixed with wistfulness in Norman Kane's voice, and frankly I was darn curious about the meeting with Stone. Still, I hesitated. Some instinct, perhaps malicious, prompted my response.

"Why not take Frieda out to dinner and tell her?"

"Frieda? Look, this is business, Eddie. Frieda's got nothing to do with my business. Not ever."

It was a strange remark, but before I could think of what to say, Norman was talking again.

"OK, buddy," Norman said. "I'll meet you in twenty minutes. Downstairs in the bar."

I had no chance to demur; Norman hung up.

On the way to the club, I thought over what he had said about Frieda. Here was a man in the midst of a big business transaction, the biggest one he had ever undertaken, and he wouldn't discuss it with his wife. "Not ever," he had said, as if that were some fundamental rule of his existence.

Why? Surely Frieda was clever enough to understand the deal. True, it was a dangerous deal, but Frieda must have grown accustomed to Norman's risky manipulations by now. In fact, I was sure she was excited by them. I envisioned Norman telling his tale to this beautiful and intelligent woman. I could sense her response, animated and enthusiastic. If a man had a wife like that, why not share his achievements with her? There was something in that thought which seemed to reflect on my own marriage. I didn't like the idea, somehow, and I drove it from my mind.

When I entered the club lounge, Norman was sitting sprawled at a table tucked away in a corner. My favorite drink and his were on the table. He wasted no time on amenities.

"I met Stone today."

"I know."

He looked at me. "Yeah, who am I kidding? I asked you to be there, didn't I? But when it came right down to it, I wanted to go alone."

"That's all right, Norman. I always thought you would."

Norman smiled. "You ever seen the old man's suite?"

"No. I've been in the Stone Tower, but never up in General Stone's own office."

"You wouldn't believe it. You just wouldn't believe it. I've been in plush places before, but this is the plushest. He's right on top of that building, you know, just like I am on top of the Cormack Tower. Except his office is a complete circle with glass all around. You can see the whole city. But the view inside is better than the view outside. There's a circular wall in the center, paneled in various woods—some he told me are a thousand years old, selected, fitted and joined by some genius so you can't even tell where the joints are. The light comes from—hell, I don't know where the light comes from—it's like a halo.

"The floor is leather. That's right, leather, laid in a parquet pattern. And colors, well, I couldn't begin to describe them. When the lights are on or when the sun comes through the windows, the damn floor glows. The whole place glows.

"The General's all alone up there. No secretary, no receptionist. Just General Stone sitting on top of the world. Everybody else in the organization works on the lower floors. If you want to get to the General, you have to take this little round elevator that opens up right in his office. But you can't get in unless the General presses a button.

"All around, beneath the windows, are low, curved benches covered with leather just like the floor. Drapes? There are no drapes. Just light-diffusing curtains, and when he pushes a button on his desk, they curl up and disappear into the ceil-

74

ing, like in a theater, you know? Or bang! There they are hanging down all around you.

"And no desk. Just a seating group here and a seating group there, some files hidden on the inside walls, maps and charts that pull out from nowhere, but no pencils, no paper, no nothing.

"And murals, incredible murals. Some curved along the inner core, others hanging in space like on sky hooks—and they move. Maybe a painting is blocking your view, see? And the General doesn't like that, so he presses this button and bang! There goes this hundred-thousand-dollar painting on a track around the room. Or maybe you'd like to see it close up, and by God, he pushes this button and before you know it, you're sittting knee to knuckle with this goddamn master-piece. Why, it scares the hell out of you. If the General gets mad, he could kill you with a painting.

"Then there's the General. He's pretty hard to believe, too. Here is this big gorgeous office with maybe a million bucks' worth of floors, walls, furniture and paintings, and up steps this little guy—well, I tell you, he makes me look like a giant—maybe he weighs a hundred and ten pounds and except for this tiny moustache, there ain't a hair on his head. Next to him, I'm the original hairy ape.

"You know he's pushing seventy-five, but you wouldn't be-lieve it. He's got skin like a baby, pink skin, no folds, not around the eyes, not around the chin, nowhere—just a little, round, seventy-five-year-old baby with blue eyes and a white moustache."

"You've seen him before, Norman."

"Hell, I never really saw him before in my life. I only saw him seated up on a platform, or maybe his picture in the paper. I saw him in a hundred places, but I never saw him up in that office. And up there, I tell you, he's something else.

"Anyway, I'm getting ahead of myself. Before I meet the General I have to get past the receptionist on the floor below. She's a middle-aged doll but nice-looking, and she smiles like she knows me all my life and says, 'Oh, yes, of course, Mr. Kane. The General's expecting you.' She presses this little button and tells the General I'm there, and the next thing I

75

hear is the sound of a door sliding open. I look behind this doll and suddenly there's an elevator and she says, 'Please take the elevator up, Mr. Kane. It opens in the General's office and he'll be waiting for you.'

"I walk into this elevator, and before I can push a button or anything, the door closes. That elevator is walled with mirrors, great big circular mirrors. You ever see yourself in a circular mirror, Eddie? Yeah, well, unless you're Cary Grant, by the time you walk out you got an inferiority complex.

"While I'm still thinking how bad I look—zing, the door opens. I walk out because I don't want to shuffle off in that mirrored coil, and then I see this little round baby with the blue eyes and the white moustache coming at me, and he's covering the floor ten feet at a stride and saying, 'Norman Kane, what a pleasure. It's so good of you to come.' And I'm saying, 'General, it's a great privilege for me to be here.'

"And he's saying, 'Forget the "General." That's for the press and the public. Let's start out with Norm and Merv.'

"Well, that makes me feel pretty good. So I say, 'Fine with me, Merv.' And all the while I'm looking around.

" 'I'll give you a quick tour, Norm.' We walk in a circle around this central core and he doesn't say anything about what's outside the windows, because you got to be a moron not to recognize what's outside the windows, and he doesn't tell me what the floor is made of because even an idiot can see that, and he doesn't tell me how much he spent for the paintings, but God knows I can figure it out myself. He just walks around and I follow him, and by the time we get back to where we started, I'm kind of at a loss for words.

" 'Like it?' he says.

" 'Like it?' I say. ' "Like" isn't the word. Tell you the truth, Merv, I don't know what to say. I've never been any place like this before and I suppose nobody else has, either.'

" 'That's right. That's the response I wanted.'

" 'Well, I have to give you credit,' I say. 'This is really beautiful and tasteful.'

" 'Bullshit,' he says. 'I got no taste at all. All I know is trucks and real estate. I ordered one of my men to get this place decorated, and everybody tells me he did a hell of a job.'

"The General talks in an abrupt way, plain and straight-forward, even vulgar. I know this son of a bitch never went beyond the fourth grade, but even so, after fifty years of living high and talking to smart people, I'm damn sure he can talk smart himself.

"So we're standing there, he's smiling up at me (which for me is a thrill anyway) and he says, 'How about a drink, Norm?' I don't know if this guy likes people to drink or not, but I figure, what the hell's the use of kidding him, so I ask for Scotch because I don't know if he can mix a martini. He makes a pass at the wall, and the next thing you know there's a bar, and he pours me out a double J & B (he never asks my brand) and one for himself, and then waves me to a chair.

"This chair is pretty well placed, and I got a strange feeling the old boy put it there himself, because when I look out that window I feel just like when I'm at home looking out at Lake Shore Drive. I can see a half dozen big buildings that this bird owns. 'Well, Merv,' I say, 'it's kind of a comforting view.'

"The General laughs. 'Yeah, it sure is comforting.'

" 'Like having your portfolio open all the time.'

"Again he laughs, and I keep talking. 'Your typical miser has to keep his gold in a safe somewhere and open it up when he wants to see it, but you can sit here like a gentleman—pull the curtains and look at yours.'

" 'I knew you'd understand. From your office you can see the south side of your buildings, and from your apartment you can see the north. You got it coming and going, huh?'

"Well, this ain't too funny, but I give him a chuckle any-way because he laughed at my line. 'That's it, Merv. That's it exactly.'

"The General smiles. 'Any time I get to feeling disgusted with it all,' he says, 'I look out these windows at all that steel and concrete rising up in the sky. It makes me feel good to know that a hell of a lot of it's mine.'

"About this time my eyes are going around the room again and I'm looking at this painting which I know damn well is by Claude Monet. Somebody has placed it perfectly. From where we sit, the mass of colors dissolves into a pond of lilies. You can catch the reflections in the water, and the whole thing makes sense.

77

" 'You like it?' the General asks me.

" 'Like it? I love it.'

" 'Great. It's yours.' He stands up.

"I laugh.

" 'No, I'm serious,' Stone says and heads for the painting.

" 'Baloney, Merv. We're not going to start that way. I guess you know my soft spot, but I'm not going to get into your debt for a lousy painting.'

" 'Lousy painting,' he yells. 'Why, that damn thing cost me a hundred fifty thousand dollars.' And his pink face turns kind of purple, but then he sees I'm smiling and he sits down again.

" 'You're OK,' he tells me. 'I see my usual tactics aren't going to work with you.' I wonder what he means by his 'usual tactics.' Still, I'm pretty shaken up because a guy doesn't offer you a hundred-fifty-thousand-dollar painting just like that, not even to buy, let alone as a gift. I begin to wonder whether he really meant it.

" 'On the up and up, Merv, tell me something. Supposing I said Yes. Would you really have given me the painting?'

" 'You would never have said Yes.'

" 'What makes you so sure?'

" 'That was the risk I had to take. If you took the painting, I would be out a hundred and fifty grand. But you would be out several million dollars. I'd never go into a deal with you. I'd know you were the wrong kind of partner.'

"He gets up and starts to walk around, then he doubles back and points a finger at me and now somehow he looks like he's six feet tall. 'I'm not saying you're the right kind of a guy because you didn't take it. I just say you're not a small-time con man.'

"I laugh out loud. 'Listen, a hundred and fifty grand for five minutes of bullshit and a drink, that's not a small-time con man. Those are pretty big chips.'

" 'You're playing for bigger ones. Besides, how do you know I'd let you take the painting?'

" 'I'm glad I didn't find out.'

"The General steps even closer than before. 'Let's cut the conversation,' he says. He waves an arm around the city.

'You're on the way up. You've done damn well. One day you might even pass me by.'

" 'I sure as hell hope so,' I say.

"He doesn't even smile. 'I still like making deals,' he says. 'It still gives me a charge. It's a way of life, making deals, putting them together—stealing them, if you like—I still enjoy it.'

" 'But why me?' I stand up and take a jolt of the Scotch, and now I'm taller than he is again and I feel a little better. 'There must be guys floating in and out of here seven days a week with big deals.'

" 'You're right.' He turns his back and walks over to the window. 'Guys are forever walking in here with deals, big and little ones, but mostly big ones. Some of the guys are crooked and some are honest. Some are smart and some are stupid. But the deals, Norman—' and he turns around—'either they're the kind I've done a million times or they're so damn screwy nobody in his right mind would try them.' He comes back from the window. 'What I'm looking for is something interesting, something different, but something that makes sense. Your deal on the Drive—office buildings on the Kincaid property—that makes sense.'

" 'Wait a minute, Merv,' I say. 'How the hell did you find out about my deal?'

" 'McGarrity told me.'

" 'About the office buildings, maybe, but McGarrity knew you were interested in my deal even before I went to see him.'

"The General smiled. 'Who do you think sent Ernest Barry to see you?'

"Well, I tell you, Eddie, I was sure surprised. I sit there with my mouth hanging open while Stone goes on talking.

" 'I told Barry, "I'm no developer, I'm a backer. Go see Norman Kane. If he's interested, I'm interested." '

" 'Why didn't you just call me?'

"The General only smiled.

" 'Anyway,' I say to him, 'McGarrity says we'll have a hell of a time rezoning the property.'

" 'Baloney. McGarrity always says No but he acts Yes. That's what counts.'

" 'I thought you were looking for deals that aren't crazy. Everybody says I'm out of my mind.'

" 'You probably are. When you come up with an idea like that, you're not just Norman Kane, you're somebody else. You're the somebody else you want to be.'

"I just stare at him. Here is this cold, hard multimillionaire —a guy who has beaten, smashed and robbed his way into being the richest man in this town and maybe the richest man in this country—and he spills this sentimental philosophy. I know he ain't drunk because he barely touched the one Scotch. I look in his eyes and I tell you they're glittering. That's right, glittering. I begin to think maybe he isn't really General Stone but some nut pretending to be General Stone.

"Suddenly he squints and then he begins to laugh like hell. He falls into a chair, slaps his knees and pounds his chest, and now I am really worried. I don't say a thing. Finally he stops laughing. He picks up his drink and finishes it. Then he gets the J & B and fills up my glass and his.

" 'You think I'm nuts, huh? You're surprised the old General is feeding you this sentimental hogwash. You can't believe that's what keeps the old boy going. Well, nobody else understands it, so why the hell should you? And what's the difference? All you want is my money and my help.'

" 'That's not true. I mean, you're not what I expected, Merv. That is, I don't know what I expected, but anyway, you're not like I thought you'd be.'

" 'You're stumbling, Norman. *You're* beginning to talk nonsense. Let's drop this psychology and philosophy. Who cares why I want to do this thing? Maybe you understand, or maybe if you don't, some day you will. I'm not looking for guys to manipulate, Norman.' And he sits down next to me. 'I'm looking for partners—oh, hell, not financial partners. I can get all the money men I want. I'm looking for cockeyed people like you who see this cockeyed world the same way I do. Guys with brains and maybe some larceny in their souls. But smart. You aren't going to take my hundred-fifty-thousand-dollar painting if you can get several million dollars out of me. And I'm not going to give you a big chunk of dough if you'll settle for paint on canvas! Maybe I got you wrong, Norman. Maybe you're just lucky. But, on the other hand, maybe you got what I'm looking for. I'm gonna take a chance on you. I'm gonna write you a check for whatever you need.'

"At that he looks away, gets up and walks to the window again, and I'm pretty glad that he does because when he says he's gonna write me a check I stop breathing for quite a while.

" 'How much, Norman?'

" 'Forty million dollars.'

"For a few minutes the General doesn't say anything, and I sit there jiggling the ice in my drink and he stands there looking out that window and jiggling the ice in his. I'm thinking to myself that forty million bucks will buy a hell of a lot of ice cubes.

" 'I want ninety per cent of the deal.'

"At that I sigh. I look at the ice cubes floating in the booze and I think to myself, *What the hell, it's been an interesting afternoon.* I take another swig of Scotch and then I get up.

" 'You know, General, I need your dough. I really do. In fact, if I don't get the money from you, I don't know where I'm gonna get it. But I never give anybody ninety per cent of a deal—not even me. I'll tell you what. Maybe you want to sell me that Monet. That way we can say we made a deal together and stay friends.'

"He turns around. 'You don't make sense, Norman. What's wrong with ninety per cent of the deal?'

" 'Well, first of all, I don't need the whole forty million dollars because my other pigeons are willing to put up half of it. And then I gotta have my piece of the action. I don't see how you can have what you want and I can have what I want and my other partners can get their share.'

"The General smiles. 'I'll tell you what, Norman. I'll give you fifteen million for thirty per cent of the deal and you can split the rest any way you goddamn please.'

"I'm so stunned I almost sit down. 'Do you mean that?'

" 'Yeah, I mean it. Fifteen million dollars for thirty per cent.'

" 'That doesn't make sense. You're taking the short end of the deal.'

" 'Now.'

" 'I don't get you.'

"The General waves his hands. 'Never mind, Norman, never mind. Forty million for ninety per cent or fifteen million for thirty per cent. Take your choice.'

" 'I'll take the fifteen.'

" 'Good, then we got a deal.'

" 'What are the strings?'

" 'No strings. That's my offer. Except there is one thing.'

"In my mind I'm thinking, *Uh huh. I knew it would come.*

" 'Only one string, Norman, and this is it. If the deal takes more than forty million dollars, everybody puts up his own share of the overage.'

" 'Of course,' I say.

" 'Don't say of course. I want everybody's stock in escrow to make sure that if the deal runs short everybody comes up with his stake. If your boys don't come up with their share but I come up with mine *and* theirs, I own their stock.'

" 'I'm not sure I understand you.'

" 'It's pretty simple. You need forty million dollars. I'm putting up fifteen for thirty per cent. The other seventy per cent will cost twenty-five million. Now suppose the deal runs up to a hundred million; that leaves you sixty million short. The guys that put up the twenty-five million got to put up seventy per cent of the shortage. And if they don't, but I do, I get to take over their equity.'

" 'Yeah, and what do they get for their equity?'

" 'Nothing. Not a dime.'

" 'You mean their original twenty-five million is wiped out?'

" ' "Wiped out" is an ugly phrase.'

" 'But accurate. I think they should have the right to remain in the deal for a smaller interest. At least give them a chance to get their money back.'

"Stone drops his hands palms down. 'No deal, Norman. Fifteen million for thirty per cent on my terms or no deal.'

"I put down my drink and I get to thinking I ought to leave. I stand up and start to move 'I'll have to think about it, Merv.'

" '*Now,*' he says. 'Make up your mind right now.' I tell you those baby-blue eyes were iron-gray.

"I stop right where I am, one foot in front of the other, a bit unbalanced—both my footing and my thinking.

"The General says it again. 'Now, Norman. Yes or no.'

"I take a breath. I look out the window at the skyline. I see those gorgeous buildings the old boy has begged, borrowed and stolen. *What the hell?* I think. *What have I got to lose?*

" 'OK,' I say. 'You got a deal.' "

When Norman finished his story, he was literally glowing with pride and excitement. Now he awaited my comments, in the evident expectation that I would be overwhelmed by what he had told me. Actually, his story disturbed me in many ways, but I was careful not to voice my doubts—at least for the moment. The best I could do was to express my amazement over his strange interview with General Stone.

"Great, huh? I thought you'd be impressed."

"I am, Norman. Quite impressed."

"Come to my office tomorrow morning, Eddie. We'll hammer out the agreements together." He leaned forward, obviously pleased with himself. "Now I'm going to celebrate. I think I deserve it." He looked around for a telephone.

"Going to take Frieda out on the town?"

Norman had the phone in his hands. He grinned at me slyly. I had seen that look before. I almost jumped to my feet.

"Got to get home, Norman. Great story. See you in the morning."

As I left, he was placing his call. If it wasn't Frieda, I didn't want to know about it.

When I reached Norman's office the next day, I immediately confessed that I did not even understand the basic financial arrangements.

"Norman," I said, "if I heard you correctly last night, the figures don't add up. You promised General Stone thirty per cent for fifteen million dollars. That's so unfair the boys will drop out of the deal the minute they hear about it."

Norman was unruffled. "Of course. You're absolutely right. If I put the deal together like that, I'd be long on stock, short on money, and out of investors."

"Then you intend to go back on your word?"

Norman frowned and drew in his chin. "What has my word got to do with it? I'm putting a deal together. With thirty-five million dollars I'm eighty-seven-and-a-half per cent home. Now all I have to do is find five million dollars more and divvy up the interests in a way that makes sense."

"If you do that you're a magician. But then, it wouldn't be the first time."

"OK, Eddie, I'll explain. The General expects to put up fifteen million dollars for thirty per cent of the deal, so for another five million he's entitled to another ten per cent— forty per cent for twenty million dollars."

"How do you know he'll put up another five million?"

"I don't. But I've got to start somewhere. Now, if the General gets forty per cent of the deal for twenty million dollars, the boys won't be happy. That is, the boys won't be happy if they know about it. So I gotta figure out a way they don't know about it. As far as the boys are concerned, the General is getting only thirty per cent for his twenty million. Of course, that's still a better deal than I offered them, so I've got to give them thirty per cent for their twenty million, too. That oughta make the boys happy—an extra two and a half per cent for nothing. But I'll have to cover up what I'm doing for the General."

"Forgive me, Norman. I don't understand a word you're saying."

"OK. Suppose that for the usual tax reasons we split up the forty million dollars into stock and notes. Let's say thirty-six million of notes and four million of stock. OK?"

"One day Internal Revenue is going to complain about the way you capitalize these deals, Norman. They're going to say you've got too little in stock and too much in notes. They're going to claim the whole investment should be considered stock, and then the payments on the notes will be taxed to the shareholders as dividends, and the corporation won't get any deduction for the payments."

"They haven't done it yet."

"But they might."

Norman did not want to hear any more about it.

"Let's get back on the track, Eddie. Thirty-six million in notes, four million in stock. Right?"

"We'll see."

"Now this is how I'll divide it." And Norman scribbled on a piece of paper the capitalization of Lake Shore Plaza.

Investor	Notes	Stock	Stock %
Stone	$18,000,000	$1,200,000	30.00
Boys	13,500,000	900,000	22.50
Kane 1	4,500,000	300,000	7.50
Kane 2	—	1,040,000	26.00
Kane 3	—	400,000	10.00
Kincaid	—	160,000	4.00
	$36,000,000	$4,000,000	100.00%

I stared at the figures without understanding them. "The numbers add up to forty million dollars and a hundred per cent of the stock," I said, "but other than that I don't get it."

Norman smiled happily. I realized he was delighted and not a bit surprised that I didn't understand his chart.

"Look at the figures, Eddie. If you add up the notes and stock for Stone, they total nineteen million two hundred thousand dollars. Now if you add up the notes and stock for the boys, plus what I call Kane One, that also comes to nineteen million two hundred thousand dollars. You see, each side gets thirty per cent of the deal for nineteen two."

"That Kane One—you're going to buy four and a half million dollars in notes with your own money?"

"Oh, for Christ's sake, why don't you hear me out?"

I shook my head while Norman continued his explanation.

"Now if you add up what I call Kane Two and Three and Kincaid, that's my ordinary promoter's percentage—forty per cent of the deal. As usual, for my promoter's share I don't have to buy any notes."

"That I can understand. Now explain the rest."

"OK. To make the General happy, I've got to give him the stock I call Kane Three, which is ten points. That way he's got forty per cent of the deal for a little less than twenty million dollars."

"You're going to give him ten points?"

"Well, not exactly give it to him. We'll make a side agreement. I won't tell the boys or they'll realize Stone has a better deal than they do. Later, when the project is up, I'll just sell him the stock for what I paid for it—four hundred thousand. In the meantime, the boys will be delighted. They'll think that between me and them and Kincaid, we own seventy per cent of the deal."

"I still don't get it, Norman. You're also buying four and a half million dollars' worth of notes. You never bought notes in a deal before."

"I don't intend to use my own money. I'm going to borrow four million eight hundred thousand dollars—enough cash to buy seven and a half per cent of the stock and the four and a half million dollars' worth of notes, from General Stone."

"From Stone? Why in hell are you going to do that?"

"Well, in the first place, who else would lend me the money? And in the second place, Stone loves deals like this. He's gonna own thirty per cent in the clear and ten per cent on the side. If I don't pay back the money I borrow from him, he picks up seven and a half per cent more, which gives him forty-seven and a half per cent of the deal. All he has to do is sway one of the boys or buy out Kincaid, and he's got control."

"What if you do pay him back?"

"So what? Then he owns forty per cent of a good deal. What has he got to lose?"

"Will you tell the boys you're borrowing from Stone?"

"Are you kidding? One of the come-ons in this deal is that I'm putting up cash to buy notes just like they are."

"I don't know, Norman. It's all very risky and not very ethical. To make it work you've got to lie to the boys and put yourself in hock to Stone."

"In hock? I won't be in hock. The only security Stone will have for that four-and-a-half-million-dollar note is the note it-

self, and the stock that goes with it. I'm not gonna sign anything personally. Besides, I'm going to get him to agree to let
me buy back the stock that goes with the note at book value.
If everything works out all right, I'll end up with thirty-three
and a half per cent of the deal, anyway."

"Norman, you've worked out screwy deals before, but this
is the worst."

"How do you figure? For one million three hundred forty
thousand dollars I end up with thirty-three and a half per
cent of a two-hundred-million-dollar deal."

I protested, but Norman had lost interest in dazzling me
with his fiscal gymnastics. "All right, Eddie, you know how
this deal has to be set up. Go ahead and draft the agreements.
We've got to pick up Delbert Kincaid's option as soon as possible. Come on now, stop worrying. The legal fees on this deal
will probably net you a couple hundred thousand dollars."

By the time I returned to my own office I was resigned to
drawing the agreements the way Norman wanted them. In
some ways this was not as complex a transaction, at least from
a legal standpoint, as many others I had worked on with Norman. In the past, our syndicates of investors often numbered
in the dozens and sometimes in the hundreds. This time there
were only nine men, which meant we could avoid the usual
multiplicity of legal agreements.

Then, too, because there were so few investors, we would
not be required to register our offering with either the Securities and Exchange Commission or the Illinois Securities Commission.

The terms were relatively simple: the group would put up a
little more than twelve million dollars now to buy the Kincaid property and cover incidental expenses. Then they
would pay eight million dollars more to buy the Simmons
property from Norman—but not until the rezoning was complete and Norman arranged his long-term financing. The
final twenty million dollars would be paid in before construction began.

As usual, Kane Enterprises, Inc., would act as the leasing and mortgage agent, construction manager and project coordinator. Norman always insisted on complete control over the development of his ventures. All of this was typical, except that this time all the stock would be pledged, and General Stone and his millions would be hovering about—waiting for a crisis.

I trotted around behind Norman as he brought the agreements to the investors. The boys were no trouble at all. As Norman predicted, they were delighted that he was giving them more for their money and requiring a smaller total investment. The notes that Norman was buying impressed them mightily.

The boys were accustomed to our forms of development agreements and they signed without question. Norman warned them the agreements might have to be amended to satisfy Stone's attorney, and this proved correct.

We met with Frank Glover and Stone in the General's incredible office. I was happy to have a chance to inspect this sanctuary of sanctuaries. Norman's description was, if anything, understated.

Glover was trim and precise in appearance and demeanor. "This deal is nothing like the one you proposed, Mr. Kane. My client was to pay fifteen million dollars for thirty per cent of the equity. The price has now gone to nineteen million two hundred thousand dollars."

I'm sure I must have betrayed my own surprise at Glover's statement. He didn't seem to know about Norman's side deal with Stone.

The General was smiling. "That's all right, Frank. Mr. Kane and I agree on that point."

Glover stared at Stone for a moment. Then he shrugged. Clearly this was not the first time his client had made private arrangements without telling him.

"These agreements," said Glover, "give you a lot of authority, Mr. Kane."

Norman smiled. "That's how I work."

General Stone waved his hand at Glover. "The agreements are fine, gentlemen. A man can't run a deal like this without broad powers. But there is one thing missing. I told Norman I want all the stock placed in escrow at the Chicago Title Company, with an agreement that if our final project cost exceeds the funds available, each man will come up with his proportionate share of the shortage or he loses his equity. I thought you might forget, Norman, so I had Frank draw up an escrow agreement." Stone nodded to Glover, who handed a blue-backed agreement to me. Norman had told me about this before, of course, but I decided to question him as if I knew nothing about it.

"Is this your understanding, Norman?"

Norman nodded.

"What about the notes?" I asked.

"The notes are pledged with the stock."

"You mean to tell me that any investor who doesn't come up with his share of any shortage loses his stock, his notes—in fact, his entire investment?"

"That's correct."

"You've never made that kind of arrangement with your syndicates before. You have always permitted your investors to stay in the deal on some basis, even if recouping their investment was somewhat deferred."

Norman stared at me. "This deal is different."

"Not that different. Are you sure the other investors will agree to this?"

"Look," said Norman, "I agree to it. And I'm putting in money on the same basis they are."

"The same basis, Norman?"

"Of course. We're all in this together."

"Yes." I said. "Everybody's feet are firmly planted. But maybe the water's too deep for some of us."

"That's enough," Norman said, taking the escrow agreement out of my hands. "I'll take this home and review it. If I'm satisfied, I'll put it up to the boys."

There was no point in making further comment. I remained silent until our meeting with Stone ended, but as soon as we had passed through the bronze doors of Stone Tower and reached the sidewalk, I took Norman's arm and told him of my misgivings.

"The investors in this project are not all on the same basis and you know it. What about your deal with Stone? The boys aren't even supposed to hear about it. And there's no use comparing the boys with Stone, anyway. Compared to him they're paupers. If the deal runs way short, they'll never be able to come up with the money."

"That's their problem."

"I'm going to tell them what I think."

"Wait a minute. Are you representing me or them?"

"I'm not going to lie for you, Norman. It's bad enough I had to sit up there and pretend I didn't know about your private arrangements with Stone. I'll be damned if I'll kid the boys about that escrow agreement."

For an instant Norman was terribly angry. But then his frown curled into a smile. "You tell the boys anything you want. The worse you make it sound, the more likely they are to sign. Anyway, you're worrying yourself over nothing. The General won't have such an easy time getting his hands on their investment. If you think Stone can just tap his finger and get the Chicago Title Company to turn the stock over to him, you're crazy. Just let the Title Company hear there's a dispute and they won't let go of the stock without a court order."

"Maybe. But Stone can stand a long, involved lawsuit better than the boys."

"Oh, hell. After a little legal maneuvering, everybody wants to settle. Stop worrying, Eddie."

"What about your side deals with Stone?"

Norman poked a finger at me as he answered, "So far as you know, there are no side deals."

"But Norman, you told me—"

"Forget what I told you. There are no side deals, understand? You haven't seen any documents covering any side deals, have you?"

"Well, no—"

"Then as far as you're concerned, there aren't any. You tell the boys whatever you want about the escrow agreement, but stay out of my private arrangements with Stone." Norman turned abruptly and walked away.

I could not decide what to do. Technically, what Norman said was true; I had no documentary proof that he was making private deals with General Stone. Of course, if the boys used their heads, they would realize Norman must be getting the four million eight hundred thousand dollars somewhere.

It seemed to me the only procedure I could honestly follow would be to deliver the agreements to the boys and advise them to have their own lawyers review them. Norman wouldn't like it, but I was not going to be responsible for these six men putting up over fourteen million dollars.

As it turned out, Norman's forecast of the boys' reactions proved perfectly accurate. When I suggested they employ their own attorneys, I set them on precisely the track I had hoped to avoid. Phil Winsley grinned and said, "You want us to hire one of those 'No' guys, don't you? A guy who'll talk us out of this deal, huh?"

It was difficult to control my temper in the face of Winsley's knowing grin.

"All I want you to do is make up your own minds. This is the biggest deal you've ever been in. You ought to study it pretty carefully."

Even George Lillis smiled. "You're a lousy liar, Eddie. There's something bugging you and you can't tell us what it is. I figure Norman is trying to frighten us out of the deal. You know it and you don't want us to be frightened."

"How did you reach that conclusion? Maybe I *do* want to scare you out of the deal."

"Well, in that case, buddy, you're carrying the ball for Norman, which is even worse."

Somehow I managed to control my anger. "Stop trying to read my mind. I don't put these deals together; Norman does. Either you trust him or you don't. Either you protect yourselves or you don't. I won't take the responsibility for your money, that's all. I'm trying to do you a favor. I hope some day you so-and-sos remember it." I threw the escrow agreements down on the table and stalked out.

But my warning had no effect. That afternoon the boys signed the agreements and returned them to Norman Kane.

———————

Norman had been avoiding Del Kincaid, but now that his financial arrangements were complete, he set up an appointment at Kincaid's office. Norman had decided against holding this meeting at his own office. Exposing Kincaid to the luxurious premises of Kane Enterprises might have an unwholesome effect on the younger man.

Kincaid's office contrasted strangely with General Stone's sanctuary. The building itself was one of the oldest on La Salle Street, a squat stone structure graced only by spiderweb grillework around its open elevator shafts and broad mosaic-paved stairways.

The halls of the upper floors were lined with bathroom marble, interrupted by office entrance doors fashioned of wood and translucent glass, topped by adjustable transoms. Some sections of the building had been modernized, but Kincaid's office was evidently in its original state, which probably meant it had not been remodeled since 1912.

Kincaid's suite was paneled floor to ceiling with a highly polished dark-brown wood. The carpet was vaguely blue in color and almost threadbare, and the solid, thick-topped desks were laced with an intricate, if random, pattern of nicks and scratches. The furniture was waxed to a high gloss, which served only to emphasize its age.

Even if all the lights in Kincaid's reception room had been lit, I suspect the room would still have been dark. But despite the late hour, the lights were off. An ancient secretary (whose sex I could guess only because she wore what must have been a dress) led us to the end of a shadowy corridor. The walls were lined with glass-fronted bookcases, but it was too dark to discern the tomes within.

After traversing this gloomy channel, Kincaid's half-lit office seemed glaringly bright. It was a vast room, "decorated" in turn-of-the-century legal style and distinguished only by an ancient and faded Oriental rug on the floor. *My God,* I thought, *what a wild extravagance that must have been in its time.*

Kincaid came bounding from behind his desk with an easy athletic stride. I had met his type before: the wealthy, youthful-looking scion of an ancient family, wearing the usual nondescript clothes and close-cropped hair. Still, my reaction was not completely fair—there was something truly ingenuous about Del Kincaid.

"Del, I'd like you to meet my lawyer, Eddie Ellison."

Kincaid looked at me quizzically.

"Ellison? Aren't you Bob Dean's partner?"

"Right."

"Bob and I are old friends. Play golf together every Sunday. I thought Bob told me you were going to join our club."

"I thought about it, but I finally decided to stay at Pinecrest. It's a family thing, you know. Three generations and all that. Anyway, my wife prevailed on me to stay."

"I've met your wife." The voice startled me. I spun around and got my first dazzling glimpse of Tina Kincaid.

She was so tiny and sparkling and perfect that she seemed out of place in the musty office: a perfect gem in a dreary setting. When Norman had described her to me, I had smugly assumed that he was exaggerating. Besides, Norman often saw things in women that I never saw. This time I had to admit he was entirely correct.

"I'm Tina Kincaid. I'm afraid Del was going to forget to introduce us."

"I'm sorry, dear. I was just surprised to learn that Mr. Ellison is Mr. Kane's lawyer." He realized that his choice of words might have been unwise. "A pleasant surprise, of course."

Tina wasn't listening to him. "Nice meeting you, Mr. Ellison. Your wife and I worked together on the St. Luke's Fashion Show. She's a very lovely woman." There was a fractional pause between "very" and "lovely." I didn't mind. I hadn't thought Eleanor was a beauty when I married her.

"I'll tell her I met you today," I said. "I'm sure she'll be pleased."

Norman more or less forced his way between us. He looked

rather irritable. I realized that our exchange of greetings had excluded him. Perhaps more importantly, it indicated a social equivalence between me and the Kincaids—a realm in which Norman obviously played no part. That was bound to annoy Norman Kane.

"Mrs. Kincaid," Norman said, "it's delightful to find you here."

Delbert Kincaid frowned. "It was her idea. You should be complimented, Kane. Tina never shows any interest in my business affairs."

Tina Kincaid smiled, which increased the lighting level in the room by several thousand lumens. Then she spoke, so sweetly that the underlying irony escaped me at the time.

"Ah, but this is a very special venture, dear. You're actually doing something on your own. I couldn't miss this remarkable occasion."

"Well," said Delbert Kincaid, setting his chin firmly, "let's get down to business."

We sat down around the huge desk, and at Norman's request I handed the papers to Kincaid.

"First," I said, "I suggest you examine the financial arrangements. We've prepared a simple statement showing the capitalization of this venture and listing the cash investment of each stockholder."

Delbert Kincaid stared at the paper. When he looked up he was wild-eyed. "General Stone? Are you serious?"

"Completely," said Norman.

"You mean General Stone is going to invest almost twenty million dollars in our deal?"

"We already have his signed agreement."

"But I . . . well . . . I never . . ."

"What seems to be the problem?" Norman asked. He spoke very softly, but he was staring intently at Kincaid. He seemed to enjoy the man's agitation.

"General Stone," Kincaid said again. "I never guessed *he* would be in the group."

"The names of the other investors are also listed," I pointed out.

"Yes, well . . . I expected the others. They have been in Kane's deals before." Kincaid turned to Norman. "Have you ever been in a deal with General Stone before?"

"No, I haven't, Del. This is the first time, but then, this is the biggest deal I've ever put together. How about you? Ever been in one this big?"

Kincaid winced. "As you know, I've never . . ." His voice faded. Then he mumbled, almost to himself, "General Stone."

"Why do you object to Stone?"

"Well, you know, he has this reputation for . . . ruthlessness."

Tina Kincaid laughed. "No one," she said, "would accuse you of that."

Delbert Kincaid glared at his wife. "Of course not. Of course I'm not ruthless—and I don't like the idea of having a ruthless partner."

Norman Kane studied each of the Kincaids before he spoke. "You know, Del, I've learned that if I want to do big things I can't always choose my associates. You and I aren't the most obvious set of partners, but we'll get along. *I* think I can get along with General Stone, and so do six other men who are putting up more than fourteen million dollars among them. Frankly, your risk is pretty small compared to theirs."

"You can't get the land without me and you know it."

"True. But on the other hand we can't build the project without General Stone. That is, unless you know someone else with twenty million dollars to invest."

Kincaid was silent for a moment. Then he shook his head. "No, I don't know anyone who would put up that kind of money."

"Then I guess we have no choice. Either we make the deal with Stone or forget it. Which do you prefer?"

I glanced at Tina Kincaid. She was sitting on the edge of her chair, leaning forward, wetting her lips.

Her husband looked at her almost covertly. Then in a quiet voice he said, "I guess we'll have to live with Stone."

"Fine," said Norman. "Why don't you review the rest of the statement? Check out the other partners and the distribution of notes and equity."

Delbert Kincaid sat staring at the schedule so long that we

all became restless. Tina Kincaid edged even farther forward on her chair. I had the impression her hairline was beaded with tiny drops of perspiration, but this was probably an illusion.

Delbert Kincaid cleared his throat two or three times. "I see that you'll have forty-three and a half per cent of the deal."

"Yes, that's true, except I'm paying the full price for seven and a half per cent. I'm only getting thirty-six per cent as a promoter."

"I'll have only four per cent of the deal."

"That's right."

"You promised me ten."

"No, that's not what I promised. I said I'd give you ten per cent of *my* interest. You're really only entitled to three point six per cent."

"But your interest will be forty-three and a half per cent."

"As I said, I'm paying for seven and a half per cent. If you're willing to put up the money, you can have as much of the deal as you want."

"That's not how I understood you."

"Doesn't matter how you understood me. That's what I said. If you like, I'll sell you my seven and a half per cent of stock and notes. Then you'll own eleven and a half per cent of the deal. Is that what you want?"

"Well, no. I mean, that's not what I meant."

"I'm beginning to wonder what you do mean. Do you want to buy more of the deal or not?"

Again there was silence. Again Tina Kincaid seemed to lean forward.

"I guess not," said Kincaid.

"All right. Then you're happy with your four per cent."

"I can't say that I'm happy, but if that's the way it has to be . . ." Kincaid recoiled, then blurted out, "Say, that four per cent will cost me a hundred and sixty thousand dollars."

Norman sighed. "I'm letting you participate on the same basis that I do. I pay for my promotional shares, too. If you stop and think, you'll realize that you and I get tremendous leverage in this deal. The others are buying not only stock but notes as well, and the dollar cost of the notes is nine times the cost of the stock. I think getting four per cent of this deal is pretty darn good—at bargain prices. And you'll still be paid for your share of the Kincaid property just like the rest of your family."

"I get paid anyway, no matter who the buyer is." Kincaid spoke defiantly. He seemed to think he had made a brilliant point.

"So what? You can't put the deal together without us. Now let me make this clear. I don't intend to advertise to the world what percentage each of us owns in this deal. As far as I'm concerned, you're my partner, the same as General Stone or Phil Winsley or Joe Woodward. We plan things together and we work them out together."

"I'm glad to hear that," said Kincaid. Then he shook his head. When he spoke again, his voice was almost a whine. "I thought I was going to get my interest in return for delivering the deal. Now you want me to pay a hundred and sixty thousand dollars for it."

Norman sat back in his chair and studied Tina Kincaid. She was watching her husband intently. Norman smiled at her lovely profile.

"You know, bringing your wife here today has softened me up. I never let anybody participate in the promotional units with me except on the same basis I do. But in your case I am going to make an exception. I'll pay for your four per cent."

Kincaid began to smile, but his wife rose from her chair.

"We'll pay for our interest, Mr. Kane. We aren't the kind of people who expect something for nothing."

Norman shrugged and looked at Delbert Kincaid.

Kincaid was watching his wife. She stared down at him with an indefinable mixture of anger, contempt and anticipation.

"Tina's right, Mr. Kane. We'll put up our share. I'll draw a check for a hundred and sixty thousand dollars today."

Tina smiled at her husband—a mechanical smile, as if someone had taken a set of forceps and pushed her lips back over her teeth. But the smile she turned on Norman was dazzling. Tina sat down in the chair, crossed her legs (which sent a flutter through my legal mind) and stared down at her hands.

"Whatever you say," Norman said. Then he spoke with

more animation. "This makes it a real partnership—everyone pulling his own load. But we don't need the whole hundred and sixty thousand now. We'll only assess the group enough to pick up your option on the property."

"You're going to exercise the option right now? I mean, the property isn't even rezoned. How do we know we'll be able to proceed?"

"A damn good question. Glad to see you're on your toes. But don't worry about the rezoning. That's my problem." He turned to me. "Let's go over these agreements. Eddie, you analyze them for Del."

I began to explain the documents to Kincaid. He seemed to understand me, and although he raised his eyebrows when I described the escrow arrangement with General Stone, he offered no comment.

While I was talking to Kincaid, I could feel Norman Kane and Tina Kincaid staring at each other. Perhaps Del saw them. If so, he chose to ignore it. He looked at me with trusting blue eyes, occasionally nodding his close-cropped head.

Finally I said, "That's about the size of it. I hope I've made everything clear."

Kincaid nodded.

"Good. I presume you'll want your lawyers to review these papers."

Tina Kincaid spoke again. "No, Mr. Ellison, that won't be necessary. Del and I trust you. And of course we trust Mr. Kane and General Stone and the other investors, too. As far as I'm concerned, we ought to sign the agreements today and save time."

"Right," Del Kincaid said, a bit too quickly. "I agree with Tina. If these agreements are good enough for you they're good enough for me." He reached for a pen and scrawled his name hurriedly in a huge sprawling hand.

Then he called for his secretary. "Bring in a checkbook, Miss Wilson, on the Kincaid Trust Number Seven." When his secretary returned, Delbert Kincaid prepared his check. "Look," he said. "There's not that much involved. Here's the whole one sixty and I'm done with it. What do you say, Norman?"

"Very generous, Del. Now why don't you turn the option agreement over to Eddie so he can study it?"

"Of course, I'll get a copy right now."

"Isn't the property held in trust?" I asked. "If so, we'd better examine the trust instruments as well."

Kincaid frowned. "It may take me a while to put my hands on all the trust papers."

Norman stood up. "In that case, Del, I guess I'll move on. Eddie will wait until you collect all the papers."

"Fine," I said.

Tina Kincaid stood up. "I think I'll leave, too, Del—now that you're getting down to details."

"All right, dear. Ellison and I can work things out together."

"Goodbye, Mr. Ellison," Tina said. "Be sure and give my best to Eleanor."

Norman Kane was scribbling something on a piece of paper. "Eddie," he said aloud, folding the note and handing it to me, "here's something for you to consider. We'll talk about it later."

Norman shook Del Kincaid's hand. Then, as Norman and Tina were leaving the office, I glanced at Norman's note. It read: "You can't beat this combination. The best piece of land in Chicago and the best piece of ass—all in one deal."

I dropped the note. By the time I picked it up and shoved it in my pocket, Norman and Tina were gone.

———◆———

When they reached the street, Tina said, "You're a remarkable man, Norman Kane."

"Based on two brief meetings? You hardly know me."

"I rarely have the same opinion of a man after the second meeting. You should be flattered."

"I am, Mrs. Kincaid, sincerely flattered."

"I seem to recall asking you to call me Tina."

Norman smiled. "Did you? I don't remember that. Still, it's important to establish the rules."

"Funny, somehow you don't seem to be the kind of man

99

who lives by other people's rules. I rather hoped you invented your own."

"At times. But every game has its rules. You can follow other people's or make up your own, but without rules the whole thing becomes pointless."

"Perhaps it depends on the game."

"I doubt it."

Tina was annoyed. "Are we going to stand here discussing rules?"

"I didn't bring up the subject."

"That's true. By now you should have offered to buy me a drink."

"I was waiting for you to ask."

If that bothered Tina Kincaid, she didn't show it. "Splendid," she said. "I'm asking."

Norman chose the quiet, dimly lit lounge in the Claridge Hotel. After ordering their drinks, he turned his most winning smile on Tina Kincaid. "It hardly seems fair."

"What's that?"

"Buying you a drink—that's damn poor compensation for what you did for me today."

"What I did for you?"

"Yep. A one-hundred-and-sixty-thousand-dollar favor."

"Come now. Surely you never intended to give Del a hundred and sixty thousand dollars?"

"Not Del. I was doing it for you."

"You're being kind."

"On the contrary. I'd say you were rather kind to me."

The smile slipped off Tina's face. Her eyes narrowed and she studied Norman with a catlike expression.

"Don't misunderstand me, Norman Kane. I didn't do it for you *or* Del. I did it for me. I wouldn't let Del cheapen himself, and, more important, I wouldn't let him cheapen me. But at least you learned I can make Del do whatever I choose."

"I never doubted that. It's no great trick for a beautiful woman to master a simpleton like Delbert Kincaid."

Tina responded angrily, "He's not a simpleton"—then caught herself. "But you know that too, don't you? I see that life with you is going to be interesting, Mr. Kane."

"We're back on last names."

"In this case it's rather affectionate. A sign of respect, you might say."

"Don't you plan to wrap me around your finger, too?"

Tina offered a dazzling smile. "Oh, I certainly expect to."

"I may even permit you the luxury."

Tina Kincaid sat back, arranging herself with a single, apparently unconscious movement into a composition of sensual grace and beauty. Norman's imagination stripped away her wool suit. His tongue explored his palate while he enjoyed this vision.

"I'm afraid you have things backward," Tina said. "I'm the luxury. The question is, can you afford me?"

"Del can afford you, but where does it get him?"

She laughed aloud. "Right. That's what ordinary people never understand. The very best luxuries are not for sale. But God knows you can enjoy them."

"I'm willing."

She leaned forward again, and his eyes followed the lines of her body beneath the gray wool suit. With some effort he avoided mentally removing her clothes again. "I'm sure you're willing. Almost anyone is willing. But it takes more than that. Money won't do it. Pretty words bore me. As for good looks, I can take care of that department myself. What have you to offer?"

"Who's offering? Still, the very fact you're here proves something—although I'm not aware just what it is."

"Don't kid me. There's nothing unaware about you."

"Maybe that's my appeal."

"Part of it."

"What's the rest?"

"I'm not sure, but we're certain to find out." Her voice changed tone suddenly. "Tell me about Mrs. Kane."

Norman was surprised. "What has Mrs. Kane to do with our discussion?"

"You've gotten to know my husband. It's only fair that I learn about your wife."

Norman smiled. "She's very intelligent, extremely beautiful, and probably the most sensual woman I've ever known."

"And her father was very rich."

Norman twisted in his chair. "I never got a dime from Frieda's father. I wouldn't take it if he offered. Whatever I have, I earned myself." He suddenly realized Tina was needling him. While he was quietly suffering over this realization, Tina spoke again.

"I understand your wife had a rather unfortunate first marriage."

Norman forced himself not to flinch. "I'm not so sure she's crazy about her second one."

This drew a thin smile from Tina. She had scored on his psyche—not once, but twice, and she knew it.

"I can see," he said, "that we're going to have to get to know each other much better."

Tina nodded.

Norman suggested, "Perhaps we can start right now."

"No," Tina said, with a triumphant smile. "Now is not the time. Nevertheless, I've enjoyed the preliminaries."

"We'll get at it in stages, then?"

"I didn't say that. There are times when I suddenly feel carried away. But this is not one of those times."

"It's hard to imagine you carried away."

"Well, then, let it be a delicious surprise."

———————

When Norman opened the door to his apartment, he found Frieda waiting. Surprised, he dropped one of the packages he was carrying, and uttering what sounded like a wounded cry, he stooped to pick it up. Despite his confusion, Norman noted that his wife was wearing a stunning hostess gown, her blond hair was piled high and her face was perfectly made up.

"You look great, kid."

"Is that what surprised you?"

The packages were unwieldy and Norman had trouble holding onto them.

"For Christ's sake, Frieda, stop interrogating me and help me get these things into the apartment."

She accepted one of Norman's oblong parcels and carried it into the living room.

"Careful now, Frieda. That's damn expensive. Put it down on the table."

"Where were you?"

"Where was I? Picking up these paintings. Where do you think I was?"

"You promised to be home for dinner for once. I prepared everything so carefully and then you didn't appear." Frieda's pout was very appealing.

Norman seemed genuinely contrite. Perhaps he was thinking about Tina Kincaid. "I'm sorry, Frieda. I just plain forgot. I was very busy at the office and then I had to hurry over to the gallery to pick these up. As it was, they had to stay open past closing time for me."

Frieda frowned. "More paintings?" She looked around the room. "Where will you put them, Norman? Every inch of every wall is covered."

What she said was true, but Norman was irritated nonetheless.

"My paintings mean nothing to you. You'd probably rather have wallpaper."

"That's not true. I—"

"Of course it's true. You've never shown any interest in my collection. Even in Paris, when I go off searching for art, you shop for clothes. You're not even impressed by the cash value of my works."

"You have spent a great deal of money on art, dear."

"Yeah, well it's worth a lot more than I paid for it. Some guys play the ponies, others blow their dough on booze, but I spend my money on art, and you don't appreciate the difference."

Frieda smiled, "The perfect, virtuous husband. No horse-playing, very little liquor. Gosh, I'm lucky."

Even Norman smiled. "Anyway, you needn't worry. They're not for me." He began to unpack the paintings. They were unframed. Norman hurried into another room, returned with an easel, and began to stack the paintings beside it.

"How do you like them?"

"Since when are you interested in my opinions on art?"

"Oh, come on now. I'm sorry about dinner." He paused to plant a kiss on his wife's cheek, then finished arranging the paintings and pulled a cloth over them.

Frieda was subdued, perhaps mollified by Norman's apology and his show of affection, no matter how perfunctory.

"I don't understand, Norman. Who are these for?"

Norman glanced at his watch. "Oh, my God. He'll be here any moment. Help me straighten up the room."

While Frieda watched in amusement, Norman scurried about, dimming lights, plumping up pillows and emptying ashtrays.

"Please tell me the name of this august personage who has the powerful Norman Kane scurrying about like a houseboy?"

"John Bennett."

Frieda was clearly surprised.

"You mean to tell me that you're doing all this for an insignificant lackey like John Bennett?"

Norman stopped in his tracks. "Are you aware that in the last several years I've placed tens of millions of dollars of mortgage loans at Fidelity Standard Life Insurance Company —all through that insignificant lackey?"

"I thought you told me Bennett was just a subordinate, that somebody named Graham or Grayson, or something that starts with a G, is the head of the mortgage loan department?"

"Well, we do listen once in a while. The man whose name starts with G is Arnold Gresham, and Bennett is his assistant."

"Then, for heavens sake, why not entertain Gresham? Why waste your time on an underling?"

"Do you suppose I haven't thought of that? Unfortunately, Mr. Gresham is not quite my type. I do perfectly well with Bennett. We have a kind of rapport, you know. And Bennett has a kind of rapport with Gresham. That's what keeps the nickels and dimes flowing in. And anyway, why the hell am I discussing corporate politics with you? Will you please go off and read a book or something and leave me alone?"

Frieda was petulant. "Why can't I stay here?"

"Because I don't need you. You'd only be in the way."

"I could help entertain Bennett."

"I'm sure you could."

"That's not what I meant."

"I'm sure it wasn't."

"This is my home, too."

"But it's my business, and besides, you wouldn't want to be degraded by having to entertain an insignificant lackey."

Frieda did not move. Norman decided to try a gentler form of persuasion. He took her arm. "Come on, Frieda, this is silly. There's no need for you to get involved in this. I'm saving you for better things. Besides, that hostess gown and that hairdo are too good for John Bennett. Especially with the four-foot cleavage."

Frieda's hand went to her breast, but she smiled.

"That's right, honey. Be a good sport. I'll tell you all about it after he's gone."

"Really?" Frieda's voice was tinged with suspicion.

"Of course," Norman said, and patted her fondly on the bottom.

Frieda closed the door to the bedroom. She really hadn't wanted to spend an evening with John Bennett. The man was a bore. It was the principle of the thing. Norman had dozens of interesting associates, brilliant, powerful men. She would have been content just to listen to their conversation. But Norman rarely permitted even that.

She wandered about the room, picking things up and setting them down. There was a television set, but she had no interest in watching television. There were books, but she didn't feel like reading them.

Over the bed was a large painting by Laurencin. She studied it for a few minutes, recalling Norman's rhapsodic comments on the color harmonies, the graceful shapes, the interlocking patterns. Frieda shook her head. The painting was pretty. It went with the decor, but she felt nothing more. *Norman's right,* she thought, *I don't give a damn for his paintings. They don't do a thing to me.*

She was saddened by the thought. Here was something they

might have shared. Frieda had read the books on art Norman had given her, and for a time she dutifully followed him through the galleries. But it didn't take. *I tried. I really did. I even like your pictures. They're nice—some of them—but what can I say after that? I'm not an intellectual, Norman, and you wasted your time trying to make me one.*

For some reason, she thought of her father. When she was a child, he had always sent her out of the room while he discussed business with his associates. Norman did the same. That was frustrating, because Frieda liked business. Not her father's business, not a chain of department stores, but Norman's business—building huge buildings, turning raw ground into tall towers. That was exciting.

Frieda had not sensed the excitement in Norman Kane immediately. When he first called for a date, soon after her divorce from Charlie Clark, she had not been flattered. Frieda remembered Norman as a short, somewhat crude and rather homely college student. Precisely the opposite of her ex-husband. Well, she had thought, perhaps that's all to the good. She decided to go out with him.

He was not one bit better-looking than she recalled, though he was better dressed and his hair was carefully trimmed. Unfortunately, even then he was beginning to lose his hair.

To Frieda's surprise, Norman drove a good car, took her to a fine restaurant and the best show in town. His manners needed polishing, but he was an effervescent companion— cheerful, talkative and rather witty. The range of his knowledge, the depth of his intelligence amazed her. Norman proved to be a much more interesting man than she had expected.

Mildly intrigued, she went out with him again. Of course, it was painfully obvious that Norman was trying to impress her. He insisted that she order the most expensive items on the menu and he tipped lavishly.

Frieda dated Norman again and again. Not because she was seriously interested in him, but because he was diverting. Even when he described his business deals, Norman managed to inject such amusing anecdotes and remarkable character sketches that Frieda never found his narratives tiresome. She realized it was all done with a purpose. Norman held her attention with wit and humor while he offered a complete description of his business accomplishments. After a few weeks of this, she knew Norman's net worth almost to the penny. That was not what fascinated her. Despite his achievements, Norman was not nearly as wealthy as her father. But one day he might be. And more important, Frieda began to realize that Norman was a dreamer. He was homely, rough-edged and aggressive, but he was a visionary.

To Norman, buildings were more than brick and steel; they were the final embodiment of his dreams. It was true that he wanted money, fame and power. But more than that, he yearned to reach beyond himself, to build better and more beautifully than anyone had ever done before. Norman wanted to be unique: a renaissance man in a reactionary world.

The realization surprised Frieda. This little man wanted to play God. To build, to create, to change the face of his world. It was a challenging thought. Frieda was in love with Norman's dreams long before she fell in love with Norman.

This new conception of Norman Kane somewhat unnerved her. She was still disturbed by his looks. Physically, he was not the kind of man she thought she wanted. But he had shattered her standards. She could no longer judge by outward appearances. A man might be a man despite a balding head and clumsy features. When Norman proposed marriage, she accepted him at once, surprising both of them.

At first it had been great fun. Norman hurrying home each night to tell her what he had done. Norman taking her on trips to see his projects. Norman inviting his associates home for dinner, where Frieda could listen to, even join in, their discussions. She got on well with his business friends. At first, they were simply taken with her beauty. She understood that and appreciated it. But Frieda wanted more. She was determined to learn all she could of Norman's affairs. Soon she could converse intelligently with Norman and his interesting friends. She got along famously with these men—perhaps too famously.

After a while Norman seemed to resent it. She had always

known he would be a jealous man; he was jealous of all his possessions. She found that he consulted her less and less. He stopped bringing friends home for dinner, stopped inviting her to join him on business trips. She was bewildered, then resentful. Didn't he want his wife to be beautiful and intelligent? To charm his associates?

After that came Norman's women. At first Frieda tried to pretend there was no problem. He still made love to her, but not as often and not as ardently.

Once she saw him leaving the Palmer House with the wife of Harper Rhodes. Frieda told herself it was only a chance meeting. But she didn't believe it. In time, the evidence of Norman's infidelities became undeniable.

Confronted, Norman denied everything. Then admitted it. Then denied it. Finally, he accused her of flirting with his friends. And more. And always, when everything else failed, there was Charlie Clark.

But that was a side issue. And so, eventually, were Norman's infidelities. Frieda never learned to forgive him, but she learned to live with him as he was. A strange, powerful, yet insecure man, who had to keep proving himself.

Most important, Frieda was excluded from any participation in Norman's business. He seldom told her his plans. She learned more about Kane's enterprises from the newspapers than from Norman's lips.

I don't want to run your business, Frieda thought. *I really don't. I just want to hear about it. To talk about it. To feel somehow that I'm part of it. Not just a clotheshorse you trot out to impress your associates on rare and selected occasions.*

It seemed to her that Norman simply refused to understand. Or maybe he did. Probably she'd never know which. But it was clear that he was determined to withhold a part of himself.

You don't want me to own you, do you, Norman? Nobody can own you. But you want to own everybody.

She sat at the vanity in her mirrored dressing room and studied herself. There was really nothing to be done, but she patted on a little powder and freshened her lipstick. *I look great,* she thought. *Better than any of Norman's paintings. And I live and breathe in the bargain.*

Smiling, she began to take down her hair. Norman didn't like it up anyway. He never had. She brushed her hair vigorously, then combed it into a soft roll at her shoulders.

That will get him, she thought. *It always does.*

Norman stood at the windows of his apartment staring out pensively at the Chicago skyline, tinged a delicate purple against the fading peach-toned sunset. John Bennett, tall, gray-haired and dignified, lounged on a sofa a few feet behind him. *Ah well,* thought Norman. *Time for the play to begin.*

"It's incredible, John, simply incredible. I never cease to marvel that you and I are able to survive in a world of financial intrigue."

He turned to Bennett and waved his hand in a broad gesture that encompassed the entire room. "We belong here, with Mozart playing in the background, magnificent paintings on the walls, and books stacked within easy reach. This is our secret, John. I never invite my business associates up here. They might laugh at me: a real-estate promoter who pretends to be a scholar. Day after day, John, we deal with a horde of ambitious, uneducated, ill-bred men and boys, all trying to make money at our expense."

John Bennett nodded his head while he continued to sip Norman's imported brandy.

"It's difficult, John, confess it. Elegance is suspect. A three-syllable word is ominous."

John Bennett smiled at Norman Kane. "There's no premium placed on such things today, Norman. I'm afraid we're the last of a dying breed."

Norman Kane smiled. "I'm happy you understand, John. Frankly, I know it is more difficult for you than for me. You must be civil to any man who comes to your door."

John Bennett laughed. "How right you are, Norman. Few of these so-called businessmen even understand their own businesses, let alone anything on a higher plane."

Norman's voice became a stage whisper. "Don't worry, John, I'll keep your secret. I won't tell them how erudite you are. I *could* blackmail you. What would Gresham say if he discovered that his lieutenant is literate? I promise not to tell, John. It would shake them to their bones. The company would order an investigation. They would insist that you sign a loyalty oath swearing you love Fidelity Standard Life Insurance Company more than Proust and Mozart."

John Bennett flushed with pleasure. "I'd have a difficult time taking their oath, Norman. I really would."

"Then let's make plans right now, John. If we're forced to take the oath, we'll go underground. I'll take my paintings off the walls and paste up posters of Tahiti and Hawaii. I'll bury my records in the basement and replace them with a thousand tapes of 'Home Sweet Home.' "

John Bennett caught the spirit of Norman's jest. "I don't think Tahiti and Hawaii are wise choices, Norman. The company would suspect you are planning to abscond with their money. Why not prints of early Chicago?"

"Splendid idea. But what will I do with the books?"

"All you need is a new set of jackets. No one opens a book any more. Surely no one would disturb your library if you put on a set of crinkly, fresh, socially acceptable jackets."

"Perfect. I won't have to store them. It will be just like my boyhood, when I slipped girlie magazines inside my textbooks."

"Yes, and then we'll have secret meeting and swear oaths to the Muse."

"I have a better idea. Instead of hiding the paintings, I'll simply turn them over and paste the prints on the back."

"Marvelous! Then we can come up here with flashlights, spin the paintings around and enjoy them together."

"By God, it sounds like fun. I almost wish it would happen."

There was a pause. When Norman Kane spoke again, his words came very slowly and ponderously. "I hate to say it, John, but that's almost precisely what we're doing right now."

John Bennett nodded his head sagely and sadly. They sat silently for a moment, savoring their martyrdom. It was a delicious moment for John Bennett. Here he was, sacrificed on the altar of Babbitt, brutality and crass commercialism.

Never before had he realized that his life possessed such stature. He was very grateful to Norman Kane.

"Well," said Norman, "I presume we must endure it all the same. Thank God, I have someone to talk to." He patted John Bennett on the arm affectionately. "And now you can do me a great favor, John. I've bought some watercolors—that is, I haven't bought them yet—I brought them home on approval. A Kandinsky, a Klee, a Chagall, a Braque and a Picasso. I can't buy them all, and I can't decide which ones to keep. I need your judgment."

This, of course, only enhanced John Bennett's opinion of himself. He spent the evening sitting on a sofa with his arms folded while Norman played the role of an art salesman, presenting first one watercolor, then another, placing them and lighting them for the master's inspection.

"I'm not terribly fond of the Picasso, John. It's dated 1956 which is about the time he began substituting squiggles for lines."

Bennett nodded sagely. "Quite true, Norman. Mustn't just buy a name, right?"

Norman removed the Picasso and mounted the Chagall. Bennett studied it thoughtfully, finger on chin, for quite a while. Then he shook his head. "Colors seem a bit strong, don't you think? All colors and no composition."

Norman shrugged and continued his presentation.

Eventually, they decided on two paintings, a violently colored abstraction by Kandinsky and an almost representational sketch by Paul Klee. It was evident that Bennett vastly preferred the Klee, perhaps because he understood it better. Norman privately considered it to be one of the artist's poorer works, but he accepted Bennett's opinion.

"You know, John, I've watched you eying that Klee, bestowing on it the attention a mother usually reserves for a child. That watercolor has affected you very deeply. Please permit me to make a present of it to you."

John Bennett's throat constricted. "Oh, Norman, I couldn't do that. It wouldn't be right."

"John, I can buy it for a fraction of its true value. It's not that expensive, and I really want you to have it."

"I couldn't do it."

"Then do me a favor: At least let me loan it to you. We'll say it still belongs to me, but you will have the pleasure of living with it. Of course, I insist on one condition. Any time I have an urge to look at it, regardless of the hour of day or night, you must permit me to see it."

John Bennett smiled delightedly. "Why, I—I guess I could accept a loan, Norman. I don't believe that would be improper. Thank you, Norman, I'll deeply enjoy having it, and as you say, any time you want to see it, you come right over."

"Then it's a deal. The Klee will reside in the home of its great admirer, and yet I can see it whenever I wish. Besides, you're doing me a favor—I really haven't room to hang another thing."

While Bennett glowed over his new acquisition, Norman poured out two more glasses of brandy and changed the records from Mozart to Beethoven.

Bennett had very little more to say.

Norman carried the conversation. He began a long rambling discourse on the Lyric Opera's problems with the musicians' union, the possibility that the entire season might be canceled or, even if it were held, that many of the great singers might meanwhile be lost to other companies. Together, Norman and Bennett had mourned these prospects before, and Bennett could see no purpose in repeating the discussion.

Just as Bennett thought Norman was finally running down, he suddenly switched to a lecture on the proposed new Museum of Contemporary Art. Norman had been asked to contribute both money and works of art. He had turned the sponsors down. As far as he was concerned, there was still too much to be done at the Art Institute. Except for the collection of impressionists and a few great Renaissance masterpieces, the Art Institute was woefully lacking in major works. "Let's have one good museum," he declared, "instead of two mediocre ones."

This, too, was familiar ground. Bennett was puzzled by Norman's rambling discourse. He listened nervously, anxious to clutch the Klee watercolor and be on his way. He could already envision it hung beside the staircase of his house. Norman had never welshed before, but then—

Abruptly, Norman stopped his pacing.

"John, last week you told me a top executive from International Materials was in to see Hobbs?"

"Ralph Churchill, the president."

"How many dollars' worth of their bonds do you hold?"

"Oh, about twenty million. It was nearly thirty once, but they've retired a substantial sum. Of course, that's more or less confidential."

"And where is their closest plant?"

"Well, they have one in Gary, Indiana."

"Where is their main plant?"

"Say, Norman, what is this about?"

"Where is their main plant?"

"Well, they have big plants everywhere—Indiana, South Carolina, California and Texas. I suppose the biggest ones are in Indiana and Texas."

"Terrific! You passed the examination."

"I'm glad to hear that." John Bennett sounded slightly annoyed.

"Do you know Churchill?"

"Oh, yes. Years ago, when I was in the bond department, I handled the original negotiations with Churchill. He was their financial vice-president then."

"Perfect. Just what I was looking for. Will you call Churchill for me tomorrow and see if you can arrange a meeting the following day in New York?"

"Concerning what?"

"We'll go into that later. Just call him and tell him what a great guy I am and see if you can arrange a meeting."

"I don't know."

"You said you knew him."

"Yes, but I haven't talked to him in a year or two."

"OK, John. If you can't help me, never mind."

"Wait a minute. I'll call him. Of course I don't know if he's in town or how soon he'll be able to see you."

Norman looked at Bennett sadly.

"But I'll try, Norman, really I will."

"That's fine, John." Norman smiled, picked up the Klee watercolor and handed it to Bennett. "That's just fine."

Frieda found Norman stretched on the couch. His eyes were open but he did not seem to be aware that she had entered the room.

"Has he gone?"

"What? Oh, Bennett. Of course."

Frieda sat on the edge of the couch. She was still wearing the hostess gown, but her hair was down—a good sign. If anything, she looked even more beautiful than before—now that Norman could give her his full attention.

"I'll never understand it, Norman."

"What's that?"

"Your relationship with Bennett."

Norman propped himself on an elbow while he replied in a pedantic tone. "We share a broad spectrum of mutual interests: art, music, literature. John Bennett and I are soulmates."

Frieda laughed.

"It's true. John is an avid and generous patron of the arts."

"Generous? For every dollar he gives, you give a hundred."

"That's not the point, my dear. John Bennett is no millionaire. I prefer to consider the identity of our interests rather than compare the size of our contributions."

"What about the paintings? Did he decide to buy any of them?"

"No. I decided to buy the Klee—and then I loaned it to Bennett."

"Oh, Norman, not again."

"Yes, again." Norman struggled up from the comfort of the sofa.

"But Norman, you've loaned Bennett dozens of things in the last several years—paintings, sculpture, drawings—his home must be full of them."

"I suppose it is." He was studying the deep plunge of her neckline and finding it a bit difficult to follow the conversation.

"Why do you say 'suppose'? You mean you know it is."

"I don't mean anything of the kind. All I know is that I've loaned a number of art works to Bennett. I have no idea whether he displays them in his home or not."

Frieda was puzzled. "Are you telling me you've never been to John Bennett's home?"

"Precisely."

"I can't believe it. How could anyone be so ungracious? To accept the gift—or loan, if you insist—of art worth tens of thousands of dollars, and then never to invite the donor—all right, lender—to his home. It's unbelievable."

Frieda's words distracted Norman from his appraisal of her throat and the exposed portion of her breast. He sighed, stood up and walked to the windows.

"Has it occurred to you that John may not have advertised to anyone the source of all these loans—not to his friends, not to his family—and especially not to his business associates?"

"You mean he pretends he owns them?"

"As I said, I don't know what he does. I prefer not to know."

"I can't believe it."

Norman spun about. "You keep saying that, Frieda. Believe me, it's just as I told you. I've loaned the art to Bennett. I have no idea what he does with it, or what he tells anyone about it. But I can understand there might be reasons he doesn't invite me to his home. Besides which, I rather suspect that Bennett, his family and his friends may not be terribly fond of Jews."

"Not terribly fond—Norman, this is too much. You're good enough to do business with, good enough to entertain him in your own home, good enough to accept presents— loans—from, but not good enough for his family and friends. It's disgusting."

"You lost me a few sentences back. I didn't hear very much after you said I was good enough to do business with. That's all that matters, Frieda. That's the name of the game."

Frieda was thinking this over, rolling it around in her mind. "Norman, it's blackmail. Just plain blackmail. You have that poor man—"

"Suddenly he's 'that poor man.' "

But Frieda didn't stop. "—under your thumb. He's got a houseful of art that he doesn't own. You could call the loans due any minute, Norman. If those things really mean anything to Bennett, he must live in constant fear."

"Why should he? I have no intention of asking for them back."

"Now."

"That's right. Now."

"It's blackmail."

"I wish you wouldn't say things like that, Frieda. It pains me. It really does. We're just two friends, John and I, who happen to share a common interest in art."

"The sharing goes only one way."

"Look. It goes both ways. I'm not forcing Bennett to keep those things. Any time he wants to he can just give them back."

"Obviously he can't bring himself to do that. Suppose I do a little guessing about Mr. Bennett. Here is a man with an institutional job—one he's held for many years. Apparently he's mired there, a subordinate with a subordinate's salary. His one claim to fame is his art collection. It's not spectacular, but it's awfully good. Some people may wonder how he managed to acquire it. Of course, he's done it over a number of years. They probably credit him with good taste and shrewd judgment. Do you suppose that one day he could just crate up his whole collection and ship it back? It would be the end of him."

"Frieda, I don't know whether your analysis is right or wrong, but it's beautiful."

"You're diabolical."

"Why, thank you, dear. That's a lovely compliment."

"And that's how you squeeze all those millions out of Fidelity Standard."

"Now wait a minute. That's not fair. I've never brought them a bad deal. They've made a lot of money on me. Do you think Gresham would approve my deals—do you think the loan committee would pass them—if they weren't good? I'm not conning anyone, Frieda. I only get what I'm entitled to."

"You don't suppose you get an edge somewhere, do you?

Maybe a little lower interest rate or a little bigger loan?"

Norman smiled, "I'm a good customer. I'm entitled to special consideration."

"That's probably true, Norman. You know, come to think of it, Bennett does have a houseful of your art. Maybe I've got this all wrong. Maybe Bennett is using you."

That was too much for Norman.

"Bennett is a complete boob," he said. "He knows less about art than a blind man. Well, that's not exactly true. Living among my masterpieces has given him some taste. But every time I offer him a choice between two works of art, he picks the inferior one."

"Maybe he's reticent."

"Baloney, he's ignorant. Bennett thinks he's outwitting me. But if you compare the values of the paintings he's turned down to the ones he picked, you'll find that he outwitted himself. The ones he passed over are worth twice as much as the ones he selected."

"So what? Even at that rate, he still has a collection worth thousands of dollars."

"Oh, no doubt. All I'm telling you is that this guy knows even less about art than he does about real estate."

"You mean you've had to create his taste in real estate as well?"

"Is that surprising? Most mortgage loan officers are boobs—guys who got clobbered in the thirties and picked the insurance companies as a safe refuge. They spent the depression cheerfully foreclosing on one building after another. When times got better, these geniuses sold some of the finest properties in America at one-third their value. But now it's a different world. We've had almost continuous good times and inflation. The value of real estate has sky-rocketed. These same boobs are still loan officers. Many of them are heads of their departments. They don't know any more than they did before, but now they're not scared. Now they make loans based on ignorance instead of fear."

"Aren't you being harsh? If it weren't for the insurance companies, you could never build a project."

"If I thank anyone, it will be the guys who sell life insurance. They create the profits that these morons invest."

"Come now, Norman. You're overstating the case."

"Maybe, but John Bennett is my pigeon. I've trained him and fed him and I'm smart enough not to ruffle his feathers. He preens himself at my expense, but he knows damn well that without me, he's just another flunkey. Some day I'm going to need that boy, and he's going to have to deliver."

At that moment, Norman felt curiously deflated. He had not intended to discuss John Bennett with Frieda. Somehow, she had provoked him into these revelations—even put him on the defensive. He stared blankly out the window, trying to think of a way to retrieve his position.

Frieda touched his arm. She was standing beside him, her eyes searching his face. He did not permit himself to look at her directly. Sometimes her eyes were enough to melt him. Sometimes he could almost feel them picking his brain. "Tell me about it, Norman."

He did not respond.

"Please, Norman, don't keep me out."

"I don't know what you're talking about."

"You do. Of course you do. You've started something big."

He shook his head.

Frieda pressed closer. She would not take her eyes from his face. "Please, Norman. You're not fooling me. I can tell just by looking at you. You get like this when you have a new deal—I can feel it."

He thought about removing her hand, but it was pleasant having her there. Warm, intense, wetting her lips, giving off some exotic essence, her breath tickling his neck when she spoke.

"Oh, hell," he said. "Why not?" The feeling of depression dropped away. He spoke with animation.

"You see, Frieda, over there, right in front of the van der Rohe glass towers? I'm buying those low apartment houses. I'm going to tear them down and build office buildings. And get this. You know that beach in front of the buildings? You can't quite make it out from here at night, but it's there. I'm going to build on it. Going to fill in part of the lake and build on that, too. Six buildings. Sixty stories high. The biggest project this city has ever seen."

They were at the window now. Norman gently placed his arm around her waist. Frieda was breathing quickly, as if she were inhaling Norman's exhilaration.

"You're finally going to do it."

He looked at her sharply. "Do what, Frieda?"

She smiled. "The one thing you've hoped to do all along. Some men yearn to build the tallest building, some the biggest, but not you, Norman. You're going to recast the face of the city. You finally found the place, the most dramatic place in this town. After you've finished, Chicago will never be the same again."

Norman couldn't say a word. He felt a surge of feeling toward Frieda, a closeness he had not experienced in years. She understood. He had told a dozen people, but none of them had gotten the point. They were concerned with options and rezoning, building costs and net return on investment. Only Frieda realized what he was trying to accomplish. He was terribly pleased and terribly frightened at the same time—as if he had nourished a wicked thought and then been found out.

Frieda seemed unaware of his reactions. "That's marvelous," she said. "Absolutely incredible. You're the only man in the world who could have dreamed it up."

He did not deny it.

She kissed his cheek. "When, dear? When will you build it?"

"I'm only at the beginning, Frieda. We don't even own the land yet. There's money to be collected, plans to be drawn, space to be leased—a million details to be completed before we can even put a spade in the ground."

She was staring out into the night, her eyes fixed on the spot he had pointed out to her.

"You'll do it. I know you will. You always do."

Norman placed his free hand on her neck, then slowly moved it down inside her bodice. His fingers traced the arc of her breast, hesitated at the tip. He bent to kiss her throat, and as he did so, the deeply slashed gown slipped from one shoulder.

"Oh, Norman," she sighed.

He was wondering whether Tina's skin would feel as smooth as this.

The next morning Norman instructed Miss Fritch to make plane reservations for New York, as if John Bennett had already made an appointment with the president of International Materials. To Norman's great satisfaction, Bennett called within the hour and proudly told him he had arranged a meeting with Ralph Churchill.

"It was rather peculiar. I couldn't tell him what you wanted. I said that you were a prominent developer and a good friend of mine, and that you had asked to meet him."

"You did splendidly, John. And by the way, while I'm in New York I plan to pick up a marvelous new Léger. I want you to see it when I get back. Thanks a lot, old buddy."

The following day Norman took an early flight to New York. As he approached the International Materials Building in a taxi, Norman realized he had seen it many times before, but until now it had been just another faceless skyscraper like many others that lined Fifth, Park, Madison, Lexington and Third Avenues. He checked the building directory and learned to his satisfaction that International Materials occupied thirty of the forty floors in the building.

One of Norman's favorite games was attempting to visualize a man he was about to meet for the first time. He was rather good at it, but he made no attempt to visualize Ralph Churchill. He did not want to build any barriers. He tried to make his mind a clean slate, fresh and ready for the morning's impressions.

The elevator carried him with incredible swiftness to the top floor. Everywhere he went he noticed the block shape *M* dotted with an *I* which was the company's trademark. This symbol was carved on walls, engraved on stone, raised on letterheads and etched into doors. *IM, IM, IM,* it pronounced everywhere. Norman said to himself, "No, goddamn it, *I* am." The childish pun pleased him. It almost started him on a variation of the visualization game, an exercise in which Norman mentally diminished the man he was going to meet. *After all,* he would think, *what has he done? So he's president of the Flugel Company and he earns $100,000 per year. I* *make a lot more than that. How did he get where he is? Did he start the whole business like I did? Hell, no. He may be capable, but he can't match my record. Look where I started from, and what I accomplished.* Thus fortified, he would build up in his mind an image of his own worthiness, while his opponent slipped down the scale to a point where Norman could view him patronizingly.

But not this morning. It was essential for him to be as flexible as possible with Ralph Churchill. He had to make the right impression and to learn to understand the man as quickly as possible.

The reception room was a high-ceilinged rectangular carton, richly carpeted and furnished with austerely modern furniture. There was nothing on the receptionist's desk except a telephone, a pad of paper and a ballpoint pen. There was no clutter anywhere; the ashtrays were clean and the coat racks were empty. Every hair on the girl's head was in place.

"May I help you, sir?" She was classically pretty and her sculptured smile was impersonally perfect.

"I'm Norman Kane from Chicago, and I have an appointment with Mr. Churchill."

"One moment, Mr. Kane. Will you please take a seat?"

Norman backed into a chair while the girl murmured into her telephone. It was impossible for Norman to judge the reaction on the other end of the line.

"Mr. Churchill will see you in a minute."

Norman settled back and looked for a magazine. There were none, which somehow annoyed him, but his annoyance did not last, for within seconds another primly dressed and pretty woman appeared to escort him to Churchill's office.

Norman followed her along polished tile floors between polished wood walls, beneath a glowing fluorescent ceiling. It was a rather long walk and Norman passed many doors, each bearing the company symbol and the title of the occupant. Vice-presidents by the handful, plus a corporate secretary and treasurer and in the smaller cubicles, assistant secretaries and assistant treasurers. In the distance he could hear the sound of typewriters, but they were electric and the chatter was a cool, distant monotone.

Ralph Churchill rose to greet him, and Norman extended his own hand as he walked across the room. *Why, he looks like Vern Hanson,* Norman thought, and immediately felt reassured.

"Good morning, Mr. Kane. I'm Ralph Churchill." The voice was clear and the phrases clipped. Not much like Vern Hanson after all.

"Good morning. I'm grateful that you arranged to see me today."

"John Bennett told me you would be in New York and I said I would be happy to meet you. Won't you take a seat?"

It took but one quick glance for Norman to appraise Churchill's huge office. *Not as big as mine,* Norman thought, *but still pretty big.* Churchill's desk, at one end of the room, was backlighted by a vast pane of glass that stared out over New York. At the other end was a long conference table, large enough to seat at least a dozen men. The walls were paneled in a rich brown wood, heavily grained and deeply polished, divided by narrow recessed strips of black plastic. Most of the chairs were black and the rug was a soft gray. Here and there touches of red highlighted the room. A few paintings hung on the wall—originals, yes, but Norman guessed Churchill had not selected them.

"What brings you to New York, Mr. Kane? Are you about to buy the Empire State Building?"

Norman forced a chuckle. "No, I tried, but Henry Crown and Larry Wien beat me to it. This is one of my regular trips East. I have many business associates here and we get together to review our affairs from time to time."

"I see." Churchill waited for Norman to continue.

"Mr. Churchill, I'll get right to the point. I see you're quite comfortable here in New York. Your building is one of the finest in the city—which is a problem, because I intend to move you to Chicago."

Churchill laughed. "Lock, stock and barrel? Do you plan to transplant the whole building?"

"No, not the building. Not even your home office necessarily. But my studies indicate that Chicago is a far more central location for you than New York."

Churchill did not seem irritated by Norman's comment.

"Well, yes," he said, "more central from the standpoint of production and shipping. From an administrative standpoint, it hardly matters. Our lease here expires soon, but we intend to renew it. It's true that we need more space. However, our landlord is willing to provide it by moving some of the other tenants out of this building. No, Mr. Kane, we're perfectly happy in New York."

"I'm sure you are, but it does seem that with your company's extensive expansion program, there are good reasons for you to maintain a substantial office force in Chicago. Let me tell you what I have planned. John Bennett says I can safely take you into my confidence."

"Of course."

"I'm going to construct the largest and most beautiful office complex ever built in the city of Chicago. Our facilities will be superior to those provided by any office building in the United States—even more impressive than you have here. Just as important, our buildings will be built on the finest site I have ever seen anywhere in the world."

"That's interesting, but I don't see what it has to do with us."

Norman did not respond directly. "I recently purchased the Kincaid property on Lake Shore Drive. I already own the Simmons property next door, and when I put those two sites together, I will own the largest, most desirable hunk of ground on Lake Shore Drive. Perhaps you're acquainted with the area I'm describing."

"Yes," Churchill said, and from his tone Norman believed him.

"Well, sir, there are restrictive covenants in the Simmons and Kincaid deeds which have prevented the construction of buildings on the lake side of the Drive for over fifty years. However, now that I own both parcels, I can merge the estates, as the attorneys say, and cancel the restriction. I will then be able to build on both sides of Lake Shore Drive."

Churchill sat back. "That does sound impressive, Mr. Kane."

"My architect will be Karl Friedrichs. I don't know whether you are acquainted with him or not."

"Friedrichs? No, I don't know him personally, Mr. Kane,

but it's surprising you should mention him. Friedrichs designed our plant in Düsseldorf, Germany, which we built in 1959 in partnership with a German chemical company."

"Oh," said Norman innocently. "I didn't realize Friedrichs had worked for you before."

"Not for us, for our German co-partner, but I've seen the plant and it's very efficient. However, it's not an office building."

"Karl Friedrichs has vast experience in designing office buildings. Fortunately he happens to be available, and I have decided that he is the ideal man to do our work."

Churchill did not respond.

"Since this will be the finest office development in the Midwest, and probably in the world, we think your company should be in it."

"That may be. I'm sure we can use additional office space in Chicago. We've talked many times about taking more space in the Prudential Building."

"I think you should have your own building, possibly even named after your company."

"I'm afraid that would not impress us greatly, Mr. Kane."

"Perhaps you're concerned about whether we will actually be able to proceed with this project, particularly in this money market. I've talked to John Bennett and he assures me that Fidelity Standard will provide the financing for our venture."

"I believe you can procure the financing. John Bennett praised you highly."

"That was kind. I'm very happy we have a friend in common, Mr. Churchill. Since I am such a good mortgage customer at Fidelity and they hold twenty million dollars' worth of your debentures, we seem to have a natural combination."

Churchill's eyes narrowed and Norman was certain he had touched a vital nerve. The moment John Bennett had told him Churchill was in Chicago, Norman had suspected International Materials was attempting to refinance its debentures. Norman hoped he had given Churchill the impression that Bennett had informed him about it.

"Mr. Churchill, I won't insult you with salesmanship. If

you're interested in my proposal, you'll eventually submit it to your research staff. Perhaps you'll let them make a preliminary study of the site, even now."

"I don't object to consulting my research people, but frankly we've never considered operating a large office facility in Chicago."

"I'm certainly talking about a large office facility. Each of my six towers will contain a million square feet. I want you to lease most of one building."

Churchill laughed. "I'm sure we don't need that much space."

Norman reached into his inside jacket pocket and pulled out a small piece of paper. "According to my information, you occupy close to one hundred thousand feet in the First National Bank Building, another hundred thousand in the Prudential, and at least three hundred thousand more in places like Gary, Des Moines and Grand Rapids. That's half a million square feet, and I'm told you're pressed for space in every location. Ordinarily, if you needed five hundred thousand feet in six or seven locations, a hundred thousand less would do the trick, once you consolidated your offices. But since you're apparently under-officed everywhere, you probably need at least as much total space as you now have—maybe more. Not that I'm presuming to tell you what you need."

"Where did you get those figures?"

"That's part of my business, Mr. Churchill. I wouldn't presume on your time if I weren't positive you belong in my development."

"I see." The cool reply irritated Norman.

"By the way, I've also heard that you plan to open an office in Los Angeles containing another one hundred fifty thousand square feet. I probably shouldn't say this, but I don't believe you need that facility. You could handle all production and selling from Chicago if you had adequate space."

"I don't agree with you, Mr. Kane. There's nothing like having your sales force on the spot."

"That's true. You may need a sales office out there, but that won't take a hundred fifty thousand feet. The orders will eventually be processed in the Middle West anyway, and it seems a waste of time to set up an entire organization in Los Angeles to duplicate transactions."

Churchill was eying Norman steadily, and with evident interest.

"I'm not an expert in your particular line of business, Mr. Churchill, but I like to think I *am* an expert on real estate. I have a fabulous location, and I will build fabulous buildings. Financing is available, but I must have the best possible tenants. I offer quantity, quality and prestige in one package."

"As I said, John Bennett spoke very highly of you."

"That is a real compliment. John is the most able mortgage man in the country."

"It's not surprising that you would think so." Ralph Churchill spoke quite dryly, and Norman wondered how much the man knew.

"Well, sir, I won't take any more of your time. If you need any additional information, please call me. I sincerely hope you decide to make our project the Midwest headquarters for International Materials."

Norman rose, the men exchanged pleasantries, and he departed. The entire discussion had taken less than fifteen minutes, and Norman began to doubt his own wisdom in choosing the direct approach. He had intended only to chat with Churchill and learn a little about him. But there was something about Ralph Churchill, perhaps his facial resemblance to Vern Hanson, that kept Norman from making small talk.

He took a cab to the airport, changed to an earlier flight and headed back to Chicago that same afternoon. The trip was uneventful and it gave him time to reorganize his thoughts.

Usually Norman enjoyed observing the flight approach to Chicago. He loved to study the pattern of buildings and streets, trees and parks, spreading out from the edge of the lake. Sometimes, when his plane began its approach south of the city, he could spot his office, his home, even some of the buildings he owned. It gave him great satisfaction to see how prominent his buildings looked from the air.

But this time he was preoccupied, and although he sat in a window seat, he hardly bothered to glance out. He had set many wheels in motion and hoped they were all rolling in the same direction. Unless he was very alert and very careful, they might run him over.

———————◆———————

Norman decided to call John Bennett as soon as he entered the terminal. He knew Bennett's business day began at 8 A.M., but never lasted beyond 4 P.M.—and it was almost 4 P.M.

Norman hurried to one of the open, acoustically treated booths along the corridor, and placed his call. The switchboard at Fidelity Standard was still open and he reached John Bennett almost at once. Bennett sounded irritable, probably because Norman had called him only minutes before his escape from the office. But when Bennett heard Norman's voice, he masked his annoyance.

"Norman? Still in New York?"

"I'm at O'Hare."

"Oh? How was your meeting with Churchill?"

"Not bad. I think we made a start. Have you heard from him?"

"No. Should I expect a call?"

"I don't know."

"Well, I haven't heard anything yet, Norman. What shall I say?"

"Look, John, why did you kid me about that company?"

"Kid you? What do you mean?"

"Why didn't you tell me you were refinancing their debentures?"

There was a moment of silence on the line. "Truthfully, Norman, I didn't think it was your business. As a matter of fact, I'm surprised Churchill told you."

"He didn't. I guessed it. But you should have told me, John."

"Really, Norman, now you've fooled me again. I thought Churchill had told you. Good heavens, if the company knew that I was passing out information like this, I would be in terrible trouble. Can't I talk to you some other time?"

"No."

"Norman, the switchboard is still open."

"You mean they listen in on your calls?"

"I don't think so."

"Has International Materials' debenture proposal gone through committee yet?"

"I don't know. I'll have to ask Hobbs. He's the man who's handling it. But really, Norman, I can't put information like that in your hands."

"Don't put it in my hands. Put in my ears."

There was a long silence.

"John, you'll have to find out how far along they are with the deal. It's extremely important. And you must do it right away."

"I hardly think I can do it today."

"Has Hobbs gone home yet?"

"Probably. I was about to leave myself."

"Trust me, John. You know I wouldn't do anything to hurt Fidelity Standard. See what you can find out—and do it as fast as you can. Call me at home tonight."

"Well, all right, Norman. I hope you know what you're doing."

———

Bennett called Norman that evening. "I found Hobbs, and I managed to talk to him briefly before he went home. He told me he's just begun to work on the deal. No commitment has been issued yet."

"I see. How many years have those debentures left to run now?"

"About ten."

"And what was the original interest rate?"

"Four and a quarter per cent."

"What does International want now?"

"They want to stretch them out to twenty years again, Norman, and they want to borrow even more than the original issue."

"That was thirty million dollars."

"Right, but International has paid it down more than I

thought—down to eighteen million. Now they want to borrow another twenty-two million—forty million dollars in all."

"What interest rate?"

"Hobbs said they offered six per cent. The market today is closer to seven. However, since we're refinancing a four and a quarter per cent debt, they're probably entitled to a lower average rate."

"How does your company feel?"

"Damn interested. Hobbs is anxious to make the deal. International Materials is one of the biggest and best in the country, and we've held their long-term debentures for many years."

"Look, John, you don't have any control over that department, do you?"

"No, I don't."

"What kind of a man is Hobbs?"

"Well, I think he's intelligent. He knows his business."

"That isn't what I mean."

"I don't know what you do mean, Norman."

"I'll repeat what I said: What kind of a man is he?"

There was another moment of silence at the other end of the line. "I don't think he likes Léger or Mozart."

Norman realized he had taken the wrong tack. "Damn it, that's not what I mean at all. I'm not asking whether's he's an art connoisseur. I don't give a damn whether he likes classical music. That's between you and me. What I am asking you is this: Is Hobbs a man you can reason with? Can you talk to him?"

"Of course I can talk to him, but I don't know what you want me to say."

"Don't say anything, John. Let me do the talking. You just arrange a meeting."

———

A few days later, Norman sat across the desk from Fred Hobbs, the gaunt, stiff-looking vice-president in charge of investments for Fidelity Standard Life. Hobbs' office was formal in every detail. In some ways it seemed like a bureaucratic version of Churchill's office. Everything was arranged in a rigid rectangular pattern. There were no paintings on the walls— only framed professional certificates and photographs of high executives in the company, signed and suitably dedicated to Mr. Hobbs. The photographs were as expressionless as the certificates.

Hobbs' greeting was cool. He was courteous to Norman, but his attitude could hardly have been called cordial. John Bennett, wearing his typically rumpled tweed suit, was nervously fingering a chain with a metal key at the end. It looked a bit like a Phi Beta Kappa key, but Norman Kane knew better.

"It's amazing to me," said Norman, "that we've never met before."

"Not too surprising. This *is* a totally different department. John handles mortgage loans. We handle bonds, debentures and other securities."

"Oh, certainly," Norman said. He worked up a smile. "I have a confession to make, Mr. Hobbs. I've done so much business with Fidelity Standard across the years, I sometimes forget that my contacts are limited to the mortgage loan department. I think of Fidelity as 'my company,' which is quite presumptuous."

Hobbs received this in silence, studying Norman with clear gray eyes that neither blinked nor wavered. Insofar as Norman could tell, his words had not even registered on this computer.

"Well, be that as it may," Norman said, "I've come to ask your advice." For an instant, Hobbs' face betrayed surprise. "I have to make a very important decision, Mr. Hobbs, and you have the facts, the knowledge and the experience that will enable me to make the right one."

"Really?" said Hobbs. "I think you're the first real-estate developer who has ever asked us for advice."

"I'm sure it isn't common. However, despite our pretensions and our learned surveys, despite the projections we assemble and the plans we prepare—despite all this evidence of scientific method, Mr. Hobbs, when you get to the nub of it, we developers are an emotional lot. We reach conclusions first and then assemble the data to support them."

"Then you admit real-estate development is not a science."

"Please, Mr. Hobbs, don't quote me. I've made some rather damaging admissions already. I simply want you to realize that—as ever—I come to Fidelity Standard without pretense."

"We appreciate that, Mr. Kane."

"However, there are many times, Mr. Hobbs, when the developer's enthusiasm is not the issue. There are times when the determinants are strictly financial. Either the deal makes sense or it does not.

"That is why I'm here today. Our present project has reached that very point. We have assembled the Kincaid and Simmons properties—for a large, yet not unreasonable, consideration. We have employed one of the world's great architects to draw our plans. We believe this to be not merely a sensible but a spectacular venture, which will bring us exceptional financial rewards and tremendous prestige.

"I must point out to you that I, myself, am not impatient. I bought the Simmons property several years ago with this very idea in mind. I have carried it all these years at no profit, hoping that one day I would acquire the Kincaid property and develop the project we are discussing."

John Bennett spoke for the first time. "Norman could easily have built on the Simmons property, you know. He had many opportunities an ordinary builder would have leaped at. But Norman was waiting for something much bigger and more important."

"Right, John. But the time has come to proceed with this enterprise. My judgment of it depends on many things—principally on the quality of the tenancy of the project. We have tentatively decided to call our venture Lake Shore Plaza. But we can call it anything we wish. If we are not able to stock every floor with leading companies, we may as well dub it Disaster Plaza."

"Well," said Hobbs, "I don't see how I can help you. I'm sure Fidelity Standard doesn't intend to move its home office to your site."

Norman chuckled over Hobbs' attempt at humor. "I didn't think you would, although it's not a bad idea. Nothing would do more for our venture. However, that is not why I have come to talk to you. At the present time we are considering a major tenant, one we believe is willing to lease several hundred thousand square feet. On the surface, this firm's record is excellent. We have studied its financial statements with meticulous care and made intensive inquiries in the financial community. Everyone tells us they are perfectly sound. In the course of this investigation I learned that your company has a long history of dealing with this corporation, and I think you are far better able to judge its financial strength than anyone else."

Hobbs cleared his throat. "We'll help you if we can, but naturally we won't give out any information that is confidential."

"Splendid. What more can I ask?"

"Name the company, Mr. Kane."

"International Materials Corporation of New York City."

Hobbs showed not the faintest flicker of surprise. *I wonder,* thought Norman. *I wonder if John Bennett has discussed this with him.*

"You mean to tell me that International Materials plans to lease a large amount of space in a new building in Chicago? I never realized they had any such idea."

"I hesitate to presume on your knowledge. However, I would like to point out that almost all of International's plants are located far from New York City and that its principal markets are concentrated in the West, the Middle West and the South. It seems that International Materials has elected to locate its home office unusually distant from both its production facilities and its customers."

Hobbs pondered this for a moment. "It *is* true that most of International's plants and many of its customers are located far from New York."

"There should be some reasonable relationship between the location of a company's offices and its business. I'm aware that much of International's business is transacted abroad and that New York is an export center. However, even though

International Materials sells to the entire world, most of its products are shipped from ports on the Gulf of Mexico or the West Coast. They ship not one package, not one pinch of powder, not one drop of liquid from New York City."

Hobbs was nodding his head; Norman was encouraged.

"Then, too, over the years International Materials has acquired several other companies. Each acquisition has carried the company ever further from New York. Today the Texas and California subsidiaries contribute thirty per cent of total sales and nearly half of their net profits."

"Who told you that?"

Norman smiled. "It's in a footnote to their latest annual report.

"Also, despite the location of its home office, International Materials procures almost all of its financing from Midwestern institutions. Do they deal with New York Life or Mutual Benefit? Have they ever placed a bond issue with Metropolitan Life or any of the New England companies? No, of course not. Almost all of their long-term financing has been handled either by you or the Pacific Insurance Company. Strange, isn't it? The head is in New York, but the body, the arms, the blood, the flesh—the very heart—everything else is somewhere else."

Hobbs sat thinking about this for a moment. "I still don't understand what you want from us, Mr. Kane—although you seem somehow to have heard that we're planning to refinance their debentures." Hobbs did not look at Bennett.

"It's very simple. I want to know your opinion of this company. I want to know whether you believe it would be wise for me to lease them the major part of one of my buildings."

"It seems to me you have just proved Chicago is an ideal location for them."

"Yes, it's right for International Materials. But is it right for me? I want to be certain I'm making the correct decision."

"Are you asking whether they will pay their rent?"

"In a way. My lease will probably run just as long as your bond issue."

"I'm still perplexed, Mr. Kane. I didn't realize International Materials was planning to consolidate its offices."

"They don't have any choice. Right now, they occupy space in several cities, plus five or six different New York office buildings. Mr. Churchill works in one place and the chairman of the board has his office in another. The operating vice-presidents of the ethical drug divisions are located four blocks away on Broadway, and the import division rents a warehouse near the docks. Believe me, they must consolidate their operations sooner or later. But they'll probably rent additional space in New York City."

"Then they're not thinking of Chicago?"

"They're thinking about it now. I discussed the matter with Mr. Churchill a few days ago. He was impressed—but not too impressed because, after all, New York is the first city and Chicago the second. Very likely the company's executives prefer New York's cosmopolitan atmosphere."

"I don't see where we come into all of this."

"Let's look at it this way, Mr. Hobbs. Here is a company you already have on your books for millions of dollars—one that hopes to borrow many millions more. This company must consolidate its offices. If they expand in New York, someone else will get the benefit. Perhaps they'll build a new and larger building. In that case, Fidelity Standard and Norman Kane will reap no advantage whatever. On the other hand, if we bring them to Chicago and put them in our building and if, as I hope, Fidelity Standard agrees to provide the long-term financing, then we've accomplished several things. First, we've gotten them to locate their offices in the city which is best for them; second, we've got them here in Chicago where we can keep an eye on them; third, instead of someone else holding a lucrative mortgage loan, your own mortgage department ends up with the deal.

"There's another advantage, but this one is a bit on the emotional side. What a coup for all of us! Year after year, major companies pull up stakes and move to New York. They leave Atlanta, Kansas City, Omaha, St. Louis, Cleveland, even Chicago, and build shiny, gleaming towers in Manhattan. But not this time. This time we take a major company, pull it out of New York and set it down right here in Chicago. A lot of people will be impressed, Mr. Hobbs."

Hobbs nodded again. He was beginning to see the point, and Norman did not press it further.

"Of course, we don't seem to have an answer to your question, Mr. Kane. You inquired whether you should lease space to this tenant. It comes down to our asking ourselves how great our risk will be once we have lent them millions of additional dollars on their debentures and they have obligated themselves on a new long-term lease somewhere."

"From a risk standpoint, I don't think it matters where they build their office."

"It does matter," said Hobbs. "If they lease space in a building we finance, we're using the same credit in our mortgage department we already used in the bond department. If they lease space in a building financed by someone else, we're spreading the risk."

John Bennett spoke. "Of course, Fred, if you don't mind my saying so, this is all rather fanciful. International Materials is a very large and very sound company. I can't conceive of them not paying their rent any more than I can conceive of them defaulting on our debentures."

"That's true," said Hobbs.

"Then," said Norman, "there *is* no additional risk, or at least the risk is minimal. It seems a pity that someone else may get the benefit of International's lease when you and I and John Bennett could put it all in a single package."

"But what if they don't want to move to Chicago?"

"I think you would have very little difficulty persuading them. It's true they have an enormous net worth. But they are planning to refund their debentures. It isn't too easy to place a multimillion-dollar issue in today's market. Besides, if they go elsewhere, they'll probably pay another half point in interest. That could mean hundreds of thousands of dollars a year—a lot of money to flush down the drain for the glory of remaining in New York."

Hobbs sat at his desk, staring straight ahead for several minutes. The silence disturbed John Bennett, and he began to twist nervously in his chair. Norman said nothing.

Finally Hobbs spoke. "This has been a very useful meeting. You've given us a good deal to think about."

"I know I've been presumptuous," Norman said. "I'm well aware you have been handling this company for years, and you obviously know a great deal more about International Materials than I do."

Hobbs waved him off. "Probably true. Nevertheless your thoughts are interesting. You've put together in one package a group of basic problems which we've been viewing as fragments. Thank you for coming in. We'll give this further thought, and you will hear from us."

Immediately after leaving Hobbs' office, Norman phoned Ralph Churchill. He repeated most of his conversation with the men from Fidelity Standard verbatim to the astonished company president.

When he finished, Churchill asked, "Am I to believe that all this actually transpired, Mr. Kane?"

"Why would I invent such a story?"

"Why did you tell it to me?"

"Mr. Churchill, I'm a rather aggressive guy, but the truth is, I don't like trouble. Oh, I've had my share of it and fought my way out of it, but I'd rather kiss my way out if I can. I figure that if Fidelity Standard decides to slice you into this debenture-office-mortgage sandwich, you'll be in a pretty tight spot. You're probably angry, and I don't blame you, because I mousetrapped you. If you can get out of the trap, more power to you. But I don't think you can. If you quarrel with Fidelity Standard, you may preserve your pride but you'll lower your profit. You don't strike me as that kind of man, Mr. Churchill. It would cost your company a fortune to break off relations with Fidelity Standard."

"That much is true, Mr. Kane."

"You see, I'm offering you a hell of a deal. I'm giving you a negotiating position you wouldn't have with anybody else. You can hammer me down on the rent and Fidelity on the interest rate. We're just as boxed in as you are."

"I still don't understand why you've told me all this."

"Call it an investment in good will. I think you're barrelled, one way or another. But I don't intend to push my advantage. I'm willing to negotiate a reasonable lease with you—one that makes sense for both of us. We'll be doing business together for the next twenty years. Of course, you can make a fool out of me just by calling Hobbs and repeating what I've told you. At that point I'm dead. Dead at Fidelity Standard and dead at International Materials. On the other hand, I think you see how this can work to your advantage. We'll all end up with a nice sweet deal and live happily ever after."

Ralph Churchill did not hesitate. "They told me you were a very shrewd man, Mr. Kane, and now I believe it. Everything you say is true. I *am* damn mad that I allowed you to box me in. On the other hand, by the time I finish chiseling you on the rent and Fidelity on their debentures, we won't be paying a hell of a lot more for their money than we are right now."

Norman laughed aloud. "That's right. That's the picture."

"And by the way, Kane, I investigated your little project and it's not so crazy after all. You may never get your property rezoned, but if you do, you'll have one hell of a development."

"Why, thank you." Norman was surprised by the compliment. "I hope your people will be happy here."

"Happy? We employ almost six thousand people in the New York area, Kane. I'll have to sell most of them on relocating. It won't be easy. Then there is my board of directors—fifteen men, not one of whom lives more than fifty miles from where I'm sitting. When I tell them we're moving the whole shop from New York to Chicago, they won't be very happy. I'm also going to have to sell the idea to my wife, and I'm not looking forward to that, either."

"Wait a minute. You're talking as if you plan to move your home office to Chicago."

"Right."

There was complete silence at Norman's end of the line.

"Don't pretend to be surprised, Kane. That's what you had in mind all along. I gave the problem to my research staff as you suggested. They reported that once we consolidated our

Midwest offices, it wouldn't make any sense to have our administrative headquarters in New York. I hoped to avoid the whole mess, but now you've locked me in with those damn debentures."

"You're being rather candid."

"Why not? It hardly matters now. Besides, as you said, it's an investment in good will."

"I appreciate it, Mr. Churchill."

"OK, Kane, I'll try to sell it here. But first, I'm going to make a suggestion. You'll love it and your pals will be flabbergasted."

"Go ahead."

"I'm going to call Hobbs and tell him I've done some investigating since you and I met in New York and that I think there's a lot of merit in your ideas about moving us to Chicago. I'm going to suggest that he come out here and bring you along."

"Mr. Churchill, Fred Hobbs will faint dead away."

"Mr. Kane, in order to faint you have to have blood in your veins. That bastard hasn't a drop in his entire system."

There was no goodbye. Only the click at the end of the line. Norman looked at the phone.

"It really grinds you, you son of a bitch."

"Did you say something, sir?" It was the long-distance operator.

"No, operator, I said all I have to say."

"I have to get you off the hook, John."

"Off the hook? What hook?"

"We both know this project is going to cost around two hundred million dollars. Even with forty million dollars in equity money, we'll still need a hundred and sixty million dollars in financing. God knows, Fidelity Standard won't lend me that much."

"Of course not, Norman. We're only going to finance the International Materials building."

"John, Lake Shore Plaza is one deal. I don't intend to slice it up and mortgage each building to a separate lender."

"But Norman, even if our mortgage limit were high enough to carry it, we'd never loan one hundred and sixty million dollars on one project. My God, if Hobbs knew that was your idea, he'd call this whole thing off."

"Simmer down, John. I don't expect you to loan me a hundred and sixty million dollars. There's only one solution. We have to assemble a group of insurance companies to participate in the deal. One mortgage will cover all of the buildings, but we'll split the notes up among several companies. Fidelity Standard can decide how large an amount it wants, but probably it will come to less than half."

"Half the total loan? We wouldn't loan anywhere near eighty million dollars."

"John, please hear me out. I think this is an idea you can sell your people." Bennett shook his head but Norman ignored him. "Let's say Fidelity leads the group and takes sixty million dollars. Then we look for other companies to absorb the remaining hundred million. I'm sure we can find four companies that will each put in twenty-five. For example, Pacific Insurance Company. They own a lot of International Materials common stock. Now if Pacific and Fidelity take eighty-five million, that leaves only seventy-five to place elsewhere. With Fidelity and Pacific spearheading the group, you'll have no difficulty placing the balance."

"I don't know, Norman. We've always frowned on split notes. We've even refused to do it on small loans. Now you're suggesting we split a big one."

"That's the whole idea. It makes a lot more sense on a big loan. There's enough gravy in this deal for everybody. And Fidelity Standard can earn a fat fee for putting it together."

"Well, that's true, Norman, but it's very unusual."

"I think Hobbs will buy it. It's just possible that a cold rectangular guy like Hobbs may have a romantic streak buried deep inside."

"I don't know. It sounds risky."

"There's no risk at all. And think of the rewards. You've been Gresham's assistant for years. At the rate you're going, you'll remain in your present position even after Gresham moves up. And why? You have more imagination in your little finger than Arnold Gresham has in his whole body, but the top men at Fidelity Standard don't know it. This is your chance to put together one of the most brilliant deals this country has ever seen."

Bennett sat on Norman's couch staring out the window. "I've never done anything like this, Norman."

"I'll help you. I'll tell you what companies to talk to. Together we can plan the whole thing. Listen, Gresham is bound to be promoted soon. Why shouldn't you be head of the department?"

"I don't know if I can do it, Norman."

"You've done things that were even tougher than this. Now look, we've got International Materials going for us, General Stone and even Fred Hobbs. How about it?"

Bennett sat quietly for a long time, thinking.

———————

Norman now controlled the property, the partners and the equity funds he required. He was close to a major lease with International Materials and he had begun negotiations for long-term financing with Fidelity Standard. All this without even a simple layout or a rudimentary sketch of the project. Norman was selling a vision. But he could not rezone his land, lease space or obtain a mortgage commitment without an architect.

If his first approach to Karl Friedrichs had been premature, Norman was now behind schedule. He had been waiting for the architect to come to him.

And Friedrichs finally did. The morning after Norman told John Bennett how to organize the financing of Lake Shore Plaza, Karl Friedrichs telephoned Kane's office. Norman was delighted, but he did not accept the call. Not until the following afternoon did he telephone Friedrichs.

"Dr. Friedrichs? Norman Kane."

"Oh, yes, Mr. Kane. I called you yesterday."

"Yes, I have your message."

"It's not really that important, Mr. Kane, but the last time we met you offered to send me some large photographs of my buildings in Germany. I don't want to impose on you but I would like to have them."

"Fine. I'll order additional copies made and mail them to you right away."

"That won't be necessary. I'll be downtown Friday afternoon. If the prints are ready then, I can pick them up at your office."

"All right. I think I can have them by Friday. I'll leave the photographs with my receptionist and you can get them at your convenience."

There was a moment of silence at the other end of the line.

"Is that all right, Doctor?"

"Oh, yes, it's fine—except that if you happen to be in your office when I come, perhaps we can talk together. I have a little something to show you."

"Just a minute. Let me check my appointment book." Norman held the phone away from his head and stared at the ceiling. "What time will you be downtown?"

"About two-thirty, Mr. Kane."

"I think I'll be in. Perhaps we can spend a few minutes together."

"Very good, Mr. Kane. Thank you."

"You're entirely welcome, Doctor."

Norman could not resist calling me. "I've got him, Eddie. I tell you, I've got him."

"We'll see."

"I'd invite you to come up here Friday, but you'd ruin the mood, you cold-eyed, fish-livered lawyer."

───────────

Norman deliberately kept the old man waiting in his reception room for half an hour. Then he was blandly apologetic. "Forgive me, Doctor. I was tied up on a long-distance call."

"That's perfectly all right. You're doing me a great favor."

Norman escorted the old man into his office.

"This is very impressive," Karl Friedrichs said as Norman

performed his usual ritual, demonstrating the wonders of his establishment.

"It's rather ostentatious, but I have my reasons."

"To be sure."

"Oh, I almost forgot the photographs." Norman hurried to his desk, picked up a large bundle wrapped in brown paper and brought it to the architect.

The old man was perplexed. "These are the photographs?"

"Of course." Norman laughed. "Let me show you." He placed the bundle on the conference table and, gesturing theatrically, pulled the string and the paper off. There, mounted under glass, was a complete set of the photographs Friedrichs had requested. Some were framed individually. Others were grouped in an ingenious pattern within a single frame so that they illustrated several views of the building at once. The photographs were so cunningly arranged that they gave an illusion of depth and perspective.

The old man stood at the table studying the photographs and shaking his head.

"You're not happy," said Norman.

"Not happy? I'm delighted. I never expected this. I thought you were giving me a few unmounted prints."

"I always intended to surprise you. It wasn't easy to get these frames ready in two days, but here they are. Please don't thank me. It's privilege enough to see them properly mounted."

"Mr. Kane, it would be impossible for me to put in words the gratitude I feel." The old man hesitated for a second. "Frankly, I'm embarrassed. After this, my own gift seems insignificant."

"A gift, Dr. Friedrichs? Don't tell me you brought a gift for me?"

The old man placed a large worn leather case on the conference table. He opened it, quickly removed a cardboard portfolio and handed it to Norman Kane.

Norman laid the portfolio on the table and opened it carefully. Inside were dozens of drawings and sketches—some in pencil, some in ink, a few highlighted with touches of color. Many were fragments torn from a roll of tracing material.

Norman sat down. He glanced briefly at Karl Friedrichs, but said nothing. He examined the drawings one at a time, handling each with care. Once or twice he nodded his head.

The only sounds in the room were the old man's somewhat labored breathing, an occasional murmur by Norman Kane and the rattle of the papers in the ancient portfolio. When Norman had studied every drawing, he closed his eyes. Then he rose, walked to a window and stared out across the city. His voice was somewhat muffled.

"Dr. Friedrichs, this is the most magnificent present anyone has ever given me."

"You're very kind, Mr. Kane, but they are merely a few old sketches."

"A few old sketches," repeated Norman. "That portfolio contains original drawing of some of your finest buildings."

"Scratches on paper, Mr. Kane. I thought they would amuse you."

Norman turned suddenly. "Amuse me? I'm inspired. With a few lines you've expressed the essence of some of the world's greatest structures. I have the privilege of seeing these buildings as you first conceived them. Your drawings are magnificent. I don't see how I can possibly accept such a gift."

"Oh, please don't turn me down. I want you to have them. Your reaction only confirms my expectations. I have other sketches—my drawers are filled with them. But I admit I selected these very carefully. I feel they represent some of the clearest ideas I have ever had." He chuckled. "Many of my sketches look much better than the completed buildings."

"The buildings are better," said Norman, "but not clearer." He returned to the drawings almost reverently, selected one which he held high in his hands. "Look at this one. The Mannheim Tower in Frankfurt. These half-dozen lines instantly call to mind that elegant building."

Norman hurried to the French doors and shoved them open. "I can almost see this building—perhaps even several just like it right over there."

The old man had followed him onto the balcony. "Yes," he said. "I see them too. Not exactly like the Mannheim Tower but similar. The proportions are not quite right, particularly if you are going to build a group of identical structures."

Neither man spoke for several minutes. The wind fluttered the drawing in Norman's hand and he held on to it tightly, crinkling the corner between his thumb and forefinger.

Karl Friedrichs cleared his throat. "I must be honest with you, Mr. Kane. I appreciate the photographs and I am very pleased to have them. I want you to have my sketches. But that is not why I came."

Again there was silence. Norman gave the old man no encouragement.

"I came here because I hoped you would do exactly what you have done now; that you would take these sketches and look out at this city and see my buildings on your property."

Norman looked at him. "Oh, yes," said Friedrichs. "I know you are buying it. And I have some idea of what you intend to do with it. I cannot help it, Mr. Kane. I see my buildings on your property. I see them rising against the lake and the sky and the city. I can close my eyes but I still see them. Isn't that silly, Mr. Kane?" The old man tried to laugh, but he could not manage it. His voice cracked. "An old man like me and I dream like a child. I bring you a present of sketches—worthless sketches—like the offering of a child to gain your favor." He hesitated. Norman looked away and said nothing. He clutched the sketch tighter in his hand while it rattled in the wind. The old man seemed to be breathing even more heavily than before.

"Forgive me," he said. "It is not that I think you are a fool. I know you are a successful businessman. And I know you don't need Karl Friedrichs for your project."

Suddenly he straightened his shoulders. "Also, I am a proud man, Mr. Kane, not given to begging or pleading. I will not plead now but I will be honest. I want to design your buildings, Mr. Kane. I know I can do it better than anyone else in the world. That is not arrogance. Simply a statement of my honest belief. I am not forty years old or sixty or even seventy, but my eyes can still see and my hands can still draw and my mind is still clear."

Again there was silence on the balcony. Then, without looking at Karl Friedrichs, Norman began to speak. "Yes, you

144

are right. It is a dream. But I have the same dream myself, Doctor. You see, I live over there." He pointed his hand toward his skyscraper apartment home. "Every morning when I awake I look at the Kincaid property and when I look I don't see those jumbled Rococo monstrosities. I see the kind of slim towers Karl Friedrichs would design.

"I could hire one of your imitators. The world is filled with men who imitate the steel-and-glass elegance created by Karl Friedrichs. But few of them understand the basic proportions that dynamize your buildings." Norman held the sketch higher in his hands. "Sometimes I shake my head and I think the vision has gone away. But then if I glance back, half in dismay and half in pleasure, I see them again. Six towers."

"Six?" The old man was surprised.

"Yes, six. I'm telling you something that is unknown to any but my closest associates. I'm going to build on both sides of Lake Shore Drive, Dr. Friedrichs. Three buildings on each side."

The old man almost ran to the parapet. "Six, you say? Three on each side of the Drive? How can you do this?"

"We will have to rezone the property. But I own land which everyone thinks is a public beach and some of which is under water. I intend to fill it in and build on it."

The old man shook his head. "Fantastic. Even more fantastic than I dreamed."

"That's the beauty of a dream," said Norman. "You can invent anything you want. And on that site—" he pointed an imperious finger— "on that site Norman Kane sees six buildings."

"You know," said Karl Friedrichs, "now that you mention it, I see six buildings too."

Both men stood at the parapet and laughed.

3

A few days later Norman asked me to meet him at Dan McGarrity's office. I knew McGarrity; almost everyone in the city did. He greeted me with a jovial smile, offering his big hand, fleshy and a bit sweaty, but his grip was firm and he slapped me on the back almost affectionately.

"By God, it's good to see you, Eddie. You don't generally come down to this part of town."

"You don't often invite me."

He laughed. "That's true enough. But if we let all you high-priced La Salle Street fellas down here, there wouldn't be much left for us poor neighborhood lawyers."

"I think it's the other way around. I'll be pretty frightened if you ever open up shop on La Salle Street."

We sat back and smiled contentedly at each other. After a few minutes Norman Kane arrived, and we settled down to business.

"Now, Norman," said McGarrity, "I know you don't need a great deal of advice in this matter, and I'm sure you're well aware that the first thing we want is a set of plans. Not too complicated, mind you. We don't want anything that will confuse the boys."

"I agree with you completely, Dan."

"Yeah, well, the site plan will scare them fair enough, but I'll have a little talk with Jimmy Dunleavy before you come in and I'll see that he doesn't turn it over to the newspaper boys until we're ready."

"Any problems in the Zoning Committee?"

"No, I don't think so. They'll refer it to the Department of City Planning for a recommendation. Now that may be a bit more difficult. Bernie Adler, the commissioner, is not a political appointee. After all that trouble a few years ago, the Mayor decided to put in one of those honorable boys and, by God, Adler is certainly that. If he doesn't like your design, you're going to have real trouble."

"What then?"

"Then we go to the City Council. The Mayor can push it through if he wants to. But you know how the Mayor feels about these things. He hates to overrule anybody. His Honor likes things nicely worked out and packaged before they get to his desk. For a boy who grew up back of the yards, he's a very fastidious fellow."

"Of course," said Norman. "We'll certainly do everything we can to ease the way. How do we proceed?"

"Well, first we pick the right architect. Now I was thinking of Graham and Graham, or perhaps Marshall, Constable and White. They've both done a lot of city work in the past and everyone knows them."

"I've already picked the architect," said Norman.

"You have, have you? Who is it?"

"Karl Friedrichs."

I would wager that few men have had the privilege of seeing Dan McGarrity with a surprised look on his face. Dan has played in tough leagues all of his life and he's seen all kinds of pitching, but suddenly a red spot appeared on Dan's forehead —almost as if he had been hit by a beanball. After a minute, he forced a smile. "Oh, come now, Norm, you're putting me on."

"No, I'm not, Dan. The architect for my project is Karl Friedrichs."

McGarrity spun his swivel chair and stopped, facing a window. He sat there, huge and momentarily silent. "I think you're making a terrible mistake. Friedrichs is not safe. He's not safe at all. Isn't he the same chap who called our lovely McCormick Place the biggest white elephant this side of the Indian Ocean? And isn't he the man who condemned the Civic Center as scrapyard architecture?"

"That's right," said Norman.

"Do you by any chance think that those kind words have ingratiated him with His Honor? The Mayor remembers his friends—and his enemies."

"I'm aware of that."

McGarrity spun back and looked at Norman. "And you still want to throw this noisy foreigner right in the Mayor's face?"

"Now hold on, Dan, he's not a foreigner. Karl Friedrichs became an American citizen years ago. And I have no intention of throwing him in the Mayor's face, as you say. I intend to tell the Mayor what I'm doing and why."

"I certainly hope you have a good reason."

"I have many. The first is the most important to me and the least important to you. I think Karl Friedrichs is the finest office-building architect in the world. But let's pass that. Dan, you've been around a long time. If we bring in Graham and Graham or some other political architects, and we throw in General Stone, everybody in this town is going to say there's graft in the project—that it's some kind of a boondoggle. But instead we're going to give them Karl Friedrichs. Upright, pious, arrogant Karl Friedrichs. God and everyone else knows he's not the Mayor's pigeon."

McGarrity sat staring at Norman, watching his lips move, and watching his eyes. Then suddenly he smiled an engaging smile. "You know, I think you're going out of your mind. That's the craziest reason I ever heard in me life." His brogue had suddenly grown thicker. "I'll be damned if I'll take the blame for this one."

"Dan, it's not a question of blame. I'll take the responsibility, and you can tell that to the Mayor."

McGarrity sat back. "He's certainly going to think I've gone mad when I try to explain to him how his worst enemy is now his best friend."

———————————————

There was trouble in the Zoning Committee of the City Council. McGarrity warned us that some of the members had learned of Norman's plans and were under pressure from their constituents. Some of them were prepared to make public statements against the project. McGarrity kept them quiet, then suggested an informal meeting with Kane and Friedrichs even before the application was referred to the Department of City Planning.

Karl Friedrichs appeared before the committee with his site plan and his sketches, and his fierce pride and amazing inspiration. They tried to tell him that his buildings didn't fit because they differed so greatly from the surrounding construction.

"Tear down the rest of the buildings," he said.

I suppose that is what other architects have said for centuries, but it sounded so arrogant—so preposterous—coming from that frail old man. His hand shook unless he held a pencil in it; then it was firm and steady and graceful. *Remarkable,* I thought, *the pencil is like a tranquilizer.*

Friedrichs finally stalked out of the meeting. McGarrity tried to placate the committee members. He urged them not to take a stand, stating he would not expect them to approve the plan and submit it to the full council without a strong recommendation from the planning commissioner. "Let Adler carry the ball," he said. "Why should you guys stick out your necks?" That made sense to the aldermen and they promised to take no action until they received a report from the commissioner.

It was no use trying to pressure Bernie Adler. Even McGarrity had cautioned us against that. All we could do was offer as attractive a presentation as possible. Once again, Friedrichs would be called upon to defend his work. We would have preferred to have someone else appear before Adler. But Friedrichs was the architect and everyone knew it. Norman spent many hours trying to convince him to hold his temper.

Bernard Adler, the nonpartisan, nonpolitical commissioner, questioned Friedrichs closely, examining every detail of his presentation. We were grateful that Friedrichs managed to control himself. He was arrogant, of course, but eloquent. We hoped his eloquence would be enough to outweigh his manner.

When our presentation was complete, Adler spoke. "I have admired the work of Dr. Karl Friedrichs for over twenty years. I believe he is one of the three or four greatest architects of our century. Possibly, he is the greatest of them all. Dr. Friedrichs' plans for these buildings are magnificent. The concept of placing them on both sides of the roadway, not as the overpowering walls of a tunnel, but almost in the shape of a triumphal arch, is a stroke of genius—as brilliant a piece of engineering as I have ever seen. Gentlemen, this project will be a great credit to our city."

I was stunned. But Norman was not. Somewhere, somehow, rummaging around in that grab bag of information he carried with him, Norman had learned that Bernard Adler revered the ancient German architect. Many months later—long after the property had been successfully rezoned—Norman showed me a thin volume Bernard Adler had written eulogizing Karl Friedrichs. "I've had this book in my library," Norman told me, "for nearly twenty years."

We signed the International Materials lease in Churchill's office with a dozen top executives looking on and several members of the press in attendance. Mr. Churchill made a little speech about the happy years International Materials had spent in New York City and how sad they were to leave. He expressed his regrets to employees of the company who would be dislocated by this move, and then finished with a brief but impressive analysis of the advantages it would have for International Materials.

The story caused quite a ripple in the New York financial

community. In Chicago, the event received even greater attention. Mayor Conlin publicly expressed a hearty welcome to International Materials and invited other progressive companies, both large and small, to join this forward-looking enterprise in America's heartland, etc., etc., etc.

The announcement gave Lake Shore Plaza new impetus. Thereafter, Norman Kane received several unsolicited inquiries from companies in various lines of business. Some may have been influenced by directors or major shareholders who pointed out that their market, like International Materials', was in the Midwest. There were also inquiries from suppliers of International Materials who were fearful that the move would affect their business. Probably Churchill himself told many of International's suppliers that it would be advantageous if they, too, relocated in Lake Shore Plaza.

We had celebrated in New York after Churchill gave his statement to the press, but our biggest celebration came after Norman announced the placing of the long-term financing with a group headed by Fidelity Standard. That afternoon the newspapers reviewed Norman's career and listed General Stone's achievements. Fidelity Standard provided its traditional press release, lauding the strength of the Middle West.

The financing was arranged on precisely the basis Norman had suggested to John Bennett. Once Fidelity Standard announced it was prepared to buy sixty of the hundred-and-sixty-million-dollar total loan, a number of other companies offered to share the balance of the financing. Eventually, instead of dividing the hundred million dollars among four companies, Fidelity parceled it out among ten. This gave Fidelity Standard even greater control over the project. At the same time, it widened the impact of the project nationally; now there were eleven companies, with home offices in various regions of the country, interested in the success of Lake Shore Plaza.

On the evening of the announcement, General Stone threw a party in his incredible office suite. The attending dignitaries included a group of city officials, Bennett and Hobbs and two or three other executives representing Fidelity Standard, Vern Hanson—even the boys and their wives. Churchill flew in from New York alone.

I, too, was alone. Norman had asked me to bring my wife,

but she had told me she wasn't feeling well enough to attend a large gathering. I knew better. Ellie couldn't stand Norman Kane. She was at least as unhappy as my law partners that I continued to represent him. Once, years before, she had remarked, "I presume you're the house Gentile." We had quite a quarrel over that. Ellie never mentioned it again, but I knew her feelings hadn't changed.

I stood near the windows of Stone's office sipping a drink, sampling hors d'oeuvres, and studying the mighty assembled. Frieda was acting as the more or less official hostess. With the possible exception of Tina Kincaid, she was the best-looking woman in the room—surely the most elegant. Norman introduced her to the guests with evident pride. He was standing tall—as tall as he could—but she was still a fraction taller, even though she was wearing her hair down. For my money it looked better up, but obviously she didn't want to tower over her husband.

Frieda seemed to be enjoying the party. I knew that Norman rarely asked her to join him when he entertained business associates. Of course, this invitation had come from Stone. Nevertheless, Norman didn't mind showing Frieda off once in a while. If he hadn't wanted her there, she wouldn't have come.

There was one unpleasant incident early in the evening. I was talking to Norman and Frieda when Ernest Barry arrived. He walked over to where we were standing, looking his handsome best.

"Norman," he said, "congratulations." He smiled at Frieda. "And this must be the beautiful Mrs. Kane. No wonder Norman never lets you out in public." He began to take Frieda's hand, but Norman abruptly pushed him away.

"What the hell are you doing here?" Norman's voice was harsh and loud. Frieda, Barry and I were astounded.

Recovering, Barry smiled. "It's a victory party, isn't it? I came to enjoy the triumph."

"Who asked you? God knows I didn't. Did Stone?"

"Well, no, Norman, but after all, I heard you were having open house—"

"Open house, your ass."

The room was suddenly silent. Frieda turned pale. Barry searched our faces in confusion.

"You're joking, Norman. After all, I did bring you the deal—"

"Brought me the deal? You big clown. You're nothing but an errand boy. Listen, when the time comes, I'll send you a commission check. Meanwhile, this is a private party, and you ain't invited."

Frieda tried to intervene. "Norman, I think we—"

"Stay out of this, Frieda. I know how to handle characters like this. OK, Barry, you said hello, and that's it. Go shake hands with the General, take one drink, and then get the hell out of here."

Barry was speechless. Norman turned his back on him, took Frieda's arm and then mine and led us away.

I was bewildered by Norman's conduct. Frieda was rigid with anger. When I looked at her, I realized that my presence was not required. I excused myself and headed for General Stone's bar.

"How could you, Norman?" Frieda said. "You degraded yourself."

"You mean I degraded you."

"At a party like this, in front of people like these, how could you be so unbelievably crude?"

"Drop it, Frieda. I've heard enough. If you keep picking at me, I'll give you some of the same."

She believed him. She felt humiliated, but she knew that goading Norman further could only lead to a greater disaster. She smiled bravely. "Very well, my hero. Shall we rejoin the other guests?"

By the time I had gotten my drink and looked around, Norman and Frieda were talking to Ralph Churchill. Frieda held Norman's arm, and she was smiling that cool, aristocratic smile. Norman seemed subdued. I looked for Ernest Barry. I was not surprised to find that he was gone.

One of the happiest men at the party was Delbert Kincaid. By ten-thirty that evening, he was more or less smashed, and he sat with me offering unwanted and somewhat humid confidences.

"You know that little bastard," he said, "I never thought he could do it. Why, that little bastard is some kind of genius. Maybe it's mirrors. I think all these Jews use mirrors."

"Well," I replied, "if they use mirrors, I'd sure like to find out who manufactures them."

"Ho, ho, ho," said Del Kincaid, laughing hugely, out of all proportion to my remark.

"Yeah," he continued, "I got to hand it to him. I was satisfied when we sold the Kincaid property. I got my dough out of the deal, and I hardly had to put a nickel into the new project. If I wanted to, I could have made Norman put up all the money. But I was too big for that."

"You were very generous, Del." Kincaid seemed to have forgotten I was sitting in his office when his wife had trapped him into paying his share.

Kincaid pulled at my sleeve. "He kind of scares you, doesn't he?" I looked into Kincaid's finely chiseled face, struck by the appearance of his eyes, usually a bit blank, but now jagged little tracers of blood seemed to have exploded from both corneas.

"Well, I've strung along with Norman for years. He generally delivers," I remarked.

"Yeah, but how many deals can you put over? I mean, this one is fantastic. My God, who else in this country would even try it? And that General Stone—he scares me too. Another little bastard. Little guys frighten me."

"Why is that, Del?"

"I don't know. A big guy, you stand up and you can look him in the eye. But little guys, you got to look down at them, and sometimes you think when you're looking down at them maybe they aren't really looking up to you. Do I make myself clear?"

"Not exactly."

"No, I guess I don't make myself clear. But what's the difference? It's all going to be all right now. We're all going to get rich. Right?" And with that he threw an arm across my shoulders. The impact pushed me forward and lifted my head, and as I looked up, I noticed Norman standing over at the window, a drink in his hand, talking to Tina Kincaid.

"Yeah, look at him. Talking to my wife. My beautiful little wife. There's something about him that gets her. I don't know why Tina likes that guy, but she does. She don't say she does, but she does. I can feel it. You know what I mean? You live with somebody for fifteen years, you get to know what they're thinking. God damn it, she likes that guy."

"Does that bother you, Del?"

"Aw, hell, that don't bother me. He's no threat, that little guy. But he makes me uncomfortable. I mean, what do they talk about?"

I couldn't have told him—then.

"You really did it," she said. "You fooled us all."

"I didn't fool me, just you."

She laughed, throwing back her head and swinging her hair. Norman's eyes followed the line of her throat, down between her breasts. It was a long line; the bodice of Tina Kincaid's dress was cut square and very low.

She slammed her glass down on the table with a gesture so violent that people standing nearby turned to look at her. Norman felt uncomfortable. But when Tina spoke, her voice was pitched too low to be overheard.

"Now," she said.

"Now?"

"Yes, now."

"Now, what?"

Her eyes narrowed and a deep crease divided her forehead. "I said I'd tell you when, Norman Kane. And 'when' is 'now.' "

Norman could not hide his surprise. "Right now?"

"You heard me."

"Shall we stretch out on the rug in front of this distinguished gathering? We'll be the hit of the evening."

"No, damn you. Stop pretending you don't understand. I said now, and I mean it, but not here."

Norman lifted his drink to his lips, hoping his hand would not tremble. "Where, then?"

"My house."

"Your house?"

"Yes, the children are all away. There's no one there."

"After the party? Is Del going out of town?"

"No," she said, almost fiercely, and Norman could see that she was stifling the urge to stamp her foot. "Now, I said, *right now*."

Norman appraised her for a moment. "OK. You're out of your mind, but OK."

"Yes, I'm out of my mind, and that's the way you want me. Now let's go, and let's go together."

"You want everyone to see, huh?"

"You bet I do."

"What thrill can that possibly give you?"

"That's the way I want it. Take my arm, Norman Kane, and lead me out of here."

Norman set down his drink quite carefully, offered his arm, and escorted Tina Kincaid from the room. Mervin Stone hurried by. "Back soon, Norman?"

"Yeah, see you later."

"Gutless liar," Tina whispered. Norman tried to smile, but the expression was tight on his lips. He continued walking out of the room and into the elevator.

As they left Stone's office, Del Kincaid turned to me. "Now, where the hell are they going? And *why* the hell are they going?" He started to get up, then wavered for a second, and sat down. "Oh, hell," he mumbled, "I must be drunk. What could she want with that little Jew?" Kincaid stood up again and staggered off to the bar.

I may have been the first to realize Norman and Tina were not coming back. After a while, others in the room began to realize it too. No one asked questions. The only man with first-rank interest in the problem was Del Kincaid, and ten minutes after his wife left, Del passed out. Fortunately, he sagged into a chair and almost no one realized he was unconscious. The General spotted him immediately and hurried over. He looked around the room, then beckoned to me.

"Put him in the other room," he said. "There's a bed in there. Let him sleep it off. Where the hell is his wife?"

"I don't know where she went."

"I'll send somebody to find her."

I took his arm. "Don't bother, I don't think she's coming back."

General Stone studied me for a moment. "Where's Norman Kane?"

"I don't think he's coming back."

———

In the elevator traveling down to the garage, Tina stood beside Kane, but she did not take his arm. When they reached the garage, Norman called for his car. The wait seemed interminable, though the car jockey hustled to bring up the Cadillac, knowing Norman was good for a heavy tip.

"Yes sir, Mr. Kane," he said. "Here she is, all bright and ready for you." Norman did not smile; he almost forgot to tip the man. He did forget to help Tina Kincaid into the car, and she had to open the car door herself.

It was all foggy and hazy and unreal. Norman had thought about this moment ever since he had first met Tina Kincaid. In erotic fantasy he had imagined seducing her under a remarkable assortment of circumstances—some romantic, others brutal. A part of him said, "This woman wants to be raped." Another part said, "She needs romance." But the truth of the matter was that he could not imagine himself in the role of either a rapist or a Romeo. Not with Tina Kincaid. She was too beautiful, too perfect to need him.

Norman drove mechanically, entering the expressway at the right place, staying within the speed limit all the way to the suburbs. It seemed important not to exceed the speed limit. Norman concentrated on holding the needle between the two 5's. It required real effort to pull his eyes up from the speedometer above the hood and onto the road.

Beside him, Tina Kincaid lounged against the seat, her head thrown back. Every once in a while, Norman permitted himself a brief glance at her. Even in the darkness he could follow the flawless line of her forehead and nose, her lips, chin and throat. The rest he could easily imagine.

Farther out, the speed limit was higher. Norman gradually accelerated until his car reached the new plateau. He tried to avoid sudden movements. This was a strange and delicate moment, and he was afraid of doing anything that might destroy it. Tina Kincaid remained almost motionless, apparently calm and relaxed. For a brief, absurd moment he wondered if she was asleep.

It took them less than an hour to reach the Kincaid home. Norman always noted the change in sound when his tires jarred the graveled drive. This time the tone seemed particularly harsh. It grated on his brain, and he wondered if it would break the mood.

They sat motionless for a moment. Only the quiet humming of the motor framed the silence.

Finally Norman spoke. "Shall I leave the car here?"

"Of course."

He keyed off the ignition and punched out the headlights. Then he shoved the keys into his pocket and opened the car door. He resisted the urge to close the door gently. He let the handle escape his hands, and the door closed with a solid *thunk*. Norman walked around the car, unhappily aware of the crunching sound his feet made on the gravel. He held the door open for Tina Kincaid. She sat quietly for a moment, then turned and looked at him with luminous eyes. A marvelous smile crossed her face.

"We're here, Norman. We're actually here." She stepped out of the car looking as if she intended to embrace him, but then she hurried up the cement steps and opened the door.

"Do you know what?" she asked, and her voice was so loud that he jumped involuntarily. Tina Kincaid laughed. "There's no one here, Norman, no one but you and me. The children are away, and Del is drunk as hell. Just the two of us, Norman. This is the night we've been waiting for."

Norman dared not speak, afraid he might betray a surge of desire so powerful that he briefly considered throwing Tina down on the floor and overwhelming her on the spot.

Tina clapped her hands and laughed a sudden, girlish laugh. "You know what we are going to do?" she asked.

Norman was bewildered. He thought it was quite obvious why she had brought him there.

"Come on." She grabbed his hand and pulled him through the house at a run. He followed her from room to room until finally she stopped beside the swimming pool, now enclosed against the cold fall weather.

"We're going to take a swim, Norman. Yes, that's what we're going to do."

Norman shook his head in disbelief. "Swim?"

She laughed aloud. "Ah, yes. *First,* we're going to swim." She ran to the wall, pulled open an electric cabinet and flicked some switches. Lights came on below the surface of the water. "Look, Norman. It's just beautiful."

"Isn't it too cold to go swimming?"

"But we're inside, Norman."

"Yes, I know, but the room isn't heated."

"The pool is."

Norman stood uncertainly, not knowing what to do.

Again, Tina hurried away. When she returned, she held a pair of men's swimming trunks in her hand. "Since you're so cold, Norman, I think you should wear trunks when we go swimming. And I'll wear a swimming suit." She laughed again. Norman felt vaguely ridiculous.

"Surely," she said, "surely, you don't want to swim in the nude."

Norman did not know what to say.

"There," said Tina, "is the dressing room. Hurry, Norman."

It was absurd, but Norman did as he was told. The room smelled of clean towels and talcum powder. Quickly, very quickly, he stripped off his clothes and pulled on the trunks. They must have been Delbert Kincaid's. Surprisingly, they fit him. He was pleased.

Tina was waiting for him. She had shaken loose her hair and it streamed down about her shoulders. And she was wearing a bikini similar to the one she had worn the first day he had met her.

Tina's face glowed with appreciation. "So they fit, do they? You know, it was all a joke. I thought you'd never get into them. I thought you were pudgy, Norman. But look at the way you're put together." She stepped close and ran her fingers across his chest and down his arm. Norman shivered.

She leaned closer. "Cold, Norman? Or excited?" And then she laughed aloud.

"Come on," she said, "everybody into the pool." With a single graceful move she dived into the water. In a second, her face appeared above the surface. Her eyes were glittering even more brightly than before, and her long hair, drenched, framed her elegant features. Norman felt his stomach contract. "Come on in," she laughed. "What are you waiting for?" There seemed nothing else to do, so Norman dived into the water. In a second he splashed up alongside her.

"I'll race you," she said. Tina split the water with a neat surface dive. Norman followed her, his powerful strokes matching her own. Up one length of the pool and down another, up one length, then down another. Finally she touched the shallow end and stood up, laughing.

"You can swim," she said. "I never thought to ask whether you could swim." He stood in the water an arm's length away, relishing the illusion that he towered over this tiny, magnificent creature. She smiled up at him, her body glistening with a sparkling film which made her flesh seem even more desirable.

She laughed. "Don't stand there staring as if you've never seen me before. Wasn't that marvelous? I'm going to do it again." Once more she split the water, swam to the far end, spun into a perfect turn, kicked away and swam back to him.

When Tina stood up beside him, Norman laughed aloud. Her eyes narrowed. "What's so funny?"

"It's you. You lure me away from an elegant party, promising all sorts of sensual delights, and then bring me home for a swim."

"Not just to swim." She pressed against him and raised her lips. Norman leaned down and kissed her, all too aware he was dripping wet and shivering with a variety of emotions.

Tina pulled away. "Isn't that better than some old party?"

Norman laughed again. "You know," he said, "among Orthodox Jews, before a girl is married, she takes a ritual bath so that she will come to her husband absolutely pure. Is that what you're doing? Is this your ritual bath?"

Her smile twisted into a grimace. "Don't talk about religion," she hissed. "Don't talk about anything but me. You're here for *me,* Norman Kane. And I'm here for you." She splashed away and climbed the steps up and out of the pool. She leaned down and the bikini became a thin string across her thighs. Her breasts swelled above the skimpy top.

"Are you going to stay in there?" Tina asked. "Do you want to swim all night?" Norman reached up, placed his palms on the ceramic lip of the pool and lifted himself out of the water.

Tina had picked up a huge towel which she threw over her shoulders so that it covered most of her body.

"Here," she said, "towel me off," and she turned her back. Norman placed his hands against the towel and began to rub her body, gently at first, avoiding her breasts and hips.

"Don't be shy," she said. "Dry me. All of me."

Norman began to apply the towel more vigorously. He brought his hands down across her breasts. At this abrupt gesture, the thin top of the bikini fell away.

Tina laughed. "That's it, get me dry, all of me." Norman continued to move the towel across her body—over her breasts, down her back, across her belly and her thighs.

"Wonderful," she cried. A tone of tremulous pleasure tinged her voice.

Tina turned, pulled the towel from Norman's hands, and threw it aside. She stood before him, bare-breasted, only the narrow G-string line of the bikini showing dark against her loins.

The sight was unnerving. Norman stared at her. Her breasts were not large, but they were cone-shaped—almost perfectly cone-shaped—and proudly erect.

"What about you?" asked Tina. "You're wet." She picked up the towel and handed it to Norman. He began to dry himself.

She stood before him, smiling now, a lazy catlike smile that warmed him. At the sight of her, he felt his entire body tightening with anticipation.

Tina laughed again. "You've missed the most important area," she said. "You can't dry yourself through those jersey trunks." And she smiled as if she had made a brilliant comment. Something about her struck Norman in a strange way. He did not remove his trunks but continued to dry his legs.

"What's wrong?" she asked, moving closer to him until her cool, firm breasts pressed against his chest. "Don't you want me?" She opened her mouth slowly. Her lips looked incredibly sweet and full to him. With a brutal gesture Norman lifted her off her feet and kissed her cruelly hard on the mouth.

Tina stepped back. "Well. How violent we are. But that's what I expected, Norman Kane. That's what I wanted from you. And now, Norman, now is the time."

He appraised her for a moment, splintered by a thousand pin-sharp impressions, impelled by a dozen conflicting desires. He still held the towel in his hands. "Here," he said, to his own surprise. "Take it. This is the end."

Incredulous, she accepted the towel, and held it below her pointed breasts. She was infinitely desirable and infinitely amazed. But her mouth hung open now. It no longer seemed inviting. "What do you mean?"

"Just what I said, Tina. It's been a lot of fun. I enjoyed the swim. Quite a ball. Invite me over any time." He turned his back and started toward the locker room. She ran after him, pulled at his arm, her nails scratching the skin. He stopped to look at his arm; he fingered it gingerly.

"You can't be serious. You said you wanted me. I said I'd tell you when the time was right, and here I am." In her voice anger and desire were mingled with confusion.

Norman could not help looking down at her, and the vision was almost irresistible. He shuddered as her hands reached up under his arms, then moved down along his sides. At last, she gently touched the front of his trunks.

"You do want me," she said. "Of course you do."

"Of course. Who wouldn't want you?" His voice cracked and he was breathing so heavily he could barely form the words. He slowly closed his fingers around her arms, holding them still, and bent over until his lips dug into hers. The kiss seemed to last forever. Inexorable, interminable, enclosing both of them. Pressed against her like this, Norman knew a desire so intense that it shocked him. Tina moved gently away and looked up at him with a smile of assurance, almost of conquest.

"You see," she said. "There's nothing else for us to do."

Norman leaned toward her once more. His hands fumbled with the ties of her bikini. She wriggled to help him, and in a second she stood before him completely nude.

"You're perfect," he said. "You're the most magnificent woman I have ever seen." He watched her eyes widen and her breasts rise in response. "I've never wanted anyone as I want you."

Norman placed one hand gently behind her back, bent down and placed the other behind her knees, then picked her up.

A deep sigh escaped Tina's lips. Now he held her against his chest, his eyes but inches from her body. Even this close, she was perfect.

Norman took three halting steps and threw her into the pool.

She came up spluttering and swearing, her face so contorted with anger that it was almost impossible to recognize her features. But Norman was laughing, laughing hysterically at the sight of this naked beauty, swimming and sinking, yelling and screaming at him.

In a moment, she scrambled out of the pool and ran towards him, a furious bundle of churning breasts and swiveling hips. She reached for his face with long-nailed hands. He grabbed her wrists and held her while she screamed and twisted. Finally she was silent, but still purple with anger.

"You're too much for me," he said. "Too much. You think I don't want you? You're mad. I want you this very second. You're the most beautiful creature I've ever seen. But you insist on telling me when and how and where. You give the orders. 'Now,' you say. You call the shots. *Nobody* calls the shots for Norman Kane.

"I could have taken you anyway. It would be a pleasure." He used one hand to twist her arm up behind her back and ran the other over her from chest to thighs. She snarled and tried to bite him, but he held her away.

"Beautiful," he said. "Too beautiful. After you, what? All his life a man dreams of having a Tina Kincaid. But it's better if it stays a dream. Once I've had you, what then? You would spoil every other woman in the world for me." Again he stretched out a hand to touch her, but this time she bit his wrist, and he hurriedly pulled away.

"No," he said, grimacing in pain. "This is better. I could have had you, and I chose not to. You offered yourself, and I turned you down. This is much better."

"You fool," she screamed. "You idiot. You fairy."

Norman laughed. "You would say that. Why not? But I had you. You offered yourself, and I turned you down. No one ever did that before, did they, Tina?" He increased the pressure on her arm until he had forced her down on her knees before him. Norman leaned close to examine her face. "You gorgeous whore. You arrogant slut. Remember this. I could have had you and I threw you away." He loosened his grip and shoved her. She fell sprawling against the tile rim of the pool, legs kicking high, arms flapping, screaming obscenities.

"Remember," he yelled, and now his own voice was almost hysterical. "I could have had you, and I threw you away." Before his emotions overpowered him, Norman wrenched himself back to reality, grabbed up his clothes and ran out of the room.

———◆———

Norman stopped his car a block from the Kincaid house and pulled to the curb. He began to laugh. First in a low chuckle, then in huge gulping guffaws. Finally in dry heaves that were close to tears. *Imagine,* he thought. *Imagine turning down a piece like that. I must be getting old. I must be going crazy. What did I prove? What in the hell did I prove?* But then he began to laugh again. Only this time he bypassed the first two stages. Dry, painful heaves racked his body. Once or twice he thought he would vomit. He could taste General Stone's crabmeat cocktail in his throat. Then he began to sneeze. He wondered why. Why on earth would he be sneezing? Then he remembered pulling on his clothes over wet swim trunks, and he began to laugh again.

Norman started the car and headed south, but after driving a few blocks he found the feel of cold swim trunks on his flesh was unbearable. He pulled over to the side, kicked off his shoes, shoved down his pants and removed the trunks. *My God,* he thought, *what if they catch me here, sitting alone in a parked car with my pants down. How do I explain it?* He began to laugh again, and to heave, and to sneeze, and to cough, all the while trying to get dressed.

That made him feel better. The wool pants were rough on his skin and they sopped up the last of the moisture which had been trickling down his legs. He started the motor, turned on the heater and drove to the expressway. The speedometer needle moved smoothly to fifty, sixty, seventy, eventually to eighty miles an hour. At any moment he expected to see a blue light spinning beside him. He wanted a policeman to come, to order him to curb his car. Norman wanted a sign of sanity, of law and order. But there was no sign. Norman realized that, as usual, he would have to supply the law and order himself.

I saw Norman re-enter the room, and of course I was astounded. The party was still in full swing, although by now everyone had noticed Norman's absence—*and* the absence of Tina Kincaid. There was some buzzing about, but not much. Most of the guests were beholden to Norman Kane or General Stone in one way or another.

John Bennett stopped Norman at the door. "Norman," he asked ingenuously. "Where on earth have you been?"

"Been? I had a little business to transact."

"At this time of night? What kind of business?"

"Look, John, we have a two-hundred-million-dollar project getting ready to explode out there on Lake Shore Drive."

"Of course, Norman, I was just kidding."

Others stopped to talk to Norman. It was some time before he reached me.

"Where is he?" Norman asked.

"In the other room, sleeping it off."

"Does he know we left?"

"He saw you go."

At that moment the door to the other room opened and Delbert Kincaid walked out. To everyone's surprise, his hair was combed and his clothes, though rumpled, were on straight. He saw me standing with Kane, and he rocked his way over to us.

"I saw you," he said. And then he realized that he had spoken quite loudly and was attracting attention. He lowered his voice. "I saw you leave with her, Kane."

"I don't know what you're talking about."

"You left here with my wife."

"Of course I did, you big oaf. You were drunk as a lord. If you couldn't help her, somebody had to."

Kincaid looked bewildered. "Help her? What do you mean, 'help her'?"

"Your wife was sick, you clown. I put her in a cab and sent her home."

There was a moment of silence. "Why didn't she wait for me?"

"You were drunk. Tina didn't want to make a scene. She just quietly got up and left. If I were you, I'd call and see how she is."

"You think she's really sick?"

"Look, Kincaid, she's your wife. You take care of her." Kincaid peered at Norman with bloodshot eyes, trying to pierce Norman's skin and brain, trying to piece together this strange puzzle. "Yeah," he said. "Well, maybe I won't call, maybe I'll just go home."

"Do you think you can drive?"

"I can drive." He stumbled out of the room with the wooden walk of a man who is truly sick-drunk.

"Eddie, that guy's not going to make it. Somebody better go with him. John Bennett doesn't live far from Kincaid."

"That's a good idea, Norman. I'll see if I can persuade John to take him home."

When I returned, Norman was sitting in a corner of the room, talking to Frieda. She was smiling, but I recognized the brittle self-possessed smile that Frieda could assume instantly, on demand. She had not seemed to notice when Norman left the room with Tina Kincaid. She continued to circulate among the guests, laughing and talking, smiling and conversing in her beautifully modulated voice. Why had she waited? For a second, I remembered her as a girl on a tennis court at the University. Like everything else she did, Frieda played tennis elegantly. Perhaps that was it. You don't walk off and forfeit the match. You stay and take your beating.

"The wild stallion returneth."

"Not much of a stallion, Frieda." Norman's voice sounded nasal. "This stallion has one hell of a cold."

"I wonder: Is it the perfume? Or the heady aroma of Kenilworth living?"

"What do you want, Frieda?"

"What does it matter? It's always what *you* want. And I suppose tonight you got it."

Norman hesitated for a second. "I could have—if I wanted it. But I'll tell you a funny story, Frieda, one you'll never believe! I didn't take it."

Frieda laughed. "Since when does Norman Kane pass up the pleasures of this world?"

"There's no point in arguing about it."

"We're not arguing. There's only one thing that puzzles me. Why did you come back? To gloat? Polish off the poor girl and then come back to the party? Isn't that rather crude, Norman?"

"Oh, I'm crude. Always have been. You remember me; the little kike running around the campus in his sloppy clothes. The guy who only shaved once a week and took his bath the same night. The kid who played tennis like he had a hammer in his hand instead of a tennis racket. Surely you remember?"

"I do indeed. You've always displayed a rather brutal charm."

"Brutal? Don't you mean filthy or low?"

"Please, Norman, you're insulting me."

"I'm trying not to, but the vision of Charlie Clark keeps floating into my head."

Frieda's hand went to her throat. Norman noted with satisfaction that his thrust had gone straight to the jugular. She angled her face into a smile. "Always the same response, Norman."

"Hard to forget."

"He was my husband."

"Yeah . . . later."

"That was twenty years ago. When will you give it up?"

"I try, Frieda. But it keeps nagging at me." He smiled grimly. "By the way, what were you doing while I was gone?"

"Come now, Norman." She waved her hand in a brief gesture that encompassed the entire room. "With a hundred witnesses?"

Norman knew he had lost ground. "Charlie Clark," he said. "Charlie Clark. I never could understand it, really. The guy was older than you—not that much older—but older. Of course, he was pretty. Very pretty. But a jerk. A gutless jerk. If it could be Charlie Clark, it could be anybody—even now."

Norman watched the frustration unraveling Frieda's smile. "It's so easy, isn't it, Norman? Just mention the name. You don't have to make sense. Just a name—and then an accusation."

"It gets me, too, Frieda." But there he was, saying the wrong thing again. Giving ground again. He hurried to renew his attack.

"Why does it get you? If it isn't true, why does it get you?" Norman nearly stopped breathing. He wasn't sure he truly wanted an answer.

But Frieda had regained control. "It is a mystery, isn't it? I'm not quite sure that I understand it myself. Maybe I'm a martyr, Norman? Perhaps I enjoy suffering."

"I doubt that. I've never seen you suffer."

"I'll never let you see me suffer."

"I believe that, too."

"But why did you come back, Norman? One night of love. Everyone saw you leave with her. Everyone knew what you would do."

"It doesn't fit, does it? You can't figure it out. If I left to shack up with her, why did I come back so soon? It's hard for you to believe I didn't screw her. You can't fit that into your little pattern. And you're always so intent on fitting things into the pattern. Well, I'm afraid you have another conundrum for your collection, Frieda."

Norman patted her shoulder and stood up. "But keep trying, dear, I'm sure that with your fine logical mind, one day you'll come up with a theory. Of course, you'll be wrong, but the pieces will fit."

Frieda Kane smiled lovingly after him as he walked away.

What art, I thought, *what art there is in that smile.* It was clear to me that Norman had worked his magic on Frieda, throwing tiny darts that pricked her vanity, scraped against her psyche, then pierced her self-respect. Norman did it with consummate skill, applying the pressure subtly or crudely, but always at unexpected points and unexpected times. Frieda was always off balance, yet she never gave way. What a waste, I thought. For a moment I felt like comforting her—of telling her how much I admired her. Yet I wondered whether she really needed comforting or wanted my admiration.

And then I was angry. Angry at Norman for torturing this lovely woman, abusing her for the sheer pleasure of establishing his mastery. If a man had a wife like that—

I caught myself. Hadn't I thought the same thing before? I was getting involved—too involved—in matters that were not my affair. Norman's business was complex enough. Now I was beginning to insert myself into his personal life. Thus far, at least, I had said nothing openly, either to Norman or to Frieda. Let it end there. It had to end there.

Norman sat down beside me. "Do you think Kincaid will buy your story, Norman?" I hadn't meant to say that. It was a mistake. Norman frowned at me.

"You too? Frieda just finished giving me the same jazz."

"Oh, come now, you don't expect me to believe you put her in a cab and sent her out to Kenilworth?" I felt foolish going on this way, and Norman was beginning to turn his annoyance on me.

"I don't have to explain myself to you, to Frieda, to Delbert Kincaid or to anyone else."

"Take it easy. Methinks you protest the lady's innocence too much."

"Oh, Christ," said Norman. "You can fracture a quotation worse than anyone I ever met."

———————————◆———————————

The morning after General Stone's party, I joined Norman in his office and together we reviewed the documents submitted to us by Fidelity Standard. When Miss Fritch called on the intercom, Norman reminded her she was under orders to hold his calls.

"I know, Mr. Kane, but there's an immense package here from General Stone."

"From General Stone? Send it in."

"Well, it's not quite that easy, sir."

"Damn it, send it in."

It was several minutes before the door opened. Two young men carried in a huge, flat, rectangular carton.

Norman looked at them in amazement. "What in the hell can that be?" He glanced at me, but I shook my head. "Pull off the wrappings, boys." The two young men began to remove the long sheets of cardboard. Inside they found additional protection, this time in the form of wooden crating.

"My God, it looks like a painting. You don't suppose the old boy is sending us an autographed portrait, do you?"

It required considerable effort to remove the crating. When one side was open, Norman instructed the boys to clear a space along the wall and lean the carton against it. Then he himself began removing the inner wrapping.

"Oh, no. Oh, my God!"

"What is it, Norman?"

"I don't believe it. It can't be."

He began ripping and tearing at the wrappings. Within moments we could see a large section of the Monet which had previously hung in Stone's office.

Norman continued to tear and pull at the wrappings. "I should be more careful," he said, "but I can't wait to see it."

In a few minutes the masterpiece was completely exposed. The young men stood close to the painting. "What is it, Mr. Kane?" one of them asked. "I can't make out a thing."

"Of course not," Norman replied, and he ran to the opposite wall of the room. "You can't see anything over there. Come here." I followed them to the far side of the room. We stood together: the connoisseur, the lawyer and the two office boys.

"To be truthful, Mr. Kane," one of them said a bit hesitantly, "it don't look like much of anything to me. Just some lily pads in a pond."

"Precisely, my boy," said Norman, looking at him with amusement and pleasure. "You have proved yourself a great connoisseur."

Norman seemed to forget everyone else in the room. He studied the painting for several minutes, sighing and twisting his hands. Finally, he remembered himself. "That's it, boys. Thank you—wait a minute. Isn't there a note or letter with it?"

"Oh, yes, there was a letter attached to the outside of the carton."

Norman ripped open the envelope while the office boys filed out of the room. He read the message, then handed it to me without a word. The note was very brief: "To America's greatest developer. Admiringly, Mervin Stone."

"You mean Stone is giving me this as a present?"

"I guess so, Norman."

"Incredible. This painting is worth a couple of hundred thousand dollars. Why would he do it?"

"He seems to be impressed with you. The note speaks for itself."

Norman moved to his desk and bellowed into the intercom, "Get General Stone, Miss Fritch, and do it right away." In moments, the General was on the line.

"General, I don't know where to start. A couple of minutes ago they delivered this—this masterpiece to my office. And with it there's a beautiful note from you. Forgive me if I sound like a damn fool, but what is this about? Surely you don't intend to give me the painting?"

"Have you got me on that damn loudspeaker telephone, Norman?"

"Yes, I have, Merv. I'm shaking too much to hold the receiver."

The General's laugh boomed into the room. "Well, all right then. Yes, Norman, it's a present—from me to you. Don't you like it?"

"Like it? Why, General, you know how I feel about this painting."

"Of course, Norman. That's why I'm giving it to you."

"But Merv, you don't just give away a two hundred thousand dollar painting!"

"Is that what it's worth? In my office you said a hundred and fifty thousand. Maybe you better send a corner of it back to me."

Norman began to laugh, but then broke off sharply. "How can I laugh? How can I say thank you?"

"You already have, Norman. I'm only sorry I wasn't there when you unwrapped it."

"Merv, I still can't believe it. What have I done to deserve it?"

"Maybe nothing yet. It's what you do from here on in that counts. But keep it up, Norman, I like your style. And you like Monet's style. You and that picture belong together."

Norman was silent for a moment. "I guess that's about the nicest thing anybody ever said to me. God knows, this is the nicest thing anybody ever did for me." His hand fluttered toward the painting.

"You still there, Norman?"

"No, I can't really say I am. I keep trying desperately to think of something to say to you."

"Forget it, Norman. Just enjoy the painting. Put it up in your office somewhere. Don't take it home. I'd like to see it every time I come over."

"Merv, I'd build a gallery to display it in, if you asked me."

"No need for that, just hang it in your office and enjoy it. Now stop blubbering, buddy, and get back to work on our deal."

That ended the conversation. Norman sat staring at the silent telephone for several minutes. "Do you believe it, Eddie?

Do you believe a guy can be so rich he sends you a two-hundred-thousand-dollar present just like that?"

Norman turned to the painting. "I'm going to prove I'm worthy of it."

I looked at him sharply, but Norman seemed unaware of how naïve he sounded.

Soon after the International Materials lease was signed, Norman called Karl Friedrichs to his office. "I want you to meet Don White," Norman said, "of Donald White and Associates. He is the finest mechanical engineer in Chicago."

"Thank you," said White. "It's a pleasure to meet you, Dr. Friedrichs." The old man shook his hand, but he was evidently perplexed by White's presence in Norman's office.

"And this is Neal McNeill of Graham and Graham. I'm sure you've heard of the firm, Karl."

"Of course." Friedrichs gravely shook McNeill's hand.

"Well, let's sit down," Norman said. "We have a lot to talk about. How are the drawings coming, Karl?"

The old man looked about hesitantly.

"Go right ahead, it's perfectly all right to discuss it here."

"I am working on the structural drawings first, of course. I expect to have the basic design completed within sixty days."

"That's fine, but could you let me have preliminary drawings in, say, three weeks, so that I can show them to White and McNeill?"

"Why?"

"Oh, I'm sorry, I'm afraid I haven't explained this at all. Don White will do the mechanical design for our building, Karl, and McNeill's office will handle the architectural detailing."

"I'm sorry, Norman, I'm afraid I don't understand you."

"It's very simple. White and Associates—mechanical engineers—will do the air conditioning and heating, plumbing and electrical design for Lake Shore Plaza. Graham and Graham will prepare the final working drawings. Naturally, they'll work under your supervision."

The old man's hands were trembling now. He held onto the

arms of the chair to control them. "I'm afraid I am confused, Mr. Kane. I have the greatest respect for Mr. White and for Mr. McNeill, but I thought I was to do all of the drawings for these buildings."

Norman looked surprised. "Why, Karl, I never had any such intention. I didn't think you would want to be burdened with all those details."

The old man sat up stiffly. "I've always been 'burdened' with those details."

Norman's voice edged up to a sharper tone. "But this is different." Then he smiled. "Anyway, all I wanted today was to have you meet these men. They'll contact you later to finalize your working arrangements." White and McNeill stood up and said their goodbyes, being careful to emphasize their pleasure at working with Karl Friedrichs.

When Norman and Friedrichs were alone, the old man began to speak, but Norman cut him off. "I was amazed, Karl, absolutely amazed at what you told those men. What is this whim of yours about doing all of the drawings? Where on earth did you get such an idea?"

The old man shook his head. "I thought that was our understanding, Norman. I always do all of the work."

"That's fine when you're designing a project of limited size. But surely you realize that is impossible here."

"I've done large projects before."

"Six buildings, Karl, six million square feet."

"Yes, but each building is a duplicate of the others."

"Yes and no. The tenancy will differ from building to building. We must allow for special conditions."

"The buildings are basically the same."

"In many ways they will be different."

"I can do it."

"I would prefer that you did. But we don't have the time. One man, alone, drawing every line? Impossible."

"I'll hire draftsmen."

"Draftsmen? Instead of mere draftsmen I'm giving you Donald White and Associates and Graham and Graham."

"I'm not complaining, Norman."

"Complaining? What have you to complain about? Why on

earth do you want to design toilets and lavatories? Is that what I hired you for?"

"Of course not—"

"Then why do you want to do it?"

"I've always done it."

"Look, Karl, don't tell me what you've always done, because Lake Shore Plaza is not like anything you've ever done —or anybody else has done, for that matter. The old rules are obsolete."

"I suppose I am obsolete too."

"If I thought you were obsolete, I wouldn't have given you this commission. I want my buildings to have the appearance —the impact—you alone can give them. That's what matters to me, and that's what should matter to you."

"You mean I shouldn't care how people use my buildings? It shouldn't matter to me whether they are warm when they should feel cool, or cold when they should feel warm?"

"Frankly, I didn't know you *did* care."

"Well, I do."

"It's ridiculous. How could one man do all the work for a two-hundred-million-dollar project in a little studio on the South Side?"

The old man moved his lips, but no sound came out.

"Do you think I'm mad? Be realistic, Karl. You can't do it all yourself. That's a delusion."

"But I—"

"No buts, Karl. If you want to back out of this project, just say so. I'll find someone else."

"You know I want this commission. I pleaded with you for it."

"Then take it on my conditions or forget it."

"I didn't think you were ruthless, Norman."

"Ruthless? I'm not ruthless, just practical." Norman threw up his hands and paced about the room. "Incredible," he said. "I must have been out of my mind. They told me not to use you, but I insisted."

"They told you—not to use me—?"

"Of course. Everyone thought I was a fool. They probably still do. 'You're crazy,' they said, 'the old man can't do it.'

Well, I thought you could, Karl. I guess I was wrong."

"Don't say that. I can do it."

"What can you do?"

The old man dropped his head. "I wanted to draw every line, every single line of those plans. I wanted no name on them but mine. How very foolish of me."

Norman's tone changed. "Not foolish, Karl, just visionary. You're a visionary and I am, too. But what use is a vision if you don't turn it into reality? I have to be practical. And so do you. The important thing for *me* is to own a beautiful and successful project. The important thing for *you* is to design it."

"I suppose you're right."

"Of course, I'm right. Now look, I don't want you to lose face with White and McNeill. Take my advice. Don't wait for them to call you. Call them. *You* arrange the work schedule. *You* control the timing of this job. You're the chief architect."

"All right," said Karl Friedrichs. "I'll do it."

"Splendid! I'm sorry there was any misunderstanding. I thought it was so clear, so obvious, yet somehow I failed to communicate it to you. Well, never mind, so long as you understand me now."

"Oh yes, Norman, I understand you. Now."

———————◆———————

It did not take Karl Friedrichs long to learn that he was not really directing the project. Only one man was in control and that man, of course, was Norman Kane. Friedrichs was invited to every conference, his opinion was respectfully requested—and that was the end of it. Norman sat at the head of the table; McNeill, White and the others reported to him like a staff to its general. Friedrichs presided at the other end, but after a few meetings he stopped offering comments and spent most of his time staring off into space. Norman barely allowed him to preserve his dignity. But he treated the others no better.

Of course, Norman was an unusual developer. Few real-estate men could claim his understanding of every phase of design and construction. Norman knew, and questioned, and understood. He permitted each man to present his suggestions and to defend his design. But Norman made the final decisions. He knew—or at least he sensed—when the engineers and architects were wrong or unwise or impractical.

Norman suggested no changes in Friedrichs' design of the exterior of the buildings. He brought Friedrichs' plans to one of the largest metal fabricators in the country. With Norman's help and direction, the company's engineers, following Friedrichs' design, developed a modular facing panel for the exterior of the buildings. The bronze panel contained fixed and movable windows, sleeves for the air-conditioning and heating units, and electrical conduits. Even Friedrichs approved the result.

"You are a remarkable man, Norman. You make architecture and construction into manufacturing—almost."

During this period, Norman was actively working on leasing the project. He used his own organization to develop and analyze possible prospects all over the country. He persuaded the Fidelity Standard mortgage group and the Chicago National Bank to front for him when he solicited prospective tenants. When there was a major tenant and major space to be considered, Norman handled the negotiations alone.

Over a period of time Norman persuaded Ralph Churchill to lease more and more space for International Materials. Now that the company was bringing all major divisions to Chicago, each group clamored for larger and more elaborate quarters. In part this was warranted; in part it was mere status-seeking. Churchill and the other top executives realized that in order to consolidate their operations and relocate them in Chicago, they would have to appease phalanxes of horror-stricken executives who had previously run near-autonomous departments in distant cities. Eventually the total space leased by International Materials rose to seven hundred and fifty thousand square feet.

Meanwhile, through the Fidelity Standard group, Norman found a medium-sized insurance company, Reserve Life of Indiana, which agreed to lease one hundred thousand feet in Plaza Two, the second of Norman's six buildings.

Despite this progress, the pressures continued to increase. Fidelity Standard expressed unhappiness over Norman's unwillingness to set a definite schedule for constructing the buildings. Hobbs told him he would have difficulty holding the lending group together unless Norman established a reasonable outside date for completing all construction and delivering the loan.

At this point Norman was fortunate enough to secure another major tenant. The National Tube Company of Pittsburgh decided to relocate its complete manufacturing facilities in the Gary-Hammond-Whiting area. Unsolicited, they offered to lease half a million square feet in Lake Shore Plaza to house their sales and administrative organizations. For Norman this was the clincher. He was certain that International Materials, Reserve Life of Indiana, National Tube and the satellites of these companies would ultimately require at least two million feet. There seemed to be no point now in delaying construction.

Norman was still negotiating his interim financing at the Chicago National Bank. At first, Vern Hanson refused to pay out interim construction money against the Fidelity Standard commitment.

"I'm not going to do it, Norman. In order to meet your mortgagee's requirements, you have to lease four out of the six million feet. So far you have leased less than two million feet. What happens if you don't bring in the additional two million?"

"We all go broke."

"If any other borrower told me that, I'd pitch him out on his ear."

"I don't blame you, Vern. But look, I've rented nearly two million feet without even putting a spade in the ground, and I'm backed by the strongest group of investors I've ever had. Fidelity Standard will never let this thing fold. Besides, with two million feet of top tenants going for me, the next two million will come along inside six months."

"Fine. Then we'll hold off construction for six months."

"Cut it out, Vern. When have I ever failed to meet a commitment?"

"So far you've always done what you promised."

"Then why this new attitude?"

"We're talking about a lot of chips—a hundred and sixty million of them. As it is, our board plans to bring in two New York banks as partners. Just believe me, they won't be as soft-hearted as I am."

"Since when does Chicago National Bank take orders from anyone? You had partners when we built St. Louis, but you ran the show."

"Perhaps. But if we make any mistakes on a deal this size, those New Yorkers will pressure us like we've never been pressured before."

"I appreciate that. I have no intention of creating difficulties for you. If it weren't for you, I wouldn't have made this deal in the first place."

Vern Hanson waved his hand in a deprecating gesture.

"Don't wave me off, Vern, it's true. What you told me about Kincaid got me this deal. Look, Vern, I want to do everything I can to make it easy for you. Tell me what you need to make this deal."

"Bring me signed leases for another two million square feet."

"That I can't do. What else?"

"Damned if I know. How about personal signatures?"

"Personal signatures? What the hell is this, a home loan?"

"You know very well the policy of this bank is to require personal signatures on all construction loans."

"By God, I thought I outgrew that requirement years ago."

"You just grew back into it."

"Vern, that's plain silly. The boys and I aren't worth a hundred and sixty million bucks. Maybe General Stone is, but you can be damn sure he won't sign your note."

"In that case, Norman, I guess it's up to you to come up with an angle."

"How about pledging our stock?"

"You already pledged it with Stone."

"Not *exactly*. It's in escrow."

"Will Stone let us hold the escrow?"

"I'm willing to ask. If he does, will you forget those other ideas of yours?"

"You're asking the bank to take a tremendous risk, Norman. Why don't you persuade Fidelity Standard to pay out when the buildings are fifty per cent occupied, instead of two-thirds?"

"Great. You tell them."

"I don't negotiate permanent mortgages."

"Goddamn it, you're trying to negotiate this one. You know Fidelity Standard isn't going to change their commitment now. When I begin to lose courage, they lose courage. And when they lose their courage, this deal folds up."

"Is their commitment good or bad?"

"You're the last guy in the world to ask me that. You know very well no mortgage commitment is worth a damn. Any long-term lender who wants out can always find a way. But these guys don't want out. I just don't think we should scare them. They have to be certain the money they're reserving for this deal will actually be loaned out."

"True."

"If we get to the end of the line and we need more time, we'll get it. But now is not the time to ask for changes in our commitment. We haven't even started construction."

"I don't know whether you're right or wrong, Norman."

"Believe me, I'm right."

"Well, even if you're wrong, they probably wouldn't change the commitment now, anyway. I'm telling you though, you'd better get your associates to pledge their stock. I can argue my committee into an extra million here or there, but one hundred and sixty million dollars is too much to play around with."

"Vern, if you need that stock, I'll get it for you. Stop worrying."

Norman spoke with far more assurance than he felt. Selling General Stone on the idea of transferring the pledge to the Chicago National Bank would not be an easy task. Still, he had no choice, so Norman called the General and arranged a luncheon meeting.

"I'll come right to the point with you, Merv. I've been over to see Vern Hanson. The bank is plenty worried about this deal."

"Worried? What worries them?"

"That damn leasing requirement in our mortgage commitment. We have to lease two-thirds of our buildings before Fidelity Standard pays out."

"What's so unusual about that?"

"Nothing. Two-thirds is the break-even point for our project. The requirement isn't at all unreasonable."

"Then what's the problem?"

"A hundred and sixty million bucks."

"You mean the risk scares them?"

"Percentagewise the risk is the same as in the usual construction deal. It's the total amount we're borrowing that worries Chicago National. They're putting up more money than they've ever loaned before in one transaction. You've been in enough construction deals, Merv. You know the interim lender is at the mercy of the permanent mortgagee."

"I find it hard to believe that Fidelity Standard would cop out on a deal of this size and prominence."

"I don't suppose they would."

"Are you worried about meeting the leasing requirement, Norman?"

"Me? Hell, no. I didn't get into this deal to make a fool of myself."

"All right then, what does the bank want?"

"Personal guarantees."

"You must be joking."

"No, I'm not. Vern Hanson asked us for personal guarantees."

"What did you tell him?"

"To shove the loan up his files."

"Right."

"Yeah, right. But we still need the loan."

"You know damn well I'm not giving any personal guarantee."

"I don't want to give one myself."

"You say, 'I don't *want* to.' You mean you would if you had to?"

"I guess that's what I mean."

"You'd personally sign a hundred and sixty million dollars' worth of paper?"

"God knows I'm not worth a hundred and sixty million dollars, but I'd sign the paper anyway."

"What good does it do the bank if you can't pay?"

"Well, I could pay part of it, and anyway they figure I'll bust my ass to avoid going broke."

"You do whatever you want, Norman. I won't sign a guarantee."

"That's up to you, Merv. But you may kill the deal."

"Then we'll go somewhere else. How about trying the Eastern banks?"

"Two of the biggest are in the deal with Chicago National. They're the ones who want our guarantees."

"What do we do then—fold our tents and quietly cancel this project?"

"No, I have an idea."

"What's that?"

"Look, our stock is in escrow already. Maybe we pledge our stock with the bank."

"What does that give the bank that they don't have already?"

"Not much, but it looks good."

"What about the notes?"

"Them, too."

"In other words, we hock our total equity?"

"Does it matter? Our equity's on the line anyway. The only assets we have are the land and the buildings, and those will be mortgaged to the hilt."

"I suppose you're right. But I'm not used to being handled this way."

"If you can do better, go right ahead."

"I guess that means I couldn't do better."

"I didn't say that."

"If you thought I could, you wouldn't suggest it."

Norman laughed.

"OK," said General Stone. "We pledge our equity."

That is how the stock and notes of Lake Shore Plaza, Inc., ended up in the hands of the Chicago National Bank. The conditions of the pledge didn't change very much. The bank became the escrowee, with no obligation to release the stock or notes until its construction loan was paid in full. Mervin Stone retained the same rights he held before, subject to the bank's claim.

This transaction pleased Norman immensely. "I got to thank that Vern Hanson," he told me. "He really did me a favor."

"What makes you think so? Vern has his hands on your entire equity."

"Better he should have it than General Stone."

While the architects and engineers were hurrying to complete the plans and specifications, Norman commissioned an artist to prepare perspective drawings of Lake Shore Plaza. Working under Friedrichs' guidance, the artist prepared a number of large full-color paintings depicting the project from various points of view.

One of the views showed Norman's six towers from the air —and thus the site planning immediately became apparent. On the "land" side of the drive was a long, low arcade curving in an arc that paralleled the roadway. Above rose three slim rectangular towers, straddling the arcade at right angles, one at each end and one at the center of the arc. Because of the curve, the towers converged inward toward the city and radiated outward toward the lake. The arcade itself provided communication and cover in all seasons. Above it was a continuous open promenade offering a magnificent view of the city.

Across Lake Shore Drive, the lake was to be filled in to form a promontory that curved outward into the water. On this promontory Friedrichs had set another arcade and three more towers, set farther apart so that they matched the outward thrust of the buildings on the land side.

An intricate system of interchanges connected each set of buildings to Lake Shore Drive. At various points the roadways dipped below ground level carrying passenger cars to vast underground parking facilities beneath the buildings. Above ground the entire site was landscaped with broad walkways bordered by intricately patterned landscaping, fountains and statuary. Despite Friedrichs' objections, Norman insisted on selecting the sculpture himself.

One of the most costly features of the project could not be seen in the aerial views. The two sections of the Plaza were to be tied together by a broad underground corridor tunneled under the Drive. In his earlier plans, Friedrichs had proposed a gracefully arched, enclosed overpass to cross the roadway (this had given the "Triumphal Arch" effect Bernard Adler applauded in the rezoning hearings). Later, Friedrichs decided that this form intruded on the lines of his buildings. He even suggested putting the arcades below ground; he preferred to have his buildings stand independently, related to each other by placement and scale, but otherwise not visibly connected. It took considerable effort on Norman's part to talk him out of that idea. But Friedrichs was adamant on the system for crossing Lake Shore Drive: it must be underground.

Ultimately Norman agreed to the tunnel. And this, of course, cost him an additional struggle with the Zoning Committee and the Department of City Planning. Fortunately, Adler again supported Karl Friedrichs.

The buildings themselves were slender, spartan spires, a dynamic pattern of rectilinear forms. Norman claimed that Friedrichs alone, of all modern architects, understood the proportions that gave harmony and power to these endlessly repeating shapes. The exterior walls were covered with the modular panels Friedrichs had designed—trim rectangles that matched the lines of the buildings themselves. The framing material was bronze, and the inserts were alternate panels of marble and glass running the full height of the buildings. Each panel canted slightly inward from one side to give an appearance of depth to the façade. Norman would have preferred an all-glass exterior but Friedrichs disdainfully stated that only a layman or a journeyman architect would propose such a trite design. That was enough for Norman Kane. Lake Shore Plaza was intended to be unique.

Under Norman's prodding, the architects and engineers completed the plans and specifications for Lake Shore Plaza and sent them out for bids in December. The very size of the project excluded any but the largest contractors. Nevertheless, several national building firms indicated their desire to bid on the work.

In view of this competition, Norman was hopeful that the prices would be in line with, or even less than, his estimates. Unfortunately, when the bids were opened some sixty days later, he found the prices were far in excess of his budget figures. The project could not proceed unless substantial changes were made in the design and several million dollars cut from the cost.

Norman was doubly distressed. Not only was he under considerable financial pressure, but he was also faced with the apparent necessity of omitting from the project many of the features he considered unique and imposing.

White urged him to omit the arcades; let the public walk outdoors from building to building. McNeill wanted to substitute aluminum for the bronze in the exterior panels and change the marble panels to glass. Norman rejected these solutions and many others of a similar nature. He regarded the authors of these proposals as sinister enemies, seeking to destroy his masterpiece.

The only happy man was Karl Friedrichs. His structural system, a deceptively simple concrete-and-steel shell, had priced out at his estimate. And, since Norman refused to omit the arcades or change the bronze and marble panels, it seemed that most of his work would remain intact.

Most, but not all. Norman decided to go back to Friedrichs' original design and use the overpass across Lake Shore Drive instead of the tunnel. Friedrichs was appalled, even though Norman showed him his own earlier drawings. Friedrichs could offer no adequate response, but he refused to submit the change to Adler. Norman made the request himself, in Friedrichs' name. Adler was bemused but, fortunately, compliant.

Eliminating the tunnel resulted in a substantial saving. Still, it was not enough. Working with the engineers, Norman found that the air-conditioning system could be modified without detracting from its efficiency. However, he would not consider any radical revisions, and therefore the cost reduction was slight.

It had been obvious to Norman from the start that his best hope of cutting the costs would be in negotiating with the contractors. He dealt with them, each in turn, seeking to persuade them to cut their profit margins. He told the representatives of each contractor that the project would be canceled unless they reduced their prices. Some contractors did not respond to this approach. They were willing to reprice the work if Norman made substantial cost-saving changes in the design, but otherwise they would not alter their bids. One by one, these contractors withdrew, until Norman was left with only three who were willing to negotiate with him. He decided to concentrate on Carrelli and Sons, a Chicago firm. Norman had worked with Carrelli before, and Carrelli knew that although Kane was a tough negotiator, he would stick to his deal once it was made.

Norman, the architects and engineers spent weeks with Carrelli and his staff, showing them how the job could be coordinated so as to effect savings in overhead and even in direct labor costs. Norman himself dealt directly with some of the suppliers who would furnish materials to Carrelli, pressuring them to lower their prices.

Then, with Carrelli's aid, Norman turned to the subcontractors, whittling their bids down to acceptable size. Eventually the combined efforts of all these men lowered the price of the project by millions of dollars, and Norman was ready to proceed.

I was not so sure.

Norman had been working around the clock for weeks, and the strain was beginning to show. He was sneezing and sniffling, and he looked frighteningly pale. When I remarked on his appearance, he smiled. It was then that he told me the whole story about Tina Kincaid and the swimming pool. He said that a few days after that adventure he had come down with the flu. The infection had lingered and then, burdened by the constant pressure of the gigantic new project, he had never quite regained his health.

"I'll be all right though, Eddie. Whipping the costs into line has done a lot for me."

"It's great to cut millions out of the cost of this project, but if something happens to you, there isn't any project."

"That's ridiculous. Lake Shore Plaza is too big and too important for anything or anybody to stop it now." But his voice was hoarse and he coughed persistently.

I tried to shrug off my feeling of concern. "Well, at least your efforts have brought the costs in line with your budget."

"That's what you think."

"I thought you negotiated the contractors down to meet your estimates?"

"Oh yes, we're within the estimates—except for the finishes."

"What finishes?"

"Well, partitioning the offices, electrical work, floor covering, painting and decorating—everything necessary to put the individual tenants in business."

"I don't understand. According to your own figures, you hit the budget on the nose."

"Yes, but only because the structural work, the utilities, the mechanical systems and the other basic items now cost less than our estimate. Unfortunately, finishing the space for tenants will cost us considerably more than we projected."

"It all evens out, doesn't it?"

"I only wish it did. You see, the only tenant work included in our contracts is for International Materials, Reserve Life and National Tube. Their work isn't cheap, but we're getting the advantage of doing nearly two million feet at one time. Finishing that much space costs a hell of a lot less than completing offices for tenants who rent only ten or fifteen thousand feet. Get it? If we're running over the budget for the big tenants, what will happen when we get to the small ones?"

"Doesn't anyone else realize that?"

"If they do they're not telling me."

"Then you better go back and make more changes."

"Too late. We can't change the International Materials and National Tube leases. You can be damn sure they won't let us cut anything out of their offices."

"What about the rest of the space?"

"All based on the unit prices in our contracts."

"Can't you renegotiate them?"

"I'll tell you a secret. I'm going to renegotiate the hell out of them, but even if I cut them another ten per cent I'd still be in trouble."

"Then what will you do?"

"Build buildings and lease space."

"What about the money you're short?"

"What about it?"

"Where will you get it?"

"I'll figure that out later. First let me build the buildings."

"That's one hell of a way to start a project."

"It's not the first time, Eddie. I'll come up with an answer somewhere along the line. But if I cheapen the project, I'll never rent the space. I'll just have to come up with more money."

"Will Fidelity Standard give it to you?"

"That remains to be seen, but now is not the time to ask for it."

"When is the time?"

"Eddie, you know that down deep inside I'm a 'how-it-feels' guy. Let's wait until I feel it's the right moment."

Even before all of the contracts were awarded, the demolition contractors began setting up barricades, rerouting traffic and clearing the site. I found the destruction rather sad. I'm not quite certain why, but somehow, the sight of men scrambling over the buildings, chopping away the marble sills and wrought-iron filigree work, was disturbing to me.

The ancient buildings were far sturdier than anyone had suspected. Norman, the architects and engineers, even the wrecking contractors, had assumed they were of simple masonry, bearing-wall construction. Instead the men found huge steel beams framed into the masonry and pilasters of rein-forced concrete. This delayed demolition. Norman's con-tracts contained penalty clauses covering such delays, but Norman feared that assessing the penalties might cause the contractors to abandon the work. Unfortunately, he had al-ready rescheduled the hours in which wrecking work was per-formed to meet the complaints of apartment and hotel dwellers in the area; this compromised him in his attempts to speed up the progress of the wrecking contractors.

The city authorities complained about the rerouting of traffic on the drive. There were now only four lanes instead of six, which created a bottleneck during rush hours. Norman was not making friends among the taxpayers. Nevertheless, brick by brick and beam by beam, the buildings came down.

Another crew was at work out on the lake, operating tall rigs mounted on barges, which drove long sheets of interlock-ing steel into the bottom. When complete, these would form a cofferdam enclosing Norman's property. Thereafter the water within the enclosure would be pumped out and the land filled. It was slow work, and the lake property would not be ready for actual construction for many months.

While the demolition was still in progress on the land side, Carrelli began sinking caissons for the first building. Long steel tubes were forced into the soil, searching downward for bearing stratum.

Once the caisson work was well under way, shipments of steel for the superstructure began to arrive at the site. Fried-richs had designed the buildings with a limited number of interior columns, suspending much of the weight of the structure from trusses outside each building. The steel sec-tions were immense, and delivering them to the site was a major problem in logistics.

Slowly the frame of the first building began to rise above the earth. Now another facet of Norman's personality came to the fore. He could not resist inspecting the construction at least once every day he was in Chicago. He loved to clamber over the rising steelwork at a not inconsiderable risk to life and limb.

"You've got a lot of guts," I told him.

"Guts, hell. I'm scared to death, but I wouldn't let these guys know it."

I wondered why he thought it so important to impress the dour-faced construction workers with his courage. Surely none of them would invest in his projects or rent space in his buildings. When I said this to Norman, he smiled and shook his head. He did not understand my viewpoint any better than I understood his.

Neal McNeill of Graham and Graham acted as field architect, and he was therefore required to accompany Norman on his tours of the building. It was evident that although McNeill was ten years younger, he did not customarily step out on steel girders to survey the city.

"That's not very safe, Mr. Kane," he would say. "We'd sure hate to lose you." But it was a waste of time, for Norman continued doggedly climbing up the rickety handmade ladders until he reached the highest point of the building.

Within six months the steel framework had risen beyond the thirty-story buildings to the south and there was a clear view all the way to the Loop and beyond. Of course, by then the contractor had installed construction elevators and it was much easier to reach the upper levels of the building.

Soon after the elevators were installed, Norman invited me to accompany him while he inspected the building—now that it was "safe." Not until I reached the site did I realize what I was in for. I tried to get out of it, but Norman almost pushed me onto the steel platform of the construction elevator. A frightening jolt and we were on our way. I kept telling myself that I was perfectly safe, but I did not believe it. The shaft was merely an open steel framework, and we were exposed to the sky. The stage rattled from side to side, making strange and unexpected noises. Altogether it was a fearful experience. Only Norman's bubbling good spirits sustained me.

As we reached the ground again, I began to relax, but Norman suddenly looked serious.

"Wait a minute," he said, pointing, as we stepped off the elevator. "Who's that with Carrelli?"

A few hundred feet away, the tall, dark-haired Carrelli was shaking hands with a large man in a gray suit whose back was toward us. At that moment the two men parted, and the gray-suited man passed behind the building. We never saw his face.

"I don't know who it is, Norman. What does it matter?" I was anxious to return to my office.

"It matters a lot," Norman yelled over his shoulder. He had begun to run toward Carrelli. I followed him at a more sedate pace.

"Who was that, Carrelli?" Norman was angry and his voice was strident.

"Who, Mr. Kane?"

"Come off it, Carrelli. The guy you just shook hands with. Who was he?"

Carrelli's smile was bland. "Oh, him? Just a friend. Always visits my jobs. Loves construction, Mr. Kane. Like you."

"Bullshit. That was McGarrity."

Carrelli's smile slipped a notch, but he still responded good-humoredly. "Yeah, sure, McGarrity. Like I say, an old friend. Loves to climb around buildings. What you think of the job, Mr. Kane? Going pretty good, huh?"

"Who do you think you're kidding? McGarrity don't give a shit for construction. He goes in a straight line between his office and City Hall. If he ever leaves that line, something's up. What is it?"

"I tell you it's nothing. What makes you think McGarrity ain't my friend?"

"He ain't nobody's friend. Not even the Mayor's. McGarrity don't want friends. He wants money."

Norman stepped closer to Carrelli. His pose was menacing, but he was so much smaller than Carrelli that the threat was almost ludicrous. "How much does he want from you? And for what?"

Carrelli gave Norman a fatherly pat on the shoulder. "I sure can't fool you, Mr. Kane. You're too smart for big, dumb Carrelli. Yeah, you're right. I gotta take care of Dan. But he takes care of me, see? I mean, he takes care of us. You know, all the little problems that come up on a big job."

"What little problems?"

"Well, for example, we're not supposed to store materials

on the street, see? McGarrity passes the word and it's OK. Then maybe we want to work some hours we're not supposed to. McGarrity clears it. Just little things, see? But they keep the job going. Right?"

Norman hesitated. "How much is he into you?"

"Just a few bucks. Dan ain't greedy."

Norman's disbelief was obvious.

"Really. Carrelli don't kid you. A few bucks here, a few bucks there. It's a big job. I can afford it."

"Sure, Carrelli, sure you can. OK, forget it. But if the pressure gets too rough, you let me know. I don't want anything hurting the job. You understand?"

"Sure, sure." Carrelli was smiling again. "You worry too much, Mr. Kane. You don't need to worry. You let old Carrelli take care of the construction. You just keep the money coming, huh?"

Now Norman was smiling. "OK, Carrelli, we'll drop it for now. Just get the building up—and don't put too much water in the concrete."

Carrelli was laughing as we walked away.

"I'm gonna have to keep an eye on that guy. McGarrity doesn't play for peanuts. If he takes too much out of Carrelli, Carrelli's gonna take it out of the job. I can't afford that, not for a minute."

"McGarrity knows how far he can go, Norman. He won't push too far. He's too smart for that."

"Maybe. But I can't be sure. McGarrity's never done this before. Maybe he's getting greedy. You never know."

I tried to distract Norman. "The building looks great, Norman. The trip up and down scared me, but it's sure a wonderful building."

"Yeah, wonderful." Norman glanced upward for a moment. Then he looked away, frowning. Carrelli had really worried him.

"Does General Stone ever come out here?" I asked.

"Yeah, once in a while. But he won't go up in the building. He says he'll wait until we top it out."

"What about the boys?"

"Oh, they stop by once in a while. What does it matter? To

them this building is nothing more than a huge metal dollar sign. They can enjoy thinking about it in their rocking chairs."

"What about Kincaid?"

"I never see him. I can't figure out what's bugging that guy, can you?"

"You're in a better position to know the answer than I am."

"Still harping on Stone's party. You and Frieda."

"Did you tell Frieda the whole story?"

"Not all of it. But the idea that Tina is—or was—available is just as obnoxious to Frieda as if I actually slept with her."

"You still could if you wanted to."

"Maybe. But I suspect that at the moment of orgasm I'd feel a knife slide between my shoulder blades."

"That wouldn't be the worst possible way to die."

"What does it matter how you die? There are no good ways." Norman abruptly changed the subject.

The only time Delbert Kincaid visited the construction site was the day they topped out the first of the six towers. Actually only the framework was completed, and it would be many months before the building was ready to receive tenants. However, in keeping with tradition, Norman designated a day for topping out. A steel beam was set in place at the roof line, but instead of welding it, the iron workers lifted it free with a crane so that it could be lowered into position at the appropriate time.

Norman invited a broad selection of local businessmen and political dignitaries to the ceremonies. Most of the investors and their wives appeared. To my surprise, Delbert and Tina were there, although they arrived separately. I doubted that Norman had expected either of them to accept his invitation.

I even managed to persuade my wife to attend. Apparently curiosity had temporarily overcome her prejudice against Norman. Unfortunately the weather was unpleasant, and when the time came to go up in the elevator, she flatly refused. I didn't blame her. It was very cold for October, and the wind spilling across the lake made it seem like midwinter. The elevator cage rising in the tower vibrated more than usual. All around me I saw panic-stricken faces that only reflected my own. As the cage bounced upward, the workman operating it studied us with open amusement.

At the top the wind blew even more fiercely than below. Newsmen huddled together, pleading with Norman to give them interviews in a safe spot near the center of the vast floor. It was quite a struggle, for Norman insisted on climbing to the topmost beams. The photographers were pleased with these views of the intrepid real-estate developer, but they remained a respectful distance from the edge. Watching Norman, Frieda was clearly in agony. Any second a capricious gust of wind might send him cartwheeling to the street sixty floors below.

Mayor Conlin huddled among the newsmen, gave his little speech, which was lost in the wind, raised the flag and then retreated to safety behind his aldermen. They were accustomed to shielding him.

Norman bounded across the roof like a child, laughing and yelling into the wind, giving the newsmen all the quotable quotes they could hear. If they missed a word or two, they invented substitutes rather than draw close to eternity. When he saw that the newsmen would not follow him, he laughed with even greater pleasure.

At last Norman returned to a safe spot again. The photographers closed in for more pictures. He was posing with General Stone when Tina Kincaid stepped into the group. She took Norman's arm and smiled at him. "Mr. Kane, you're absolutely marvelous," she said.

Norman was surprised, but he recovered quickly. "Here's what you need, boys, a little feminine charm to offset all this cold steel and concrete."

The photographers delightedly snapped pictures of Norman and Tina.

In a moment Frieda appeared, smiling grimly, and tried gracefully to lead Norman away.

"Wait a minute," one of the photographers yelled. "That's

terrific. The big developer with two beautiful dolls. Who are you, lady?"

"Mrs. Kane."

"Oh, yeah? Great." And while Frieda stood there, a smile frozen on her lips, they continued taking pictures. It was a strange tableau. Norman looked from Tina to Frieda. He was enjoying every minute of it.

The newsmen were ready to leave then, but Norman insisted on regaling them with his plans for the future. He was careful to give full credit to Karl Friedrichs as the architect and to General Stone as the principal investor. He did not forget Mayor Conlin or the great citizens of the city. Nonetheless he managed to impress us all with his own importance. Meanwhile, neither Tina nor Frieda left his side.

When Norman finished his speech, the newsmen clustered about General Stone. Norman managed to disengage himself from the two women, and once again wandered to the limits of the building. He paraded along the edge as a king might circle his kingdom. Firm-jawed, he gazed at the city beneath him.

At that moment I was distracted by Delbert Kincaid. At first Del had remained with the group huddled in the center of the floor, ignoring all attempts to interview him, glaring as his wife tried to charm Norman. Now he seemed to be moving toward the edge. Kincaid hunched his shoulders against the cold, but when he glanced back for a moment, his expression seemed strangely agitated. I was reluctant to leave the group that sheltered me from the slicing wind, but I felt I ought to keep an eye on him and I followed him as he moved hesitantly toward the open margin of the structure. Once or twice he looked back. Fortunately he did not see me. I followed him, but worked a shorter angle. Near the edge of the floor slab the wind seemed harsher, and my own fears sharpened. Norman, still pacing the ramparts, was beginning another circuit of his building. I could not understand why he felt compelled to pace that dangerous perimeter, even after he had assigned his audience to General Stone.

Kincaid moved closer to the edge. I hurried until I was almost alongside him. He was so intent that he was completely unaware of me. Norman's back was still turned. Kincaid began to run; his face was contorted with an emotion I could not fathom. Suddenly I realized what he intended to do. I lunged forward, grabbed his shoulder and spun him around. He stumbled, and I had to hold him tightly to keep him from falling. His eyes seemed large and luminous but strangely out of focus.

"What do you want?" he mumbled, his words barely intelligible. He tried to pull away.

The wind was so high that I had to yell to make Kincaid hear me. "Stop," I said. "Stop it, you fool." He tried to push past me, but I held him.

"What good will it do? What will you prove?" I shook him violently. He staggered back and almost fell. At that moment Norman came running up.

"What's the matter?" he cried.

"Del is sick or something. We better get him off this building."

Kincaid stared at both of us, his eyes still wide and his lips moving.

"He's sick, Norman, very sick. We have to get him out of here."

"OK. I'll get his wife."

I did not relinquish my grip on Kincaid, although by then his fit had run its course. I could feel him trembling.

"It's very cold, Del. You must be sick; you shouldn't have come up here. Come on, I'll take you down."

His expression softened; the flush left his face. He felt like a sack of bones in my hands. Kincaid nodded and I led him to the elevator cage. Norman was talking to Tina. She hurried to us, her face drawn.

"What's the matter?" she asked her husband.

Del stared at her. "What's the matter?" He mimicked her in guttural tones. She looked at him for a moment and then turned away.

"Come on," I said. "Let's get out of here."

I pushed Kincaid into the elevator. Norman waved to me and I waved back casually, as if nothing was wrong. As we started down in the open shaft, Kincaid leaned over the side and vomited into the wind. Some of it blew back onto the stage, and I turned to avoid it, but I did not loosen my grip on his trembling arm.

On the sixtieth floor Frieda Kane was talking to Tina Kincaid.

"Is your husband ill, Mrs. Kincaid?"

"He'll be fine. I'm afraid he had one too many drinks for lunch, and that, combined with this cold wind, seems to have upset him."

"I didn't think he looked well. Which is a shame. Your husband is such a handsome man."

Tina smiled. "Thank you, Mrs. Kane. Yes, Del is rather handsome, but not very strong, I'm afraid."

"Quite a contrast with Norman. Not very handsome, yet he's amazingly strong. But then, I'm sure you've noticed that."

Frieda walked away before Tina could answer.

My car was parked at the foot of the tower, but my wife was not in it. I hoped Norman would explain my absence.

I decided to take Kincaid to my office, which was only a few minutes away. When we reached my building, the only place to park was in a no-parking zone. *What the hell,* I thought, and backed into it. I helped Kincaid from the car and led him inside. He was weak now and docile. His blue eyes were almost gray. His coat was flecked with vomit, and the other people in the elevator stared at him coldly. He was unaware of their inspection, and I did not care.

When we reached my floor, I pulled him out of the elevator and led him stumbling to my office. I did not stop in my secretary's office, just pushed Kincaid through the door of mine, slammed and locked it. He slumped onto the couch—a long, leather couch, the only piece of comfortable furniture there. Kincaid sat bent forward, listing to one side at a sharp angle.

"Are you going to be sick again?"

He nodded. I helped him up and led him to the washbasin

in my closet. I could not even turn away; I had to hold him while he vomited again and again. A final spasm racked his body. He stood with his hands braced on the porcelain, unable to move. I ran the water and flushed down the mess, took out a towel and wiped his face and his coat. Shuddering, I threw the towel into the wastebasket. Then I led Kincaid back to the couch and stripped off his suit jacket.

Once again his head sank to his knees. Despite his cropped hair and buttoned-down collar, his youthfully cut suit and bow tie, he looked like an old man. He was gray, all of him— his skin, even his hair seemed gray. He rolled back against the couch and lay there, head back, mouth open. He was breathing heavily and unevenly. I realized that he was crying.

It was getting dark. I left Del for a moment and told my secretary she could go home. When I returned, Kincaid was still lying there awkwardly. One arm rested on the back of the couch, almost casually, but the other was locked, somehow, under his leg. His head lolled back, his eyes were half-closed and his mouth was still open. But the tears had stopped.

"Can I get you anything?" I asked. After a long pause he slowly shook his head.

"Do you need a doctor?"

Again he shook his head.

"You probably have the flu or something. You shouldn't have gone up on that building, Del."

He mumbled something.

"I didn't get you."

"Not that," he said, "not that."

After a moment his head snapped down, as if he could only move it with a violent gesture. He pulled one hand from under his leg and dropped the other on the couch. He leaned forward as if he were going to fall. I reached for him.

"I'm OK," he said in a quiet but somewhat steadier voice. "I'm OK now, thanks to you."

I nodded my head.

"You shouldn't have stopped me," he said.

"Stopped you from what? How could I stop you from being sick?"

"You shouldn't have stopped me." He was staring at me

with large, heavy-lidded eyes, no longer gray and vague but blue and intense.

"Cut it out, Del. I don't know what's on your mind, but whatever it is, it's crazy. Forget it, just forget it."

"My wife," he said, "my wife."

I said nothing.

"My gorgeous little wife and that ugly son of a bitch."

"I don't know what you're talking about."

"Of course you do." His voice was clearer. "The whole world knows. Norman Kane and Tina. I should have killed him." His voice rose to a shriek. *"I should have killed him!"*

"Stop it, for God's sake." Everyone in my office had gone home, but I could not help glancing toward the door. "Someone will hear you."

"I don't care. I'm going to kill that bastard. One day I'm going to kill him."

"Don't be silly. You don't know what you're saying."

He laughed a dry, harsh laugh. "Don't know, huh? You know. I know. Everybody knows. That little bastard's been screwing my wife."

"You're crazy."

He was growing violent again. "Crazy? You think I'm crazy?"

"Listen, Del, don't get mad at me. I'm only trying to help you."

Suddenly his eyes dulled again. "Right. You're trying to help me. You stopped me. I should be mad at you but I'm not." There was a pause. "That little bastard with my wife. What does she see in him? She's so pretty. Such a pretty little thing." He talked in slurred, uneven tones.

"You're not making sense, Del. What you're saying is silly."

"Not silly. That night at Stone's party, he took her to our house."

"He sent her home in a cab."

Kincaid laughed again, a laugh so hideous I shivered.

"Sent her home in a cab, huh? You must think I'm stupid. He took her home himself."

"How do you know that?"

"She told me."

I could not hide my surprise. "She told you?"

"She told me. They took a swim. Can you imagine that? I'm lying there in Stone's bedroom, smashed, and they took a swim."

"You believe that?"

"Believe it? I know it. I know when Tina's telling the truth. She's a damn good little liar, but I know when she's telling the truth. Yeah, they took a swim."

"All right, so they took a swim. So it's crazy. So what?"

"Then she offered to lay him. You get me? He didn't try to make her. She tried to make him. And you know what? That little bastard turned her down. I couldn't make her till I married her. And believe me, she was no virgin. But *me*—I couldn't make her till I married her. And man, was I trying! I was trying hard. But Kane, that little bastard, he turned her down. Even now, married to her, I've got to get down on my knees to get a piece from her, down on my goddamn knees. And Kane turned her down."

"Quiet," I said as authoritatively as I could. "Does that make sense to you, Del? The story doesn't hang together. What does a beautiful girl like your wife need with Norman Kane? And why would he turn her down?"

"I don't know, but he did, I tell you. He snaps his fingers and he can have her. I get down on my knees and I can't. Why do you think I hate him?"

"What about your wife?"

"I hate her. But she's mine, and I'm not giving her up. She shits on me, but I'm not giving her up—not to Norman Kane, not to anybody." He was still talking in a drunken singsong voice.

I threw up my hands. "I think you're sick, Del. I think you're out of your head. Did you have a drink for lunch?"

"Not a drink, Ellison, five drinks. I wasn't going to that damn topping out. It was Tina. She said she was going whether I did or not. Going to see her little hero. Left without me. Left me there drinking. Then I figured out what I had to do. Get up on that building and shove Norman Kane off. I'd have liked to hear him laugh then."

I took his shoulders and shook him. "You're a damn fool. I

don't think there's a word of truth in this. Either you're lying to me or your wife is lying to you. First you tell me your wife is sleeping with Norman. Then you say she told you she didn't sleep with Norman, but that she offered to and he turned her down. Either way, it's pretty hard to believe, isn't it? A homely guy like Norman Kane and a beautiful girl like your wife. Del, she's trying to torture you, and you're falling for it. You tell me you hate your wife but you don't want to lose her. Now what do you suppose would happen if you shoved Norman off a building? Do you think you'd get a medal? They'd put you away for the rest of your life. No Kane, no wife, no nothing. What's so good about that?"

"You're trying to save him."

"Him *and* you. I don't like murder, no matter who does it, or who they do it to. Come off it, Del. If you want to get rid of your wife, divorce her. But for God's sake, man, don't push a guy off a building."

There was a long silence. The room was quite dark now but I didn't want to turn on the lights.

"I guess you're right," he said.

"Of course I'm right. None of this will do you any good. Frankly, I think your wife told you that cock-and-bull story just to make you jealous."

Kincaid looked up at me and even in the semidarkness I could make out the hopeful expression on his face. "Do you really think so?" he asked in his little-boy voice.

"Yes, that's what I think. She told you that story to make you jealous."

"You could be right."

"Of course. Now let's forget this afternoon. We'll pretend it never happened. Whatever you have against Norman Kane, stop letting it eat into your soul. Stay away from him."

"I did stay away from him—until today. I couldn't stand the sight of him. I don't know. Being up there on that roof, watching him prance around and play the hero—it was too much. I couldn't take it."

"You've got to take it. That's all there is to it. Look, I've spent all the time I can with you, Del. I have to go home. Let's forget this whole thing. I know I will. Anybody can get excited—start out to do something rash. Thank God, you didn't go through with it."

"Thanks to you." He offered his hand, rather shyly. I shook it, resisting the urge to shudder at the damp lifeless feel of it. I withdrew my own hand quickly and clapped him on the shoulders. "Now go home. Don't think about this and don't talk about it. Not to yourself and not to your wife. Forget it. It's all over."

I knew I must warn Norman. I would have preferred to do exactly what I told Delbert Kincaid—forget the entire matter. But how could I be certain Kincaid would not repeat his attempt to harm Norman?

On my way out of the office I noticed a sheaf of telephone-message slips on my secretary's desk. Norman had called seven or eight times. Surprisingly, my secretary had not put him through. I was grateful.

I avoided Norman that evening. I wasn't very anxious to tell him about Del Kincaid. Then, too, I was a little annoyed with him. I certainly couldn't blame him because Kincaid tried to push him off the roof. Still, if he had ignored Tina—refused to pose with her at the building—Kincaid might not have done what he had done. I didn't really believe Norman wanted to have anything more to do with Tina. For him the whole affair had ended in a strange but nevertheless satisfying triumph. Yet he had used Tina's latest overture as a means of irritating his wife. I was disgusted when I thought of Frieda, trapped into posing with Norman while Tina still clung to his arm. Norman enjoyed little games like that. I didn't admire him for it.

But I couldn't put Norman off forever. Next morning, when I reached my office, he was waiting on the line. He was irate over my failure to return his calls, and I could not blame him. He asked what had happened to Kincaid. I told him Del had been sick and that I had taken care of him. Norman insisted that I come to his office. From his tone it was evident that he did not believe my explanation.

The moment I walked through his doorway, Norman was jabbing at me. "You better come clean, buddy. What's the pitch with Kincaid?"

"I told you this morning. He got sick and I kept him company until he felt better."

"You expect me to believe that?"

"You expect me to believe you never laid a hand on Tina Kincaid?"

"So that's the connection."

"Norman, do you mind if I sit down?"

"OK, sit down. But start talking."

"Let's get this clear. Kincaid *was* sick. He threw up once in the elevator and again at my office. Of course, there's more to it than that."

"Go on."

"You've got to realize that Kincaid is very hostile toward you."

"Why in the hell should he be? What did I ever do to him besides get him into a terrific deal?"

"He's not angry about the deal, and you know it."

"What, then?"

"Now *you* come off it, Norman. You know damn well he's upset about you and his wife."

Norman leaped up and began to pace the room. "I told you all about it. I didn't lay that babe. I hardly touched her. Kincaid should thank me. I kept his beauty queen pure and virtuous."

"Don't you think that may seem even worse to him?"

"Worse? Wait a minute—why would he think it's worse? He doesn't know a damn thing about it."

"You're sure of that?"

"Who would tell him?"

"Tina."

"Tina? I don't believe it."

"It's a fact, Norman. She told Del she made herself available but you turned her down."

Norman stood stock-still. "You know, every time I think I really understand people, and especially broads, something like this happens."

I shrugged my shoulders.

"By God," Norman said, "she must really be a sadist. She loves to torture that poor bastard."

"I suppose so, Norman. I imagine she really hates him."

"Or loves him. Who knows which?" Norman walked back to his desk and sat down behind it, rocked in the upholstered chair, and rattled some papers. Then he spoke again. "What the hell does she want from her husband? What does she expect him to do?"

"All I know is that he's dangerous. I'd keep an eye on him if I were you."

"What can he do? He has no control over my deal. Anything he does to harm me will hurt him, too."

"I'm not sure Kincaid is thinking quite that clearly."

"Wait a minute. There's something you're not telling me, Eddie. You wouldn't warn me this way if you thought Del represented just one more business risk. No, sir. There's more to it. OK, we'll piece it together. We're up on the building, and I'm running around looking at beautiful old Chicago, and the next thing I know you've got this character by the shoulders and you're shaking him. Is that how you handle a sick man? What's the pitch, Eddie? Level with me."

I did not see how I could avoid a direct answer. "I know this is going to sound crazy, but the reason I grabbed Del Kincaid is that he was about to shove you off the building."

Norman turned pale.

"I guess he got pretty worked up when he saw his wife fawning all over you. I know it sounds ridiculous, but he was edging toward you, wild-eyed. He had his hands out and your back was turned. Everybody else was listening to General Stone. So I grabbed him. It didn't take much to stop him. I don't think he really had the stomach for the job. I hustled him out of there and over to my office. As I said, he got sick on the way down in the cage and sick again in my office. I talked to him for hours, and he more or less admitted that he wanted to kill you. By the time we finished talking he agreed the whole idea was absurd. Still, he might have done it."

There was a long pause before Norman spoke, and when he did, I noticed he was hoarse again. "I hate to sound corny, but I don't know how to thank you, Eddie. I guess you saved my life."

I tried to play it down. "It's nice of you to say that, Norman, but you're making more of this than you should. I'm only telling you to make sure that nothing happens. After all, it's a lousy way to lose a client."

Norman tried to laugh, but it turned into a cough, and when he spoke again his voice was little more than a hoarse whisper. I told him he was pushing himself too hard and that he ought to go south for a little warm sunshine.

"No time for that. Too many things cooking here. Besides, we've got plenty of trouble."

"You mean Kincaid?"

"No, I think you took care of him. This trouble may be even worse. The building is settling."

"How can that be?"

"Damned if I know. After the ceremonies yesterday McNeill showed me some marks on the foundations. He also showed me where a few of the welds are opening up on the lower levels. We checked the bench marks together and apparently the building is settling. Not only that, but it isn't settling evenly. The northeast corner is dropping the most of all, and that's putting a kind of torsion on the rest of the structure. The welds all the way up are under tremendous strain. Frankly, I'm worried."

"Is there something wrong with Friedrichs' design?"

"Perhaps, but I don't think that's it. Maybe we didn't sink the caissons deep enough. You know soil conditions are pretty tricky when you're working near the lake. Or maybe the contractor cheated. If he did, McNeill should have caught him right away. We've got sixty stories of steel and concrete standing on those caissons."

"My God. Is there anything you can do about it?"

"We're investigating several possibilities. Meanwhile, we'll have to shore the building."

"Forgive my ignorance, Norman. Is it possible you could lose the building?"

Norman laughed that dry, half-choked laugh. "No, I don't think it's going to fall into the lake. But the cost of correcting this condition could be tremendous. And I'm having trouble with Friedrichs. He claims that if he had written the specifications himself, this wouldn't have happened. Maybe he's right. Anyway, he's arrogant again."

"You don't think he knew this was going to happen, do you?"

"Hard to believe, but if Kincaid would push me off the top of the building, why wouldn't Friedrichs stand by while somebody undermined the bottom of it?"

It was not a joke, and neither of us laughed.

"Norman, I'm sure you'll figure it out. But in the meantime I'm more concerned about your health than ever. What the hell good is Kane Enterprises without Norman Kane?"

"Don't be silly. I'm fine." But his voice came out in a half-croak that frightened me more than Kincaid's wild eyes.

4

Forty-eight hours later, Norman was in the hospital with pneumonia. They kept him in an oxygen tent for several days and fed him such massive doses of drugs that he was only half conscious for almost two weeks. It was a frightening time for everyone.

The building continued to settle, almost imperceptibly, but with ominous regularity. Friedrichs and McNeill planned to solve the problem by shoring the structure temporarily and then sinking additional, deeper caissons which they hoped would support and stabilize the building. Then the architects and engineers realized that the other buildings might develop the same problems. They decided to enlarge all the caissons and sink them much deeper into the soil than they had originally planned.

Norman was not available to authorize these changes. McNeill brought the proposals to General Stone, who reviewed them and then instructed the contractors to proceed with the work.

During that period it became clear to me just how desperately the project required Norman's attention. General Stone was an experienced real-estate developer, but it had been twenty years since he had taken personal charge of a project. It was questionable whether he really understood the schemes the architects proposed. Perhaps he did not want them to think he was indecisive. The entire project probably should have been delayed, but no one suggested that. In retrospect it seems to me the architects and engineers took advantage of Norman's absence to impose their own theories on the General and thus on the project itself.

This may be unfair. Norman's bout with pneumonia was a serious one, and we all feared he might be unable to function for a period of months. No one was willing to delay the project for an indefinite period. The lenders, particularly, would have been distressed to find that in Norman's absence the project was without sound leadership. Perhaps General Stone and the others followed the best course, but they reached conclusions different from those Norman would have reached had he been able to participate in their discussions.

I visited Norman as soon as they would let me, which was during the third week of his stay in the hospital. He lay propped on the pillows, trying to look cheerful and alert, but I was shocked by his pallor, the slackness of his skin, the dull look in his eyes, and the fidgety movements he made with his fingers. He croaked even more hoarsely than before, and now there was a disturbing quaver in his voice.

"Eddie, you've got to tell me what's going on. I've been cooped up here for more than two weeks and I don't know what they're doing. I can't take a call. I can't place a call. Stone tells me they solved the caisson problem, which sounds good, but when I hear how they worked it out I'm not so sure."

"Norman, I'm sure the architects know what they're doing."

"Bullshit. They don't know nothing, those clowns. What are they doing to my buildings?"

"I'll talk to your doctor, and if he says you can see the drawings and talk to the architects, I'll arrange it. By God, I warned you, Norman—I said you were going to get sick and you wouldn't listen to me. Now stop pressing or you'll never get back to work."

He sighed and lay back on the pillows. It was apparent he did not have the strength to continue speaking. "Wait," he said. "Wait a minute." So I sat and waited, looking about the antiseptic room with its modern steel furniture, gay bouquets of flowers, and a view over the lake.

"You always get a room with a view, Norman."

There was no response.

"OK," he said. "I can talk again. Listen, Eddie, I've got to get back to work."

"I couldn't agree with you more, but look at it this way: you've lost two weeks. If you push yourself too hard, you might lose two months or more. How will that help the project?"

"I suppose you're right." His answer betrayed a profound physical weakness.

"They can't have done a hell of a lot of damage in the past two weeks and there isn't a lot more they can do in the next two."

"Two more weeks? That's impossible. That could be the end of me."

"Two more weeks *will* be the end of you if you don't take it easy. I know you've never taken it easy in your whole life, but now you have to. You're not worth a good goddamn in an oxygen tent."

Again there was a break in the conversation. Norman turned his head and stared out the window. He was un-shaven and his hair was not as carefully arranged as usual. Norman looked sixty-eight, not forty-eight.

After a while, he spoke again. "Just get the plans in here, will you?" Then he turned his head away, and since he did not speak another word, I realized our meeting was over.

I talked to Dr. Franklin. He expressed grave doubts about permitting Norman to meet with his architects and engineers in the hospital. I told him I felt the same way, but that I knew Norman pretty well, and I feared that if he were kept away from his work for another two weeks, the stress might actually delay his recovery. I explained that Norman was convinced his architects and engineers were making serious errors. As long as he harbored these thoughts, he would brood, and the brooding might affect his recovery. The doctor seemed to see the point. I suggested that if the architects met briefly with Norman and explained their plans, it might relieve his mind.

Dr. Franklin shook his head. He said he could not accept responsibility for the patient's progress on this basis. I gave up trying to persuade him and called Frieda Kane. I explained my point of view and then she, too, called Dr. Franklin and confirmed what I said. At this point the doctor capitulated.

We were able to promise Norman that in a few days the plans would be brought to him. This was enough to relieve his mind. Until then Norman apparently believed there was a plot to keep the information from him.

———————————

Knowing how volatile Norman could be, Dr. Franklin asked me to sit in with the architects and engineers while they were in his hospital room.

When we arrived, Norman was sitting up in bed, face shaved, hair carefully combed, and wearing a new bathrobe. He was still hoarse, but at least there was a hint of a sparkle in his eyes. I had evidently made the right decision.

We brought a cantilevered service table to his bed and spread the plans so that he could examine them. He put on a pair of spectacles (I had never seen him wear them before) and examined the drawings at some length. Then he turned to McNeill.

"Have you stopped the settling?"

"Too early to tell, but we certainly think so. There may be a fraction of an inch more settlement left in the northeast end, but that's nothing compared to what's happened up till now. The shoring will support the structure temporarily. We're drilling new, deeper caissons on each side of the weak point and we'll bridge them with a concrete beam that will carry the grade beam. In the meantime, we plan to encourage some settlement on the opposite side. When we're finished, we believe the entire building will have settled equally at every corner, which will relieve the torsion at the northeast corner. Then we can reweld the steel where necessary."

"Karl," Norman asked, "what will this do to your structure?"

"My structure will sustain itself. The trusses were designed to withstand a great deal of stress. If the settling has really stopped, we won't have any further difficulty."

"What will it cost us, McNeill?"

"That's hard to say."

"Hard to say?"

"We had no choice but to let the work on a time-and-material basis to Carrelli."

"No fixed contract?"

"No. You know there's a caisson clause in our specifications. If the caissons go deeper, or if we need additional caissons, the owner pays for it."

"Yes, that's true. But what does that have to do with this?"

"Well, Carrelli had us over a barrel. We were afraid we might lose the entire building, so we authorized him to go ahead. We'll get the bills when he's finished."

Norman looked more distressed than angry. "Neal," he said, "do you realize what this man can do to us? Wasn't there some other way than an open-end contract?"

McNeill shrugged his shoulders. "We thought this was the best way, Norman. It was our duty to save the building."

"How many men has Carrelli got working on this?"

"I don't know exactly, but more than fifty."

"Are they working overtime?"

"Yes. Not only days, but weekends as well."

"You're keeping time, I suppose?"

"Oh, yes. We check in every load of concrete, and we keep time on every man. We won't let a dime get past us, one way or another."

"But it's working, you say."

"We think so."

"How deep will we have to go with the new caissons?"

"Until we hit bearing stratum."

"How deep is that?"

McNeill hesitated. "We can't be sure, Mr. Kane. Obviously the rock isn't able to support the load we have put on it. We'll just have to keep going deeper until we're absolutely sure."

"We took test borings, didn't we? We knew what was down there, didn't we?"

No one spoke. Norman turned to Friedrichs. "Well, Karl?"

"I'm beginning to think the reports are not reliable. And I'm particularly concerned about the borings we took out in the lake. I hate to think about it, but I have a suspicion that the rock is a narrow shelf that cuts in sharply across our land. Beyond the shelf, there may be only muck down there for another—well, I don't know—maybe another hundred feet or more."

"On every caisson? On all of the other buildings?"

"I'm afraid so."

"Over one hundred feet? At forty dollars a foot? My God, that will cost a fortune."

"What else can we do?" McNeill asked.

"We should scrap the whole system and float a slab under every building."

I began to laugh. Norman turned on me. "What the hell is so funny, Ellison? These guys are breaking me, and you're laughing."

"I'm sorry. It just sounds odd—floating a slab in Lake Michigan. Will you need an anchor to keep the building from drifting away?"

The others were laughing now, and after a moment even Norman joined in. "It does sound funny, but I'm dead serious. Listen, Karl, the bearing is no good, and we don't know how deep we'll have to go to find good bearing. Can't we give up the caissons altogether and try something else?"

Friedrichs had taken a pencil from his pocket and was scribbling on a piece of paper. For several minutes he worked at his computations, shaking his head from time to time and mumbling incomprehensible phrases. Then he sat motionless for a minute, staring straight ahead.

"It's not impossible, Norman. We have three floors of parking and equipment rooms with concrete walls and floors underground; they're spread across the entire site, enough to distribute the load. We could add reinforcing steel to strengthen the underground structure, tie it all together, something like a concrete cage, and float it, as you say, on whatever's down there. There's enough weight underground to protect us against the wind loads above grade." He smiled. "Our buildings won't tip over. You know, it would take study, but I think it could be done."

McNeill was sputtering. "That sounds crazy to me. Nobody's ever used that kind of construction on the lakefront before."

Friedrichs was knotting and unknotting his hands. "Mr. McNeill thinks we should use deeper caissons."

"Yes, Karl, but what do you think?"

"I prefer the floating foundation—or slab, as you called it —but Mr. McNeill thinks we should use deeper caissons."

McNeill was angry. "Look, Friedrichs, you never said a damn thing about floating a slab. You approved these drawings."

"I approved nothing. Show me my signature on your drawings."

"You didn't sign them, but you didn't object, either."

"You nearly shoved them down my throat." The old man was livid.

"Just a minute, gentlemen," I said. "Mr. Kane has invited us here despite the fact that he's been very ill. There's no point in quarreling among ourselves."

Norman ignored me. "Well, what the hell then, why don't we float a slab?"

There was a moment of silence.

"Why not, Karl? Why can't we do it right now?"

Friedrichs did not reply.

McNeill's voice was almost a whisper. "General Stone signed a new contract three days ago. We're stuck with the deeper caissons."

"Stuck? How are we stuck? Carrelli hasn't done the work yet. Why can't we get out of it?"

"He refused to accept our change order on Plaza One unless we guaranteed we would proceed with the deeper caissons on the remaining buildings."

"And you fell for that kind of blackmail?"

"It's not blackmail," said McNeill. "I honestly believe it's the right thing to do. And so does General Stone. Friedrichs did too, until he came up here today."

"Don't speak for me, Mr. McNeill. You know you never asked my opinion. You just brought me a set of drawings that showed caissons going down another hundred to a hundred and fifty feet."

"One hundred and fifty feet?" asked Norman.

"Right."

I was watching Norman closely. He looked as if he might have a stroke right then and there. At that moment the idea of bringing these men to see him seemed incredibly stupid.

"Take it easy, Norman. What's done is done."

Norman threw up his hands. He seemed to be talking only to himself. "I knew it. I knew it would happen. Leave these guys alone for a few weeks and you're dead. Keep sinking those caissons. For Christ's sake, one day they'll go through to China." He looked at McNeill. "I suppose there's a caisson clause in the new contract."

McNeill brightened. "No, we have a guarantee from Carrelli that none of the caissons will go deeper than the extra hundred and fifty feet."

"Swell, you really protected yourself. And I suppose it's on a time-and-material basis, too."

"No, it isn't, Norman. The same unit prices as the other caissons. Of course, these will take a little more steel than we originally planned. I mean, you can't go down that far without beefing up the caissons."

"How much more steel?"

"Well, I haven't completed my design yet."

"You mean you let the contract, but it isn't based on a fixed design?"

"Not exactly. The contract is based on a maximum poundage of steel per foot of caisson. Actually we get a credit if there's less steel. I'm trying very hard to keep the costs down."

"And you've drawn this new contract to cover all of the remaining buildings?"

"Yes, that's right. We thought it was the right thing to do."

"But you didn't ask me."

"How could we? You were lying here sick."

"You could have waited."

"We didn't dare."

"That's a lot of crap, McNeill. I understand why you acted quickly to save the building that's already up. But what about the other buildings? Why didn't you wait until you could talk to me?"

"Norman, let's face it. We didn't know when we'd be able to talk to you. Dr. Franklin told us you could be laid up for months. Look, there's plenty of risk putting up buildings on a sandy beach right alongside the lake. Dropping those caissons down is a lot safer than floating a slab."

"What are you afraid of? Do you think Ellison is right—that the building will float out to sea?"

There was no reply from McNeill. Karl Friedrichs smiled.

"Go ahead and smile. This is a big joke to you, Karl. Bears you out, doesn't it? You should have had control of the whole project, right? How could you let them do it? A man of your integrity. How could you let these clowns order deeper caissons? Do you realize what they're doing to the cost of this project?"

Friedrichs nodded his head. "Yes, Norman, I know, but you purposely placed me in an inferior position. It's not a case of ego, no matter what you think. These are the men you put in control of the job."

Norman sank back against the pillows. He stared at the ceiling for a long time. The men began to shift about uncomfortably. Norman reached out and seized the drawings on the little table. He crumpled them a bit, then pushed them off onto the floor.

"Get out," he said. "Get out, every one of you."

I told Dr. Franklin that his fears had been justified; Norman was badly shaken by the information his visitors had given him. "I'm afraid, Doctor, that now he'll be more anxious than ever to be up and running this deal."

"You know, Mr. Ellison, I'm not sure you did him any real

harm. Knowing the exact scope of this crisis may give him the added push to get him out of here." He hurried down the hall.

When Dr. Franklin reached Norman's room, he found him lying back on his pillows, eyes closed, just as we had left him some fifteen minutes earlier. Without opening his eyes, Norman began to speak.

"You want me to get better, Doc? You put in a telephone. You put it right here next to my bed." He opened his eyes. "Don't you believe that bullshit in all the B movies about a guy needing a reason to live?"

"Mr. Kane, you're nowhere near death."

"Believe me, Doctor, those birds are trying to kill me."

"You exaggerate, Mr. Kane."

"Maybe, but just to make the point. Now, if you want me to get better, you put in a telephone. You set it right here where I can reach it nice and easy. If you like, you get me a pretty nurse to hold the receiver to my ear when I talk, and I'll fondle her while I'm working. But you get me that phone, Doc."

"Couldn't someone place the calls for you?"

"Yeah, I suppose so. You might get my secretary over here. But for God's sake, give me a telephone."

Norman was sitting up in the bed with his elbows resting on the little hospital table. He looked bug-eyed and feverish.

The doctor made a snap decision. "OK, Mr. Kane. I'll have a phone brought in and I'll let your secretary work here. I'll permit you to use the phone for one hour in the morning and one hour in the afternoon. The rest of the day, you leave it alone. Is that clear?"

"OK, Doc, anything you say. Just get me the phone and Fritchie."

The following morning, Miss Fritch and the telephone were installed beside Norman's bed. Dr. Franklin came in to inspect his patient.

"Look at me, Doc. Don't I look better already?" The truth was that he did. The sight of his secretary, the telephone, the pads of paper and the pencils were like medication to him.

"You see, Doc, now I'm alive. You leave me stretched out

on a bed with nothing—no phone, no broads—" the doctor glanced at Miss Fritch, who was smiling benignly—"and you might as well kill me. You're a nice guy, Doc, but you've been killing me, and now, thank God, you're bringing me back to life."

By three o'clock that afternoon Carrelli, the general contractor, was in Norman's room. Visiting was forbidden without the doctor's special permission, but somehow Norman had smuggled Carrelli into the hospital.

Norman sat propped up on his pillows again, eyes glittering, trying to look tough. "Now look, you bastard. You can fuck around with General Stone and Neal McNeill and old man Friedrichs, but you can't fuck around with me."

The contractor offered an innocent smile. "Excuse me, Mr. Kane. I don't know what you're talking about."

"Cut the crap, Carrelli. You sold those suckers on deeper caissons. You know goddamn well those caissons will cost us a fortune."

"Please, I only do what the architects tell me. I don't design the caissons."

"Oh, hell, you know more about caissons than all the architects in captivity."

"Well, I do put in a lot of caissons."

"I don't mind your putting in caissons. I don't mind your making a buck. But when you take those caissons and shove them up my ass, it's too much, Carrelli."

"How you figure?"

"Look, buddy, you're just kidding yourself. You're running the cost of this project up to where you ain't even gonna get paid. Now you can slap a lien against the building if you like, but you're going to have to fight me and General Stone and Dan McGarrity and City Hall. I think that's a pretty rough combination."

Carrelli feigned anger. "You got no right to talk to me this way. I only give your people an offer and they give me a contract and I sign it. I just do what I'm told."

"It ought to be a floating slab, and you know it."

"Kane, like you say, I sink a lot of caissons. I float a slab or two, but an engineer I ain't."

"Now cut it out, Carrelli. You're the one who put the caisson bug in McNeill's ear."

"Mr. McNeill is a very fine gentleman."

"You would think that. But let's face it, pal. I'm the guy who's lining your purse, not McNeill. I got six buildings to build and I intend to do it, but I'm not going broke underground, you understand?"

"Sure I understand. But I don't see why you're mad at me."

"Because you're shoving those caissons up my ass, and in my condition, they don't feel so good."

"You pretty funny for a sick man."

"You gonna be pretty sick yourself, Carrelli, if you don't stop it."

The man leaped up. "Kane, you go screw yourself. I got a contract. You don't like the caissons, that's too goddamn bad. I got my contract. I got my guarantee. I don't need you for shit."

By now Norman was almost out of his bed, and Miss Fritch was struggling to restrain him.

"Get the hell out of here, Fritchie. Let me talk to this bastard alone. You heard me—get." Miss Fritch scurried from the room.

"You talk pretty dirty in front of that lady."

"That's none of your business, you bastard."

"Goddammit, Kane. I'm not going to take this from you. I don't do anything dishonest. You gotta stop screaming at me."

Suddenly Norman sat back. When he spoke again, it was very quietly. "OK, Carrelli, you walk out of here. You try and sink those caissons. I'll have you off that job in three days. I don't care what kind of guarantee you got. It ain't gonna hold up in court. So maybe I'm stopped. But it's better for me to be stopped than to go broke. And I figure by now I must owe you a couple of million bucks anyway. You'll sweat your way through hell getting that dough. So go ahead, Carrelli, get your ass out of here."

The man hesitated. "Look, I didn't come up here to fight with you. What you say ain't fair. I just sign the contract. Anyway, I'm kind of stuck, you see. I give the same guarantee to the caisson man. It's not so easy to stop this like you think."

Norman leaned forward again. "Put a price on it, Carrelli. What do you want to get out of it?"

"I don't know. I only figured on going ahead with deeper caissons."

"Believe me, we ain't going ahead with deeper caissons."

"Well, let me talk to my man. Let me see what I come up with."

"OK, you do that. But do it mighty fast. Three o'clock to-morrow afternoon you come back here. You bring that caisson crook with you. You bring your lawyer. You bring those lousy contracts. I'll be here with a checkbook. If the price is right, I'll buy you out of this damn thing."

Carrelli smiled suddenly. "Now you talk sense. One thing I gotta say, you yell and scream a lot, but when I listen close, you talk sense. I don't wanna hurt you, Kane. You give me a lotta work."

"That's right, Carrelli. Now *you're* talking sense. You go home like a good boy and figure it out and when you come back here tomorrow, I'll have the releases, the waivers, and everything else ready."

"OK, Mr. Kane. I'll see if I can do it by then." He hesitated a minute. "You get better, you hear?"

"Yeah. Thanks, thanks a lot. I really need *your* good wishes." And he turned away from the smiling contractor.

Within twenty-four hours Norman Kane bought his way out of the caisson contract. He was trapped on the first building, but he eliminated the caissons on the others. Friedrichs would have to design a floating slab, but that didn't worry Norman. He was certain Friedrichs could do it, certain the new design would cost far less than the caissons.

After settling with Carrelli, Norman asked Dr. Franklin to release him from the hospital. The doctor refused, so Norman walked out on his own. Thank heavens he went home; I was afraid he would go straight to his office. However, he called Miss Fritch, and she arranged to have extra telephone lines run to his apartment. Miss Fritch herself arrived with stacks of files and unanswered correspondence. Frieda was less than happy about the arrangement. Here was Norman sitting at a desk in the middle of her beautiful living room with papers, boxes and files strewn about.

I tried to handle Norman's affairs from my office, but he insisted on my coming to his apartment day after day.

"I don't make house calls," I told him. Norman merely laughed.

It was not a joke to me. The trip from my office to Norman's apartment and back took hours out of each day. Besides, it wasn't professional. I could feel myself being drawn into Norman's personal life. Representing him had created many problems for me before, and now these were multiplied by daily dealings with him in his own home.

And with Frieda. She was greatly concerned over Norman's health. Each day she begged me to prevail upon him to stop working so hard. I agreed with her in principle, but I disliked being caught between Norman and his wife. I felt I was being used.

"I don't know what to do," she told me, standing in front of Norman and talking over his head. "I can't keep him in bed." Norman, busy on the telephone, ignored her.

"Listen," I said, "you're lucky he's home."

"Home? The only difference between this and his office is the cooking."

"That's something."

"I suppose. But he works just as hard here as he does at the office. You can see he's not any better."

Norman cupped his hand over the receiver and told her to be quiet.

Frieda took my arm and led me into another room. I found the conspiratorial atmosphere rather distasteful.

"On top of everything," Frieda said, "there's Miss Fritch. Oh, my God, who can stand Miss Fritch? She watches over Norman with that smug proprietary smile."

"It's tough for all of you, but it's toughest for Norman. We have to ride along with him. No one can keep Norman in the hospital, and no one can keep him in bed."

"Look," Frieda said, as she led me to the window, "he can see the job site from here, and every time he looks at that building he starts swearing. Sometimes I think he's going to leap right through the glass."

"Frieda, we've both known Norman for a long time. He is what he is. All you can hope to do is keep him as quiet as possible."

"You've got to help me." She was appealing to me in every sense of the word.

I grew even more uncomfortable. "I don't know what to say, Frieda. Maybe you should have Dr. Franklin over here every day."

"You know, that's a good idea."

"A man in Norman's condition, with Norman's problems, could take a turn for the worse at any time, and you and I might not even notice it."

"All right," she said. "I'll do it." She marched off to call the doctor, and I escaped from one more entanglement.

It was not easy to persuade the prestigious Dr. Franklin to call on Norman every day, but Frieda talked him into it. Norman was annoyed, but he grudgingly submitted to having his pulse taken and his blood pressure checked. The doctor would shake his head and warn him that he was not recovering as quickly as he should, and Norman would say he was better off at home than at the hospital, and the doctor would try to persuade him to rest, but his words went for naught.

"Keep an eye on him," the doctor said, and Frieda smiled wryly. "Of course, Doctor, I'll keep an eye on him. Both eyes on him. But what good will it do me?"

———◆———

Despite her concern over Norman's illness, Frieda was secretly pleased to have him at home. The few weeks he spent in his apartment recovering from pneumonia offered her the best opportunity to be with her husband that she had enjoyed in many years.

It was true that Norman was a troublesome patient, irritable, quarrelsome and demanding. It was also true that the apartment was a command post, and that Norman had streams of visitors, interspersed with innumerable phone calls. Nevertheless, Norman was home, and Frieda could observe him almost continuously. She had believed she knew a great deal about Norman's business, despite his attempts to keep her uninformed. She was not intimidated by big figures; all of Norman's deals had involved millions of dollars. Now, however, she was exposed to the problems of Lake Shore Plaza on a day-to-day basis. In a few days she learned more about Lake Shore Plaza than Norman had told her in all the months since the inception of the project. She was awed by the immensity and complexity of the undertaking, astounded at her husband's ability, despite his illness, to manipulate hundreds of people and millions of dollars through complex transactions. He made his judgments quickly and dispensed his decisions with remarkable clarity and dispatch. Frieda could not help wondering how Norman conducted his business when he was well. Could anyone be more decisive or more efficient? She doubted it.

Around 6 P.M. each evening, the assaults thinned out, and eventually ceased altogether. Miss Fritch and the others in Norman's retinue dispersed until morning. Occasionally a phone would ring late in the evening, or Norman would feel the necessity to place a call. Nevertheless, by nightfall, all forces were more or less disengaged.

Norman seemed to grow unhappy, almost frightened, as the day drew to a close. He resented the departure of his staff, the silence of the telephones. Apparently he viewed the rest of the world as deserters under fire. He tried to keep everyone at the apartment as long as possible, dictating a last flurry of memoranda, issuing instructions, calling the job site until only the watchman answered the phone.

When he was finally convinced that nothing more could be done, he would stagger from his desk and fall, exhausted, on the sofa. But he always lay facing Lake Shore Plaza. He seemed unable to wrench his eyes away until the loss of daylight defeated him. Then, only the lights strung on the building could be seen. And they were faint indeed.

Now Frieda's hour began. She would mix a mild drink for Norman, then join him on the sofa, waiting patiently until he was ready to speak. Eventually, he would begin. For the most part, it was a rambling monologue. Frieda was not expected to respond, merely to listen. At times, she could not follow him at all. His words would be technical, his ideas expressed in fragments. She could not piece together these shards cast up by his restless mind. No matter. She was content to be with him, to be worthy of being his audience. After dinner, Norman was physically spent, and he would drop into bed and fall asleep at once. Frieda would be on her own until the close of the following business day.

After a few days, Norman seemed to look forward to their evenings together. Soon he was talking directly to her. He even explained his problems and the solutions he proposed. For Frieda it was like being in on a secret—the secret of the operation of Norman's mind. She had long been denied a glimpse into this holy of holies. She was both impressed and grateful.

After about a week, Norman began to ask for Frieda's reactions to his ideas. She couched her replies carefully. She did not want this new relationship to be shattered by some inappropriate comment. She cautiously indicated her sympathy for his problems but never dared to give a direct response to his queries. She realized she was only being used as a sounding board, anyway.

But eventually, perhaps inevitably, Norman demanded a direct response. "Tell me what you think, Frieda. Go ahead. Don't be afraid to express your opinion."

"I'm really not qualified to judge."

"You've been around me for days now. You've heard everything that's been going on. Do you think I should call Hanson over here for a meeting or not?"

"I don't know. All I can go on is your past conduct with the man. Thus far, you've made a point of not getting him involved in your personal life. You don't entertain him socially, and he doesn't entertain you. You told me that's the way you wanted it. I'm afraid all I can do is turn the question back to you. Why do you want to change the pattern now?"

Norman slapped his knee. "You're right. Vern and I get along great. It's all based on mutual respect and performance. There's no reason to change the rules."

Frieda was silent.

"By God, you really helped me, Frieda."

"I only told you what you've been telling me. You really knew the answer yourself."

He was pleased by her deference.

Gradually, across the days, their discussions took on more warmth. Frieda lost some of her hesitancy. She responded to Norman's questions carefully but directly. When he agreed with her, she glowed.

Norman began to relish their evening rendezvous. He no longer limited his remarks to direct points of business policy. At times he let go and described to Frieda his hopes for the Plaza. He admitted that he viewed it as being in every way the very pinnacle of his career. Perhaps he would go on to even bigger things. Perhaps not.

"It will be tough to top Lake Shore Plaza," Norman said. He spoke with great satisfaction.

"Maybe," he said, "maybe when this is complete I'll take a trip around the world. Go looking for real estate just as good as the Plaza." He waved a hand at the flickering skyline. "Maybe I can change the face of Paris or Rome, just like I'm changing Chicago."

"That would be wonderful, Norman."

"Yeah, wonderful. The little guy from Chicago who re-molded a dozen cities. How's that for a dream?"

"Perfect." Frieda moved closer to Norman on the sofa. "Could I come with you when you go abroad? Could I help you find these places?"

To her surprise, Norman frowned. "I'm the real-estate gen-ius, Frieda. I find the locations."

"Of course. I just want to *be* there. I'd love to be there."

Norman got up from the couch and stomped away.

"What's the matter, dear?" Frieda's voice was uncertain. She was frightened.

Norman spun around and planted his feet.

"You want to take over, don't you? You want to get in and

run my show. You'll help pick real estate for me. Oh, great. Just great."

"Norman, I don't mean to interfere—"

"You think because I've been sick, I'll stay weak. You think because I've had to live in this apartment day and night that I'm getting dependent on you. You've been damn clever, Frieda. Damn clever. Softening me up. Giving me the gentle caress and the melting look. Waiting to pounce in and grab a piece of my show. Well, it won't work, kid. It won't work at all."

Frieda was close to tears. How had she managed to destroy their renewed closeness? What had she done wrong?

"Please, Norman. That's not what I meant at all."

"Baloney. That's just what you meant." He could see she was giving way, and somehow he enjoyed it. "There's only one good thing about my being here, Frieda. Just one thing." He waited to launch his final missile. "For the first time in years I've known where the hell you are twenty-four hours a day."

Frieda began to cry.

Norman called me at my office about two weeks after he left the hospital. "Guess where I am, sweetheart."

"Oh, no, Norman."

"Yep. Over at the club, waiting for Gilbert of Western Machine and Foundry." I heard a cough at Norman's end of the line. "You gonna come over and join me, pal?"

"Yes, I'll come over." It was no use remonstrating with him about leaving his apartment.

When I inquired for Norman at the club, they told me he was in the Men's Grill. This was surprising, as Norman generally preferred the elegant main dining room. But when I walked through the swinging doors of the Grill, I realized at once why Norman had chosen this room. The Grill is rather dimly lit, with dark painted walls, heavy furniture and appointments. There is a bar at one end and a number of tables and booths are scattered about in shadowy clusters.

After a few moments I recognized Norman sitting in a booth in the darkest corner of the room. Even in the darkness he looked pale and thin.

"Don't get up, Norman."

"Hell, I won't waste my courtesy on you. I'm saving it for the boys from Western Machine." I was pleased to hear that his voice sounded stronger than it had in months, and I commented on it.

Norman smiled. "If you knew how much effort I expended getting my lungs into this condition, you'd think I was out of my mind. But, as I said, I'm not going to waste words. Listen, if during lunch you hear I'm about to conk out, you break into the conversation."

"Norman, don't answer me. Don't say one word. I must tell you I think this is utter madness. You know damn well you're not healthy enough to be here. You keep this up and you'll be back in that hospital."

Norman started to speak, but I raised my hand. "I know all the answers. You can't lease space lying in a hospital bed and you can't lease it from your apartment, and there's nobody else capable of dealing with Western Machine, and who can pass up half a million square feet."

Norman patted me on the shoulder approvingly.

We spent the afternoon in the Grill, negotiating with the men from Western Machine and Foundry. They were a tough lot, but Norman stayed with them, masking his weakness with food, drink and good humor. I jumped in now and then when I saw Norman was wavering. Mostly it was Norman's show. I knew what it cost him, but it meant half a million feet, and he might have been a lot sicker without that half a million feet.

———◆———

As the weeks passed Norman spent less of his time at home, and more of it at his office and club. He was not yet back to a full work schedule, but the tempo of his activity was clearly increasing.

After closing the deal with Western Machine and Foundry, Norman negotiated several other deals with prominent national concerns. None of them planned to occupy anywhere near as much space as International Materials or Western Machine, but the leases were substantial, sometimes covering a floor and sometimes more. Thus, as fall turned into winter, Norman brought his total leasing up to three million square feet—50 per cent of the rentable area.

Meanwhile, the buildings were going up. Friedrichs had solved the problems of the floating slab, and since there was no time lost in drilling caissons, the second and third towers came climbing up out of the ground at a remarkably rapid rate. Soon the steel framework of Plaza Two matched the soaring height of Plaza One.

Within the first building, craftsmen were carrying the electrical and plumbing lines, the great runs of freckled gray sheet-metal ductwork up from floor to floor. The building was a maze of wires, tubes and rectangular ducts spiraling upward, spreading out, infiltrating the structure.

On the exterior, gigantic spidery cranes crawled up the steel columns, raising bronze panels upward in endless succession, swinging them against the steel, where workmen quickly bolted them into place. It was impressive, yet it seemed marvelously simple, like snapping together the pieces of a child's building set.

Norman could not stay away from the job. Each day some new material was delivered to the site, some new system placed in operation. Norman had to see it all—to feel his buildings grow. He hurried from floor to floor, dodging sparks from the welders' guns, leaping over tangles of multicolored wire, crawling under ducts and over piles of material. The scene was noisy and dusty, and to me it seemed chaotic. But somehow the buildings were going up.

Time and again, Frieda called me at the office and begged me to drag Norman away from the building site. I felt like an overgrown errand boy. But there was no one else willing to do it.

The watchmen recognized me now and let me pass without question. I would wander about from floor to floor (the intercom system could seldom be heard over the sounds of the construction) searching for Norman. Eventually I would find him kneeling on the cold cement, covered with dust and perspiring freely under a yellow metal hat.

I could not always persuade him to leave. Sometimes he was angry and I left without him. Then Frieda would be angry, too—whether at me or Norman I never quite knew.

Still, there was more than Frieda's unhappiness to worry me. I learned that Norman had stopped leasing space in the building to be occupied by Western Machine. Instead, he began renting space in two of the other buildings. He even transferred tenants who had agreed to occupy space in Plaza Two into buildings not yet under construction. Even though Norman had leased almost half the total space in the center, only one building, the first, was close to being fully rented. Barely 60 per cent of the second building was under lease, and thus far the third was to have only Western Machine as a tenant. Norman split the remaining three-quarters of a million square feet he had rented between two of the other three unbuilt buildings. I did not hesitate to advise Norman that I considered this procedure reckless.

"Eddie, there's no need to worry about the second building. It's almost two-thirds rented. It's never tough to fill a building, once you get near two-thirds. Western Machine is taking only fifty per cent of Plaza Three, but with Western Machine for a key tenant, I won't have any difficulty filling it up. The result is I've got a leg up on two of the other three towers. Hell, there's almost four hundred thousand feet rented in each of those buildings, and you know enough to realize that a tenant would rather go into a building that's already partly rented than into an empty one."

"Norman, I admire your ability to transfer those tenants into the unbuilt structures. It probably wasn't easy."

"Well, one of the companies didn't need its space right now and so I suggested they go into a building that would be completed a little later."

"That's swell. But why don't you stop kidding me? This means you're going to start on buildings four and five far ahead of schedule."

Norman hesitated for a minute. "That's right. Not only four and five, but six as well. As a matter of fact, I'm going over to the bank right now to complete the construction financing for all the buildings."

"That's what I was afraid of."

"What's to be afraid of? Hell, we're fifty per cent rented already. I don't know what's worrying you."

"You've already told me that your costs are creeping up. The caissons you couldn't eliminate have cost even more than you expected. The floating slab costs less than deeper caissons, but it's still an extra, and the work that Stone authorized while you were sick had to be paid for. Then you made deals with Western Machine and other companies where you're required to provide a lot more interior work than you figured. Your cost of construction keeps going up and up and up."

"Right."

"It seems to me that when you build six buildings you have a wonderful opportunity to learn as you go along. If you space out the construction, you can profit in later buildings from the errors you made in the earlier ones."

"Very good, Eddie. I'm happy you put so much time and thought into construction."

"Don't be sarcastic, Norman. I'm just trying to understand. It seems to me that your contracts call for completing two buildings a year. You're not going to get any concessions from the contractors by accelerating the schedule. In fact, some of them may not be equipped to handle all six buildings simultaneously."

"That's right, too."

"Then what's the point? You're running short of money, but you're plunging ahead with the entire project right now. It looks like sheer madness."

"I don't know why. Now that I have leased a substantial amount of space in five out of the six buildings, I'm in a position to complete the project much sooner."

I studied him for a few moments. Norman's expression was so bland, it was obvious to me he was hiding something.

"I'm beginning to see what's on your mind, and now I really think you're crazy. Norman, you're doing this for only one reason. You want to open the construction loan on all six buildings. You want to take the dough for buildings four, five and six and use it to finish buildings one, two and three."

Norman smiled.

"Oh, yes, you've done it before. You rob Peter to pay Paul —take money from one project to shore up another—but this is the first time I've seen you do it within the same development. I don't see how you can get away with it. Don't you have to furnish contracts to the bank?"

"Sure. But there are so many variables in those contracts, the bank doesn't really know where we are. They have to go along with what I tell them."

"For how long?"

"Until they realize I'm not going to make it."

"When will that be?"

"I hope it takes a long time. At least until I work out some additional financing."

"But Norman, the bank knows your costs on Plaza One and Two. There aren't many variables left. Don't they know you've run over your budget?"

"Not exactly. I worked the figures around so that some of the finishing costs on Plaza One are listed under buildings two and three, and I've sold the bank a bill of goods that the cost of completing the Western Machine space will be offset by an improved rental market for the rest of the space."

"Why on earth should they believe you?"

"There are more reasons than you think. First of all, I've established a pretty fair record with them. My costs have run over on other projects, but I always came up with the difference. Second, they're hooked into this thing pretty deeply. They're afraid to call a halt. I'm getting the buildings up and I'm renting space. The mortgage commitment is still good, and it looks like I'll meet the terms. Now, if they start stalling me they could end up in a one-hundred-and-sixty-million-dollar barrel. And the only guy who can pull them out is me. So why should they cross me, Eddie?"

"You once told me that this was too big a deal for the Chicago National Bank to play games with. You said they wouldn't take the same risks they took on smaller projects. What happened to that line of reasoning?"

"That was all true *before* they got into my deal. Until then, they could be as cautious as they wanted. They could demand anything. But now they've paid out nearly fifty million dollars. It's true I signed loan agreements maybe a hundred pages long. The bank has every right in the world—even the right to take me up on top of Plaza One and drop me into Lake Michigan. But why do it? Who can finish this deal better than me?"

"In other words, you're blackmailing them."

"Don't say that. It's just good business. Opening the loan for the other buildings gives me a breather. Besides, do you really think the boys at Chicago National are morons? Do you think they sit there with five billion dollars in assets and don't know what's going on? They know. But I assure you Vern Hanson isn't going to go up to his committee and say, 'Listen fellas, Kane is running out of dough.' Maybe he blinks his eyes or turns his head when he sees these costs coming in, but he understands the problems. If he thought we were about to make a bad move—*bang*—we'd hear about it. He knows I'm right. Why the hell don't you?"

"How does Stone feel about this?"

"You can't fool an old pro. Stone knows I'm short of money. He's waiting to see what I do. If I don't work it out, he's ready to jump in and straighten it out himself. But in the meantime he doesn't interfere."

"OK, so you're going ahead. Where are you going to get the long-term money?"

"I'd like to get it from Fidelity Standard, but I still don't think the timing is right. If they suspect I'm in difficulty, they may start pestering the bank. And then the whole thing may go up for grabs."

"You really love to walk the tightrope."

"I hate it. But as far as I know, there's only one path for me and that happens to be on a tightrope."

"Of course, Norman, but you've been sick and you've never completely recovered."

"I wish I felt better, but I don't have any choice. Every time a big tenant comes along, I have to handle the deal. Every time a major decision has to be made, I've got to make it. There's no one else to do it."

"Where's your organization?"

Norman tapped his head. "Right up here. I've hired men. I've trusted men. I've given them responsibility. Once in a long while someone comes along who has the stuff, but generally those guys leave in a hurry and go out on their own. As for the rest, I've got plenty of loyal people, and some are even smart, but they haven't got the guts to make the key decisions. This business is an art, not a science. The scientists are the architects and the engineers, and they're half artists and half phonies anyway. The finance men think they are scientists, too, but they're only gamblers in black suits betting other people's money. It all comes down to guts and, unfortunately, one man's guts."

"It's more than guts, Norman. You've got ability, too."

"No, it all comes down to guts. I could take you around this country and introduce you to a dozen real-estate developers who are smarter than I am—men who know more about construction or more about leasing, but they couldn't handle Lake Shore Plaza." He tapped his stomach. "It's all right here. The ability to take it. Sometimes I got brave guts and sometimes I got scared guts, but I always got guts."

I realized that Norman was running on without saying very much. He was more garrulous than incisive. I began to suspect that he was running scared.

"Norman, I still wish you'd take off a few days. I don't think you're completely yourself, and I'm sure that if this project is to be a success, we're going to need one hundred per cent of Norman Kane. Stop kidding yourself. Rest for a few days. Get back your strength."

"I guess you don't listen to me, Eddie. I don't have time. If I walk out of here for a few days, the whole damn project might fall into Lake Michigan."

Each passing day made it more obvious that Lake Shore Plaza could not possibly be completed at a price anywhere close to the budget. Sophisticated real-estate men generally say that one should expect a construction project to exceed its estimated cost by from 5 to 10 per cent. Thus, the investors in such a project must be prepared to deal with excess costs of this magnitude. Unfortunately, a 10 per cent overage on a two hundred million dollar development means twenty million dollars.

Even so, had the nation's economy continued on a stable basis, Norman would probably have had no difficulty in meeting the leasing requirements and then restructuring his financing. But this was not to be. That spring the stock market suffered a severe drop. Norman's hopes to lease space melted away with the Dow-Jones averages. Fifteen or twenty major companies which had previously indicated serious interest in the project now advised Norman that, temporarily at least, they planned to mark time or to retrench.

Norman correctly surmised that the downtrend, though frightening, was a short-term one—but he was unable to convince anyone else that he was correct. Some tenants who had executed leases for space in the Plaza, but had not yet occupied it, sought to escape from their commitments. With the economy in an uncertain state, they were afraid to assume new and heavy fixed charges. Norman redoubled his efforts to complete construction of all leased space as quickly as possible. He could not afford to miss guaranteed occupancy dates and thus create defaults which would enable tenants to cancel their lease obligations.

Plaza One was totally enclosed now, a great bronze, glass and marble shaft piercing the sky. The electrical, plumbing and mechanical systems were in operation, and crews of carpenters were raising prefabricated partitions, dividing each floor into a maze of corridors and offices. Above, other men were fitting acoustical ceiling materials into a suspended metal grid, while electricians hung lighting fixtures, and sheet-metal workers adjusted ceiling diffusers and controls.

International Materials had begun to move personnel into the lower floors. The rest of their staff would follow later, moving upward with the building as each floor was completed.

Now the roads were even more congested than before, as a steady stream of materials, lighter than the steel and concrete, but much more bulky, flowed into the buildings. As other tenants occupied their space, the traffic would increase. Moving vans had already begun to arrive, carrying furniture, carpeting, draperies, files, typewriters, computers—all the paraphernalia of modern business.

The building elevators were now in operation, some used by the construction workers, others filled with tenants' property. Each day was beset with a new crisis.

It was perhaps inevitable that labor difficulties would multiply Norman's problems. His position grew ever more precarious as it became obvious that he would have great difficulty delivering the offices to tenants at the dates specified in their leases. The labor walkouts were short-lived, but the effect was to delay the construction schedule. Norman therefore felt compelled to authorize the contractors to work overtime to insure that the buildings would be ready for occupancy when promised. Of course, the overtime expense was substantial and added considerably to the costs.

Several times Vern Hanson called Norman into conference at the bank. At first, Hanson asked for little more than Norman's reassurance that he would keep his commitments. While he did his best to allay the banker's fears, Norman offered no new enforceable promises. What his own fears were I cannot say, for at times like this—when his projects seemed in dire straits—Norman, typically, exuded the greatest confidence. But now the stakes were higher than ever, and it was not easy to sell the Chicago National Bank with a smile, a quip and an optimistic schedule.

In addition, Norman's hopes to recast the mortgage commitment evaporated with the decrease in stock-market values. Fidelity Standard knew that Norman's leasing program had reached a standstill and that his construction schedule was lagging. Furthermore, they themselves were heavy investors in the stock market, and as their investment values decreased they assumed a new rigidity and conservatism. The atmosphere was hardly conducive to a discussion of liberalizing Norman's mortgage commitment.

While the Chicago National Bank reached the point of concern and Fidelity Standard assumed the posture of conservatism, the boys descended to sheer panic. Not a day went by without one or more of them calling Norman.

"For Christ's sake," Norman would say, "nothing's happened since yesterday. What the hell can I tell you? No, I know it's not only you. If it isn't you it's somebody else. You're all driving me out of my mind."

But nothing stopped the boys. They feared their funds were in jeopardy. Nor did they forget that their stock was pledged with General Stone and the Chicago National Bank.

Stone viewed the situation with apparent equanimity.

"I don't think it's because he wants to steal the project from us either," Norman said to me. "I really think the son of a bitch is smart enough to realize we got a hell of a good deal here. If we're patient, we'll work it out."

"Mervin Stone has patience, Norman. Time and money and patience."

"Eddie, let's face it. This guy wasn't born rich. He must be able to recognize a good deal. We're doing fine. OK, so we've had a few setbacks. They're temporary. In the long run this deal can only get better."

"What about the short run?"

"Murder. I've been scrambling all over the country. I've lost pretty nearly every prospect we had. One thing I've learned down through the years: when you have to sell this hard, it's better not to sell at all."

"What does Stone say to that?"

"He encourages me. 'Take it easy, Norman,' he tells me. 'Don't go running off in all directions. You'll work this thing out if you take your time.' "

"I don't know, Norman. I think he's lying in the weeds—waiting."

———————◆———————

The lag in leasing dragged through the spring, into the summer and early fall. Even after the labor troubles were settled, construction did not proceed as rapidly as it should have. Norman always said that overtime was intrinsically dangerous because it often led to demoralization of the crews. When you cut off the overtime the men were resentful; they had learned to expect the additional pay.

In September the stock market began to edge cautiously upward. "I knew it wouldn't last," Norman said. "Those jerks who talk about the market 'bottoming out' don't know what it's all about. You'll see. Sales will shoot up and productivity will increase. This country isn't in any trouble."

Thus encouraged, he began to intensify his leasing program. There was still resistance but it was clear that potential space buyers felt renewed optimism and that, with patience, Norman would convert many of the prospects into customers. Somehow the tempo of construction picked up again, too, and as the months passed, one tenant after another occupied its space and began to pay rent.

All six towers were under way, two of them nearly completed. The parking areas beneath the buildings were made available to workmen and tenants, and the road network linking the Plaza to Lake Shore Drive was paved and opened to traffic. Gradually, Friedrichs' dramatic site plan was coming to life.

Norman's project was now famous from coast to coast and even overseas. Major newspapers carried photographs of the six towers. Two national magazines interviewed Norman and printed the story of his new project. Of course the reporters and columnists were unaware of his financial problems. They could not see beyond the six huge buildings growing along the lake front. To them, these graceful towers were the limits of Kane's world.

Some of the articles were planted. Soon after the construction began, General Stone had assigned Don Freeman, a leading public-relations man, to Norman for the purpose of publicizing Lake Shore Plaza.

At first, Norman simply enjoyed all the attention. Every few days he would send me a clipping from one publication or another along with a scribbled note stating that this "exposure" (a word he learned from Freeman) was bound to be good for the project. I don't think he really believed it until he was contacted by several major prospective tenants who had learned of his venture from a magazine article. Norman was delighted. Being a national figure was not merely fun—it was good business.

In early November, at a press conference called by General Stone's man, Norman fainted dead away in the middle of a sentence. Not until I read about it on the front page of the *Daily News* that evening did I learn that Norman was ill. According to the story, he had suffered a heart attack. Even as I sat at my desk, stunned by this new calamity, the phone rang. The caller was Don Freeman, the General's publicist.

"Christ," he said. "That was a close one."

"What do you mean, a close one? How is Norman Kane?"

"Oh, he's OK."

"OK? I thought they took him to the hospital."

"Yeah, but it isn't what they thought."

"What did they think?"

"Heart attack."

"Well, what is it?"

"They're not sure, but it isn't a heart attack."

"What do you want from me?"

"The press wants a statement. I asked Mrs. Kane to say something but she wouldn't, and of course General Stone don't want any part of this. I thought maybe you'd say something."

"Say something? What could I say? I didn't know anything until I read the paper."

"Yeah. That was lousy timing."

"What was lousy timing?"

"Kane fainting dead away with all those reporters watching."

"Boy, you've sure got a weird conception of timing. Listen, Freeman, I'm not giving a statement. You find somebody else." I started to hang up. "Say, just a minute," I said, "where is Kane?"

"Michael Reese Hospital."

"Can I see him?"

"How should I know?"

I was about to shout an obscenity, but thought better of it. I simply dropped the phone onto its cradle.

Norman Kane had infectious hepatitis. Dr. Franklin explained that he had never completely recovered from his bout with pneumonia, which made him an easy mark for this dismal disease. His case was particularly severe. It would be many weeks before he could return to work. Although Dr. Franklin did not consider his case critical, Norman would require constant attention.

I was shocked by the course of events. I had watched Norman Kane march from one triumph to another, conquering what often seemed overwhelming odds. Though not a large man, he was rather muscular and had always enjoyed robust health. Now, suddenly, pneumonia and hepatitis had struck successive blows. At the moment when Norman most needed his strength, he was lying flat on his back, unable to control his fate.

I remembered Norman's previous illness all too clearly. The architects and engineers had plunged ahead, making decisions that had cost the project millions. General Stone had proved ineffectual, or at best indecisive. The boys had merely wrung their hands.

It seemed that delaying tactics were called for. Surely the men at Chicago National Bank would be disturbed by Norman's current illness. I decided to talk to Vern Hanson at once.

"The important thing, Vern, is for you to sit tight."

"Impossible. Everybody around here is screaming. They want us to take action to protect ourselves and the quicker the better."

"It doesn't make sense to act hastily. It won't be long before Norman is up and about, and then he's sure to work out every problem."

"Frankly, my committee has written Norman off. To them, he's as good as dead."

"That's ridiculous, Vern. All he has is hepatitis. He'll be back at work soon, better than ever."

"My committee thinks we should take over the project, finish it as best we can and sell it to Fidelity Standard."

"Impossible. You're not equipped to do it. You take over now and the whole deal will collapse. The bank will lose millions."

"Then what should we do?"

"I know it sounds childish, but you're better off stalling. A few weeks could make a hell of a lot of difference."

"Maybe you're right, Eddie. But I've got to take some action—and right now."

"OK. You still have to follow the regular procedure. I checked the agreements myself. If you don't mind my suggestion, I think you ought to apply Article Fifteen of the construction loan agreement and make a straight request for additional cash or collateral. Under Article Fifteen, when the statements show that our costs exceed the budget, the bank has the right to withhold further advances until the owners cover the shortage."

"I know all about Article Fifteen, Eddie. What good will that do us?"

"Well, in the first place, you can spend a few days preparing your notice, which will give us a little time. You'll be able to show your associates that you're taking some kind of action, and you'll establish a default for the benefit of your legal department. We'll reply to your request for collateral, although it's obvious we don't intend to put any up now. Anyway, you will have protected your rights, and no one at the bank can complain you're not following through in accordance with the terms of the agreement."

"You have a point. Following the procedures will take some time, and at least I'll stick to the formalities."

"Vern, as I understand it, we're not due to make a payout for almost thirty days. Even then we should be able to stall the contractors for another two weeks without alarming them. Maybe by that time we'll have a solution."

"You mean maybe you'll be able to talk to Norman."

"That's it."

"You know, Eddie, I'm not sure even Norman can work his way out of this one."

Frieda responded to this new crisis with amazing strength. The last time, she had reacted with surprise, followed by fear, and then had made an anguished attempt to slow him down. Now she seemed to realize that her tactics had been a failure. She did not intend to repeat the mistake.

She called me occasionally, always apologizing for each call, and then questioning me as to the status of Norman's affairs. She seemed to know a great deal more about Norman's business than I had realized—perhaps even more than Norman realized, particularly since he had done so little to enlighten her.

I explained things as best I could. Our conversations were rather odd. Frieda talked to me as if I were operating Norman's business. She never said this directly, but the inference was obvious. When I thought about it, I viewed her attitude with mixed emotions. I was flattered that she trusted me— even more flattered that she thought I could manage so vast an undertaking. At the same time, her assumptions were unsound. I had neither the intention nor the desire to run Norman's business, let alone the knowledge and skill. I should have said, "Look, I'm just Norman's lawyer. I do what I can, but I'm no businessman. I can't run this show."

I never said it. I let Frieda cherish whatever illusions she held. I told myself it couldn't hurt to have her think everything was under control. What was the harm? I did not follow that thought any further.

As a practical matter, I was dealing in hope. I had no program. My one goal was to hold on as long as possible. I believed that with so many people holding a substantial stake in this project, eventually someone was bound to find a workable solution.

But nobody did, and gradually, by a process I had not anticipated, I found myself assuming greater and greater responsibilities. As time passed, more of the problems of Kane Enterprises were directed toward me. Perhaps I could have avoided this. I told myself I neither coveted nor enjoyed this role. Perhaps I could have persuaded General Stone to take over the administration of Lake Shore Plaza. However, I hoped Norman would be up and about at any time. I knew that Norman's assessment of my abilities as an entrepreneur was not very flattering, but I was sure he would rather have me handle his affairs than General Stone.

I admit that my own ego influenced my decision. I suppose I wanted to impress Frieda, too. Not that I wanted to be a hero, but I did hope to turn everything back to Norman in at least as good condition as he had left it. Still, these were secondary considerations. Primarily, I felt that I was the only person everyone else regarded as impartial.

I did not attempt to participate in the engineering or construction phases of the project. Friedrichs and the others carried out these duties quite acceptably. The leasing, unfortunately, was at a standstill. Norman had been dealing with several prospects when he was stricken. We maintained contact with these companies, but were unable to consummate the deals. I had no experience in dealing with major tenants—or even minor ones, for that matter.

I carried on a cat-and-mouse correspondence with the bank. In compliance with my suggestion, Vern Hanson sent us a notice of default. I replied by letter, stating that the costs to complete the project were estimates only, and that there was no certainty that the total allowance would be exceeded.

The bank replied with a twenty-page letter proving, at least to its satisfaction, that the costs would be substantially higher than the budget, and that therefore a default existed.

By then I knew the figures as well as the bank, but when I saw them aligned row after row on page after page, they looked ominous. I replied to the bank that the project was still under construction, that there were obligations to contractors, and that these could not be avoided. I stated that we would explore the possibilities of furnishing additional cash or collateral. Had I stated otherwise, the bank would have been forced to act. But I talked to Vern Hanson each time before I sent him a letter, and in some cases made changes based on his suggestions. Temporarily, at least, we kept the bank from taking any action.

Of course, the next request from the contractors for a payout might bring us up against a stone wall. In order to defer that crisis as long as possible, I called in the members of

Kane's construction organization, as well as White and Mc-Neill. I would have invited Friedrichs, but I was afraid the old man's arrogance might create additional problems for us. I explained to the architects, engineers and construction super-intendents that we had to hold off requests for another payout as long as possible. I asked them to inspect the contractors' work with greater care than ever before and to turn back any statements that were not in precisely the form required under the contracts. I said I did not expect anyone to invent defects, but if there were errors, this was no time to be lax.

I told the men to explain this new firmness to the contrac-tors in terms of the bank's concern over the project, not ours. I cautioned them to say only that the bank wanted to be cer-tain the building complied with the plans and specifications in every respect, so there would be no difficulty when the time came to disburse the permanent mortgage proceeds.

The men assured me that, without arousing the contrac-tors, they could probably delay the payout for two or three weeks, but this would be the outside limit. Thereafter, Car-relli would be in a serious financial bind and his subcontrac-tors would be clamoring for payment.

Perhaps my greatest surprise was that these men did not seem offended at having a lawyer instruct them in the niceties of dealing with contractors. But Kane's men understood; probably Kane had given them similar instructions during the construction of past projects. In any event, they accepted my orders without apparent resentment. Perhaps they hoped I would provide the "strong" hand to guide the venture while their leader was ill.

I talked to Dr. Franklin every day, but it was three weeks before he permitted me to talk to Norman. Even then, I was limited to a phone conversation. The doctor would permit Norman no visitors whatever.

The Norman Kane I spoke to on the phone was a new Nor-man Kane, and a frightening one.

"Hello, Eddie. How's the boy?"

"Just fine, Norman. How are you?"

"I've been better."

"Yes, I know, but Dr. Franklin tells me you're coming

242

along very well and that with proper rest and treatment you'll be up and about very soon."

"That's what he says."

"I'd like to come in and see you, but Dr. Franklin says I shouldn't do that for a while."

"No. It's not a good idea." There was a pause.

"Anything I can do for you, Norman?"

"Not much, pal."

"Well, I guess the most important thing is to take care of yourself and get well."

"Yeah." Pause. "Anything I can do for *you*, Eddie?"

"No, everything's fine, Norman."

"Good. If you need me, Eddie, you just call me."

"Sure, Norman, but everything's under control."

"Good." Pause.

"Well, I guess that's all for now, Norman. I don't want to talk too much and get you tired out. I'll call again in a couple of days. Just as soon as Dr. Franklin says it's all right."

"Sure, Eddie. Regards to everybody." And that was the end of our conversation.

I was frightened and bewildered. The Norman Kane I had last seen three weeks before knew very well how precarious his financial position was. Whether *this* Norman Kane did was unclear.

"I suppose I shouldn't be talking to you, Doctor, but I'm sure neither Frieda nor Norman would mind."

"Probably not."

"I have the responsibility of handling Norman's affairs while he's in the hospital, and therefore I'm quite concerned about his condition."

The doctor explained the symptoms and treatment for infectious hepatitis. Much of it was jargon to me, and all I learned was that Norman was very weak and very tired, and that he would require a long convalescence.

"What do you think the schedule is?"

"Depends on Mr. Kane. He's quite different from the man

who came in here before with pneumonia. He was darn sick, then, but he was fighting like hell to get back on his feet. Something about this hepatitis—whether it's physical or mental I don't know—has gotten him down. When he had pneumonia, it used to irritate me terribly to visit his apartment and watch him beat his brains out. However, I must admit I admired him. Other men as sick as Kane wouldn't have been able to do what he did. Now he doesn't display any of that determination. It's not too surprising. He's been hit with two pretty serious illnesses in a relatively short period of time."

"I'm sure this won't last, Doctor. I've known Norman Kane for thirty years. I've seen him down once or twice myself, but he always snaps back, and I'm sure he will this time, too."

———◆———

Two days later Dr. Franklin allowed me to visit Norman.

I had been given a shot of gamma globulin weeks before, when the doctor had first diagnosed his case. There seemed little danger, but I approached the meeting with some trepidation. I entered Norman's room prepared for the worst and found him looking a good deal better than I expected. As a matter of fact, it took me a little while to realize how sick he really was. Norman was sitting up in his bed, freshly combed and shaved. His face was ruddy, though still a little bit on the yellow side, and his eyes seemed clear.

He greeted me cheerfully, and for the first few minutes I was put off by his enthusiasm.

He looked at me sharply. "You thought they finally had old Norman flat on his can, didn't you? You walked in expecting to find me half dead, and here I am filled with pep and energy."

"OK, Norman, you're right. I was expecting the worst. I'm glad to see you looking so well."

"I'm not feeling so well. There's no use kidding you. I'm plenty weak but not so weak I can't think. Eddie, there's a lot of work to be done, and we'd better start doing it."

"Are you sure this is OK with Dr. Franklin?"

"Yes it is—and the hell with him anyway."

"But are you sure?"

"Goddamn it, I'm sure. If you wanna talk to him yourself, go ahead." He picked up the phone and handed it to me.

I shook my head. "Never mind, Norman. If you say it's OK —it's OK."

"Frieda tells me you're doing a great job keeping things going."

"Frieda told you that?"

"Yeah, she was really impressed. And Frieda don't get impressed very easily."

"That's very nice, Norman. I'm flattered. But really, I don't think Frieda actually knows what's been going on. All I did was talk to her over the phone a few times and try to reassure her."

"You sound like you're apologizing, buddy. You don't have to do that. Thanks for keeping her happy. I appreciate it."

Norman was still smiling. I couldn't determine whether he really meant what he said. I decided to change the subject.

"Listen, Norman, you've been out of touch for a while. Let me fill you in."

He waved his hand. "No need to. This morning I talked to the boys at the shop, to all our architectural buddies, to General Stone and Vern Hanson."

"You did?"

"Yeah, they all said you did a great job. A real take-charge guy."

"Wait a minute. I'm just your lawyer. That's all I want to be—and sometimes I don't even want that."

"Hold on, Eddie. I'm grateful. Really I am. Somebody had to do it, didn't they? Better you than Stone, right?"

"That's how I figured it." Somehow I sensed that was not the right response.

"Good. So let's get down to cases. We have to get the show on the road again. We're in plenty of trouble and we have to get out of it."

"Of course. What do you intend to do?"

"Well, I'm not quite sure. I want to review all the figures. There must be a way out of this mess."

He sounded optimistic, but it was all words. No plan of action. I took a deep breath before I spoke.

"Stop kidding me, Norman. You know what you have to do. You just won't face up to it."

The smile vanished. Norman looked at me warily. "What's that, friend? You tell me."

"Why the hell do you want to make me say it?"

Norman seemed to have lost his enthusiasm. He stared around the room as if searching for some escape from what he knew was inevitable.

"Yeah, you're right," he finally said. "I gotta cut the construction costs. And to do that, I gotta chop some things out of the project. I hate to do it, Eddie. You understand that. I've been dreaming of a deal like Lake Shore Plaza all my life. It was going to be perfect." He slammed his fist on the service table beside his bed. "Can you imagine a guy has two hundred million dollars to spend and he still can't have it just the way he wants it?"

For a moment I was silent.

"Norman, I'm sure you can figure how to cut the costs without really hurting the project. There must be places where you can save money where no one will notice."

"I'll notice. What matters is that I'll notice."

"Do you want the whole deal to go down the drain?"

Norman smiled suddenly. "Now you're talking like me. By God, Frieda was right." Then his expression changed. "OK. I'll do it. I hate to, but I'll do it. And I know just what to do. I've been lying here figuring it out for days."

He was sitting up straight now and talking rapidly.

I could feel a tremendous weight lifting from my shoulders. I should have realized Norman was terribly ill. But he made everything seem so easy and so right. Most important, it was such a relief.

"First, we're going to make a lot of changes in buildings four, five and six," Norman said. "Changes that don't show but will save us a lot of money and speed up the job. We're gonna redesign the air-conditioning system radically. I talked to White today and I feel we have learned enough from Plaza One and Two to know that we over-zoned the first three buildings. The savings in duct work, controls and equipment ought to be substantial.

"I talked to the elevator people, too. We don't need as much speed as we put in that equipment, and we're gonna leave out some of the signals and some controls. I've cut down on the cabs, too. If the interiors aren't as fancy as in the other three buildings, who gives a damn?

"Then I talked to Friedrichs and told him to omit the marble from the first floor vestibules. We'll use steel and formica and sculpture."

"Aren't the tenants going to complain?"

"The tenants don't have any right to complain. I never promised them any of those things. We're gonna leave out a lot of other junk, too. Things we can add after we rent the space. When I go back to Chicago National I'll show them our total cost is down four, maybe even five million dollars."

"That still leaves you millions of dollars in the hole."

"I know it, but I'm cutting what I can, where I can." He laughed. "Hell, I talked to the plumbing contractor this morning, and just by changing the valves on the toilets and buying cheaper dividers I can save a quarter of a million dollars."

"Are you sure you're not cutting out things you shouldn't?"

"Let me worry about that, Eddie. I only wish I'd done these things before. Those buildings were so beautiful, you know. So perfect."

"They'll still be beautiful, Norman."

"Yeah, sure. Anyway they'll meet the requirements of my mortgage commitment, and as far as the public can tell, they'll seem just as pretty as the other buildings. Look, we're in trouble. I'm not going down the drain for a pile of marble and plaster."

"When will you go back to Fidelity for more money?"

"When I have something to offer—something for their money. First I'm gonna make one or two more major leases— show them we're still active and we've got a hot market. Then I'm gonna come back at them with some kind of a new deal. A deal where they'll do even better than they expect."

"You mean you'll increase the interest rate?"

"I don't know what I'll do, but it's gotta be something. I have to make it worth their while. But first I gotta go out and make leases."

"Go out? You can't go out."

"All right, so I can't go out. Then I'll have those birds come in."

"Good, that's the right attitude."

"Yeah, I suppose I'm stuck here, at least for a while. I can't play that dark-corner-of-the-club bit any more. I'll just have to bring them here and do my best. Maybe I'll hire a makeup man and have him paint me healthy."

———◆———

Norman's improvement was remarkable. Even Dr. Franklin was surprised and pleased. "It's hard to believe," he told me. "Maybe Norman is sicker than he seems, but according to every test and every outward symptom, he's recovering far more rapidly than I expected."

"You're not going to let him out of the hospital?"

"No, I've convinced him he has to stay here. The pneumonia and the hepatitis frightened him. I think he's almost conquered that fear now, and some of his old energy and enthusiasm are returning. Nevertheless, I won't let him out until I'm absolutely certain he's recovered."

It was amazing how much Norman could accomplish from a hospital bed. Even Hobbs and Bennett came to see him, and he promised them he would deliver the loan to Fidelity Standard. He said he might need an extension, but that he would not ask for it until he could offer sound value in return. They were thankful for that.

It was not easy to put off the bank; their money was already on the line. Nevertheless, Norman prepared a revised estimate of the costs to complete buildings four, five and six, which he backed up with new proposals from the contractors. Norman's new figures indicated that even after allowing for the cuts he had made, the overall costs had increased fifteen million dollars above the budget.

"Norman," I said, "the bank may think it's less than that."

"That's what you think. Hanson sent me figures showing us in the hole thirty million dollars. First I'll show them it's only fifteen, and then I'll convince them I'm gonna cut the costs even more. But they gotta give me time to work it out."

I must have looked dubious.

"All right, Eddie. *You* I don't have to convince. But just for the sake of argument, pretend you're a banker at Chicago National. You think a deal is in the hole thirty million dollars. Then you find out it's only fifteen. You're still pretty unhappy, but you feel a hell of a lot better than when you thought it was thirty. That's what I'm gonna sell, Eddie."

He did. At least he sold them on giving him a ninety-day extension. However, twenty of those days had already passed, and Norman gained only seventy days. He accepted the extension, short as it was, expecting to ask for more time after he renegotiated the commitment with Fidelity Standard.

The only people Norman refused to talk to were the boys. "I can't take it, Eddie. I've got too much to do. I can't negotiate with those characters. You'll have to front for me. You tell them everything will be all right."

I did my best to mollify the boys. They were annoyed by Norman's refusal to see them, particularly since they knew that I was in almost daily contact with him. Lillis and Woodward weren't too difficult to handle. To Winsley I said, "You know this hepatitis thing. It's infectious, see? You want to get hepatitis?"

"Can you catch it over the phone?" he asked.

"Now cut it out, Winsley. Even though he's in the hospital, this poor guy is beating his brains out to make your deal successful. If you call him, the only thing you'll manage to do is annoy him. You want to make him even sicker?" Eventually I persuaded Winsley not to call Norman.

The leasing problem was more difficult to solve. Norman couldn't see prospects in person because of his illness. Despite his handicap, using only the telephone, Norman leased another hundred and fifty thousand square feet in less than two weeks.

"You see," he said. "Even from a hospital bed I can rent

space. Hell, you characters who've got your health, your brains and everything else can't do it face to face." Not until later did I learn that some of this space would be occupied by tenants Norman had moved from his own La Salle Street office buildings to Lake Shore Plaza. Ignorant of this, we were all impressed by the continued leasing progress.

Next, Norman asked Fidelity for an extension of time. He displayed his leases, backed up with a list of prospects for another three-quarters of a million square feet. Some of the list Norman invented; some of it was real. But he documented his presentation so meticulously that even I was thoroughly convinced of its authenticity. Once again Norman did most of the work by phone. After some negotiation, Fidelity agreed to give him an additional six months.

Unfortunately, this did not satisfy the Chicago National Bank. Vern Hanson came to see Norman in his hospital room a few days after Fidelity issued its new commitment. He looked tired and rather old.

"You don't look so good, Vern. Maybe you need a vacation like I'm getting right here."

The older man did not smile. "I'm going to retire, Norman."

"You're gonna what?"

"I'm going to retire. I have to quit anyway when I'm sixty-five, and I can do it voluntarily right now at sixty-two. I'd like to stay another three years—among other things, I'd like to see you get your project buttoned up and out of the bank. But they brought in another man. They hired some hotshot from a West Coast bank. I'm supposed to train him for three years. Well, you know what that means."

"No, really, Vern. I don't know."

"It means I'm a lame-duck officer. Everybody knows this guy is going to take over sooner or later, so why should they listen to me? I can already see what's happening. There's a change in everybody's attitude. The old man is on the way out."

"You're selling yourself a bill of goods, Vern. The only reason they're bringing this man in is because they finally realize your department has expanded so much that you need help."

"Yeah, that's what they told me."

"Of course. But you don't believe them."

"No."

"I don't understand you, Vern. When I first did business with you, you had one assistant and one secretary. You used to grumble because you had to do everything yourself. Now you've got a hundred men and God knows how many secretaries, but you're still crying. Maybe you *are* ready to retire."

Norman's needle failed to stir Vern Hanson. "Norman, there's no use kidding. I'm on the way out and everybody knows it. The man who's replacing me is too capable to sit around for three years and play errand boy. And God knows I won't be *his* errand boy."

Norman drummed his fingers on his blanket. "I won't tell you what to do, Vern. I certainly can't ask you to stay until this deal is finished, just to please me. Still, I think you ought to give yourself more time. If things get rough, you can always drop out."

"No, I'd rather quit now, before it gets rough. I don't want to limp out of there whimpering."

"You never whimpered in your life."

"That's right. And I'm not going to start. Only one thing bothers me, Norman. I don't want to leave you hanging high and dry. Right now you've got terrible problems."

"Why is that?"

"The bank's not satisfied with your new commitment."

"It gives me another six months."

"I know, but they're not satisfied."

"What do they want?"

"More collateral or more cash."

"You mean they want me to come up with fifteen million dollars?"

"No, I don't think they'll lean on you for the whole fifteen million just yet. But they expect a good part of it."

"How much?"

"Maybe half."

"Seven and a half million dollars? Ridiculous."

"How much can you come up with?"

"You want to know the truth?—not one thin dime."

"That's crazy. You don't have to come up with it all yourself. You have partners."

"You think the boys are gonna write million-dollar checks? You know better."

"Do they want to lose the deal?"

"Look. In a situation like this they sit tight and let old Norman Kane sweat."

"What about Stone?"

"You've seen our pledge agreements. If Stone comes up with the money, we're all screwed. You think we want to get screwed out of this deal for seven and a half million dollars when we've got twenty million in it already?"

"Norman, I don't understand. Surely you have other collateral you could pledge."

"Suppose I don't feel like doing it?"

"Then you're in trouble with the bank."

"Well, suppose I *can't* do it?"

"Then you're in trouble with the bank."

Norman's tone softened. "I'm not blaming you, Vern. I'm sure you want to help me. But I can't come up with seven and a half million bucks—at least not yet. Stall your pals, Vern."

"I can't stall them for very long."

The two men did not shake hands when Hanson left. After he was gone, Norman sagged deeper into the pillows.

———————◆———————

"I don't know what to do, Eddie."

"I don't know how to advise you. Would you really consider putting up additional collateral?"

"This has been a bad year. I've had to go deeper into hock than ever. We were in trouble in St. Louis. I never bothered you about that. It took a lot of money to bail out St. Louis— everything I got out of the Simmons Building—and then I had to pledge my equities in Newark and Los Angeles on top of it."

"Norman, you took eight million dollars out of the Simmons deal alone."

"Not eight—three. There was a five-million-dollar mortgage on that building and I had to pay it off before we tore it down. I only netted three million on the deal. I needed six in St. Louis, so I borrowed three more by using my Newark and Los Angeles equities as collateral."

I was too surprised to respond.

"Yes, it's fact, Eddie. But I'm not worried. Everything will be all right because now the income from St. Louis is free and clear and there's enough to pay off those Newark and Los Angeles notes at maturity. Still, it means that I'm tied up everywhere. I own other properties, but a lot of them are in trust for Frieda, and I wouldn't dip into those, even if I could."

"Can't you refinance some of your other real estate?"

"I don't know. Right now it's hard for me to find conventional sources of financing. I guess I made a mistake placing so many loans with Fidelity. I can't bring my other deals to them because they know I'm angling for Lake Shore Plaza. With other companies I just can't hope to move fast enough to make a deal within the sixty days I have left."

Norman shook his head, then suddenly smiled. "Wait a minute. Maybe the thing for me to do is try the banks—not here, but in New York. You know, there's always Jerry Davis. That son of a bitch has been pleading for some of my business for years. I hate brokers, but maybe this time a broker can help me. I wonder if he knows how much trouble I'm in? I bet I can still snow that son of a bitch."

Norman grabbed the telephone. "Jerry! You old so-and-so. How the hell are you? Yeah. I'm fine. Of course I'm fine. I had this damn hepatitis, but I'm over it. Look, I've got secretaries, partners, lawyers and accountants running in and out of here all day long. Hell, I'm working harder than I do at my office. How's the family? That's good. Mine too. Sure, I know you would've called. No, it was really nice of you not to call. Some of my friends keep me on the phone for hours over nothing." He winked at me.

"Say, I was just thinking about you. Yeah. For years you've been asking me to let you turn a trick. Uh huh. I'm glad to hear that. Well, here's what I want. I want to place a bank loan, but not in Chicago. Sure. Why not? That's a hell of a bank. Yeah, I know him. Of course I could talk to him myself, but they won't let me travel for a few weeks. I think face to face is better, don't you?

"Five million. That's right, Jerry, five million dollars. But only for a year. Oh, I know this isn't much of a deal. You can't make a lot of money on it. But at least we start working together, right? We start with something small—" Norman winked again—"and then we go on to a big one. That's right. I tell my partners Jerry Davis turned the trick.

"Collateral? Who the hell needs collateral? I'll give you a financial statement showing a net worth that'll make your eyes boggle. Kane Enterprises will sign it. Yeah, Kane Enterprises, Incorporated. Call Eddie Ellison for the papers. By God, if we can't borrow five million on our statement, we ought to get out of business.

"I don't know. What's the market? OK. Seven. It ought to be six and a half, but seven is all right. Now if you've got any doubts, fella, just say so. OK? Fine. Go to it, buddy. Yeah. Nice talking to you. Regards at home." Norman slammed down the phone.

"Well, five million ought to hold Chicago National for at least a little while."

"You mean you're going to put it all up yourself?"

"I'll take notes from the partnership. What the hell is the difference? It's only twelve months. I'll bet you Davis delivers, the crazy little bastard."

———◆———

We sat in a white leather booth far back in a corner of the main dining room of Norman's club. It was the height of the lunch hour and the room was crowded, but even the mass of people and the babble of voices did not shatter the impression of elegance. High, ornate ceilings, antique mirrored columns, deep carpets, fine tableware. Uniformed captains glided up to our table from time to time. It was clear Norman was one of their favorites. They were vying to serve him, but he waved them all away irritably. Norman should have stayed in the hospital, but neither Dr. Franklin nor I could restrain him. So there we were.

"The son of a bitch is late. The son of a bitch is always late."

"If he's always late, what's bothering you?"

"I've known him for years. I've eaten lunch with him a thousand times, we've gone to a thousand shows and five thousand functions together, and that son of a bitch is always late."

I decided not to reply.

"Can you understand a guy who's always late? Is he trying to insult you? Is he careless? What is it?"

"Norman, you're awfully irritable. When Davis gets here you'll be so worked up you'll punch him in the jaw."

"Yeah, I might. For ten years I've thought of punching him in the jaw."

"Well, I think this is a poor place for it. Of course, I still don't understand why you came here."

"The son of a bitch loves it here. For ten years he's been telling me how he loves my club. For ten years he keeps saying, 'I should be a member, Norman, I love the place.' And you know, he's never joined. I used to send him an application every six months, but he never sent it in."

"Why?"

Norman laughed harshly. "Why? Why? Because if he belonged to the club he could sign the checks, and that cheap son of a bitch never picks up a check."

"Not in ten years?"

"Well, almost. Maybe one out of five. No, I take that back. One in ten. If he bought my lunch every day for the next ten years, I still wouldn't be even."

"But you keep taking him to lunch, Norman. Why do you do it?"

He shook his head, stuck the end of his spoon into the tines of his fork and jammed them together. "I can't figure it out. There's something about him, you know. He's so engaging. He's so friendly. No, I've just been a mooch for this bird for ten years. But today, I'm mad."

"Look, maybe you should have punched him in the jaw ten years ago. But today's not the day. You need him."

Norman disengaged his silverware. He broke a roll, buttered it, then put it down on his plate. Then, as if he had forgotten the first roll, he broke another one, buttered it and set it on his plate. He looked at the two rolls in surprise.

"I suppose you're right. God, how I need his help. What a joke. I never thought the day would come I'd need a favor from Jerry Davis."

"I don't see why you decided to rely on him anyway, Norman."

"Rely, hell. Just try. That's all I'm doing. I've exhausted every other source. Jerry always says to me, 'Give me a piece of the action, Norman. Let me work on your deals. I'll make terrific loans for you, believe me,' He's told me that for ten years. For ten years I've turned him down. I didn't need him, see? I didn't want the favor, see?"

He shook his head and shoved the spoon into the fork again. "Besides, I didn't believe he could do it. All these years I heard he was a hell of a mortgage broker, but I didn't believe it. I suppose he knows his business. He built his firm up from nothing. But I aways figured I knew more than he did. God, to think I'd ever have to ask him for a favor. I'm twenty thousand lunches up on him, and now I need a favor. If I paid him a hundred-thousand-dollar fee and deducted the lunches, I wouldn't owe him a dime."

I tried to laugh, but all I could manage was a smile. Now I understood that Norman was afraid. Only fear could have induced him to deal with Jerry Davis. Otherwise he would have called the New York banker himself.

Another waiter edged up to our table, and this time Norman ordered a drink. It was his third, and Norman never had three drinks at lunch.

"Why did you invite me, Norman?"

"You've got to settle me down, Eddie—hold me in line. This guy may come in with some screwy offer, and by God, I've got to swallow it."

"Seems to me the whole trouble is your ego. If Davis gets you five million dollars, what do you care how he does it? For ten years you've been telling yourself he hasn't got it, and now maybe he's going to deliver and you can't stand it."

"Maybe."

Norman picked up one of the rolls and took a bite, crinkled his nose in displeasure, and set it down again. "God," he said.

"They never have fresh rolls here." He pushed the plate away in anger. His movement was so violent that the rolls bounced off the plate and onto the floor. A busboy picked them up. He smiled at Norman. Norman did not even notice him.

We kept looking at the door. The two of us sat in the booth and waited for nearly an hour.

Then we saw him. He was impossible to miss. There was something about Jerry Davis. I suppose part of it was his tall, wavy-haired good looks—his bright, straight teeth and flashing eyes. Then I realized with a start that most of his hair was gone now, yet he still looked wavy-haired and bright-eyed. As much as anything, the illusion was due to his walk. Davis had a cocky stride, bouncing on the toes and bouncing on the heels. It was almost a waggle, not quite a waddle. But he carried it off with such energy and enthusiasm that it wasn't ludicrous.

"There he is now, the son of a bitch," Norman said, "Smiling and bouncing along like it was the happiest day of his life, and here I am, dying."

Davis picked his way through the tables, nodding to friends here and there, stopping to shake hands. His face was creased with his own special closed-mouthed, dimpled smile. His eyes flashed and his invisible wavy hair ducked and bobbed.

At first he did not see us. Then a captain pointed to our booth and Davis turned his bright, cheerful eyes on us.

"Norman, buddy," he said. "How the hell are you? You're looking terrific." He shook Norman's hand vigorously, then turned to me. "Eddie. Didn't know you'd be here. How yuh been, buddy? How yuh doin'?"

"Fine, Jerry, and of course it's easy to see you're doing fine, too."

"Yeah, that's right," he said. "Jerry's doin' fine." He slid into his seat as we backed into ours. Almost in the same motion he turned his head. "Where's that captain? Say, Tony," he called. Norman shook his head and mumbled under his breath, "Always the same. Just like he owned the place. They all know him."

Tony came over to the table. "Yes, Mr. Davis?"

"Tony, I'm parched. Get me a drink, will yuh? The usual."

"Yes, Mr. Davis. Be right back."

Again Davis turned on his smile. "You know *me,* boys. Can't think without a martini."

"Doesn't stop you from talking, though," Norman said.

Davis laughed good-naturedly. "Nope. Nothin' stops me from talking. If I ever stopped talking I'd go broke. Well, fellas, how's everything?"

Norman started to speak, but Davis broke in. "Say, Norman. I meant to ask you something. You see that article in *The New York Times* on Sunday? They're bringing over a group of paintings by that Dutch painter, Piet van der Lin, for an exhibit in the Albert Gallery on Fifty-seventh Street next month. Don't you own one of van der Lin's paintings?"

"Yeah, that's right."

"By God, you must have owned it for ten years now. I'll bet it's worth a fortune."

"I suppose so," said Norman.

Davis turned to me. "This guy's amazing. He's got an eye for art like no one I've ever met. He buys paintings when these guys are nobodies. Suddenly everybody discovers them and there's old Norman Kane with a wall full of masterpieces. Are you going East for the show, Norman?"

"No, I haven't the time."

"Did they ask for your painting?"

"Yes, but I turned them down."

"I don't understand."

"I don't do that sort of thing any more. What the hell do you care if I turned them down?"

"For heaven's sake, don't get mad. I just thought you'd be proud to have an early van der Lin in that exhibit, since you were smart enough to recognize his talent long before anyone else."

Norman was silent, but nothing stopped Davis. "Gee, I'm sorry to hear that. You know, I'm going East myself and I thought maybe if you were going we might spend a few days together. Gosh, you and I haven't taken a trip to New York for years. You sure you're not going, Norman?"

"I'm sure."

"Too bad. I was going to suggest we take the girls and make a holiday out of it."

"I'm in no mood for holidays!"

"That's not like you, Norman. By God, I think you're finally getting old."

At that Norman's face purpled slightly. He began to speak, but Tony came rushing up with a drink, and Davis raised his hands and said, "Before you shoot me, Norman, let me have my drink." Norman sat tense and flushed while Jerry Davis worked on his martini.

"You know, there's something about this place. I don't know what they put in these martinis. I can't figure out how they make them taste like this. A guy told me it's because they chill the glasses and mix the drinks in chilled containers without using a lot of ice, but I tried it at home myself and it doesn't work."

Norman was getting angrier and angrier.

To head him off, I spoke to Jerry Davis. "I think we came here to talk business."

Davis looked at me wide-eyed. "You too? I think you're both getting a little creaky. No, old Jerry ain't gonna talk business until you put some food in him. Come on, let's get Tony and order lunch."

Somehow Norman managed to restrain himself. We sat quietly while Jerry Davis cheerfully ordered himself the equivalent of a full dinner at Maxim's. Norman and I ordered sandwiches, but nothing seemed to faze Davis. He bubbled on about the art show in New York and the trip he planned. Then he told us that he would probably travel from New York to Rome. It was supposed to be business, he confided, but actually it was all pleasure.

Our meal was served, and while we ate, Davis talked on and on. Once in a while he extracted a grudging comment from Norman or from me, but he did most of the talking himself. Once or twice he asked a question, and while Norman tried to answer it, he went right on talking.

I could not eat my sandwich and Norman only picked at his.

Two drinks, six courses, three cups of coffee and a cordial

later, Jerry Davis pushed himself back from the table. "Like I always say, Norman, they really know how to serve food in this joint. By God, I don't know why I don't join this club."

"Oh, for Christ's sake, Jerry, for ten years you've been saying that." But Norman's voice was almost a whisper.

"Well, I'm serious. By God, I must still have one of those applications you've sent me. This time I'm going to fill it out."

"That's fine," I said. "I look forward to having a lunch on you some day, Jerry. But in the meantime, what about our business?"

"Yes," said Norman. "What happened with the loan?"

Davis' smile did not leave his face. "I went to the First Manhattan Bank and sat down with old Harry Dunsten. I told him the setup and gave him the facts. Laid the whole package right in front of him."

"Well?" said Norman.

"Well," said Jerry. "I turned the son of a bitch down."

For a moment Norman was speechless. "You what?"

"I turned him down. That goddamn Harry Dunsten is getting senile. He hasn't got the slightest idea how to make a deal."

"Now, just a minute, Jerry. Just a minute. What do you mean, you turned him down?"

"You told me to go out and get you five million bucks, right?"

"Right."

"And you told me Kane Enterprises would sign the note?"

"That's right."

"Well, that's what I offered Harry Dunsten. And you know what he wanted?"

"No."

"He wanted seven and one-half per cent interest, a five per cent discount and your personal guarantee. Can you imagine that? From a man like you? A five per cent discount and a personal guarantee?"

"What did you do, Jerry? Come on now, tell me what you did."

"I told the son of a bitch to shove the loan up his ass."

"You what?"

"I told the son of a bitch to go shove his loan."

Norman's voice burst from him in a strangled shout. "You're out of your mind." His voice was so loud that heads turned at several adjacent tables.

"Quiet, Norman," I said. "For heaven's sake, hold it down."

"You're out of your mind, Jerry. You turned him down?"

"Of course I turned him down. I knew you wouldn't take a crazy loan like that. I would have been too embarrassed to bring it back to you. You'd think I flipped my lid."

"Look, Jerry," said Norman, his voice cracking, "you didn't really turn him down?"

Davis looked bewildered. "Why, of course I did, Norman."

"Now goddamn it, you get on the phone and call Harry Dunsten and you tell him I'll take the loan."

"You'll take it?" Davis looked confused. "What do you mean you'll take it?"

"Listen, Jerry, listen close to what I'm saying. I'll get a phone over here. You call Dunsten and tell him I'll take the loan."

Davis stared at him. "I can't do that. The man pretty nearly threw me out. He'd never make the loan now."

"I got to have that loan, Jerry."

"You can't get it, Norman. I never dreamed you'd want it. I don't believe you. You're putting me on, Norman. Aren't you putting me on?"

"You son of a bitch. You miserable, filthy, mealymouthed, stupid son of a bitch. You ruined me. How could you turn down the deal? Did you ask me? How did you know what I'd take or what I wouldn't take?" He leaned across the table glaring at Davis, who sat staring back at him in fascination. "I'd take that loan. I'd take it at seven and one-half per cent and I'd take it at ten. I'd pay ten points. I'd take it on any terms. I need five million bucks, Jerry, and I need it fast. Now pick up that phone and get it for me. Do you hear me? Get it?"

"It's too late. I couldn't do it. I assure you the deal is dead."

Norman leaned back, almost shrinking into the uphol-stered booth. His head dropped between his shoulders. I thought that he would not speak again, but his voice drifted up from somewhere deep in his chest.

"You fink. You miserable rotten fink. For ten years you've played my friend. For ten years you've drunk my liquor, eaten my food and played with the broads I got you. And now for once I give you a deal—one stinking, lousy, rotten deal. But a deal I had to have. And what do you do? You blow it. Oh, yeah, you're a hero. A big hero. You put the First Manhattan Bank in its place. You put down Harry Dunsten. I've watched you for years. I've watched that goddamn arrogant walk of yours, listened to your stupid stories and laughed at your moronic jokes. I've talked about art and music with you as if you knew what it was all about. You have no taste. You never had any. You don't understand anything. But I talked to you, Jerry. I was your friend and I liked you. Despite your cheap, sniveling ways, I liked you."

Davis leaned forward as if to speak. Now his face, too, was turning purple, and his eyes roamed the room from side to side as if he were fearful that Norman could be overheard.

"Don't say anything, Jerry. Don't say a goddamn word. A guy who's got a friend like you don't need any enemies. You ruined me, you bastard. You just ruined me. Now I'll tell you what you do, you cheap son of a bitch. You get up right now and turn around and walk out. I'll pay the check like I have for ten years, and that won't bother me at all. No sir. I don't mind. I always knew you were no good, but this is the last check, buddy, the very last. Straighten your collar and pull down your jacket, and get the hell out of here."

I didn't know what to say. Davis sat looking at Norman for a moment. His smile was gone. His color was gone. As I watched him, his face shrank. I could no longer see the wavy hair flopping across his forehead. Slowly he pushed back his chair and stood up. Then he straightened his tie and pulled down his suit jacket, as Norman had said. He began to turn away, but then he came back. And when he looked down, there was a trace of the same old smile on his face.

"You said your piece, Norman. Now shut up, stay where you are, and let me tell you something. I didn't ruin you. You ruined yourself. You put yourself in the hands of General

Stone. You put yourself and everything you've got right in the pocket of that crafty bastard. You think you're smart enough to dig a hole in his pocket and drop right out, but you'll never do it."

Norman started to stand up.

Davis shoved him down into the booth. "I said stay there and I mean it. Now get this, and get it clearly. Oh, yes, I went to the First Manhattan Bank. Sure. And I talked to Harry Dunsten. Yeah. I offered him your loan. I offered him your statement. But I'll tell you a secret. He wouldn't take the deal. Not even for eight per cent. Not for five points or ten. He didn't want your loan. He told me I was a damn fool for bringing it to him. But I spent the whole day there, Norman, and I came back the next day. I tried to make a deal for you—I tried to figure out every angle there was. In the beginning they laughed at me. By the time I left, they were mad. You didn't lose a thing, Norman. You couldn't borrow money at that bank if you wanted to. I didn't mean to tell you that, old buddy. I didn't mean to at all. I decided to tell you they asked for ridiculous terms and that I turned them down. I wanted to give you an easy out. I didn't want to tell you they think you're finished. But that's what they think, Norman. And after what you said to me, I think so too. You're writing me off, buddy? It's too late. You can't write me off because there ain't any ink in your pen."

Davis straightened suddenly. "Nice to see you, Eddie. Good luck. You've got yourself a real charming client." Again he pulled down his suit jacket, turned and started out of the dining room. For a moment he walked a bit stoop-shouldered, but then he began to waggle, and there was that cocky step again, the little bounce from head to toe. Davis stopped at tables here and there to shake hands. When he looked around, I could see that invisible wave bouncing on his forehead.

———◆———

Frieda called me at my office.

"I'm sorry to bother you, Eddie. I called your home and

263

your wife told me you were working late this evening. I don't think she wanted me to disturb you."

"That's all right, Frieda. Why are you calling?"

"It's Norman. I haven't heard from him since early this morning. I called Dr. Franklin, and he said Norman left the hospital without his permission. Norman told him he wouldn't be back tonight."

"I don't think that's anything to worry about. Norman obviously has an appointment somewhere. He probably intends to come home tonight."

"I don't think so. He told Dr. Franklin he was going out of town. He didn't say where."

"How can I help you?"

"Do you know where he went?"

"No."

"Is there any trouble, Eddie?"

I hesitated. "The usual problems. Long on projects and short on money."

"Did you talk to him today?"

"I had lunch with him. There was some unpleasantness with Jerry Davis. But Norman is accustomed to that."

"Eddie, you're covering for him."

"Don't be silly, Frieda. I'm not covering anything. I haven't the slightest idea where Norman is or what he's doing."

My voice sounded very loud to me in the silent office. Frieda's response was a long time coming.

"I'm sorry to have disturbed you, Eddie." Her voice was very low. "Thanks, anyway."

"Wait a minute, Frieda. Look, I'm worried about Norman, too. I'm sure he'll be all right, but I do wish we knew where to find him. I'll be down here a while yet. If you hear from him, please call me. All right?"

"All right," Frieda said, still subdued, and then hung up.

I sat there for quite a while, thinking. *I don't want to get involved,* I kept telling myself. *I just don't want to get involved.*

I tried to work but I couldn't. I decided I would call Frieda back in an hour, but the time passed very slowly. Only thirty minutes had gone by when I dialed her number. "Have you heard from him?"

"No. I'm really worried." Her voice sounded rather child-like. "Eddie, would you do me a favor? I have a feeling Norman went to New York. I'd like to try and locate him there. Would you come over and place the calls? I'm too embarrassed to do it myself—calling hotels and asking for my husband. It would be different if a man called."

"It's rather late, Frieda."

"I know. I really shouldn't ask you. You've done enough." There was no hint of challenge in her voice, but I felt one nonetheless. "All right, Frieda. I'll be there in twenty minutes."

"Oh thank you, Eddie. You're a doll."

I sat there thinking, *I'm a doll.* Just great. My client's wife says I'm a doll. What an accolade. What the hell am I getting into?

Frieda answered my knock. She was wearing a robe, long with full sleeves, buttoned to the throat and belted at the waist. Her hair was down, loose and unarranged. She wore no makeup. Her face was pale, her eyes were bright. She was beautiful. For a moment, I thought of turning on my heel and running.

"Eddie, have you heard from Norman?"

"No, Frieda. And you?"

She shook her head. The long blond hair swung across her face. She looked helpless. I felt quite the same.

"Come in, Eddie." Reluctantly, yet with a vague sense of anticipation, I followed her inside.

"Here, I've listed the hotels where Norman usually stays. I've got the phone numbers, too. Please start calling."

"You know, Frieda, he may be out somewhere meeting somebody."

"It's eleven P.M. here—twelve midnight in New York. I doubt he would be out doing business this late. And he must be tired now. Very tired. I'm sure he's in a hotel."

I began by calling the Plaza—Norman's favorite. He wasn't registered. I had him paged anyway, but there was no response. Then I tried the St. Regis, another favorite. While I was calling, Frieda brought me a cognac, then poured one for herself. It looked to me as though it was not her first. Norman was not at the St. Regis. Frieda began to pace the room. Perhaps she had picked that up from Norman. Anyway, it made me nervous. At first, when Frieda had called, I thought she was unduly alarmed. Now I was beginning to wonder.

I tried the Pierre and the Regency. Same answer. No Norman Kane. Frieda lit a fresh cigarette each time I placed a call. She refilled her glass and mine. She was drinking much too fast for cognac, and I told her so. To no avail.

Then I remembered I had not called home. Ellie would have no idea where I was. I began to dial my own number, then hesitated. How would Ellie react to the news that I was taking care of Norman's wife?

"What is it, Eddie?"

"Nothing."

"Calling home?"

"No."

Frieda smiled for the first time since I had arrived. "Afraid to tell her where you are?"

I nodded. Frieda came over and touched my face gently. Her long blond hair grazed my cheek. "You're very sweet, Eddie. You really are." Then she was moving away, pacing the floor again. I felt more than faintly ridiculous.

I picked up the phone and called Ellie. I didn't say much—just told her where I was and what I was doing. I hung up as quickly as I could. That would be tomorrow's battle.

I called every hotel I could think of—any place that Norman could possibly be. I wondered whether he was out with a woman. I didn't voice my thoughts to Frieda. Anyway, I didn't really believe Norman was with a woman. He was interested in money now, not babes.

"What are you thinking, Eddie?"

"Nothing, Frieda—well, something. I'm trying to think of other hotels."

A few came to mind and I called them. In an hour and a half I must have called twenty hotels, perhaps more. I was sure I had exhausted the list of hotels where Norman might be found.

"We've had this line tied up for a long time, Frieda. If Norman tried to call us, he couldn't get through."

"There's another phone in the den. If this line was busy, Norman could always call on the other. Keep trying, Eddie. We've got to find him."

There was a Manhattan Classified in Norman's den. I found a few other hotels whose names had escaped me. I called, but Norman was not registered anywhere. I began to realize it was hopeless. Plenty of brandy, cigarettes and Frieda. But no Norman Kane.

"We're just wasting our time, He's not in any New York hotel. He probably never left Chicago. Or maybe he's staying with a friend in New York. Maybe he's on the way home—on a plane—right now. Anyway, there's no use calling again and again. I'm down to the fleabags—second-rate hotels. Norman would never stay at any of these places, not if he were dying." It was a stupid thing to say, but I was tired and the cognac was getting to me.

"Frieda, Norman can take care of himself. I think I better be going home."

She almost ran to me. "Please, Eddie. Don't leave me alone. Stay here with me till Norman calls—or until he comes home."

She took my arm and gently eased me back onto the couch. "Here," she said, "I'll refill your glass."

I didn't want the cognac, but I took it. Frieda sat down beside me and offered a pathetic imitation of a smile. She tipped her glass against mine and drank. I did the same.

"He'll be all right, won't he, Eddie?"

"Of course. The phone will ring any minute. You'll see. Norman's fine."

She smiled at me, a lazy, curling smile. A sensual smile, although I doubt Frieda intended to be sensual. I attributed it to the liquor.

We sat together on the couch, sipping cognac. Now I was even smoking Frieda's cigarettes—and I seldom smoked. The minutes passed. The phone did not ring.

Frieda asked if I wanted to hear some music. I didn't know

what to say. She shrugged, turned on the phonograph, picked a record from the shelf and placed it on the turntable. It was something classical, something I didn't recognize. Norman's style.

The time passed, the record played out. Frieda replaced it with another, poured more cognac. The phone still did not ring.

I had taken off my suit jacket and loosened my tie. That wasn't like me. But hell, everything was out of whack, anyway.

Frieda was half sitting, half lying on the sofa, her head resting on the cushions. From time to time she sipped her drink.

"Have you any idea what it's like, Eddie?" She paused. Her words were slow and slurred. "To love somebody, to need him—and yet be shut out of his life?"

"Frieda, you're very tired. I think you ought to go to bed."

She wasn't listening. "I'm not the bird in the gilded cage. I'm outside, beating my wings to get in. Norman's in there, in that special golden world he's built for himself. He can get out—any time he wants to. But he won't let me in."

It was maudlin, of course. But probably true. Frieda's anguish was real. I didn't want to hear it. Didn't want to know how Norman handled—or was it manhandled?—his wife. In fact, I didn't want to hear about Norman at all. Still, I didn't seem to have any choice.

"It's always been like that, Eddie, since the beginning. I really wanted Norman—more than any man I ever met. It was strange. I thought I wanted someone pretty, like Charlie Clark. I took Charlie, but it wasn't any good. He wasn't a bad guy. Just weak. Norman was right about Charlie. He called him a gutless jerk. It always bothered Norman that I could fall for a man like Charlie Clark. It bothers me, too. A flaw in me somewhere." Frieda shook her head. "What I really needed was somebody strong." She laughed. "The first time I saw Norman, I almost laughed at him. He certainly wasn't pretty. I never imagined I could love anyone like that. I'm still surprised. I get into bed with him—"

"Frieda, please—"

"When he'll have me." She laughed again, then looked at

me. "Can you imagine? After all these years our lovemaking is still a battle. For Norman, a conquest. For me, submittal. Never to come together freely, without reservation. Always the unstated assertion of his superiority and my weakness. It's degrading, don't you think? Oh, yes, you do. You know it. It's degrading." She took a jolt of the cognac, coughed a bit and went on. I was horrified, but she didn't seem to notice.

"Always on the outside. Never sharing his life. Never."

She was crying softly, the tears running down her face. I felt terribly sorry for her, and something more. I wanted to take her in my arms. Comfort her, and something more. I pushed that something out of my mind. How had I gotten mixed up in this? I should never have come.

"I'm a fool," she said. "I should leave him. Leave him with his business, his paintings and his women. But I can't. I'm helpless. Don't you see?" She turned her tear-stained face toward me. She was close, very close. Her face was fuzzy and I was struggling to contain myself. I wanted to tell her she didn't have to put up with all this. She didn't need Norman. She could have anyone she wanted. Even—

The telephone rang. My head snapped back at the sound. I grabbed it.

"Hello." My voice came out hoarse and cracked.

"Who the hell is this?"

"Norman, is it you?"

"I said, who is it?"

"Me. Eddie."

Norman's voice thundered through the telephone. "Eddie? What the hell are you doing at my home?"

"Waiting for you, Norman. We were worried, Frieda and I. We called every hotel in New York trying to find you. Are you all right?"

"Of course I'm all right. Couldn't you call from your own office? Your own home?"

"Listen, Norman, don't shout at *me*. I just came here to help. You didn't tell anyone where you went. Dr. Franklin said you were out of town. We didn't know where. Tell me, where the hell are you?"

"The St. Regis."

"I called there. They said you weren't registered."

"I know. I was damn tired. I registered under another name so I could get some sleep before coming home." His voice changed tone. He was suddenly all business. "Eddie, set up an appointment tomorrow morning. The boys, Stone and Jerry Davis."

"Davis? He'll never talk to you again."

"I gotta see him. You get him to my office. I don't care how you do it. Just get him there."

"Hold it. Make it my office, Norman. I think he'll come. I won't tell him you're going to be there. I'll make up some excuse."

"Great. Just get him there."

"All right, Norman. What about you?"

"I'm coming back tonight. Plane leaves in an hour. Tell Frieda I'm coming home. Wait a minute, I'll tell her."

I handed the phone to Frieda.

Before she could say a word Norman was talking. I couldn't make out the words, but his tone was angry. Suddenly, Frieda was smiling—in control and smiling.

"No, he's been just wonderful. A wonderful friend, Norman. I don't know what I would have done without him."

There was another burst of angry sound from Norman's end of the line.

"Why, Norman," Frieda said sweetly, "that's positively ridiculous. But very flattering nonetheless. Have a good trip, dear. I'll wait up for you." She gently replaced the phone on the receiver.

Frieda was smiling at me. The tears were gone. Her eyes were shining with pleasure. "Isn't that incredible, Eddie? He suspects that you and I are having an affair."

I tried to share her laughter.

I didn't sleep very well that night. Ellie was waiting up for me, eager to express her own views on the Kane-Ellison-Kane triangle. I didn't hear half of what she said, but it didn't help me rest, either.

I left home early, before Ellie could start in on me again. For once I caught the 7:15 train into Chicago. I sat in one of the coaches, ignoring the other commuters, rocking with the roadbed and my disordered thoughts. When I reached my office, it was not yet 8:30. For the first time in many years, I had to use my own key to let myself in.

All was peaceful at Hardwick, Burns, Ellison and Dean. Very peaceful indeed. I wondered why I ever left those tranquil precincts.

I strolled along the corridor to my own office, savoring the solid, substantial look of it all. Nothing too old, nothing too new. Nothing too bright or too dull. The carpet soft underfoot, but not ankle-deep. The corridors wide, but straight. The nameplates on each door neat and discreetly sized. I pushed open the door to my office. Large, but not vast. Impressive, not ostentatious. Everything in geometric order. I began to relax.

For half an hour I did absolutely nothing. After a while I could hear the secretaries coming to work, putting away their coats and cosmetics, uncovering their typewriters, chattering a bit, but in hushed tones. Soon the associates, then the junior partners, then the senior partners would be arriving. Within minutes the whole organization would be humming—softly.

I realized I had not turned on the lights. It would not do to be found by my secretary sitting alone in the semidarkness. I opened the blinds and turned on the lights, then spread some papers about the desk for effect. I had destroyed the harmonious desk-top arrangement, but that was to be expected. My life was beginning to lose its clear, mathematical precision. Norman Kane, Lake Shore Plaza, Frieda.

The office sounds had a musical quality, almost like a hymn. I was a high priest of this hierarchical, semidevout society. Nevertheless, its creed had not always comforted me. Strength, stability and prestige were not always reassuring.

Once, a dozen years before, I had contemplated heresy: I proposed to abandon the faith of my father (who had also been a senior partner) and set out on my own. The thought had been exhilarating and not terribly dangerous at that. Many of the firm's clients would have followed me. Perhaps my income would have dropped for a while, but surely I was bright enough, and well enough connected to bring it up again. And I would be free. Free of this safe and solid but nonetheless cloying existence.

Eleanor talked me out of it. If she was shocked, she did not show it. Ellie merely enumerated the risks: loss of income, loss of prestige, loss of face. Particularly if I should fail. After all, how could I be absolutely certain that clients of long standing would leave the firm? Besides, the remaining partners would undoubtedly feel hostile, and they were men of substance, economically, politically, socially. Then, too, what would our friends think? If we had any left. And what would happen to the children? Would they still be able to attend the same private schools? Would they be wrenched away from the friends they cherished? Would we perhaps even have to give up our fine home? Give up membership in our club?

Ellie marshaled her arguments quietly but effectively. And in the end I was convinced. I remained among the faithful. And I prospered.

For a long time I hated myself for my capitulation. Eventually the feeling faded. Still, there was a lingering doubt. Perhaps Ellie was right. Very likely she had prevented me from undertaking a dangerous course of action. But if she had supported me, encouraged me, I might have done it.

I shook my head. It would not do to blame Eleanor for my own cowardice. But I could not help comparing her to Frieda Kane. Frieda had always encouraged Norman, no matter how wild his dreams, no matter what the risk to her own welfare. Even now, after two severe illnesses, her faith seemed unshaken. I would not have blamed her had she urged Norman to give up Lake Shore Plaza. She might easily have taken the position that his health was more important than his dreams. But she did not. Perhaps the idea crossed her mind, but she never voiced it. She seemed as certain as Norman that he would conquer all obstacles, ill health included, and go on to accomplish his objectives.

I realized *that* was what I admired most about Frieda Kane. True, she was a lovely and charming woman with a deep strain of sensuality—but more important, she had total faith in her husband.

All right then. The question was answered. I knew now what fascinated me about Frieda Kane. Having puzzled out the problem, could I let it rest? I would have to. I was Norman's lawyer and his friend, and there was work to be done.

Nine o'clock. Time to call Jerry Davis. I was brusque with him. I told him my firm needed his consultation on an important matter. I would tell him what it was when he arrived. I believe he was about to ask whether it involved Norman Kane, but I didn't give him a chance. I told him to come at 2:30 and hung up. I was banking on the prestige of my firm's name to get him there. Happily, I didn't have to lie to him about Norman. But I would have done so if necessary.

Then I began calling the other men, telling them that Norman considered it urgent for them to be there not later than 2 P.M. I wanted everything set up before Davis arrived.

I decided to use my own office for the meeting instead of the conference room. My office was at the end of the corridor, and if there was going to be any disturbance, I didn't want the noise to carry.

Norman was the first to arrive. He smiled, his greeting was warm, but he looked wary. I was afraid he would mention Frieda, but he didn't. He talked about many things, but not about his wife.

I could sense he was measuring me—not only mentally, but physically as well. Once, he stepped rather close to me and straightened his shoulders. He seemed to be checking to see how much taller I was. A moment later, when I turned to look at him, his eyes were fixed on my forehead, studying my hairline (all intact). Perhaps I should have been amused, but I wasn't. I simply felt uncomfortable.

The other men began to arrive. General Stone was the last, and he was obviously angry.

"Dammit," Stone said. "What's all this mystery?"

"Look, Merv. I hate to take up your time, but believe me you'll be happy when you hear what I have to say."

"What is this about Jerry Davis? What the hell has he got to do with us?"

"Let me handle this my way. I got reasons, believe me. Now I want to tell you something before Davis gets here. Vern Hanson came to see me the other day. He said we'll have to put up more cash or collateral. The bank won't accept the Fidelity commitment as it is."

"What'll we do?" asked Winsley.

"Well, one thing for sure, we won't put up fifteen million dollars because we ain't got it, right?" Everybody nodded but Stone.

"OK. I talked to Hanson. I talked him out of the fifteen million but he insists on five, so we're gonna put up five million bucks, temporarily."

"Yes?" said General Stone. "Where are we going to get it?"

"I ain't got my share," said Winsley. "At least I ain't gonna put it up. You must think we got bottomless wells for pockets."

"Now look, Phil, if we don't put up the five million, the bank is gonna stop making payouts. And then Carrelli will stop building the buildings. And the tenants will stop moving in. And other tenants will stop making leases. And Fidelity Standard will stop extending their commitment and then we all go down the drain. So just shut up and listen."

My phone rang. I picked it up and the receptionist told me Davis had arrived. I told her to send him in. He entered the room hesitantly, uncertain what to expect. Norman bounced up from his chair and fairly ran across the carpet to greet him.

Davis took a step backward. "Norman, what the hell are you doing here? Ellison, you told me your firm wanted to consult me on something. What kind of game is this?"

"Wait a minute, Jerry," Norman said. "Don't get excited. I knew you were mad at me, but I had to get you here. Listen, I'm sorry. Understand? I'm telling you in front of all these men, I'm sorry. It was damn nice of you to try and make that deal for me. I know you did your best. Really."

He put out his hand. Davis didn't take it. He looked about warily from face to face. He learned nothing.

Norman was talking again. "These are my partners, Jerry. You know Winsley and the other boys. And this is General Stone."

Norman did not wait for the introductions to be completed.

"Jerry's one of the best brokers in this town, you know. That's why he's here. I asked Jerry to go East and borrow five million dollars for us. He talked to our old friend Harry Dunsten, at the First Manhattan. So tell them what happened, Jerry."

Davis looked bewildered. "I don't understand."

"Go ahead. You tell them what happened."

Davis spoke very quietly. "They turned down the loan."

"Completely?" asked Norman.

"Completely. They said they couldn't make it."

"What did you offer them, Jerry?"

"Seven and a half per cent interest and five points."

"Five points?" General Stone was outraged.

"Yeah, five per cent of five million dollars. Two hundred and fifty grand as a bonus for making the deal—and they still turned me down."

Stone turned to Norman. "I'm surprised at you. Offering seven and a half per cent and five points. Are you crazy?"

"Now wait a minute. I didn't offer that. Jerry did. but I don't blame him. Everybody in the country knows we're in trouble. Jerry did the best he could, and you all know Jerry is one of the best brokers in Chicago."

"Well, Norman," said Jerry, "you don't have to say that."

"No, dammit, it's true. You turn the tough tricks. But you couldn't turn this one, right?"

"I did everything I could. They wouldn't listen to me."

"I wanted you fellas to hear this. I wanted you to know how tough it is. Is that right, Jerry?"

"Yeah, that's right, Norman."

"Well, look, Jerry. There's something I want to show you."

Norman reached into his pocket and pulled out an envelope.

"Come over here, everybody." The men gathered around the desk. Norman removed a letter from the envelope and carefully unfolded it. Inside there was a check drawn on the First Manhattan Bank payable to the order of Kane Enterprises, Inc., in the sum of five million dollars. Jerry Davis looked at it and turned white.

Norman was staring at him intently. "Read the letter, Jerry. Go ahead." Davis picked up the letter, and it seemed to me his hand was shaking. He began to read it to himself.

"No. Read it out loud. I want everybody to hear it."

Davis hesitated.

"Go ahead, Jerry. Nice and clear so everybody can hear."

"'Kane Enterprises, Inc. Attention: Norman Kane, President. Gentlemen: This is to acknowledge receipt of your note in the amount of five million dollars. Interest at the rate of seven per cent will be due at maturity one year from the date thereof. Will you please acknowledge receipt of the check in the space provided below. Kind personal regards. Sincerely, Harry Dunsten.'"

Davis' voice trailed off. Everyone was staring at him. He looked around, and fear was scribbled on his face. "Look," he said. "I tried very hard, I mean . . . I don't understand."

Norman broke in. "No points either, Jerry. No discount. Nothing, see? Just five million bucks at seven per cent. Pretty impressive, huh?"

"I gotta hand it to you," Davis said slowly. "That's fantastic. Just two days ago this same guy told me he wouldn't lend you a dime. I don't understand."

"You don't understand. Look, you son of a bitch, yesterday you walked into my club swinging those silly hips of yours and smiling with those pearly whites and you told me I was full of crap. You said nobody wants my loan. You told me Harry Dunsten says I'm finished. That's what you said, isn't it? Now here I am, you jerk, twenty-four hours later, holding onto the money. You think it was tough? It was nothing. I could have done it myself all the time. I was just giving you a break. Letting you make an easy buck. But you couldn't turn the trick. A lousy, crummy little deal like this, a lousy five million bucks. I thought you were big time, but you're not. You're just a clumsy, rotten, helpless little pimp. You got nothing on the ball, Davis. Nothing."

"Look, Norman—"

"Don't ever talk to me again, you bastard. Imagine a punk like you trying to write me off. Why, it makes me sick just to look at you. I've taken all I can stand, Davis. Get the hell out of here. Turn that silly ass of yours and wiggle your way out the door."

Davis flushed, turned and hurried from the room. He was careful not to straighten his tie or the shoulders of his jacket, and he walked in a clumsy stiff-legged gait.

General Stone offered his hand to Norman. "You're a fantastic guy. I don't know how you do these things, but I sure admire you. So you're putting up the money?"

"Yeah, I'm putting up the money. But not without taking back a note from the company—a note that has priority over all the other notes."

"You want to be ahead of us?" said Winsley.

"Listen, Phil, you wanna put up the five million? You put it up. Otherwise, I'm ahead of you."

"OK," said Winsley. "I just wanted to know."

"Well, now you know. Ellison will be over to see you with subordination agreements this afternoon. Now you sign them real fast or maybe I'll take this five million and use it myself. There are plenty of places I could use five million bucks." After some grumbling, Winsley and the other boys left my office, but General Stone remained.

"You know I'm not going to subordinate my note," he said.

"I know it. But at least mine will be on a par with yours. That's fair."

"Yes, it's fair. It's better than fair. In fact, you don't have to put up the whole five million, Norman. You put up enough to cover yourself and those boob partners of yours. I'll put up my share."

"That's damn nice of you, Merv."

"All I want is a fair shake, no favors. I'll have my check over here this afternoon."

After Stone left, Norman and I were alone in the office.

"OK, buddy," I said. "Let's have it. How did you pull this one?"

"I pledged St. Louis."

"You what?"

"I didn't have anything else to put up, so I pledged St. Louis."

"Wait a minute. The other day you told me you needed the

277

money from St. Louis to pay off your loans on L.A. and Newark. Now you pledged your St. Louis property to take care of this deal."

"That's right."

"God damn it, Norman, you're getting in deeper all the time. Right now everything you own is pledged. Why the big grandstand play?"

"You can't afford to have a fink like Jerry Davis out on the streets telling everybody you're dead. Not when he knows something. Not when he's tried to make a loan for you and been turned down. I had to clear the air in New York and Chicago. First thing you know, the First Manhattan calls the Chicago National, and then I really am dead. Meanwhile, Jerry Davis is running up and down La Salle Street telling everybody Norman Kane's credit is no good."

"Who the hell listens to Jerry Davis?"

"These days everybody listens to everybody. Anyway, I'm off the hook. For just a minute they had me, but old Norman wriggled away."

———————◆———————

It sounded good when Norman said it, but of course, when Norman said things they generally sounded good to me. I understood the importance of silencing Jerry Davis, but I wondered if it had to be done in the dangerous and expensive manner Norman had chosen.

I appreciated the effect Norman's announcement had on his partners. I was willing to concede this might be important at a time when their morale was sagging. Still, it was a terrible price to pay—and this was not the end of it. If the project was actually short fifteen million dollars, Norman had two jobs to do: first, to sell the bank on accepting the five million dollars as a stopgap measure, and second, to come up with the missing ten million.

Norman had judged the bank's position accurately. The proffered five-million-dollar cash advance bought him his additional six months' extension, but it had no effect whatsoever on his permanent mortgage arrangements.

I did not see what Norman could offer Hobbs and Bennett. He had improved the leasing situation considerably, but he was still far short of the break-even point, and all six buildings were now under construction. Fidelity Standard could hardly be unaware that Norman was in a terrible bind. It was unlikely that they would offer him a way out.

Norman tried to secure additional funds in the second-mortgage market, but the reaction there only confirmed his expectations. His deal was too large for all but a few second-mortgage lenders, and those who could handle it demanded a staggering price for their money.

Besides, General Stone was under no obligation to permit the use of a second mortgage. Under the development agreements, Norman had a free hand with first-mortgage loans and interim financing, but no second mortgage could be placed upon the property without the consent of all the investors. The General was unlikely to consent unless the second mortgage was his own.

Stone was probably surprised that Norman Kane did not ask him to furnish secondary financing. This was the usual pattern in Stone's deals. After his partners ran short, they usually asked him for financing, and he lent them money on a basis so onerous that he often ended up owning the entire property.

Norman was determined to solve his problems without Stone's assistance. Thus the General waited for Norman to show signs of weakness, and Norman struggled to avoid asking Stone for the help he needed.

Norman had lived through many deals in which the financing ultimately proved inadequate, but the size of those deals had been manageable. Lake Shore Plaza presented a different problem altogether. Norman had no hope of finding a company or group of companies that would put up more than one hundred eighty million dollars on short notice. Norman had to secure help from Fidelity Standard or supply the deficit himself. He had, of course, paid in most of the funds he had borrowed from the First Manhattan Bank, but he had no intention of leaving this money in the deal. He could not afford to. The loan was due in one year. Actually Norman could not afford to keep it outstanding for more than a few months, because he needed the income from the St. Louis property to take care of his problems in Newark and elsewhere.

Only further leasing would enable Norman to pry more money out of Fidelity Standard. Additional income from high-quality tenants was bound to impress the insurance company. Also, it would give him more cash to cover the operating expenses of the buildings and thus avoid further deficits.

But there was a serious obstacle to putting this program into action. Norman's forays to his club, to his office, and to New York had sapped his strength. Following the meeting with the boys, Stone and Jerry Davis, Norman had staggered back to the hospital of his own volition. He was not willing to remain there full time, but he realized he was in no condition to live at home.

Dr. Franklin considered it vital that Norman remain subject to the hospital regimen. He therefore arranged for Norman to become a combination inpatient-outpatient. Norman lived in the hospital most weekends and several days every week. On other days he would travel. Generally he tried to arrange his schedule so that he could return in time to spend the night in his hospital room.

Dr. Franklin had to battle the hospital administration in order to establish this procedure, which seemed to flaunt every rule of sound therapy. Nevertheless, he realized that if he sought to impose more stringent controls, Norman might check out of the hospital altogether. Somehow the good doctor managed to convince the hospital authorities that this unorthodox procedure was the only way to deal with a most unusual patient.

When Norman left the city, I sometimes traveled with him, as much to protect his health as to assist with his negotiations. It seemed to me that each day he was getting weaker. Technically speaking, the virus was under control, but Norman was thinner, paler and patently less energetic. He had to accomplish great volumes of work during remarkably brief periods of time.

Of course, this procedure was not always successful. There were prospects who either refused to negotiate on a hurry-up basis or who sensed immediately that some desperate compulsion was driving Norman Kane. They played a waiting game, and when Norman came up against this form of resistance, he simply gave up and directed his effort where he could get faster action.

Norman planned his trips and prepared his presentations with infinite care. Day after day, from morning till night, he poured over financial statements and field reports, detailing the operations of various companies with whom he was negotiating. He wanted to know everything he could possibly be asked before he went into a meeting.

Despite the research and preparation, despite the careful planning and ingenious presentations, Norman's program was almost self-defeating. I told Dr. Franklin that these trips, following one another in rapid succession, were weakening Norman more and more. I thought he should be restricted to his hospital bed for several weeks until he could regain his strength. Dr. Franklin agreed, and together we tried convincing Norman. It was impossible. He complained that on top of battling banks, insurance companies and tenants, he now had to struggle with his friends as well.

It was a difficult time for Dr. Franklin. In his heart he believed that, strange as Norman's program might be, it was still the best that could be provided for this particular patient.

One day Dr. Franklin unburdened himself to me. "Mr. Ellison, Norman Kane is the most difficult patient I've ever had. I don't know whether I'm killing the man or keeping him from killing himself. Every day I make up my mind to resign from the case. But I can't take a chance, you see. He might say, 'OK. Forget it,' and leave the hospital. Then there would be nobody to look after him. At least I feel I'm doing him *some* good although I'm frank to admit that what is going on here is absolutely incredible. I find myself making decisions which are neither logical nor rational. Once you start doing this sort of thing with one patient, it's bound to influence your handling of others. Next thing you know I'll be totally worthless as a doctor. I'll be some kind of medicine man."

Each day when I came to see Norman in the hospital I brought an assortment of papers to be reviewed and signed. Other men might have balked at the vast mass of documents that passed across his hospital "desk," but Norman never complained. His hospital room was a command post. People hurried in and scurried out at an amazing rate. Miss Fritch tried to screen his visitors, but the hospital wouldn't permit her to set up her desk in the hall, and unless the door was locked, people darted into the room before she could stop them. Some were friends, some business associates, some enemies come to watch Norman painfully struggling with his fate.

Norman arranged to have several phone lines installed, and his "desk" was continually strewn with plans and papers. Gradually the documents were spread all over the room, piled on window ledges, stashed in file pockets on the floor, even crumpled between the covers of his bed.

Other patients complained. The traffic to Norman's room was disrupting the hospital. Dr. Franklin moved Norman to a corner room on another floor where he would create less of an uproar. But still the parade of men and documents and telephone calls continued. There were three phones in his room, and it was not unusual for him to be using two of them at once.

At times he seemed almost to be himself. Almost, but not quite. He could talk for a while with great animation, but then he would sink back into the pillows and pretend to be reading a paper or a plan. Miss Fritch and I knew he was resting. Every day, Frieda, the doctor, Miss Fritch and I watched him fading.

We tried to reason with him. He overwhelmed us with glib attempts at self-justification. "No kidding," he would say, "I feel ten years younger after making that deal"; or "Boy, that one gave me a lift. I was feeling kind of sick the last few days, but signing up Felstan Steel was the best therapy in the world."

Dr. Franklin stopped by every evening and routed the remaining assault groups from the room.

"Just five more minutes, Doc. If we work it out, this guy won't have to come back tomorrow." Dr. Franklin was adamant. The torture period must be limited from ten in the morning till eight at night (except for hour-long breaks for lunch and dinner). After 8 P.M. only Frieda was allowed in the room. Not even Frieda was permitted to stay past ten.

Norman continued negotiating with Fidelity Standard. I'm sure Hobbs and Bennett thought Norman's approach was oblique. They knew he needed changes in his financing, but Norman never quite discussed that aspect of Lake Shore Plaza. He told them in detail of the latest developments in his leasing program. He reported the progress of the construction from day to day. Hobbs and Bennett thanked him for this information. With difficulty they restrained themselves from asking whether or not they were ever going to get the loan.

Norman never raised the point. He would say, "When we deliver the loan," or, "After the requirements are met," or, "After you boys take over the security." The final loan papers had been approved months before. But Norman discussed various details in the mortgage, the mortgage note and related documents as if there were still unsettled questions. He never raised the slightest doubt that Fidelity Standard would be the ultimate holder of the security.

The meetings with the men from Fidelity always took place outside the hospital. Norman had noted John Bennett's morbid fear the day he first visited the hospital, and Norman had no intention whatever of repeating that unpleasant experience. Although Norman did not look like a well man, he did his best to talk and act like one. Listening to his persuasive words, there seemed no reason to suspect that his recovery would not be complete.

Before and after the meetings with Hobbs and Bennett, I questioned Norman about his tactics. He never explained them. I began to wonder whether he really knew what to ask for. Still, I could not believe that Norman had no plan. He never did anything without a plan.

I must say that Norman's behavior in the hospital worried me more than his rare and carefully organized public appearances. Dining with prominent businessmen, bankers and the like, Norman seemed to be under tight control. He retained that special flamboyance which not even serious illness could destroy. Apparently the outside world was a stage for which Norman expected to be costumed and made up to play his special role. He followed his lines and the business required of him with little deviation.

In the hospital, he seemed to relax. And when Norman relaxed, he gave vent to every form of verbal and physical display, including fits of anger and even hysterics.

Once I asked, "Norman, why aren't you as restrained in the hospital as you are outside?"

"Don't be silly, Eddie. I can put on a show maybe two or three times a week, but if you think I can live that way, you're crazy."

"I don't like to say this, Norman, but that may be the only way you're going to live."

He turned white and spoke to me angrily. "Don't ever say that, Eddie. Don't even joke about it. Norman Kane is gonna make it, and the way for Norman Kane to make it is for him to be Norman Kane."

———◆———

But it was not easy for Norman Kane to be himself. Physically he was much thinner and very pale. It seemed to me his hairline had receded somewhat since this siege of illness had begun. No amount of careful combing could cover up the retreat. This made Norman look older, and he was aware of it. Worried by it. He knew he was not handsome, but he had always looked young, vigorous and virile.

Mentally he was still as sharp as ever—that is, from time to time. At other times he was depressed. His manner was careless, his thought patterns random. Then, suddenly, he would be filled with enthusiasm—as he was a few days later, when he invited me to accompany him on a business trip to New York. Norman did not usually relish these forays, but this time he seemed to look forward to the trip. I was not eager to go, but there was no way to refuse him.

On the plane, Norman was quite jovial, talking a great deal, eating and drinking a bit too much. I was too pleased by his good spirits to reprove him for these relatively petty offenses.

Norman tried to engage one of the stewardesses in conversation. She smiled mechanically in response to his banter but did not linger near his seat.

"Oh, well," he said to me, "never try to kibbitz a twenty-two-year-old babe when she is looking down into your bald spot." He laughed, but I wondered whether he was really amused.

We checked into the St. Regis. The room clerk greeted him by name and the assistant manager came bustling out to escort us to our rooms. Norman tipped the bellman lavishly.

Our suite was enormous, two huge bedrooms connected by a spacious sitting room. The furniture was fragile-looking and elegant. The predominant colors of the walls, the upholstery and the carpeting were gold and white. I tried to compare this ornate period treasure trove with Norman's severely modern apartment. Apparently he felt equally at home in each.

We rose early the next morning to have breakfast in our suite with several men from Eastern Steel Specialties Company. Norman greeted the men graciously, inquired as to the health and welfare of their respective families, and altogether played the perfect host. During our sumptuous breakfast he engaged the men in cheerful, if trivial conversation. He was quite entertaining, especially when he told rollicking and somewhat ribald tales about his experiences in leasing the Plaza. By the time the last cups and saucers were trundled out of the room, everyone seemed to be in splendid good humor.

Eventually the discussion turned to the business at hand. Instead of stimulating Norman, this seemed to depress him. When asked for details about the Plaza, Norman repeatedly deflected the conversation with an amusing but irrelevant quip. For a time the men from Eastern Steel responded good-humoredly. After a while, they seemed confused. They glanced at one another. It was clear that they were wondering why Kane had invited them to his suite. He apparently had no interest in transacting business.

Finally the conference broke up. Norman's guests departed, a little bewildered and perhaps annoyed. Norman was obviously happy to see them go.

"What was that all about?" I asked him.

He did not even bother to put me off. "No stomach for business, Eddie. No stomach at all. Those guys bored me. No class, see? No class."

"Since when does it matter whether a tenant has class?"

He waved a hand at me. "I had to get out of Chicago. I was dying there. This was just an excuse. I wasn't even trying to sell those guys."

"But you made me come with you. This is ridiculous. Come on, Norman. Pack your things. We're going back to Chicago."

"No, not yet. Look, we'll spend the day here. Go to the Metropolitan, the Museum of Modern Art. Maybe an opera. Have a good dinner, sack out here, and go back tomorrow."

"Norman, I didn't come to New York for a picnic. I thought you were serious about doing business. You should have been. Those men were talking about leasing over a hundred thousand feet. Now I think you've lost them altogether."

"So what? I'll find someone else." Norman had followed me into my room. I was beginning to pack my suitcase. He took my arm and turned me to face him.

"Come on. Be a pal. Stay here today. What the hell is one lousy day? I got to do something different. Don't you see? And I don't want to be alone."

He was taking my clothes out of the suitcase and putting them back into the dresser drawers.

"My shirts go on top, Norman. And the underwear in the second drawer."

He smiled and followed my instructions.

———◆———

It was a dull day for me. I was not a habitué of art museums. But Norman was very happy. As we trotted through the galleries, he gave me a running commentary, describing styles and techniques, exclaiming extravagantly over each masterpiece. He was oblivious to my indifference.

We ate lunch in the fountain court of the Metropolitan, then renewed our viewing. I was relieved when closing time arrived.

I tried to talk Norman out of going to the opera. Instead, I suggested that we have dinner in the room; it had been a tiring day. Norman refused. He wanted to eat at the Four Seasons. That was our compromise: no opera, but a rich dinner at the Four Seasons.

The food was superb, but Norman barely picked at it. We had walked so many miles that day that he was exhausted. I was tired too, but the exercise had spurred my appetite. I attacked my dinner with real enthusiasm, while Norman studied the other patrons in the restaurant.

"Look at that broad over there, Eddie. How do you like that construction?"

I agreed that the girl was beautifully put together.

"Yeah, well, I'd like to take her apart." He studied the girl ravenously.

"Listen," I said, "let's not get any ideas. We may not be here on business, but we're not here to get laid either."

"Oh, sure, sure. But I can look, can't I? Even Frieda lets me look."

Finally we finished our dinner. Norman suggested that we walk back to the hotel. I refused.

"It's early, Eddie."

"Yes, it's early. But both of us are tired, and you especially should get to bed."

"You know, you're right. OK. You hail a cab. I have to make a phone call." He stepped into a booth and shoved the door closed.

I waited for him in the cab for several minutes. The driver began to grumble. Then Norman appeared, loping across the sidewalk, grinning widely.

"Sorry to keep you waiting. St. Regis, driver." We shot off into the traffic.

When we reached our rooms, I urged Norman to go straight to sleep.

"No. I'm going to read for a while. But you go to sleep. Don't worry about me. I feel fine."

He apparently did. Norman was inexplicably cheerful and energetic.

"All right. Just don't sit up all night reading."

I left him sitting on the edge of his bed, fully dressed, smiling guilelessly and looking very healthy indeed. His transformations never ceased to amaze me.

I undressed quickly and got into bed. I read for a while myself. Finally I turned off the reading light and fell asleep.

Voices awakened me. I was groggy, and several moments passed before I realized they were coming from Norman's room. Perhaps he had become ill and called the doctor. Frightened, I jumped out of bed, grabbed my robe and started for Norman's room. Halfway across the sitting room, I stopped. One of the voices was female. Then I was angry. The little son of a bitch. That's who he called—some whore. And now he had invited her over in the middle of the night. I wasn't going to put up with that. Angrily I walked toward the half-open door to Norman's room. I was going to throw the slut out.

But I didn't. I could see into Norman's room quite clearly from where I stood. The girl was Tina Kincaid.

"How did you know I would come?" she was asking. She stood in the middle of the room, fingering a long strand of pearls as she watched Norman mix a drink.

"You're here."

"Yes, but how did you know?"

Norman turned, handed her the drink and smiled. *"Salud."* He tipped her glass. She did not drink from it, but she returned his smile.

"You're really quite an amazing man."

"That's why you came."

Tina shrugged and sipped from the glass. She looked about the room. I stepped back into the shadows, but she did not glance my way. I was shaking with a mixture of emotions. The strongest was fascination.

Tina set her glass on a table and stepped toward Norman. "You haven't even greeted me properly. I didn't fly eight hundred miles in the middle of the night for a martini."

Norman placed his drink down next to Tina's and put his arms around her. It was a long kiss and a passionate one. Tina's back was toward me. I watched Norman's hands slide slowly down the small of her back and across the curve of her hips.

After a while, Tina gently pulled away. Norman loosened his hold reluctantly. I could still see the faint indentations on Tina's dress where Norman's hands had held her. *I should get out of here,* I thought. I couldn't. I was disgusted with myself, but I couldn't.

"No swimming pool?" Tina asked.

Norman laughed. "Not this time."

"But we do have a bed," Tina said. She began to walk toward it, loosening the zipper on the back of her dress as she walked.

Norman took her hand and pulled her around. "The hell with the bed," he said. He took hold of her dress and began to pull it down from her shoulders and over her arms. He let it fall to the floor.

"No bed?"

Norman shook his head. He pointed to the carpet.

Before Tina could protest, he kissed her again, this time even more fiercely than before. Then slowly, he forced her down on the carpet, still holding her in a tight embrace.

When he released her, she lay back, still wearing her black brassiere and panties, stockings, and the strand of pearls around her neck.

"Aren't we overdressed for the occasion?" she asked.

Norman began to remove his clothes. Tina sat up, unsnapped her brassiere and laid it on the carpet. She slipped out of her panties and stockings. Norman never took his eyes off her. Neither did I.

Tina lay back on the carpet, then suddenly rolled over and raised herself on her elbows. Her full breasts swelled against the carpet. She was looking straight toward me.

"Where does that door lead?"

"To a sitting room and another bedroom."

Tina froze. I could tell that she didn't see me, but I dared not move.

"Why do you need another bedroom?"

"For Ellison."

Tina scrambled to her feet. "Where is he?"

"In there, sleeping."

She turned to look over her shoulder, then looked back at Norman.

"You expect me to make love to you here on the floor, with Ellison sleeping in the other room?"

"Why not?"

"But, Norman—"

"It's only Ellison."

"What if he wakes up? What if he finds me here?"

"Eddie? He sleeps like a log. Anyway, he's a friend. He wouldn't say anything."

"How can you be sure?"

"I know him. He's perfectly faithful. Eddie would never do anything to hurt me."

"It's not right, Norman. It's just not right."

"Since when do you care about right?"

She hesitated. He was directly in front of her now, his hands holding her arms.

"It's more exciting this way, Tina."

She shook her head. "I'm going to close the door."

Norman held her tightly. "That would take away the excitement." He drew her to him again.

I stood there helpless, trembling with anger and humiliation. I watched them embrace. I watched Norman ease her to the floor again. Tina was breathing heavily now, her breasts rising and falling in quickening cadence, her knees rocking from side to side. Then Norman was over her, on her—

I stumbled away. They wouldn't hear me now. They wouldn't hear anything.

I crawled into bed. I could imagine them making love, fiercely, crudely, on the carpet. I couldn't erase the vision from my eyes. I thought I could hear them rolling about on the floor. I imagined their sighs of pleasure, their moans of contentment.

I lay in bed for hours, unable to sleep. In the morning, as dawn lightened the room, the visions and sounds, imaginary and otherwise, receded. I could hear traffic in the street below. I dozed a bit but never fell completely asleep.

I realized I couldn't lie there forever. I got up, washed, and dressed. I walked into the sitting room. There was no sound in Norman's room. *Thank God,* I thought, *that tramp has gone back to Chicago.* I could see the spot on the carpet where Norman had taken her. No one was there, but the vision of them leaped back into my mind. I shrugged it away. I was building my anger. Norman was going to hear about this.

I pushed open the door and stepped into the room. Norman and Tina were lying on the bed, naked, awake, as if they were waiting for me.

"Good morning," Norman said.

Tina pulled a sheet up over her thighs. She did not bother to cover her breasts. She was watching me curiously.

"What's the matter, Eddie?" Norman said, sitting up. "You feel all right?"

I was trembling again. "Get her out of here, Norman."

Tina smiled. "I think he means me."

"Get her out of here."

Norman slid out of bed and pulled on a robe. Tina still sat there watching me. If she had only pulled the sheet up. It was a ridiculous situation. I felt unbearably absurd.

Norman was walking toward me.

"Surely you don't expect me to send the lady home without a good breakfast?"

Tina had slipped from the bed and was gathering up her underthings. I couldn't keep my eyes off her. No matter how she moved or bent her body, she couldn't make it appear graceless or crude. She seemed to enjoy my scrutiny.

"Why don't you have breakfast with us, Eddie?" Tina asked.

I forced myself to speak. "I'm going downstairs for breakfast, Norman. I'll be back in an hour. She'd better be gone when I return."

I stepped back into the sitting room and slammed the door. I could hear them laughing on the other side.

I didn't eat much of my breakfast. I was too busy rehearsing the speech I intended to deliver to Norman. But my thoughts kept wandering. I couldn't come up with the right denunciation to hurl at Norman Kane.

When I returned to the room, Tina was gone. That, at least, was some relief.

Norman had packed his things and was sitting comfortably

in a chair, waiting for me. I stood in front of him, looking down into that damn bald spot.

"You did it deliberately," I said. "To humiliate me."

"Don't be silly, Eddie. Humiliate *her,* maybe. But not you."

"You wanted me to know. You left your door open. You knew I'd wake up and come after you."

"Then you were watching." He barely masked his smile.

"Yes, I was watching. I got out of bed because I thought you were sick. When I could make out the voices, I knew you had a woman with you. I was going to throw her out."

"But you didn't."

"I didn't realize it was Tina until I reached the door to your room."

"I see. Tina's different. Some ordinary tramp you'd throw out, but not Tina."

"I was too surprised. I didn't know what to do."

"So you stood there and watched us."

I was beginning to turn red. I could feel the color suffusing my face. "I couldn't go back and I couldn't go forward. You might have heard me."

"Who was hiding from whom?"

"God damn it, Norman, you had me trapped, and you know it. I didn't want any part of it. I didn't want to get involved."

"Why didn't you close your eyes?"

"And cover my ears? Hear no evil, see no evil, speak no evil. That's what you want of me, is it? Well it won't work. I refuse to be your accomplice in lechery."

"You already are."

"I'll tell Frieda."

Norman laughed. "You'll only confirm what she already believes." His tone became gentler. "Sit down, Eddie. Let me explain a few things. Please sit down."

Reluctantly I complied. This wasn't going right at all.

"I thought you would understand, Eddie. I was down. Way down. I needed something to build up my self-respect."

"A broad?"

"Not any broad. Tina. Look, I haven't had a woman for a

292

long time. That might not matter to you, but it does to me. A guy like me thrives on dames."

I stared at him impassively. "What about your wife? She's a woman."

He shook his head. "Not the same. It wouldn't prove a thing."

"What did you prove last night? I told you before you could have Tina any time you wanted her."

"You said that a long time ago. Things have changed since then. Look, you probably think I planned it this way. I didn't. I didn't even know whether she'd come. I got the idea last night as we were leaving the restaurant. I had to call and see if she would come."

"It was childish, Norman. And stupid."

"All right, I agree. But I needed it badly. A lift. A lift for my ego. Lake Shore Plaza has been knocking me out. Killing me. I had to prove I was still a man."

"Of course you're a man, Norman. You didn't have to screw Tina Kincaid to prove that to me."

"Not you. Me. I needed the proof. I feel better now. A whole lot better."

"What's the use of arguing? You did it. Now, of course, you'll have more problems. Wait until Tina gets back to Del. She ought to love shoving this story in his back."

"Maybe."

"He'll never believe she didn't sleep with you before. He'll think you took her that night at his home. I'm not so sure I believe you any more myself."

Norman's features seemed to sharpen. "I believed *you*. The night I got the five million from the First Manhattan I called home and you said you were only helping Frieda track me down. You were alone, alone with my wife, but I didn't doubt you."

Then I knew why Norman had wanted me to see him make love to Tina. He wanted *me* to know that he was still "a man." It was a warning.

"I see. All right, Norman. We believe each other. That's good. That's the way it has to be. Any time you feel differently, any time you don't trust me, say so. I'll get out."

Norman was on his feet now, smiling. "Of course I trust you. You're the best friend I ever had. You wouldn't cross me, ever. I know that." He patted me on the back. Point made. "Come on now, Eddie. Let's get out of here. Enough of this high living."

We didn't talk much on the trip home. Now that he had achieved this double triumph—over himself and me—Norman seemed to go slack. His brief escapade was over. Norman was going back to all the unsolved problems of Lake Shore Plaza. Perhaps he realized it had been an illusion—conquering his fear of fading manhood was no help whatever in saving his project.

I drove him straight to the hospital. He seemed relieved to be back. Dr. Franklin did not remonstrate with him for failing to return the previous night. He could see that Norman was very weak.

Norman stayed at the hospital continuously for the next few days. I talked to him by phone, but did not offer to visit him, nor did he ask me to come. I was happy to have this brief respite. I couldn't possibly have known what was coming, but it was good to be out of Norman's orbit, even if only for a little while.

A week later, Miss Fritch called my office and begged me to come to the hospital at once.

"What's up?" I asked.

"Please do me the favor of coming right over. I'll meet you in the hall at eleven o'clock." I had no chance to answer because she hung up.

Miss Fritch was waiting in the hall as promised.

"Mr. Carrelli will be here any minute. He has another battle going with Mr. Kane. Mr. McNeill and Dr. Friedrichs will be here, too. I've been through these meetings before, Mr. Ellison. Even when times were good, they always ended up yelling and screaming at each other. Now Mr. Kane can't take it. I won't sit here and watch him kill himself. You'll have to help me."

"That's quite an order, Miss Fritch. Norman never listens to anybody."

"Sometimes he listens to you, Mr. Ellison. Every once in a while."

I followed her into the room. Norman was surprised to see me, but before he could ask why I had come, Carrelli and his men were at the door. As soon as they entered, Norman leaped from his bed, pulled on his robe and started pacing the room.

"You fellas got to stop this. You just gotta stop it, Carrelli. I've had too damn much trouble with you already. I'm not putting up with any more."

Carrelli looked puzzled. "I don't understand, Mr. Kane. What are you talking about?"

"Don't give me that crap, Carrelli. You know what I'm talking about. I got the inspection report on Plaza Three and I know God damn well what you've been doing. Now come off it."

Carrelli's face turned purple, but he controlled himself. "Look here, Mr. Kane, I know you're not feeling well. I didn't come here to fight with you. I heard you want to talk to me and to the subs, so I brought my boys along. I don't think we should start fighting with each other."

Norman glared at him for a moment, then sat down on the edge of the bed. "You're absolutely right. It doesn't do any good to fight. I'm not gonna yell or scream at you. I'm just gonna issue an order."

A knock on the door interrupted him. Miss Fritch admitted McNeill and Friedrichs to the room.

"Just in time," Norman said. "Carrelli's playing innocent. Pretends he don't know why I'm mad at him." Norman's voice took on an exaggeratedly gentle tone. "Let's make it very clear, Mr. Carrelli. You're in for a payout, the biggest you've requested so far. Something like six million dollars. Mr. Carrelli, your payout request is hereby disapproved. Mr. McNeill, Dr. Friedrichs and I, we don't approve it."

Carrelli walked a step closer to Norman's bed. "What you mean, you don't approve it?"

"Very simple. On the bottom of the form it says 'Payout Request Approved,' and there are lines for signatures—by the architect, the engineer and the owner. We're supposed to send it to the bank tomorrow. I'm gonna fill it in, Carrelli, but I'm gonna write the word 'Not' before the word 'Approved.' And then we're all gonna sign it."

"You must be kiddin' me. That's six million dollars."

"That's what I said."

"Why you don't approve it?"

Norman started to stand up, thought better of it and sat down again. "OK. We'll talk like gentlemen. I'll tell you why I don't approve it, Mr. Carrelli. I've had the boys inspect the building. I would say you must have installed a hundred and fifty thousand lineal feet of partitions in Plaza Three. According to the specifications those are Gen-Metal partitions, type 860. Now it's just possible, Mr. Carrelli, that even though you've been in this racket thirty years, you still can't read specifications. I won't bore you by reading them in detail. I'll just tell you that the way *I* read the specs, a type 860 partition should be twenty-gauge steel on both sides and three inches thick, filled with sound-absorbing material, with channels for electrical and plumbing lines. Also, it should be eight foot six inches high—that's why they call it 860, see?— and be designed so you can put it through the ceiling and add a panel to extend it up to the underside of the construction. That's how you separate one tenant from another. That's the whole idea of this 860 partition. Now, also as I read it, the specs say, 'vinyl fabric both sides,' and there is a description of the vinyl fabric and a number showing the gauge and quality.

"I'm sure you're completely unaware of what I'm about to tell you, Mr. Carrelli. A fine, honorable contractor like you wouldn't be party to any such thing. But my men have gone through Plaza Three, and they find, to their amazement, that we don't have a type 860 partition. Well, it *looks* like an 860 partition, but it ain't. You see, it's not quite three inches wide, it's more like two and a half inches. And it ain't twenty-gauge steel. Somehow or other it's only twenty-four gauge.

Then, when they look at the top of the partition, our men find they can't fit another section on top of it.

"Now, Mr. Carrelli, here is the biggest surprise of all: the vinyl. The vinyl, Mr. Carrelli, isn't the one specified. It isn't the same thickness and the quality is not quite as good.

"My friends are quite surprised when they inspect this building and find you have made this mistake, because they think to themselves: A hundred and fifty thousand lineal feet Mr. Carrelli has put in, and he must not realize he has been getting the wrong kind of partition. How unhappy Mr. Carrelli will be when he hears this because Mr. Carrelli is a fine, honest contractor and wouldn't cheat his grandmother. They call and tell me this very sad story. They say, 'Shall we go over and talk to Mr. Carrelli and tell him about the bad mistake made by the nasty men who sold him the partitions?'

"I tell them, 'Boys, let us not call Mr. Carrelli. Let us call the Gen-Metal company and see what they have to say.' So I pick up the telephone and I talk to Mr. Gunther at Gen-Metal. He tells me a funny story. He tells me Mr. Carrelli came to see him six months ago and asked if he could modify the type 860 partition. Mr. Carrelli says it need not be three inches thick; it can be two and a half inches. There needn't be as much insulation, and the adjusting plate at the top won't be necessary at all.

"Mr. Gunther asks Mr. Carrelli, 'Are you sure this will be all right with the owners of the building?' 'Believe me. Trust me,' says Mr. Carrelli. 'They are looking to save some money and this will save some money.' 'Of course,' says Mr. Gunther, 'this will save your owners some money. We are happy to help you.' 'By the way,' says Mr. Carrelli to Mr. Gunther, 'you have a very expensive grade of vinyl fabric which you use to finish these partitions. Is there not some less expensive grade we could use?' 'Of course,' says Mr. Gunther, and then he suggests a less expensive vinyl fabric.

"I think this is very nice of Mr. Gunther and I thank him for being so kind about figuring out ways to save me money. I ask Mr. Gunther, 'How much, Mr. Gunther, would you say the difference in cost is between these two kinds of partitions?' Mr. Gunther is surprised to hear me ask the question. He assumes I know the difference. But I urge him to give me a figure. Mr. Gunther cannot be too accurate because he does not have the contracts in front of him. So I say, 'Mr. Gunther, this is my dime and I am willing to sit here and wait, so you go find your contracts.' After a few minutes Mr. Gunther comes on the phone again and he says the way he figures it, this fine new partition is costing us about a dollar and thirty cents a lineal foot less than the regular type 860 partition. I say, 'My goodness. That is really wonderful. I am delighted by this wonderful saving.' I say, 'Unfortunately, Mr. Gunther, today is the first I know about it. Mr. Carrelli has somehow neglected to tell me.'

"Mr. Gunther is amazed. He is certain Mr. Carelli told him Mr. Kane wanted to make the change. I tell Mr. Gunther I am sure this is what Mr. Carrelli told him, and it is a shame that Mr. Carrelli has not told me the same thing."

I watched Carrelli. He looked from Kane to his subcontractors to us. His face grew even darker.

"Now," said Norman, "I have made a simple little computation here, Mr. Carrelli. I figure that with a hundred and fifty thousand lineal feet of partitions, you have saved me a hundred and ninety-five thousand dollars. Ordinarily I would be very grateful. But since you neglected to tell me about this marvelous saving, I figure it is only coming to me as a wonderful surprise when we get to the end of the job. I know you always planned to tell me, Mr. Carrelli. Isn't that right?"

Carrelli said nothing.

"Of course, I have ruined your little surprise. I am sorry, because I know what a soft-hearted gentleman you are, and for me to hurt your feelings by letting everyone in on your secret is really very cruel."

Norman stood up again. "Mr. Carrelli, I am very grateful for your little surprise, and I am delighted to have one for you in return. I appreciate your kindness in going to all this effort to find this wonderful inexpensive partition for me. But I regret having to tell you I cannot accept it.

"So this is where we stand. You have put in one hundred and fifty thousand feet of this lovely new partition which I understand is called 860 F. I do not know what the F stands for, but may I assume it means 'flimsy'?"

Still Carrelli said nothing.

"No, Mr. Carrelli, I'm sorry. Your little surprise has back-fired. I have a very simple suggestion. All you have to do to make me happy is to take out the whole one hundred and fifty thousand feet and replace it with type 860. You get that, Carrelli? The whole hundred and fifty thousand feet."

Carrelli's lips were trembling. "Wait a minute," he said. "I give you the credit. I give you the whole credit. I saved two hundred grand putting it in. I give it all to you."

"No, thank you Mr. Carrelli. I do not want your little present. All I want is my type 860 partitions. Like the ones in the specifications. You remember the specifications, Mr. Carrelli? We all sat down around the table and signed them. It was a very happy day, Mr. Carrelli. I'm sure you recall it."

"Look, I do better. I not only give you the credit, I give you another fifty thousand dollars cash in the bargain. Only don't make me take out the partitions."

"That would be cruel, wouldn't it? I imagine taking them out would probably cost you another two hundred thousand dollars. And you think that would be unkind and unfair. When you decided on this little surprise you said to yourself, 'Suppose Kane finds out. This is a good partition. What will he care? I give him part of the credit and he lets me off the hook.' But you're wrong, Carrelli. I'm not letting you off the hook. This is the last word, you son of a bitch. *Take out those goddamn partitions.*"

Carrelli stood motionless. One of the subcontractors spoke. "Mr. Kane, it's a perfectly good partition. Why don't you work out something with Carrelli? I know he doesn't mean to be unfair."

"Who is *that* jerk?" said Kane, pointing to the speaker.

"I'm Arnold Glassen. I'm the subcontractor who installed the partitions."

"Oh, congratulations, Mr. Glassen. You did a lovely job. In fact, the boys tell me the way you arranged things with the other subcontractors, it's a miracle we were able to discover you didn't put in the right partitions. Permit me to compli-ment you, Mr. Glassen, on your lovely work."

Glassen stood there, his mouth open, but no sound issued

forth. Carrelli looked around and then spoke to Kane again.

"Give me a break, Kane. It's worse than what you say. There's nothing I can do with that partition. I rip it out and there's no place to use it. I'll have a hundred and fifty thousand feet of partitions I got no use for. I could take a loss of hundreds of thousands of dollars."

"That is very sad, indeed, Mr. Carrelli. But you should have thought of that before you put the partitions in. Now you listen to me, you lying bastard. You take those partitions down. Every fucking foot of them. You hear me? Every foot. And the next time you do anything like that, you son of a bitch, I'll not only make you fix it, I'll sue the shit out of you."

Carrelli's lips trembled again. "You bastard. You dirty little bastard. You do this to screw me. You don't care about the partitions. You don't care about nothin', you son of a bitch. You want to fuck Carrelli."

Norman roared with laughter. "Me fuck you? Why, you rat, am I the guy who cheated on the partitions? Am I the guy who put them in without telling the owner or the architect? Who screwed who?"

"You never get away with this, Kane. I don't take them out. I carry this to court. I get you somehow. I never take them out."

Norman turned to Friedrichs and McNeill. "Tell me, gentlemen. Does he have to take them out?"

The architects nodded.

"You see? You gotta take them out. I think you better get out of here right now. I think you better start taking those partitions down right now. I want every foot of that crap out of my building in three weeks. And in five weeks I want all of the right partitions back in. You get me? Five weeks, you son of a bitch. I don't care if you have to work three thousand men around the clock. You get that crap out of my building."

Carrelli swore again and took a step toward Norman, who stood up too, as if he figured there was going to be a fight. But Glassen grabbed Carrelli, and then a couple of men stood between them.

I moved in too. "Hold on. Are you men out of your minds? You listen to me, Carrelli. If you cheated on the specifications you have no right to threaten anybody. You do anything to hurt Mr. Kane and I'll see you're put behind bars for the rest of your life."

Carrelli looked around. "OK," he said. "OK, you crowd of Jew bastards. You think you screw Carrelli, but you find out."

"Get out," yelled Norman. "Not another word, you son of a bitch, or I'll sue you whether you take the partitions out or not. Get out, you bastard."

Carrelli got, but slowly. He walked as if every step was agonizing. As if he could barely restrain himself from turning around and strangling Norman Kane. In a minute the door was closed, and Norman and I and Miss Fritch were left in the room with Friedrichs and McNeill.

Norman sat down on his bed. When he spoke his voice was trembling. He talked to the room, not to any of us.

"You hear that? What kind of a man is he, anyway? Tries to cheat me and then calls me a son of a bitch. You hear that? What is this world all about? Scum like Carrelli come in here and yell and scream at *me* for cheating *me*. This guy thinks I done him wrong. Can you believe it? And then what? Then I'm a Jew bastard. You hear? In fact, we're all Jew bastards. I'm the only Jew in the room but we're all Jew bastards. You hear that? Somebody's crazy here. Either me or Carrelli."

"Norman," I said, trying to calm him down, "you've had contractors try to cheat you before."

"But Carrelli. You realize Carrelli has been building for me for fifteen years? Until this deal I never had a bad word with him. Never had a problem with him. Fifteen years. Paid him on time. Paid him bonuses. And now he sees me sick in this bed, and what does he do? Like a vulture he says, 'I'll swallow him. I'll chew him to bits.' "

"Take it easy, Norman. There's no use getting excited."

"You think this is the end? We'll have to watch Carrelli nine times as carefully as before. How can we trust him? This guy is gonna try and cut something out of that building every chance he gets. My God, what are we coming to?"

McNeill cleared his throat. "We found this one, Mister Kane. We'll find anything else he tries. He won't get away with a thing."

But Norman wasn't listening. "You heard what Carrelli

said? I gave him a contract. Over a hundred million dollars. A chance to get rich on one deal. And he swears at me and calls me a Jew bastard."

Miss Fritch walked over to his bed. "Now, Mr. Kane, I think you ought to rest."

Kane pushed her away and jumped from the bed. "My God, I don't understand it. They're all waiting for me to drop. Every one of 'em. All vultures. There's Fidelity Standard and the bank both waiting for me to fail. Carrelli waiting for me to fall on my face. All the tenants trying to bleed me. General Stone waiting for me to drop into his lap. The partners screaming and hollering while I do all the work. What am I doing all this for? I'm in this hospital. I lie in this bed. I beat my brains out day and night. For who? For them? They're waiting, you see. They're waiting for me to lose my grip. They think now maybe I *have* lost it. Maybe Norman Kane won't pull through. Maybe this time he tried too much. They're standing there, waiting for me to trip. Fall on my face. Slow up. Explode." He was on his feet now and pacing about the room. For a moment he looked almost like the Norman Kane who had started this project not so many months before. We watched him, amazed at his towering anger and his incredible display of energy.

Norman stopped for a minute and looked out the window. "You see those buildings? Even from here you can see my buildings. I built towers you can see for miles. What did those guys ever do? What did those pigs ever do but live on somebody else's leavings? *I* built them. Nobody else. People have been trying to stop me all my life. But nobody's ever gonna stop me. I'm gonna put those six buildings together. I'm gonna lick Fidelity Standard, the Chicago Bank, General Stone and everybody else."

He turned to look at us. "There ain't nobody who can lick Norman Kane. You just remember that. Nobody in this whole world."

He pitched forward on his face and lay still.

For a fraction of a second we could not believe it. Then we rushed to him. Miss Fritch ran down the corridor, screaming for a doctor.

It didn't matter. Norman Kane was dead.

5

At first everyone was very courteous, very sympathetic and very helpful. Hundreds of Norman's associates and admirers came to his funeral, and a smattering of his enemies as well. How they must have enjoyed it—to see Norman Kane, age forty-nine, stashed away in an early grave. But, for the moment, the expressions of sympathy seemed sincere.

Even the first meeting of partners in Norman's office after his death was notable for the same atmosphere—the same awareness that the "leader" was gone, that everyone must be cooperative and sensible and try to work things out as well as possible. This climate of good will, possibly superstitious in origin, soon disappeared. It was not long before the partners were at each other's throats, or at least at each other's pocketbooks.

In the beginning the partners assigned me to represent them in analyzing and reporting on our situation. There was no talk about using other counsel, no threats of lawsuits, no questions of foreclosure, none of the bitter battles that would soon erupt.

I was busy winding up Norman's estate as well. This was a complicated procedure; probably his estate would not be finally closed for years. In the meantime, many matters required immediate attention.

Most important, Carrelli's men continued to complete the construction of the building. At first we had feared he might slow down the work, or even pull off the job. But Carrelli was too shrewd for that, with millions of dollars due him at each payout date, and tens of millions more riding on the construction still to be completed. Of course, he regularly presented his bills for payment. We hedged, approving everything except the sums requested for the partition work. Carrelli accepted the lesser amounts. He was too vulnerable to protest—at least for the time being. Meanwhile, he persisted in using the cheaper partitions. When the showdown came, the sums at stake would be considerable.

Chicago National Bank continued to pay the contractors, but with increasing reluctance. Each payment represented a major crisis. We never knew when the bank might balk and bring the entire venture crashing down.

This uneasy truce ended when Ernest Barry filed a claim against Norman's estate alleging that he was entitled to a 10 per cent equity interest in Lake Shore Plaza for his efforts relating to the purchase of the Kincaid property. Of course, had Norman lived, Barry would never have put forth such a claim. But Norman was dead, and Barry hoped he might be paid something now that there was no one alive to dispute his claim.

It would be unfair to say that Barry precipitated the deluge, but soon afterward, others stepped forward to present their demands. Some were no more valid than Barry's; others were perfectly proper. Thus began the assaults of partners, creditors, lenders, contractors, subcontractors, suppliers, employees, agents, brokers. Each day I found myself more involved in the affairs of Kane Enterprises. It soon became clear that I would have time for little else. Still it was difficult for me to make the move from my own office to Norman's premises. "Just until things settle down," I told my partners, but we all had our private doubts.

Norman Kane's huge office was barely large enough to contain the meeting. The boys were there—Lentman, Rhodes, Winsley, Lillis, Woodward and Klein—and they brought their lawyers with them. Not too surprisingly, each man had his own lawyer now.

Frank Glover represented General Stone. He sat to one side flanked by two younger men from his office. Even Frieda Kane was represented by separate counsel (at my request), although technically I was her lawyer, and strictly speaking, I was still the attorney for Lake Shore Plaza.

Delbert Kincaid and his attorneys sat quietly in the rear of the room. The largest group of lawyers, accountants and executives represented Fidelity Standard Life Insurance Company. I noted a few men from the Chicago National Bank. Others in the room were complete strangers to me.

Miss Fritch sat alone taking notes, even though we had hired a court reporter who was supposed to be copying down every word. God knows it was impossible to catch every comment made during the meeting.

The only investor not present in person was General Stone. This was not surprising; the General seldom appeared at our meetings. Somehow it was more ominous when Frank Glover said, "the General thinks," or "the General suggests."

Norman's massive conference table was not large enough to accommodate this mob. I had the table placed against the wall along with most of the other furniture and ordered a few dozen folding chairs brought in. I worked at Norman's desk, and some of the others spread their papers on the conference table.

August Lentman stood up. "Gentlemen," he cried, "I would like to make a statement."

"A statement?" said Phil Winsley. "Another statement? You've been making statements for six months."

"Look, Winsley," said Lentman, "if I want to make a statement, I gotta right to do it. I got two and a half million bucks in this lousy deal. Since when can't I open my mouth?"

"Just a minute," said Joseph Woodward. "I'm sure we'll all have a chance to speak. I'd like to ask Mr. Lentman one question. Are you going to tell us anything different than you told us at the last three meetings?"

"Not exactly," said Lentman. "But I'm going to put it a different way."

"Well," said George Lillis, "if you're only going to repeat yourself, what the hell is the use?"

"Listen," said Lentman, "if I wanta talk, I'm gonna talk. When I got into this deal in the first place, it was represented to me that we had a commitment from an insurance company plus all the necessary leases." Lentman spoke on and on, reiterating what everyone else knew. The men moved restlessly about. Lentman's voice was loud and irritating, but after a few minutes nobody was listening.

"Shut up, for God's sake," yelled Stanley Klein, rising to his feet. "I've heard that same goddamn story so many times I can't stand it. Shut up already. I got two and a half million dollars in this deal, too!"

In the background, the men from the bank and the men from the insurance company looked at one another and sadly shook their heads.

Woodward's attorney began to speak. "Gentlemen, I'm sure we can work out our difficulties together."

"Who says?" yelled Lentman. "You goddamn lawyers get us into trouble, and then you want to be paid to get us out. You couldn't work out a thing, you moron."

"Just a minute," Woodward said. "Insults are unnecessary."

There was general disapproval of Lentman's statement. I let them quibble for a time longer, waiting for Frank Glover to speak. But Glover only looked down at his pad and tapped it with his pencil.

Eventually there was a moment of silence.

"Gentlemen," I said, "I suggest we call the meeting to order. We are here for a specific purpose. When we met before, we reviewed a draft of a settlement agreement prepared by Mr. Glover and his associates. Briefly, under the terms of this document, General Stone agrees to provide the additional funds required to complete this project—up to a stipulated maximum amount—in return for certain concessions to be made by the other investors. Naturally, all of this is subject to our making satisfactory arrangements regarding the permanent financing.

"A great many objections to various portions of the draft agreement were voiced during our last meeting, and it was suggested that each attorney file with the others a written copy of his comments. This resulted in rather considerable correspondence, and I took it upon myself to correlate these memoranda and prepare a single paper summarizing the objections of the parties. I sent that paper to you several days ago. I assume that by now you have all had a chance to review it."

No one protested, so I continued. "Before we go further, may I ask whether anyone here feels his position has been misstated in my memo or whether I have left any points uncovered?"

Mendelson, Winsley's attorney, spoke. "Well, uh, I would say, on the whole, you did a pretty good job. I'm not exactly crazy about some of the language you used, but still I think that generally speaking, you summarized our objections pretty well." Lentman's attorney made a similar statement.

"Thank you," I said. "We may not know where to go from here, but at least we know what we disagree on. All right, then, I'll use my memo as the starting point for our discussion of the settlement agreement. If you don't mind, I'll refer to Messrs. Lentman, Rhodes, Winsley, Klein, Woodward and Lillis collectively, as the 'minority equity holders.' Now, under the terms of the proposed agreement, any funds advanced by General Stone would have priority over the investment of the minority equity holders. As I understand it, the basic objection seems to be that the minority equity holders are reluctant to subordinate their notes."

"The basic objection," said Winsley, "is that we are being wiped out!" There was a grumble of agreement in the room.

"Mr. Winsley," I said, "I understand you are not happy

about the situation. You should recall that I'm the attorney for the Kane estate as well as the company's counsel, and that the Kane interests will be subject to exactly the same risks as yours. I'm no happier than you are, but we have to do the best we can.

"Now then, as I said, your prime objection seems to be the subordination provision. Most of your investment is in the form of short-term notes. These notes were always subordinated to the mortgage debt of the company and to any other institutional loans. However, the current agreement would also subordinate your notes to the debt this project will owe General Stone."

"You can call it whatever you like," Lentman said, "but let's be realistic. Most of the income from this project goes to make the mortgage payments and cover the operating costs of the buildings, including a nice fat management fee to the General's own real-estate company. Now, after paying off everybody else, we have to pay General Stone, and then, if there's any money left over it goes to us. But if there's nothing left we get nothing. And even if we're paid something, unless our notes are paid off inside of ten years, we never get the rest of our money back."

"I think," I said quietly, "you have accurately stated the order of priority."

"So what's the hope? The way this building's going, the income will never be enough to pay off General Stone in ten years."

One of Glover's assistants spoke. "In our opinion, the General has been very generous. After all, he's putting up millions of additional dollars. He holds a pledge of all of your stock and notes, and if he wanted to, he could foreclose on them at once. Now, if you accept our plan, you have an opportunity to recoup your money or at least a goodly portion of it. In fact, if the project is successful, and we see no reason why it should not be, you may get all your money back plus interest and still retain your equity."

"Look, wise guy," said August Lentman, "we got six buildings up. Two are completely empty and four are only partly filled. We have to rent another million square feet just to break even. So how do we get anything out of this deal?"

"It it not my intention," I said, "to defend General Stone. However, Mr. Glover's associate is correct. We have nothing now. If the General chose to foreclose on our pledge, I can think of no legal basis on which we could effectively resist him."

Harper Rhodes' lawyer rapped his pencil on a table. "I resent that, Ellison. When you make a statement like that, you don't speak for my client. I'm beginning to wonder who you do represent—Kane or General Stone. We refuse to concede that we have no position. We refuse to surrender our rights just like that. My client has invested millions of dollars in this project and we're not ready to let it all go down the drain. If we chose, we could make it damn hot for General Stone. He won't collect on our pledges quite so easily. So let's not give away the ball game, Ellison."

Others in the room nodded. Rhodes' attorney had apparently restored some of their courage.

"I don't think it's useful to make charges and countercharges. If you believe my statement is detrimental to your client, you have every right to object. You may do whatever you wish to redeem your pledge and prevent your stock and notes from going to General Stone. However, speaking for my client, I don't intend to put on a bold false front. In my opinion, if we can negotiate an agreement which will give us a decent chance to come out of this thing whole, I'm in favor of it. But I don't expect to impress anybody—not Mr. Glover and surely not General Stone—by talking tough. The time to talk tough, sir, was long before our clients pledged their equity."

There was a murmur of voices and a few disgruntled comments. Then Joe Woodward rose.

"I've consulted with my attorney, and frankly, he feels that the General seems to have a strong position. We're not saying that if this thing were explored more deeply we wouldn't find out we have rights we don't even suspect. However, this could all end up in protracted litigation with costs which would eat away our chance to recoup our capital. Right now, I've forgotten about profits. All I want to do is get back as much of my money as possible. Therefore my attorney and I feel we should try to work something out with General Stone. His offer gives us some hope of recovering our investment."

"Some hope!" exploded Phil Winsley. "This whole thing is a sham! Who are we kidding? The General just wants us to go along with him so he can get hold of this project without lawsuits and without bad publicity. We're getting nothing. This bullshit about kindly, generous old General Stone is too much for me to swallow."

Winsley turned to Glover. "Don't be so generous, sweetheart. It don't look good on you. You been doing Stone's dirty work for twenty years, and if you look under your nails, you'll find plenty of mud not even those five-dollar manicures can clean out. I say, let's tell the General to try and foreclose. The hell with this fake little gentleman crap."

Glover stood up and smiled thinly at Phil Winsley. "All right, Mr. Winsley, if that's your final word, that's what we will do." He turned and looked around the room. Everyone stared at him, but no one spoke. Winsley's jaw dropped open.

"Good day, gentlemen. I regret you've chosen to take such a harsh view of the General's offer. I'll tell him that in your opinion there's nothing for him to do but foreclose on his pledges." Glover nodded to his assistants and they left the room together.

There was a moment of frozen silence. Then George Lillis shoved back his chair and ran to Phil Winsley. "Damn you, Winsley. Since when did you get so fucking brave? Well, you made your speech, you son of a bitch, and now we all have to suffer for it."

August Lentman hurried to Winsley's side. "Listen, Lillis, stop yelling at Winsley. At least he showed some guts."

"Guts," laughed Lillis. "You'll see his guts. His guts will be spread all over the floor."

And then there was a general scramble as men left their seats and began yelling and screaming at each other. I looked toward the back of the room. Frieda Kane and the representatives of the bank and insurance company sat quietly. Vern Hanson was studying his hands.

In the midst of it all, Winsley's lawyer handed me a piece of paper. "Take a look at this after the meeting, will you, Eddie?"

It took me several minutes to quiet the group. "I thought we were here to negotiate a settlement with Stone, but now I don't know what your intentions are. If our position is as strong as Mr. Winsley seems to think, then let's act on it. Let's not threaten Mr. Glover. I don't think he scares very easily, and you can't scare the General at all. But I see there's no point in continuing this meeting. Please go back and talk this out with your attorneys. I hope it's not too late to talk to Glover again. I also think you ought to decide whether or not you want me to continue representing the group. I suggest you appoint another spokesman. I never again want to find myself asserting a position only to discover you don't agree with me."

Woodward's attorney spoke. "I do agree with you, Ellison, and I think the attack on you was unwarranted."

"Thank you, but that's behind us now. Let's each confer with our own clients." I began to tuck my papers in my brief-case, although I did not intend to leave Norman Kane's office.

The office cleared in a few minutes. Vern Hanson murmured a few kind words on his way out. Frieda Kane pressed my hand, but that was it. In a moment I was alone in the office except for Miss Fritch.

I remembered the note Winsley's attorney had handed me. I opened the envelope and read these words: "My client will return to your office twenty minutes after the meeting breaks up. Will you please hold your schedule open, so he can speak to you?" I looked up to see Miss Fritch staring at me with a compassionate expression.

"Miss Fritch, we're going to have a visitor. Mr. Winsley is going to return to the office. When he does, please bring him in at once. I'm going to do something Norman Kane used to do. You sit at your intercom because I'm going to turn on the one in this office. Will you please record our conversation?"

Miss Fritch's eyebrows rose, but all she said was, "Yes, sir."

Phil Winsley returned in ten, rather than twenty, minutes. He looked as if he wanted to shake hands but was afraid I might reject his offer. I decided to let him keep thinking I was angry with him.

"Listen, Ellison, let me make my position clear. I think the

General's got us over a barrel. I think we're screwed. I think if he forecloses on those pledges, he'll wipe us out."

"For heaven's sakes, then, why did you say what you did?"

"I come from a neighborhood where if you're scared shit-less, you talk tough."

"I'm afraid, Mr. Winsley, you're in a different neighbor-hood now."

"I ain't so sure. The General came from the same neigh-borhood. But there's more to it than that. I not only wanted him to think I'm thinking tough, I wanted the other guys to think I'm thinking tough, too."

"I'm afraid I don't understand you."

"We're screwed. We got nothing. Kane got us into this deal, but Kane ain't here to get us out, and the General ain't gonna get us out and *you* ain't gonna get us out. Now when you're in a spot like this, I say cut your losses, boy, cut your losses. What I want is a favor, see? I want you to go to the General for me. I think you can talk to him. I don't say you're in cahoots with him, because I don't believe that bullshit either. But I do believe you can talk to him. Right?"

"I suppose."

"Well, here's the idea. I don't want my notes. I don't want my stock. I don't want no subordination agreement. I want out. Let the General give me a check right now for a million bucks and I'll walk away from the whole thing."

"You mean that our group ought to take forty cents on the dollar?"

"I don't mean nothing of the kind. The others can do what they want. You represented Kane, so I figure you must be a smart guy. What I want is for me, and believe me, I'll take good care of you for doing it. Stone can buy me out for a million dollars. Let the others make whatever deal they can."

For a moment I was speechless. Then I remembered the intercom was on in Miss Fritch's office, and suddenly I was sickened by the whole affair. I closed the switch on mine.

"Permit me to explain something to you, Mr. Winsley. You have the right to do whatever you want. You can go to the General yourself. You can send your own lawyer. You can make any kind of offer you want. You can work with the group or you can work alone. But don't ask me to represent you. I'm not going behind the backs of the other men to make an offer to General Stone. I don't know whether he would take it or not. But if I do what you ask, it must be for the whole group or not at all."

"Are you crazy or something? What is this ethics bit? I've got millions buried out there. So I blow more than a million. So that's murder. I'll cry for a long time, but at least I'll get a million out of it and I'll get it now. Those poor shmucks will spend the next ten years praying the buildings will do better. Well, that kind of crap is not for me. I want out, I tell you. I want out!"

"You're going to get out, Mr. Winsley. You're going to get the hell out of my office right now."

Winsley stared at me.

"I don't get you, Ellison. I thought if you worked for Norman Kane, you must know the angles. But you keep coming up with this pious bullshit. I'll give you one more chance. Are you gonna represent me or not?"

"Listen, you son of a bitch, I wouldn't represent you if you were the last man on earth. And that's the first time I've ever sworn at anyone in a business meeting in my whole life. But you're no client of mine, Winsley, and you never will be. I'll give you one more chance. Get out of here before I throw you out."

Winsley's expression ranged from anger to disbelief, but his eyes still held mine. Even after the door closed, I could still see his eyes.

I found myself standing at the desk. I did not realize I had risen to my feet. I looked down to see that my hands were gripping the desk and my fingers were white.

Ridiculous, I thought. *I'm getting as emotional as Norman Kane. My God, what's come over me?* I sank back into Kane's chair. *What is it? Is it this room? Do I think I'm Norman Kane just because I work at his desk?*

———

I didn't notice the door opening. In fact, nothing pierced my reverie until my eyes focused again and I saw Miss Fritch standing in front of my desk.

"You turned off your intercom, Mr. Ellison. I hardly heard anything. I thought it might be a mistake and I wanted to tell you, but I didn't know how to do it."

"That's all right, Miss Fritch, it was intentional. Mr. Winsley's remarks were so sickening that I didn't want our discussion recorded. As far as I'm concerned, you can throw away your notes."

"Oh. I'm sorry, Mr. Ellison. I know it must have been very unpleasant for you."

"Unpleasant is not the word, Miss Fritch. I'm afraid I'm terribly shaken by the whole thing."

Miss Fritch almost smiled. "Just a minute. I'm sure if Mr. Kane were here he wouldn't mind." She scurried off to the paneled wall and pressed a button. Two doors swung open to reveal Norman Kane's elaborate smoked-glass bar—almost a duplicate of the one in his apartment.

I watched Miss Fritch while she took down a bottle of gin and set a glass on the counter.

"Is a martini all right, Mr. Ellison?"

"Well, I think it's a little early, Miss Fritch, don't you?"

"Oh, no, not when you've had a meeting like that. Mr. Kane always liked to have a martini after a meeting like that."

"You may have a point." I sat patiently in my chair while Miss Fritch mixed me a martini.

"Olives or onions, Mr. Ellison?"

"Olives."

"On the rocks or straight up, Mr. Ellison?"

"Straight up."

"Oh, good. Just like Mr. Kane." Smiling proudly, she brought me the martini. "Do you want to drink it at your desk, sir? How about the couch with the little coffee table?"

I struggled up from my chair, walked to the couch and settled into it gratefully. Miss Fritch stood before me. I could tell that she was waiting for me to evaluate her skill. I picked up the drink and took a heavy jolt. "Excellent, Miss Fritch. Absolutely excellent."

"I'm so pleased. Mr. Kane always said I was a good bartender."

"You are, Miss Fritch. No doubt about it—in addition to all of your other talents."

"Now, just put your feet up on the table. Oh, go ahead. It's all right. I'll pull off your shoes."

"Wait a minute," I protested, though perhaps a bit feebly.

"No, I can tell you need it. Go right ahead. Put your feet up."

I did what I was told, holding the drink in my hand, while Miss Fritch pulled off my shoes.

"Now, why don't you loosen your tie and relax?"

"How about you, Miss Fritch? Would you like a martini?"

"Oh, no, sir. Thank you very much." She leaned over and began loosening my tie.

I took another pull on the martini and the ugly memory of Phil Winsley began to recede.

"If you put down your drink for a second, we can take off your jacket."

"Oh?" I said, rather brilliantly. Miss Fritch gently took the glass from my hand and helped me out of my suit jacket.

"Now rest."

"Fine."

"I'm sure you'll feel better. Here's your drink again."

Gratefully I reached for the drink. By now I was nearing the bottom.

"There's more in the pitcher," she said.

I wanted to protest. In fact, I felt it was a positive necessity for me to protest. But somehow I could not force myself to do it. In a moment Miss Fritch was back with the pitcher, and she refilled my glass to the brim.

"Just fine, Miss Fritch. Just fine. I'm struggling to force Phil Winsley out of my mind. What a horrible man."

"That's exactly what Mr. Kane used to say. But Winsley always wanted to be in his deals, you know. And he had all that money. Sometimes Mr. Kane needed him."

"I understand," I said, but actually I was past the point where I understood much at all. The agitation of the afternoon, combined with Miss Fritch's martinis (to which I was unaccustomed), was beginning to take effect. I shook my head, trying to regain control.

"Oh, you're frowning, Mr. Ellison. I know what you need. It always relaxed Mr. Kane."

Her words puzzled me. I watched her walk to the far end of the room and turn her back. It took me a few moments to realize that Miss Fritch was removing her clothes.

I was stunned. *Oh, no,* I thought, *not Fritchie. Not plain, reliable, trustworthy and sensible Fritchie. Norman Kane and almost anybody, but not Miss Fritch.*

I rose to protest, but the martinis had nearly mesmerized me and I sank back into the soft cushions. All the while, Miss Fritch was efficiently removing her dress, her shoes and her stockings. She folded her clothing and placed it neatly over the back of a chair.

I was not so drunk I could not focus on her. And the vision amazed me. Stripped to her bra and panties, Miss Fritch was a marvelous sight. How could I have ever imagined that beneath her bulky tweed suits and heavy stockings Miss Fritch was hiding a splendid bosom, a trim waist and magnificently tapered hips and legs? But it was true. Clearly and unmistakably true. A new emotion, desire, began to overcome my surprise.

Miss Fritch advanced upon me, her ample bosom trembling above the white cotton brassiere. All I could think of saying was, "The door, Miss Fritch. What about the door?"

She smiled, and when she did, her severe features softened almost to prettiness.

"I locked it when I came in. I had a feeling you would need me, Mr. Ellison. I just had a feeling." Miss Fritch waggled her gray-brown curls in a maternal way, but she kept coming closer, and in a moment she had settled beside me on the couch.

"Do you want to remove my brassiere and panties yourself? Mr. Kane always did."

That struck a jarring note. "Must we speak of Mr. Kane?"

Miss Fritch smiled. "No, I suppose not. Oh, well, I'll do it myself." She reached back to unsnap her brassiere. Miss Fritch's bosom, no longer compressed by the restraining elastic, sprang forward. I sat motionless, watching her in paralyzed fascination. The incredible Miss Fritch sat naked beside me, smiling sweetly.

She was even more nobly proportioned than her simple underclothing had led me to believe. Her skin looked very smooth and soft. I could not resist reaching out to touch her. My hands rested tentatively on her shoulders, then drifted of their own volition across her breasts.

Miss Fritch covered my hands with her own. She smiled again.

"You still have your clothes on, Mr. Ellison. You ought to at least remove your pants." She began to fumble with my belt. I pushed her away.

"That, at least, I can do myself." I stood up and removed my clothes.

Miss Fritch looked at me approvingly. "I knew I was right," she said. "I just knew it." She took me gently by the hand.

Miss Fritch leaned close and smiled at me. "Feel better now?"

I nodded, "And you?"

"Oh, yes," she said. "I feel fine."

"Good," I said. "I would have hated to disappoint you."

"I knew you wouldn't. And anyway, it wouldn't have mattered if you did. After all, you're a friend of—" she paused. "I'm not supposed to say that."

"That's all right, Miss Fritch. It's rare that devotion such as yours extends beyond the grave."

Miss Fritch blushed. "Thank you, Mr. Ellison. Not everyone would understand."

I couldn't think of anything to say.

"Do you want to take a nap now? There's a blanket in the cabinet. I'll get it for you."

"Oh, no," I said anxiously. "I'll just sit here for a moment. You've done more than enough for me already."

"Are you sure, Mr. Ellison?"

"Miss Fritch, I'm positive. Now I think that it's time for me to get back to work."

"Very well," said Miss Fritch, and she put on her secretarial face, which seemed rather amusing perched above her voluptuous body. Miss Fritch was not affronted. She knew her place.

I dressed as rapidly as I could, but long before I was finished, Miss Fritch had put on her clothes, straightened her hair, and closed the bar.

As she left the office, Miss Fritch nodded pleasantly, but her expression was remote.

———◆———

The next morning I had a surprise visitor: Dan McGarrity. He arrived without an appointment, but I was not about to stand on ceremony. I immediately instructed Miss Fritch to bring him in.

As usual, McGarrity was filled with good cheer. "Well, Eddie, this is quite a spread you got here. Real impressive."

"It's not mine, Dan. It's Norman's."

"I know, I know. But you seem to fit in real good. You look mighty comfortable."

"I wish I were, Dan. But the truth is, this is still Norman's desk, and it doesn't quite seem to fit me."

"You're very nice to say that, Eddie. I'm sure old Normie would appreciate it." There was a moment of respectful silence.

"Sit down, Dan. Tell me what brings you here." I took a seat next to McGarrity. I knew better than to face him across Norman's desk.

"Just a friendly visit, Eddie. Wanted to see how you're doing. Wanted to offer my help to you. Norman was a dear friend and I miss him. But we all have to carry on, don't we?"

"Right. We all have to carry on. I'm sure you realize it's not easy." McGarrity was taking his time getting to the point.

"The rumor is, your deal is having trouble, Eddie. Bank's bothering you. Partners up in arms. Must be quite a burden."

"It is. I don't exactly know how I got on the hot seat."

"But you're the perfect man for the job, Eddie. Calm, sensible, reasonable. A good lawyer. No, I think everything is working out just the way it should."

"I hope you're right, Dan. It's quite a struggle. Some days I feel like chucking the whole thing."

"Don't do it. They need you. But there's no use killing yourself, Eddie. And there's no point taking wild chances. There are big people in this deal. Mighty big people. You just do what's right, and it'll all turn out OK."

"What's right, Dan?"

"I think you know."

"Tell me."

"Well, there's no point being rough on Carrelli—"

"He was pretty rough on Kane."

"Yes, but you know these excitable Italians. He didn't mean any harm to Norman."

"Are you here on behalf of Carrelli?"

"Hell, no. I just hear things, you understand. In a town like this, word gets around. And we both know that if you push a contractor too far, it hurts the job. I'm not defending Carrelli. But you have to get the buildings up, don't you? Of course."

"Of course. I think we have that under control, Dan. You don't have to worry about it."

"Good. Glad to hear it. I know you won't do anything crazy. You're not the type."

I waited for McGarrity to go on. I remembered Norman's concern about Carrelli's getting mixed up with McGarrity, but I couldn't believe that was the only thing that had brought Dan to my office.

"Well, then, I won't bother myself about Carrelli," McGarrity said. "There's more at stake, isn't there?"

"It's all part of the picture."

"And a big picture it is. Big people in a big picture. No use fighting everybody, is there, Eddie?"

"I'm not fighting anybody."

"Good. I wouldn't want to see you climbing out on a limb. I know it's tough to keep Norman's old partners in line, but you're the man who can do it."

"I hope so."

"I know it. Well, I won't take any more of your time. You're OK, Eddie. You're on the right track and you're going to go a long way." McGarrity stood up and looked around the room. "Yes, it's mighty pretty here, and you look mighty good in these surroundings."

McGarrity left me then, and I was faced with the problem of interpreting his innuendos. He was obviously telling me to go slow. Was he fronting for Stone? Perhaps. Carrelli was obviously a side issue.

The more I thought about it, the more it seemed to me I was being told to play the General's game. I didn't like the idea, but was there really any choice? What could I do but help the partners work out a settlement? Stone's terms weren't generous, but they weren't unbearable. There was still hope the boys would end up with something.

Perhaps McGarrity was right. I was a lawyer, not an entrepreneur. With luck, I could wind things up in a few months and get the hell out of Kane's business. Yes, it made sense. Wrap it all up and get back to Hardwick, Burns, Ellison and Dean. That was where I belonged. Anyone could see that. Eleanor was certain to see it.

Of course, McGarrity had told me how "natural" I looked in Kane's office. As if someone—Stone?—was trying to suggest that I could really follow Norman. Take his place. Run his business. And if McGarrity was right, I would have "friends" to help me. Was that what I really wanted? It was terribly confusing. I sat down in Norman's chair and tried to puzzle it out.

———◆———

While I was still trying to organize my thoughts, Miss Fritch rang. Frieda Kane was waiting to see me. Another complication. I wasn't ready to talk to Frieda, but I couldn't turn her away.

When Miss Fritch escorted her in, I suddenly realized that I was sitting behind Norman's desk in Norman's office. For some reason I felt embarrassed, and as Frieda entered I scrambled to my feet and tried to move away from the desk.

"Please stay where you are," she said. "If Norman had his choice he would want you there." Echo of Dan McGarrity.

We both sat down. "Eddie, you're the best friend Norman ever had." I began to protest, but Frieda shook her head. "No, I mean it. You stood by him through everything, despite the objections of others and the temptations they offered you. But I'm not here to flatter you. I simply want to understand what's happening, Eddie. You're the only one who can tell me."

"That's quite a broad question, Frieda. Perhaps you can narrow it down."

Frieda smiled. "Ever the lawyer, I see. Well, first of all, tell me where I stand financially."

I was certain her own attorney had answered that question by now, but I responded anyway.

"You're well taken care of. Norman pledged many of his investments and he took many risks, but he never did anything to impair the assets he reserved for you."

"I know that. I'm really trying to lead up to this gently."

"Why not be direct, Frieda?"

She hesitated, turning her head as she groped for words, presenting her profile for my examination. Her blond hair was drawn back in a severely simple style, which served only to emphasize her elegant features. She wore little makeup, but emotion had tinged her face with color, and determination shimmered in her blue-green eyes. Frieda Kane had never seemed more beautiful to me.

"It's funny," she said. "Norman never accused me of being sentimental, but it's not easy to talk about this. People think I'm cold and aloof. Maybe they're right. I do have a certain icy strain that no one except Norman ever warmed out of me. Norman taught me how to live and breathe. Whatever heart there is in me, Norman Kane put there.

"You know what?" she said, leaning forward. "I never even told that to Norman. I didn't think he wanted to hear it. There were times when I needed him badly and I had to pretend that I didn't. I couldn't disappoint him by showing weakness any more than one of his buildings would have dared to disappoint him by collapsing." She seemed close to tears.

"I'm sorry, Frieda. What do you want to know?"

My response seemed to irritate her. "I've sat through all your meetings, I've listened to my attorney and to you dozens of times. I've heard Phil Winsley yell, and seen Vern Hanson shake his head. What I want to know is, what will happen to it all? To Norman's twenty-five years?"

"Forgive me, Frieda, but can't you be more explicit?"

"For heaven's sake, you know what I'm talking about. What will happen to St. Louis and Newark?" Suddenly she began to laugh, but only for an instant. She held on to the chair arms tightly and then began to speak again in a flat, low-pitched voice. "St. Louis and Newark—that's Norman talking. He built one building in each town and thought he owned the whole city." Her voice almost broke, but once again she won the struggle to control herself. It was painful to watch.

"Since you insist, I'll spell it out. In twenty-five years Norman built dozens of buildings. He pyramided one deal on top of another until he controlled hundreds of millions of dollars of real estate. Now tell me, as plainly as you can, what will happen to it all."

I was beginning to understand. "To Kane Enterprises, you mean? To the Kane Empire?"

Frieda nodded her head.

"It's not easy to say. I've spent months trying to untangle the knots in Norman's legal arrangements. I'm still not completely sure what he pledged for what, and I don't know when and how we can get the properties back—if at all. I'll rescue everything I can—for you, for the investors—even for General Stone. But frankly, I don't know if there's any point in trying to hold it all together."

"You don't know? After all these years, you don't know?"

"Please, Frieda, not you, too." Suddenly I was angry. "Damn it, what's the difference? What does it matter now?"

Frieda drew back her lips in an angry grimace. "What does it matter?" For twenty-five years a man struggles and builds. He creates projects no one has ever dreamed of and develops

322

them in ways no one ever tried before. He takes fantastic chances, and by enormous effort he acquires all these marvelous buildings, and you say 'What does it matter?' "

Before I could answer she rose from her chair, turned her back and walked a few steps away. She kept her back turned while she spoke. "I still remember driving down Lake Shore Drive with Norman years ago, long before Lake Shore Plaza. He was depressed that day, very depressed. He seemed to have problems everywhere—nothing was going right."

Frieda turned and walked back to me. "I told him, 'Look, Norman, look at what you've done.' I pointed to the apartment buildings we were passing. 'You built them, Norman. They're here only because you created them. No one can take that away from you.' Then I said the wrong thing. 'They're a kind of monument,' I said. Norman banged his hand against the steering wheel. 'Who the hell cares about monuments?' he said. 'What does it matter once you're dead? The only thing to do with life is live it. After I'm dead I don't care if every damn building I ever built falls to the ground!' "

"I'm sorry, Frieda, but if that's true, I don't understand what you want of me."

She wrung her hands. I didn't know how to comfort her.

"I'm trying to explain. I wouldn't mind if it happened gradually—if we sold the properties one by one across the years. But *this,* Eddie, this is killing Norman all over again. We're not selling Norman's buildings, they're being torn out of our hands."

I said nothing. Frieda took a deep breath before she spoke again.

"I loved him, Eddie. I can't stand by while heartless men destroy everything he created. Part of Norman wore off on me. When those men tear down Norman Kane, they're peeling off my skin."

It was a raw phrase and it hit me very hard. I stared down at my yellow legal pad. I couldn't look at Frieda.

Frieda was striding back and forth again. "What is it, Eddie? Why do they feel this terrible urge to ruin everything he ever did?"

"I don't think it's that personal, Frieda. These men have a

lot of money invested and they're afraid they will lose it."

Frieda literally ran to my desk and leaned across it, bringing her face almost level with mine. "It's not true. Not a word of what you say is true. They want to destroy him. They can't wait to destroy him."

"Frieda," I said, "Norman is already dead."

She recoiled only a fraction. "Do you think I'm an utter fool? A completely sentimental fool? Who knows better than I do that Norman is dead?"

Frieda stood erect. "I see I'm wasting my time. I thought you felt the same way about him that I do. But I was wrong. He was just a client. You were paid a fee—I'm sure you earned it—but that was it."

"Yes and you were his wife," I answered angrily. "I'm sure you earned it, too. But that didn't stop Norman from sniffing after every skirt in town." The moment the words escaped me, I felt like slitting my own throat. But it was too late.

Frieda projected her special smile—the one she might have given Norman had he spoken as I did.

"You're right, Eddie, he cheated on me. But he never cheated *me*. I don't suppose you'd understand the difference."

I got up from behind the desk and walked toward her. "I'm sorry, Frieda. I shouldn't have said that. But you're not being fair either. You may not believe it, but I'm human too. You must know how I felt about Norman, and, of course I'm fond of you." It was something of a declaration and I thought I'd better hurry on. "I'm doing my best to save everything I can. What on earth do you expect me to do?" We were standing so close together that our faces almost touched. I was nearly overcome by the same conflicting emotions that assaulted me the evening I spent alone with her in the Kane apartment.

Frieda backed away, half smiled, and pulled on her gloves.

"Do what Norman Kane would have done, Eddie. You followed him around for years, you watched everything he did. You drew the agreements that document his life. If you strung his legal papers together, they would read like a novel. Go back and read the book, Eddie. Go back and read the book."

The meeting with Frieda left me feeling weak and inadequate. Her words were devastating. Even as she left the office, I realized she had shattered my entire strategy. I would have to re-examine everything I had done, even the most basic procedures. I realized that I had erred in calling everyone together to discuss General Stone's offer. I should have known that a face-to-face confrontation, with all parties gathered in one large room, would only end in a shouting match and eventual disaster. Anyway, I wasn't going to let it happen again. Nor was I going to sit back and let events take their course as McGarrity had more or less suggested. No, it was time to take action. I would work with each of the parties individually and reach what agreements I could. I would talk to the lawyers—not to their clients, if I could help it—and see if we could find some common ground, some basis on which to approach General Stone. This seemed logical, sensible and sound. I was amazed that I had not followed this procedure in the past.

An hour later I was sitting in the anteroom one floor below General Stone's office. I arrived without an appointment, without telling anyone of my plans. I looked about in bewilderment, wondering what impulse had brought me there. Only minutes before I had decided to negotiate individually with the attorneys of each partner and then present my plan to General Stone. Now, ignoring my own good sense, I was waiting for admission to the General's office. My God, the man might keep me waiting for hours. And what would he think? A lawyer does not talk to another lawyer's client without permission. The sudden inspiration had been overwhelming. *Frieda is right,* I had thought. *Let's "Norman Kane" it. Let's go to General Stone and straighten this thing out here and now.* Thus inspired, I had rushed out of the office and hurried up to the General's private suite.

As I waited, my courage began to dribble away. I accused and tormented myself. I thought of leaving. No excuse—just bolt. I could feel myself about to lift up out of my seat, a missile about to be launched from its pad. Abruptly the fires subsided. How could I explain my coming and going? It was all too absurd. I was trapped.

"Mr. Ellison, General Stone will see you now." I nodded

and headed for his private elevator, the electronic carpet that would lift me onto the sacred plane with General Stone.

He was waiting at the doors—so close that I almost stepped back.

"Eddie Ellison, imagine you coming up here. I'm delighted. Come on in." The General's cheerful greeting increased my anxiety.

"You've been here before, I know. I don't have to impress you with the Cook's Tour. It's all the same. I never change it. Of course, the Monet's gone, the one I gave Norman."

"I know. He treasured it greatly."

"A moment of madness. When he put through that fantastic financing with Fidelity Standard, I was astonished. And like a sentimental old fool I gave him the painting. I'll bet I surprised myself more than I surprised Norman." He chortled over the memory, savoring it.

"Sit down, Eddie. How about a drink?"

"Oh, I don't think I—"

"Don't be silly. This is an occasion—you coming up here to see me. What'll it be?"

Reluctantly I told him. The General hurried to his electronic bar, waving his hand at the magic wall like a child. I watched him. The zillionaire bartender.

We chatted for a few moments, discussing irrelevant subjects. I searched for an opportunity to take a bold stance. It was not easy, sitting there immersed in those plush cushions with that damn drink pinning down one hand and a piece of my brain.

The General took me off the hook. "Glover tells me they're giving you a rather bad time of it. Sorry to hear that, Eddie. Glover says you took it rather well."

"That was nice of Mr. Glover. I admit I had a few unpleasant moments, but I understand how those men feel, General Stone. They've invested a lot of money, probably more than they can afford to lose. I suppose in like circumstances most men would act the same way."

"Of course. Most men would, and that, sir, is the trouble with most men."

Abruptly the tone of the General's voice had chilled. I

struggled uncomfortably in my feather cushion prison. This was not what I wanted at all.

"I know what you mean, General. If you reacted like Lentman and Winsley and the others, you wouldn't be where you are today."

"I'm glad you understand."

"Oh, I do. But first, let me say I know I shouldn't be here. I should have called Glover and asked him to arrange an appointment. But I had this impulse to talk to you. I know, no matter what Mr. Glover or anyone else says, you make the final decisions."

"I don't mind at all. Go ahead, Eddie, speak your piece."

"Thanks. You know this thing could drag on for months, even years. Let's say your position is strong." The General seemed about to rise in his chair, so I hurried ahead. "Let's say it's very strong. Nevertheless, hotheads like Winsley can make it unpleasant for everyone. Don't think for a moment I'm threatening you. That would be ridiculous. I know you're not one bit afraid of litigation. But, let's face it, it's still tiresome."

"So what?" The General's voice was disturbingly harsh.

"General, our project has had its problems, but now most of them are behind us. Oh, yes, the costs ran over our budget quite considerably. We all know that. But now the buildings are up. They're not completed, but they're up. And a great deal of the space has been leased. Once we settle our differences and concentrate on developing this project, I'm sure the rest of the leasing program will move right along. You can't dump six million feet of space onto the market all at once and expect to rent it overnight. You know it and I know it, and of course, so did Norman Kane."

"Norman Kane isn't here now."

"Still, the fact remains that the buildings *are* here. The conception is still sound, even brilliant. Lake Shore Plaza is probably the most fabulous office complex in this country."

I suddenly found I was talking to the General's back. He had risen from his chair, carrying his drink, and had walked to the windows.

"Why go over all this, Eddie?"

327

"I have to start somewhere. Let me tell it my way."

The General said nothing.

"All right then. The buildings are up. The construction loan hasn't been retired, but it can be. The Fidelity group still wants the permanent mortgage. International Materials has taken possession of its space and so have many of the other tenants. It will all work out one day. Why turn this thing into a dogfight?" I walked over to where the General was standing. Talking to his back was unbearable. I put my hand on his shoulder and half turned him toward me.

"Why squeeze out the other investors? Let them stay in the deal, General, give them a smaller piece of the equity. But let them stay. After all, you have the use of their money. Isn't that fair?"

The General glared at me. "Fair? What the hell is fair?"

"Why, *that's* fair."

"Ellison, you saw those pledge agreements. You knew what our deal was. Why are you trying to change it?"

"Because it's not fair. Those men invested a lot of money. Even Norman Kane put up some money. And he put together a fabulous project. If you don't care about Winsley or Woodward or any of the others, what about Norman Kane?"

"Norman Kane's not here."

"Goddamn it, I know he's not here. I was with him in the hospital when he died. I was his pallbearer. I watched them throw dirt on his casket. I'm the executor of his will. Don't you think I know he's not here?"

"What the hell do I care, then? Why should I do anything for a dead man?"

"Look, General. You're saying things you don't have to say. It isn't right."

"Right? What isn't right? You mean the agreements aren't legal?"

"Of course they're legal."

"Then you think I'm breaking some kind of law?"

"No, you're not breaking any law."

"Then what are you suggesting—that I should be kind to those other guys? I should be charitable?"

"Yes, I guess that's just about what I'm saying. Give them a break."

"The hell with them. The goddamn hell with them. They mean nothing to me. They knew what they were doing when they put up their money. They blew it. Well, ain't that too damn bad?"

"But they're men, General. Human beings. Why can't you see the justice in what I'm suggesting?"

"Justice? There is no justice. Those guys are nothing but parasites, night crawlers. I wouldn't do a damn thing for them."

"I don't understand you. The project was in trouble long before Norman Kane died. You didn't try to foreclose on their pledges then. I don't get it."

"You don't get it. You don't see the difference. To you Norman Kane was the same as Phil Winsley."

"Of course, they were different."

"How different?"

"That's a silly question."

"Silly? Not to me. I didn't need those guys. I didn't need their money. I didn't object to having them in the deal, but I didn't *need* them. Norman Kane I needed. As long as Norman Kane was alive, I strung along. But when Norman kicked off, that was the end. When Norman Kane died, they died. To me they don't exist."

"But that's crazy. Of course they exist."

The General stared at me. His eyes seemed to bulge from his face. He no longer looked like a cherubic child. I could see the hot fury boiling up inside him. And even I, who had little to lose, felt a momentary stab of fear.

"Norman Kane is dead," the General said, "and with Norman Kane dead, they're all dead."

He walked past me to the bar and refilled his own drink. All resolution left me. I had expended everything I had in making my plea.

When the General turned to me again, he was not the same man. The flush was gone from his face. Once more he was the smooth financial genius. But his voice was curiously flat. "I thought you were different. I figured you couldn't spend all those years with Norman Kane without learning something. When Glover told me what you said at the meeting the other day, I was pretty surprised. I couldn't believe you were taking this so mildly. I told Glover, 'Keep an eye on that boy. Norman Kane didn't keep no jerks around him.' But I guess I was wrong."

The General walked away again, and I could feel anger pushing aside the fear in me. But the General wasn't finished.

"When I heard you had come over here today, I got pretty excited. Seemed I was right all the time. I thought you had a proposition. Something interesting. Oh, I knew I shouldn't talk to you. I knew I should get hold of Glover. But I thought to myself, this has turned into a rotten, crummy, miserable deal. Maybe this guy's got an angle. So what's your angle, Ellison? I'll tell you what it is: faith, hope and charity. What a package! I turned that one down forty years ago."

"Look, General—"

"I *am* looking, and I don't like what I see." He shook his head. "I thought you might be like Kane. I said to myself, maybe I could do things with this guy. You see, men like Kane excite me. They got vision. They got guts. I've always had guys like Kane dealing the cards. I give them the deck but they deal the cards. What has Winsley got? Or Klein, or any of them? Can they build a building? Or design one? Can they plan a project? Guys are always coming up here asking me to write checks. And I write plenty of them. Sometimes I write a blank check. I wrote one for Norman Kane. He had a blank check on me. But Norman Kane is dead. And those other crumbs I don't need."

The General stopped a minute. Before my eyes, the chilling reserve had disappeared. Once again he was the angry street fighter. *"You* I don't need. *You* with your pious talk and your dumb proposal. You're a pushover. You got no guts, you never had any. How did you stay alive after Kane died? What keeps you breathing?"

I was breathing rather heavily. The urge to punish Stone physically was strong. I fought it down, and I fought down the urge to dispute his view of me. I felt myself shrinking under his withering look and crude words, but I stood there and listened.

"Nothing to say, huh?"

"I guess you've said it all, General. Don't you think it's unwise to show your contempt for me so clearly?"

"No. I *want* you to know. I *want* you to understand. It's good for a punk like you to know what a man like me thinks of you. It keeps you from making mistakes. Bad mistakes that could hurt me, too. So you play nice-nice, Eddie. Be a tidy little lawyer. You bundle your clients up in a neat package and deliver them to me. I'm not going to hurt you. You got nothing I want. You're safe, see? As long as you don't cross me. But don't bother me again. Just lay your people out in a box and deliver them up here. You get me?"

"I get you."

"OK, sonny, that's it. The interview is over. Blow."

I set my drink down on a coffee table and walked toward the elevator. Behind me the General began to laugh.

I tried to do my job as if I had not met with General Stone. I reviewed the papers again—drafted and redrafted them. I polished the words, changed the phrases. I did everything I could to preserve, with words, as much as possible for the other partners. Unfortunately, when I sat back and analyzed the agreements, I realized they amounted to little more than formalized unconditional surrender. Frieda was right. So were the boys. They would never get a dime out of this deal. Everything would end up in the hands of General Stone. Maybe Winsley—yes, even Phil Winsley—was right. Better to fight the son of a bitch than hand it to him on a platter. It was a terrible thought—I had been drafting the documents of capitulation. Almost proudly, I had played the honorable, sensible attorney, the man who could represent both sides in a complex deal. Unwittingly, day after day, week after week, I had been engineering a disaster.

Once again I had a vision of Norman Kane as a college student—an ungainly little guy with bushy hair, bouncing up and down across a tennis court, retrieving the ball. Not very stylish, but somehow hitting the ball back.

Norman would have sworn like Winsley. He would have struggled and squirmed until he solved the problem. He wouldn't have sat patiently and piously as I had done, calmly and pretentiously preparing the documents of surrender.

There. I pushed the papers away. They scattered around the room. Some of them typed, some in longhand. Interlineations. Paper clips. References. Insertions. Piles and piles of papers.

On the wall, the Monet. The strange painting that up close is a bewildering splash of colors, but at just the right range becomes a masterpiece.

The right range. What was the right range? I looked at the papers. What was the right distance from them? When would they cease to be an incomprehensible mass of words and turn into the pattern of something worthwhile? Somehow, Norman knew how to find the pattern. He knew just how far back to stand. And when he looked, everything became clear.

Of course. What had Frieda said? "Read the book." I had been reading and living it for more than twenty years. Preparing Norman's legal papers, sitting in on his conferences. Had I learned nothing? There must be a pattern.

Somewhat dimly, I began to see it. This was no story, no history, no biography. It was a textbook. Yes, even the broads and the booze, the battle with Carrelli, the bending of Karl Friedrichs, the weaning and wooing of Hobbs and Bennett.

It's all in the book. A living text, made up of the master's words and deeds. Some of it on paper, some still ringing in my ears. I was not the creator, only the observer. But now was the time to analyze my observations. If I didn't, all my efforts up to now were worthless.

———◆———

I invited John Bennett to my own club. I bought him a big lunch and several drinks and we reminisced at great length and in maudlin style over Norman Kane. Bennett assured me that Norman was a brilliant, cultured man with impeccable taste, a great art collector who had demonstrated exquisite judgment.

I urged Bennett to tell me more. "I'm a lawyer, you know. This art stuff doesn't do very much to me. But I always thought art collecting was out of character for Norman Kane."

"Oh, no. You're wrong. Absolutely wrong. You only saw

his crudities. Like most people, you noticed only his aggressive mannerisms, his vulgar speech and brutal tactics. But if you had studied him carefully, you would have found that Norman was a man of great subtlety."

"What about Fidelity Standard and the mortgage?"

Bennett looked at me sharply. He apparently thought I had only intended to reminisce about our late associate. "The mortgage? What about the mortgage?"

"Are you ready to pay out or not?"

"It's not up to me, you know," said Bennett, almost visibly withdrawing. "It's up to Hobbs and our loan committee. But frankly, I don't see how we can pay out. After all, Norman didn't meet the leasing requirements."

"True in part, and part not true, John. In dollars and cents —that is, in quantity—Norman never met the leasing provisions. But the quality of tenancy is far higher than you had any right to expect."

"Yes, but try and sell that to a loan committee."

"You mean they're not impressed by a thirty-year lease from National Tube?"

"Don't get me wrong. There is a certain flavor here that would be helpful if we had something else to hang our hats on. But to pay out a loan when the borrower has fallen hundreds of thousands of dollars short of meeting his rental requirements is impossible."

"What about the works of art Norman loaned you?"

John Bennett suddenly sat upright. He started to speak, then stopped. I waited until I was certain he was not going to respond.

"What's the matter, John? Aren't you feeling well?"

"Well, perhaps I have had a bit too much to drink. Maybe I should get out of here, Eddie."

"You didn't answer my question."

"Question?"

"Yes. About the works of art. The ones Norman loaned you."

"You mean the works Norman *gave* me."

"I didn't know they were gifts. You mean to tell me Norman just plain gave you that art?"

"Why, yes."

"What would you say the value of it all might be?"

"I don't think that's any of your business."

"Ordinarily I wouldn't think so either, but you see, I'm the executor of Norman's estate, and one of my duties is to tally up his assets. Now, if those works of art were loaned to you, then of course, I'll have to ask you to return them. On the other hand, if they were gifts—"

"Of course they were gifts."

"You told me Norman had exquisite taste. I therefore must assume the works he gave you were very valuable. I have a list (I reached into my pocket and pulled out a long sheet of paper) of all the works that Norman either gave or loaned to you. I found it among Norman's effects."

"He kept a list?"

"For a man who was reputed to act in reckless fashion, it's absolutely amazing how well Norman documented his affairs. Of course, I'm not an art expert and I can't evaluate these items. However, many of the artists' names are familiar even to me. If these are original works I'm sure they have considerable value."

"They were gifts."

"Well, if they were, Norman must have failed to report them on his gift-tax returns, and Norman was very careful about filing a gift-tax return every year. I'm sorry. I didn't find your name as a donee on any of Norman's returns for the past ten years."

"Of course not. Norman would never treat such things as taxable items."

"You mean their value was so small it didn't matter?"

"I didn't say that."

"Well, then, how would you value the works Norman gave you?"

"I've never taken an inventory."

"Why don't you look at this?" I handed him the paper. "Perhaps you'd like to jot down the approximate value alongside each of these items."

Bennett shoved the paper back at me. "I would never do any such thing. What are you up to, Ellison? I thought we were here to have a pleasant lunch and talk about an old friend."

"That's what we are doing, John. I don't know why you're upset. I told you before what my problem is. As executor of Norman's estate I'm what they call an 'officer of the court.' When his will is probated I have to be certain that all of his assets are accounted for."

"They're not his assets."

"Then you are sure they were gifts?"

"Of course."

"Tell me, John, does your company know about these gifts?"

Again Bennett straightened, this time as if a sharply pointed weapon had been jabbed between his shoulder blades. "Why would I tell my company about personal gifts exchanged between friends?"

"What did you ever give Norman Kane?"

There was silence.

"I see. Generosity flowed in only one direction. I suppose your company has some knowledge of this."

Again there was silence.

"Well," I said, "I think we're in a bit of a quandary. If these items were loaned, you'll have to give them back. But if they were gifts, you should have reported them to your company. Wouldn't it seem odd to your superiors that one of the company's most important borrowers had given so many art works to a mortgage loan officer?"

Still there was silence. John Bennett stared at me with what is usually called cold fury.

"I believe you ought to give this some thought, John. I have no desire to do you any harm. I know Norman was very fond of you. But Norman isn't here to help us."

"I still don't understand what you want, Ellison. I wish you would tell me."

I stood up. "For the moment, not a thing. Not a thing at all. Come on, John. I certainly enjoyed our lunch. We should get together more often."

We walked through the halls of the club in silence, took our coats from the checkroom and walked to the door. Bennett seemed anxious to leave.

"Just one thing, John. See what you can do to keep Fidelity Standard from taking hasty action."

Bennett stared at me, turned, and walked away down the street.

"I know you've never been here, Vern. I thought it might give us a little different perspective on things."

Vern Hanson spun around in the comfortable swivel chair studying the office. "I heard about it. A lot of people told me about Norman's office. I've been in some pretty fancy-looking places around the country, but this is really something. I don't know how I stayed away. Norman invited me up here a thousand times."

"Why didn't you come? You were always a good friend of his."

Hanson laughed. "You know, I had a hell of a time turning Norman down when I sat behind my own desk. If I had ever come up here I'd have given him the bank. Anyway, I'm here. What do you want of me?"

"I had lunch with John Bennett yesterday. I think he'll do everything in his power to keep his company from canceling their commitment."

"What did you tell Bennett?"

"Let's just say I softened him up."

"All right. What's your proposition?"

"The important thing here is that we must have more time."

"You didn't invite me here to tell me that."

"Vern, I could have told you everything I'm going to say over the telephone. I just wanted you to come up here."

"Get me in the right frame of mind."

"Not exactly. You've always been in the right frame of mind. Norman never had a better friend."

"It was good business for the bank."

"I'm sure. But I'm not sure every other banker would have realized that. You're the reason Norman put almost every deal through Chicago National."

"I'm aware of that and I appreciate it. Unfortunately—and I hate to say it—I don't think the bank can expect any new business from that direction."

I was silent for a moment. I let Vern Hanson grow uncomfortable listening to the echo of his own words.

"What does your bank plan to do now, Vern?"

"We're waiting for you. We assume you will work out something to take us out of the deal."

"Well, yes, that is our general plan. Of course, until yesterday I thought there was only one way to do it. Now I'm hopeful there is another method."

"Isn't it a bit late to be working up new alternatives?"

"I won't waste anybody's time. I'm still processing the agreements we've been discussing. But I represent the venture, and it's my duty to do the best I can. I have to think of all the partners, dead and alive."

"Look, I'm with you. Good luck. But time is running short."

"That's right. All I want from you is a simple declaration—the same kind I got from John Bennett. An acknowledgment that the bank won't take precipitous action."

"Damn it, Eddie, everyone over at the bank is getting jumpy."

"You too?"

"Hell, what do I care? I'm just a few months away from retiring."

"Don't kid me, Vern. You don't want to walk out of there with your tail between your legs."

"Eddie, I think you're an honest man, but I don't believe you give a good goddamn what happens to Vern Hanson."

"Now, wait a minute. That's unfair. I've never done anything to hurt you."

"No, you haven't. And believe me, I'm not going to let you start now."

"I guess I'm not handling this right, Vern. I'm not Norman Kane. I can't find that special combination of words that makes people understand precisely what I want. I'm afraid that, without meaning to, I managed to get your back up."

"Well, damn it, what do you expect? What's the use of your sitting here protecting a dead man?"

"I'm not protecting a dead man. If you stop and think for a second, you'll realize that I have more at stake at the bank than you do. In a few months you retire. Even if they're angry when you leave, they can't cut off your pension. But think of me. Many of my clients do business with the bank. If I do something that hurts Chicago National, what do you think my status will be over there?"

"That makes sense."

"Thank God. I'm finally making sense."

"I'd still like to know, what do you want?"

"Just hold them off. I think I have found the angle."

"Tell me what it is."

"I would if I could. All I ask is that you hold them off."

"Based on what? Promises? Dreams? Some crazy scheme you cooked up in the last twenty-four hours?"

I shrugged my shoulders, stood up and walked around the room. I studied the Monet on the wall. I made a circuit of all the windows.

"You know, if you study this room, you'll eventually notice a strange thing. Nothing that Norman actually built is displayed here in any form—not one of his developments. Now that's unusual. You walk into the office of any other builder and you'll be overwhelmed with drawings, photographs and models. But Norman didn't do that. Why? Because he was modest? Bullshit. Norman didn't give a damn about pictures, models and sketches, because they were only imitations. All Norman cared about was the real thing. A building wasn't a picture hung on a wall. It was a lobby you walked through, elevators you rode in, lights that turned on, and air conditioning that worked. Maybe that's an odd way of seeing things. But as far as I can tell, it was Norman's.

"I'll tell you something else—that's a kind of honesty. Here was a notoriously shrewd salesman, a guy who could sell you anything in the world, and yet he kept his walls free of advertising."

"I don't get the point."

"I'm trying to say something, Vern. You don't want to walk out of that bank pegged as a man who loused up his last and biggest deal. And you don't want to walk out of there a coward, a fool or a fraud."

"What the hell do you mean by that?"

"You're getting angry again, Vern. The point is you don't want to be considered a fool or a phony. Now, if I can find a

338

solution that gets the bank off the hook and lets you walk out with your integrity and your self-respect intact, that's the plan you ought to fight for. Don't say anything, Vern. Just think about it."

So far so good. Two men holding the line. I hadn't scored a victory, but now neither Bennett nor Hanson would take the kind of action that might lead to defeat. What next? I couldn't hold them off forever.

I called in Friedrichs and McNeill and asked them to review the construction situation. I wanted them to compile a statement covering all expenses incurred to date and to estimate as closely as possible the eventual cost of the completed project. It was not an easy task, but I pushed and cajoled both men, and they completed their estimates in a few days.

Then I knew where we stood. If we received a sizable credit from Carrelli, our total shortage would be approximately twenty million dollars. Norman had said fifteen, but he probably knew it was twenty all the time. Anyway the architects undoubtedly had added something to their estimates to be safe.

Again I conferred with Friedrichs and McNeill. I asked them for their honest opinion of the partition that Carrelli had substituted in the building. They told me Norman was right: the cost and quality were somewhat below that of the partitions specified. Also, the substitute partitions would require more maintenance in the future. Even now, there would be problems with soundproofing and the installation of electrical service. However, when I asked whether the substitute partition was basically serviceable and attractive, both men readily conceded that it was.

I was ready to talk to Carrelli.

Carrelli was neither boisterous nor arrogant. He came in with his head hunched forward and sidled into a chair.

"You know, Carrelli, you're in one hell of a spot."

"Yeah?"

"All you managed to do was knock off the man who paid the bills."

"Look, Mr. Ellison, I'm sorry about Mr. Kane. But I no kill him."

"I'm not saying you murdered Norman Kane. But if you hadn't done what you did, there's a damn good chance he would be alive today."

"Now wait a minute, Mr.—"

"I'm not here to argue the point. I just want you to know what I think. Nevertheless, Norman Kane is gone and we have to complete the buildings. If Kane were here, he'd make you rip out those partitions, and he'd be right. But I'm not a builder, Mr. Carrelli—just a lawyer. I'm trying to wind up Mr. Kane's affairs. If we all press too hard, this thing may explode in our faces. That would leave you holding the bag. With Mr. McNeill and Dr. Friedrichs to back me up, you'd have one hell of a time trying to collect on your contract."

"I been putting those partitions in for months. I put in another hundred thousand feet since Kane died and you guys been letting me do it."

"That doesn't mean anything, Carrelli. We've taken exception to the partitions on every payout. You've just been digging a deeper hole for yourself every day. Still, I'm prepared to give you an easy way out, but for only one reason—to keep this project moving. I'll let you leave those partitions in."

Carrelli sat up in his chair. "You kidding me?"

"No. I'll even let you use the same partition in the rest of the buildings. In return, I want a credit, and not only for what you're saving by substituting the cheaper partition. I want a kicker."

"What's that?"

"I want a credit for what it would cost you to tear out everything you've put in up till now."

Carrelli looked at me. "That's a lot of money."

"You can have it either way. Rip out the old partitions and put in the right ones, or give me the credit and leave the partitions where they are. According to Mr. McNeill, if you have to pull out those partitions, you'll be so far behind schedule, you'll never meet the completion dates, and every day you're late is going to cost you a thousand-dollar penalty under your contract."

"You got me in a box and you know it. How much you want?"

"You tell me, Carrelli. What will you give me?"

"I don't know. I never thought about it. The cheap partition cost about two hundred eighty thousand dollars less, so far, and then there's the cost of ripping it out and replacing it. I figure maybe another hundred thousand dollars. I give you a three-hundred-eighty-thousand-dollar credit and you forget the whole thing, OK?" His eyes lighted up with anticipation.

"You're lying, Carrelli. It would cost a lot more than that to tear out those partitions."

"OK, I give you four hundred thousand dollars."

I shook my head.

"Four twenty?"

I shook my head.

Carrelli hesitated. "Just a second," he said. He pulled a piece of crumpled paper from his pocket and began to scribble on it. "Four hundred fifty thousand," he said, "and that's it." He threw the paper into a waste basket.

I looked at McNeill, but he offered no help. I looked at Friedrichs and he stared back at me blankly.

"I think you're conning me, Mr. Carrelli." He started to stand up. "Now, don't pull your tough act on me. You're in a lot of trouble, and if you start throwing your weight around, you're going to be in even bigger trouble."

Something in my voice must have impressed him. He sank back into the chair.

"I'm not gonna play this game," he said. "You can't get me to keep upping my price and then say No. You tell me what you want."

"Five hundred thousand dollars."

"You must be nuts."

"That's the price."

"It's too much. You're pushing too hard."

"Well, Carrelli, I'll put it this way: we've got to get along together and finish this building. I think five hundred thousand is a fair price, and you think four fifty is a fair price.

I could ask you to split the difference, but I won't. I want you to walk out of here happy. I'll tell you what, Carrelli—I'm going to take your four fifty. But you make one more mistake on this job and you'll wish that Norman Kane was still alive."

Carrelli smiled broadly. "OK," he said. "You got a deal."

I pushed a piece of paper toward him. "Here's the change order. Sign it."

"I should have my lawyer."

"If you don't sign right now, you're going to *need* a lawyer."

Carrelli signed the paper.

"That's fine, Mr. Carrelli. But from now on we're going to check you more closely than you've ever been checked before. Outside of that, don't expect any more trouble from us. All we want you to do is to perform your contract. Is that clear?"

He nodded his head.

"OK, then. It's done."

Carrelli nodded again, put out his hand to me, thought better of it, turned and left the room. He closed the door quietly behind him.

"Well, gentlemen, what do you think?"

"I think you got a good credit out of Carrelli," said McNeill. "You really handled him well."

"I'm new at this. I'm not a builder and I don't intend to become one. However, I did think you could have helped me a little."

"Help you? I was happy when Carrelli said three hundred eighty thousand."

"Good. Happy to hear it."

"Yes, that's an extra savings," said McNeill. "It should help."

"Mr. McNeill, we're so short of funds that the extra money I dug out of Carrelli hardly means a thing. Nevertheless we can't spend one dollar more than we have to. If there's a chance to save a few bucks on that twenty million, why, God bless you, go out and save it. But don't cheapen the building. Norman Kane wouldn't want a cheap building."

Both men agreed.

"McNeill, I want you to do something for me. This thing is touch and go. I want a report from you every day. Not in writing; you can give it to me over the phone. And once a week I want our project cost estimate brought up to date. You let me know of any trend, good or bad."

"Happy to do it."

I turned to Friedrichs. "What about you, sir?"

Karl Friedrichs raised both hands and let them drop in his lap. "I really haven't had much to say in this project."

"Dr. Friedrichs, I know you're unhappy because you weren't permitted to design the entire project. But it's too late to brood. You have to do what your own heart tells you is right. As far as I'm concerned, you were the architect—the only architect. The rest of the world will feel the same way. But there is no use my trying to sell you on that."

"Mr. Kane would not have permitted Carrelli to leave in those partitions."

I managed to suppress my anger. "That's right. He wouldn't. But Mr. Kane isn't here, Doctor. If you want to sit in Kane's chair and make the decisions you are welcome to do so."

"That's just talk, Mr. Ellison."

"That's all you're giving me, Doctor."

Miss Fritch prepared a detailed report listing all prospective tenants. The list was surprisingly long, but the correspondence did not reveal what phase Norman's negotiations had reached. No one in Kane's organization knew the answers.

Then I had a thought. A screwy thought and a dangerous one—but now was the time to take chances. I invited Ernest Barry to Kane's office.

"I don't know what you want, Ellison. You should have called my lawyer instead of me. I don't think much of your ethics."

"Don't worry about my ethics. Anyway, you came here, and I know why."

Barry looked at me apprehensively. "You do?"

"It's very simple. Your lawsuit stinks. It doesn't matter what your lawyer tells you, you haven't got a chance."

Barry stood up. "If that's all you have to tell me, what's the use? We'll fight it out in court. This state treats real-estate brokers pretty good."

"Yes, it treats brokers pretty good, but it doesn't give you a license to steal."

"Are you kidding? Don't you realize I brought this deal to Norman Kane? He never even knew about it until I told him."

"Who told you?"

Barry hesitated. "What does that matter? I told Kane."

"I'll tell you something very funny, Mr. Barry. I have a transcript here of some interesting notes taken by Miss Fritch. Maybe you'd like to hear them?"

"I'm not sure I want to stay here."

"The door's open, Barry. You can leave right now."

He sat down.

I called Miss Fritch on the intercom, and she brought in a set of typewritten notes.

"Please start reading, Miss Fritch, at the place I marked this morning."

Miss Fritch began to read in a steady, expressionless voice, " 'Over there, Norman, beyond the Palmolive Building—east of the Drake where the drive curves sharply, that's 191–231 East Lake Shore Drive. You can buy the entire parcel right through to Walton Street.'

" 'That's the Kincaid property.'

" 'Right.'

" 'But the estate's been in the courts for years. You can't get clear title.'

" 'Wrong.'

" 'Wrong?'

" 'You heard me. My friend Charlie Ross at Laffler, Ross and White tells me the heirs have agreed to a settlement. And the settlement requires a sale of the property.' "

Barry jumped to his feet. "Why, those are the notes of our meeting. That sounds like the talk I had with Kane."

"Yes, it is."

"How the hell did he do it? Was the room bugged?"

"Not exactly. There's an intercom here in the office and one out on the balcony. Norman just flipped the key, turned up the volume, and Miss Fritch wrote it all down on her little green pad."

"Goddamn it, that's a chintzy way to do business."

"I agree. I was surprised Norman did things like that."

"Anyway—so what? It only proves what I've been saying. You just established the day and the hour I offered the property to him."

"You're right, but you didn't let Miss Fritch finish. Skip down a few lines, Miss Fritch, and read the other material I marked—where Mr. Kane is asking Mr. Barry a question."

"You mean where Mr. Kane asked, 'Who else knows about this?' "

"Right. What did Mr. Barry reply?"

" 'You asked me that, Norman. I swear I haven't told a soul.' "

I looked at Barry.

"Of course," he mumbled. "Only being ethical."

"Of course. Now, Miss Fritch, let's go on to the telephone call."

"The one between Mr. Kane and Mr. Hughes?"

"That's the one."

Miss Fritch flipped through her notes, found the spot and began to read.

" 'Barry called this morning with a proposition he wants me to submit to Leventhal and Company. I asked him why he didn't talk to you, since you're in Chicago. Barry said you were too busy, but the more I thought about it, the more convinced I became that the deal exactly suited you. I decided to call you first on the outside chance you might be interested.'

" 'Very kind of you, Alan.'

" 'Not at all, Norman. It seems like a natural.'

" 'What seems like a natural?'

345

" 'The Kincaid property—' "

"That son of a bitch." Barry was on his feet again, yelling. "That dirty son of a bitch."

"My goodness, Barry, you certainly are excitable. I don't think I'll bother having Miss Fritch read the part where Alan Hughes told Norman what he thought of *you*."

Barry was sputtering.

"I thought you'd find our transcript interesting. It seems— excuse my choice of words—that you were double-dealing Mr. Kane."

Barry sat down in his chair and stared out a window. "What the hell does it matter? It doesn't mean a goddamn thing. First of all, the fact remains I did bring him the deal and you know it. Second, you can't use this kind of evidence in a court of law."

"Suppose I told you Mr. Hughes is willing to come here and testify."

"He wouldn't."

"Oh, yes, he surely would."

Barry stood up again. "I should have known better than to come here alone. I should have brought my lawyer. You want to fight a lawsuit, but I'm not going to fight it here. I think you made a bad mistake, Ellison. You tipped your hand. Now I know what you're up to."

"Go ahead, Mr. Barry. You get your lawyer and you subpoena anybody you want, and you defend yourself as best you can. No matter what you do, your reputation is shot. You'll be pegged as a cheap double-dealing crook."

Barry hesitated. "Why are you telling me this?"

"I haven't even gotten to the point and you're running out on me. Why don't you sit down and relax? If you like, you can listen to the rest of Miss Fritch's transcript."

"I've heard enough."

"Very well. Miss Fritch, will you excuse us?" Miss Fritch left the room.

"What do you want, Ellison?"

"You're going to be very surprised when I tell you. Despite the way you tried to outfox Kane, I still think you're a capable broker. Right now I'm a guy who needs a broker. I have millions of feet to lease. I'm not equipped to do it and neither is anybody else associated with this project. Norman Kane would roll over in his grave if he heard what I'm about to suggest. I want to use you, Barry. I'll give you a chance to make some money out of this deal, money you never would have made if Kane were alive. I'll give you a list of the hottest prospects you've ever seen, and you go out and rent space in Lake Shore Plaza."

"That's preposterous."

"Maybe, but I'm on the hot seat, and I intend to get off it in a hurry. I don't know what you can do in a few weeks, but if you accomplish something you can make yourself some money and save your reputation."

"This is mighty peculiar."

"I agree. Damn peculiar. Not only that, I have a release for you to sign. A release which provides that in return for our giving you the exclusive right to lease the Plaza for ninety days, you surrender any claims you may have arising out of the Kincaid deal."

"You want me to sign away my rights here and now?"

"You have no rights. You've got nothing. I'm giving you something for nothing. You know, even if you were willing to drop that lawsuit, I might not let you do it. I don't like the way you do business, Mr. Barry. I hate having to use you. But I figure that if I give you a chance to make a buck on me, maybe we'll all end up better off."

"This is crazy."

"Yes, it sure is crazy."

"All right, I'll do it. Give me those papers and I'll bring them to my lawyer."

"We haven't time to screw around. You get on that phone and tell your lawyer to come over here. We're going to wind this up this afternoon."

That was how I hired a leasing agent—a guy with larceny in his soul. But then, most brokers are like that. And I managed to get Barry off my back, and that was worth something, too.

Once Barry could smell the money, he was off and running. It was about a week before I heard from him again—a week of arguing with lawyers and stalling them about final drafts of final agreements. No one understood what I was up to. They probably thought I was getting punchy.

Glover was particularly difficult to handle. I appealed to him as one professional to another. "I hope you will understand, Mr. Glover, I'm in a strange position. My original client is dead. His ventures are in serious trouble. I probably should have stopped him from doing some of the things he did. Anyway, he did them and he's dead and there's nothing I can do about it now, except I *can* see that we work out a fair settlement. I hope you understand that."

Glover's voice was bland and urbane. "Oh, yes, I understand your position perfectly. No one can blame you for the peccadillos of Norman Kane. I don't know why you feel guilty. Nevertheless I understand your problems. Of course, you have to understand mine. General Stone wants this matter settled at once."

"General Stone knows that lawyers take time to get things done. Give me a few days, a week, ten days at the outside, and I'm sure all of the papers will be in shape for final signature. You know there are a lot of parties to deal with, and they're not easy to satisfy."

Glover laughed. "I don't envy you, Mr. Ellison."

"Yes, but here I am, and it's my duty to see it through to the end. If it were up to me I'd drop the whole thing. But I want to complete my task and still maintain my dignity. Please don't insist on our executing these papers in less than a reasonable period of time."

"All right, Ellison. I'll try to placate General Stone."

"That should not be difficult. I had a little discussion with General Stone a couple of weeks ago. I don't believe he's concerned over Edward Ellison."

There was a pause. "The General told me he had talked to you."

"I see. Well, I appreciate your cooperation, Mr. Glover. If you have any further problems, let me know."

"You can be sure of that."

Barry's first call came from San Francisco. "That was a stinking list you gave me, Ellison."

"Really?"

"Yes, a stinking, lousy list. Kane never even talked to half those people. And the other half were only slightly interested."

"Oh?"

"Yeah, it was like starting from scratch."

"I see."

"Yeah, but I applied a lot of pressure out here and I think I got us a pretty good tenant for Plaza Five."

"Great. Who is it?"

"Colorado Smelting and Refining. They have their home office here in San Francisco, but they've made several acquisitions in the Middle West and they're thinking of opening a large branch office in Chicago. They may take a hundred and fifty thousand feet."

"That's wonderful, Barry. You're certainly making progress."

"No thanks to you and Kane. This is murder."

"You have my sympathy. I can't help you very much, but you have my sympathy."

"Thanks for nothing."

"What should I do?"

"Draw up the lease. For Christ's sake, what do you think I'm calling about? Draw the lease. I've got these guys on the hook."

"Shall I come out there?"

"Are you kidding? I was signing up tenants before you were born."

I had not begun to solve our most crucial problem. Even if Ernest Barry leased all the space in all the buildings overnight, we would still be short twenty million dollars. The question was, where to get it?

I realized I would have to assess our position from a fresh point of view. I decided to remove from the files every legal document—the development agreement, loan instruments, mortgage commitments, construction contract, every piece of paper relating to Lake Shore Plaza—and review them as objectively as possible. Perhaps somewhere in these stacks of papers I would find the answer.

The research was tedious. There were so many instruments to examine that I constantly had to nudge myself to stay alert. The words read like a familiar song lyric. I could recite them almost by heart, but without feeling and, at times, without understanding. I forced myself to read the lines over and over again, to construct possible interpretations for each phrase.

Almost everything proved to be a dead end. I came up with a thousand angles, some of them pretty good. But each plan would take too long to work out.

Where was the opening that would permit us to wriggle out of this mess? I continued reading and rereading. Eventually I began to repeat phrases aloud to myself. I was almost mesmerized by the sound of my own voice. Finally I realized that the solution, if any, would be found within a few basic instruments. The most important of these was the development agreement. It was not particularly long, as such documents go, and the provisions were relatively simple. I dug back into it with greater care, reviewing the portions that seemed so routine and unimportant that I had never really studied them before.

After a while the paragraphs spelling out the duties and responsibilities of Norman Kane and Kane Enterprises caught my attention. I knew that these clauses contained not only Kane's obligations but his rights as well. I found this research wryly amusing. Here I was reviewing a document I had been using in one form or another for ten or fifteen years. Now, for the first time in years, I was analyzing it with infinite care.

I kept coming back to the same paragraph—the clause on permanent financing. In brief, the agreement gave Kane Enterprises, Inc., authority to procure permanent financing for the project. I read it over and over again, and finally—very gradually—I realized I might have the answer.

I met with Hobbs and Bennett in Hobbs' office. Both men seemed ill at ease. I knew they were under tremendous pressure from their own company. For a brief moment their obvious fear infected me, but I shrugged it off. I could not permit myself to be deflected by the weakness of others.

"Gentlemen, I know that you share my concern over Lake Shore Plaza. It would be a serious blow to Fidelity Standard if for any reason the terms of your commitment were not met."

"It won't be a bed of roses for your clients." The asperity in Hobbs' voice surprised me.

"Of course. I'm not here to dally with you. Our venture has innumerable problems, and you are as fully aware of them as I am."

Hobbs seemed mollified. "This has been a trying time for all of us, Mr. Ellison. Frankly, we wish we had never heard of Lake Shore Plaza."

"I'm not surprised. At times I feel like that myself. However, it's easy to exaggerate the problems of Lake Shore Plaza at the expense of its remarkable underlying strength and quality. In the first place, construction of the six towers is almost complete. Together they represent the most remarkable, the most impressive and the best publicized office complex in the United States. These days it's difficult to pick up an architectural magazine—in fact, any magazine—without seeing some reference to Lake Shore Plaza.

"Of course, one might argue that Norman Kane should not have built all six buildings at virtually the same time. When he realized he was short of funds he should have stopped and waited until he had raised the additional money. But he was convinced that such a delay would be disastrous to the venture. He was certain that, one way or another, he would work his way out of every difficulty."

"That's true," said John Bennett. "Unfortunately Norman is not here." I had heard this statement over and over again, but I knew it would not pay to be annoyed by it.

"You're right, John, but we still have his blueprints. Not merely for the buildings, but his blueprints for the overall development of this project. Apparently many people believe that Norman was a brilliant but somewhat careless business-man. They think he was impulsive and emotional. Perhaps. I worked with Norman Kane for many years. He had flair and imagination and sometimes he moved too quickly, but the fact remains that Norman never did anything without analyzing it thoroughly and planning every detail."

"That may be so, Ellison." It was Fred Hobbs talking. "But in this case he seems to have left things in pretty much of a mess."

"That's not true, Mr. Hobbs, and I'll prove it to you. I instructed our architects to review the cost and the progress of our construction in detail. I can now project the total final cost within an insignificant percentage of possible error. The interesting thing is that Norman told me what the cost would be—almost to the penny—long before I authorized these studies. He was not playing in the dark with millions of dollars. I had to have this analyzed for me by a whole crew of architects, engineers and accountants. When they were finished, all I managed to do was confirm the figures Norman gave me months ago."

"How much are you short?"

I chose to ignore the question. "Then there is the leasing problem. Some people thought that only Norman had the special skill needed to rent this project. Again, I don't intend to knock Norman Kane. He was the most brilliant lease negotiator I ever met. But the fact remains that Norman built up a leasing organization and a leasing program. I happen to have the written outline of that program with me today. It shows the deals that have been made and all of the prospects still available, including the ones who are actively interested.

"Norman realized that if he was not around to finish the job, it would take somebody with special talent to complete the leasing. A long time ago Norman told me that if anything happened to him I should employ the man he considered best suited to do the job—Ernest Barry."

Both men showed surprise.

"Ernest Barry? Isn't that the broker who filed a lawsuit against Norman and his group?"

"The same. But we've settled that suit and Barry has given

us a full release. It's true that Barry and Kane disagreed. Nevertheless, Norman did say he wanted Barry to lease the project if he himself could not."

"Doesn't make sense. Barry obviously was Norman Kane's enemy."

"John—" I turned to Bennett—"you have the Colorado Smelting lease?"

"Of course."

"It's a pretty good deal, isn't it?"

"Yes, it is. It doesn't solve your problem but it helps."

"Who do you think negotiated that lease?"

"Ernest Barry?"

"Right."

"When did he start working for you?"

"Two weeks ago."

"Two weeks ago? When did he make this lease?"

"I told you, Barry is an able man. He made that deal the first week he began working for us. Imagine that—within one week after I turned the list of prospects over to Barry, he delivered a one hundred and fifty thousand square foot tenant. And he has several more on the line."

Fred Hobbs sat back. "You're still far short of meeting the leasing requirements. You're up over three million feet, but that still leaves you nearly a million to go."

"Gentlemen, Norman Kane, with the recent help of Ernest Barry, rented over three million square feet in less than three years. Who would have believed it could be done in Chicago, the most conservative market in the country? But it *was* done, and the reason is very simple: Lake Shore Plaza is the most exciting project in America. It offers facilities and amenities unmatched by any other office complex anywhere. That's why we're able to rent it. Don't misunderstand. We won't reach four million feet next week or next month. But I guarantee you one thing: this will be the most successful development Chicago has ever seen."

Hobbs and Bennett were looking at me strangely. I realized what was affecting them and forced a laugh. "Forgive me, gentlemen, I know I'm talking more like a promoter than an attorney. However, I've finally learned to understand what this project is all about. There's something here that has inspired even me."

"That's all right," said Hobbs. "We're happy to hear someone is still enthusiastic about Lake Shore Plaza. All we've been fed is a very disturbing blend of evasion and pessimism."

"Anyway," I said, "that's the leasing picture. I've prepared a chart that shows the types of tenants, their net worth, the space they occupy, their term of lease, the rentals, et cetera. I've also taken the trouble to review your commitment, and I've charted our figures alongside yours. If you compare these figures, I think you'll be amazed. Although our annual rental is less than you require, across a period of twenty years our combined total rentals are far in excess of your requirements. And more important, there are more companies in this project with a net worth of over fifty million dollars than in any other multiple-occupancy building in the city of Chicago."

I handed copies of the chart to Hobbs and Bennett. After a few minutes Hobbs looked up. "This is very interesting. But just in case you think we're morons, let me show you something *we* prepared." He reached into a desk drawer, pulled out a folder and handed it to me. I leafed through it. The folder contained schedules listing substantially the same information set forth on my chart.

"Mr. Hobbs, I know you know your business. I certainly didn't think you were merely filing leases in drawers. All I'm trying to prove is that I understand the problems, too. We operate on the same wave length."

"That's true. Your figures are remarkably like ours."

"Well, then, we agree. The leasing job that's been done is phenomenal. In the big picture, that indicates tremendous stability for the project."

"John Bennett and I agree with you. But our opinion isn't the final one. We have our own people to convince. That's why we prepared these schedules. If something can be done to rescue this project, we want to do it."

"Wonderful. We're all moving in the same direction."

"Yes, but the fact remains that the yearly rentals are not enough to pay the annual operating expenses, taxes and insurance, and cover the mortgage payments as well."

"How do we get over that hurdle?" asked John Bennett.

"Really, it's quite simple."

They stared at me as though I were a strange apparition. I smiled. "It's not exactly simple, but there is an answer." I paused. "Cut the mortgage payments," I said.

Hobbs laughed.

"I'm quite serious. It's obvious the mortgage payments must be pared down. The term of the loan must be extended from twenty-five to over thirty years. When you do that, you'll find your present rental income pretty much covers the payments you mentioned."

"That's a deceptively simple solution. On what basis do we sell it to our people?"

"You have it right there in black and white. If you were willing to give us a twenty-five-year mortgage based on lease terms averaging twelve years, then you must be willing to take a thirty- to thirty-five-year mortgage based on twenty- to thirty-year leases."

Hobbs shook his head. "We'll never sell it."

"Anyway," put in John Bennett, "that doesn't solve the basic problem. You're still short a lot of money. Where will it come from?"

"From you."

Both men were silent for a moment. Then Hobbs spoke to me. "You're talking in riddles now. First you tell us to cut down the mortgage payments so that your present income will cover the expenses and fixed charges. Then you say, Give us more money. If we do that, the mortgage payments will go right back up again. Isn't that right?"

"No, it's not right. Because you're not going to *lend* us the money."

"Not going to lend you the money?"

"No, this time you're going to be an equity investor."

Hobbs sat up abruptly, and his swivel chair clinked.

"You expect us to buy twenty million dollars' worth of the equity in Lake Shore Plaza?"

"I see you know precisely how much we need."

"Of course we know what you need. For Christ's sake, it's all over town. You're short twenty million dollars and you expect us to put it up?"

"Why not? You've taken equity positions before. Never

with Norman Kane, because he never let you in. But you've done it with other developers. Why not Lake Shore Plaza?"

"What you're proposing is impossible. Your deal is in difficulty. The rental income is less than it should be, and the costs are higher than they ought to be. Now you say, since things are so bad, why don't we put risk capital in it? How in the hell do we justify that?"

"Wait a minute," said John Bennett. "Let's not get any more involved than we have to. Who says you can do all this, Mr. Ellison? Where is your authority?"

"I represent this project."

"Yes, but it's a corporation, isn't it?"

"Of course."

"Have the directors voted you special authority to negotiate this kind of a deal?"

"Special authority isn't necessary. Our rights are spelled out in the development agreement."

"Sounds confusing to me," said Hobbs.

"It's not. One of the shortest agreements I ever drafted, and I'm not noted for short agreements."

"Long or short," said John Bennett, "tell us where you get your authority."

I removed two copies of the development agreement from my briefcase and handed them to Hobbs and Bennett. "If you men will glance at paragraph six, I think you'll see what I mean."

They read paragraph six, but when they looked up their faces were blank.

"I don't get the point," said John Bennett.

"Paragraph six provides that Kane Enterprises shall have the authority to procure long-term financing for the project on such terms and conditions as shall be necessary or desirable to insure its completion."

"Norman Kane is dead."

"Yes, but Kane Enterprises, *Incorporated,* isn't. The corporation still has the rights and duties specified in the agreement. Thus it is the responsibility of Kane Enterprises, whom I happen to represent, to arrange the required mortgage financing."

"But you already have a mortgage commitment. What you are suggesting is a totally new commitment."

"Gentlemen, I could guide you through this agreement clause by clause. I am sure I could convince you the Kane organization has the right to arrange any reasonable type of long-term financing and that nothing—absolutely nothing— prevents the transfer of a portion of the stockholders' equity interest in return for additional funds."

"I still don't like it," said John Bennett. "We could be involved in all kinds of lawsuits."

"We don't want lawsuits any more than you do. But it doesn't matter, because the other investors are behind me one hundred per cent."

"All of the investors?"

"All of the investors."

"Including General Stone?"

"When you issue your revised commitment I will provide you with not only the written acceptance of the corporation, duly authorized by its board of directors, but also the individual written consent of every stockholder."

"On that basis we will have no difficulty."

"I am not looking for trouble, gentlemen."

"That still doesn't solve the primary problem," said Hobbs, "which is how to convince our committee to make these radical changes in our financial arrangements. I'm not convinced myself."

"I understand. In order to help persuade you, I have prepared projections of income and expenses for an extended period of years. I think you'll find that your investment in this property will be tremendously profitable."

"You still haven't given us the details. What percentage of the equity are you offering in return for twenty million dollars and a revised mortgage payment schedule?"

"How much do you want?"

"It will have to be substantial to interest our committee."

"Again, I ask, how much do you want?"

"I'll be frank with you," said Hobbs. "We would like to work this out, but you'll have to offer us something that makes sense. We've never gone into a venture on an equity

357

basis where we took less than twenty per cent of the deal. What's more, we have the other members of our lending group to consider. The other insurance companies will have to be consulted, and if they are interested in proceeding on the basis you suggest, we'll have to offer part of the equity to them, too."

"They may not want a piece of the equity."

"I hope they don't," said Hobbs. And then he realized he had said something he should not have. "I mean, I don't know what they will do. They may not approve of our taking an equity position."

"Why should they object? You will only be making their position stronger. If you're willing to put up equity money, the project must be good. Don't you think that will impress your group?"

"I'm sure it will. But let's talk about Fidelity Standard. As I said, twenty per cent is the least we've ever taken. In these circumstances, I don't think it's enough."

"Mr. Hobbs, you know one thing as well as I do. If you offer your committee too much, they'll think there's something wrong."

"That's true," said Hobbs, and he sat back in his chair, musing. "I don't know, Ellison. I'll have to think about it."

"There isn't much time. But I'll tell you this. My frank opinion is that you shouldn't ask for more than twenty per cent. However, if you need twenty-five, I'll get it for you. Keep that in the back of your mind."

"All right. That gives us something to work on." I could see Hobbs was pleased. He believed his hesitation had extracted the extra five per cent from me. He did not realize I was ready to go to thirty per cent or even more if necessary.

"There's still another question, Ellison, and a very important one. How much of our twenty million will go to the present stockholders?"

"It all goes to the corporation."

"I don't understand."

"You're not going to buy anything from the present investors. We're going to issue new stock and new notes. The present investors' equity interest will be diluted, but they won't get a dime of your money. Every penny will go into the company."

"Are you certain the stockholders will agree to this?"

"Absolutely."

"That helps a great deal," said Hobbs. "Our committee is always afraid these equity transactions may cash out the investors."

"Which is only right. In this case the investors will still have forty million dollars invested. Your twenty million will buy up to twenty-five per cent of the deal, which isn't a tremendous premium for you to pay."

Bennett finally spoke. "I don't know whether we can sell it, Eddie."

"Gentlemen, I think you can—and I think you should. It's the one sound solution for everybody."

After leaving Hobbs' office, I almost stumbled down the corridor. I hoped that neither man had realized how nervous I had been. I steadied myself and walked down the street for a block before I paused to lean against a building. I stood there for a few minutes, breathing rapidly and shivering. A few people stared at me. Perhaps they thought I was drunk. Or sick. In a way, the latter guess would have been right. I *was* sick, almost violently ill, after my interview with Hobbs and Bennett. Norman Kane had done the same thing a hundred times in his life, but I had never done it before. And I had carried it out in my own imitation of Norman Kane's style. I had no authorization whatever from Stone or any of the other investors.

Our meetings on the Stone settlement agreement had taught me how dangerous it was to call the boys together, but there was very little time. I called a meeting of all the investors—all except Stone.

We met in Norman's office. There was bickering and backbiting even during the first few minutes of conversation. It was obvious that the boys were not a very cohesive group.

"Just a minute. I'm not going to sit here and listen to you knife each other. You're all in pretty bad trouble, and I'm the one guy in the world who can get you out of it. If you want to listen, fine. If you want everything to go down the drain, keep yelling and screaming at each other."

They looked at me strangely.

"I'm laying it on the line, boys."

"Why?" I don't recall who asked the question.

"I'm not sure, especially when I listen to you quarreling. If you try hard enough, you may be able to talk me out of helping you. Go ahead."

No one spoke.

"All right, let me explain the deal." I handed out resumés of the projections I had given Fidelity Standard. I explained briefly my proposal for diluting their equity in return for the extra cash.

The boys and their attorneys seemed bewildered. Each man began whispering to his lawyer. Together they gave out a strange buzzing sound which would have amused me had it not been somewhat tragic.

Finally Winsley's attorney spoke. "I'm afraid we don't understand. Oh, we can read, but it looks like you're going to give Fidelity Standard thirty per cent of our equity."

"That's right. You understand perfectly."

"For what?"

"I guess you don't understand. They're going to give us twenty million dollars."

"They said that?"

"They didn't say a goddamn thing. *I* told them."

"What makes you think they'll do it?" It was Woodward speaking.

"I don't know if they will or won't, but I gave them my best sales pitch. I'm not Norman Kane, but I offered them a Norman Kane-type deal. Maybe their memories are still good."

"What the hell. This is just conversation."

"Yes, that's right, but as far as I can see it's your only way out."

The attorney for George Lillis stood up. "You know, I think Ellison's got something. If Fidelity Standard will go for this, it's the perfect way out. Our equity may be cut down, but we won't be wiped out."

"I don't mind a little water in my Scotch," said Winsley. The other men chuckled, mostly because they were relieved that Winsley was not protesting in his usual violent fashion.

"Why should Fidelity Standard buy this deal?" he asked.

"What the hell do you care why they buy it? I'm not going to sit here and repeat the story I told Fidelity Standard, but I want you to know that I think it's a good deal for them. And I know it's a good deal for you. Everything will be fine once Barry gets the buildings leased up."

"Barry?"

"Yes. I hired Ernest Barry."

"You mean Barry is out leasing our buildings?"

"Yes. He's the man who made the Colorado Smelting lease."

"Norman Kane would turn over in his grave."

"Maybe, but as long as we keep plugging away, the project stays alive. Barry made the Colorado Smelting lease and I think he'll make some others."

"Who gave you the authority?" It was Winsley again.

"I gave it to myself. If you want to take it back, just say so."

Again there was silence. One of the attorneys finally spoke. "I think Barry made a very favorable lease with Colorado Smelting. I don't know why or how you happened to hire that son of a bitch, but as long as he's making leases why should we throw him out?"

"I received a letter from him this morning. It looks like he's got another tenant lined up. Not a big one—maybe fifty thousand feet. But there was a time when I thought fifty thousand feet was a hell of a lot of space."

"What about that lawsuit? Didn't Barry sue Kane?"

"Not just Kane. He sued the whole lot of you and you know it. But I settled the lawsuit in return for giving him the exclusive leasing of this project for a limited time."

"How long?"

"Ninety days."

"You mean he gave up his lawsuit for a ninety-day exclusive?"

"Yes, but I'm going to renew his contract when the ninety days are up."

I turned the conversation back to a discussion of the Fidelity Standard commitment. The boys and their lawyers asked one question after another, and I explained how the proposal would work.

"Where's Kincaid?" Woodward asked. "He should be here, too."

"Don't worry about Kincaid," I said. "I'll take care of him."

"What about Stone?"

"That's the problem. Who's going to handle Stone? I don't suppose any of you boys want the job?" I waited for volunteers. "I didn't think so. I'll have to do it myself."

"Why should Stone buy it?"

"Maybe he won't. He threw me out of his office once before."

"What if he turns you down?"

"Let's not think about that. What I want now is your agreement to proceed with the offer I made Fidelity Standard."

"It's OK with me," said Winsley, and the others agreed.

"I'm not going ahead on verbal authority any more. I prepared an agreement I want you all to sign. It gives me the authority to do what I'm doing. It's more or less a power of attorney."

"It's no good without Stone," one of the lawyers said.

"Listen—nothing's any good without Stone. But at least you guys won't back out on me. Now you can check these agreements, but I want them signed, and I mean today."

There was some grumbling among the men, and the lawyers protested that they should have more of an opportunity to review the documents.

"Go right ahead. Take all the time you want. But don't expect me to represent you and don't expect me to talk to General Stone."

"I don't get it," said Phil Winsley. "What's in this for you?"

"Everybody asks me that sooner or later, but I don't know the answer. Why don't you stop worrying about it? Let's just say I'm doing it for the legal fees."

"How much will they be?"

"I can promise you my bill will be staggering."

No one protested. After some discussion, each of the men signed the documents. They wished me luck with General Stone. I could tell they did not expect me to be successful.

After the boys left, I called Kincaid. "What happened, Del? You were supposed to be at our meeting this afternoon. Why didn't you come?"

"I'm tired of the whole thing, Ellison. Sick and tired. Your meetings lead nowhere. Stone has us over a barrel, and frankly, I don't care any more."

"It's not as hopeless as you think. Come on over and I'll tell you what we're planning. You're in for a surprise."

"Some other time. I'm too busy."

"The hell you are, Del. You get over here right now." I slammed down the phone.

I waited for almost an hour, but eventually Miss Fritch brought Kincaid in. He looked wary—hostile and wary. And I could smell liquor on his breath. Perhaps he had stopped for a couple of quick ones on the way to my office. He didn't seem drunk, but he was obviously feeling surly.

I decided to be conciliatory. "Sit down, Del. I didn't mean to sound abrupt, but I've been working night and day on this thing. It looks to me like there's a way out."

"I don't believe it. Anyway I don't care."

I ignored him and went on to describe my dealings with Fidelity Standard and the boys.

Del listened impassively. He was obviously not impressed. "All right, Ellison. What do you want from me?"

"I need only two signatures to put this through—yours and Stone's."

"You'll never get Stone's signature."

"I think I will."

Kincaid seemed to come to life. "You'll never get mine." His little-boy face was twisted into an angry grimace. "I'll never sign your damn power of attorney."

"Why not?"

"What's in it for me?"

"You'll save your investment in the deal."

"Oh, hell. What do I care? I wrote off my hundred and sixty grand a long time ago."

I tried to be patient. "Why write it off? It can be saved. You'll end up with a damn good investment."

Kincaid was up on his feet, pacing the floor. "Damn good investment. Even with all your shenanigans it will be years before I see a dime. The hell with it. Let the whole deal go down the drain—you, Stone, the boys, everything." He actually looked pleased at the prospect.

I realized my patient, logical explanation wouldn't work. Kincaid was beginning to feel important. Needed.

"That would please you, wouldn't it, Del? To see the whole thing blow up. To drag the whole deal down. Destroy Norman Kane's dream. And you think now that maybe you can do it—insignificant Delbert Kincaid with his insignificant four per cent of the deal. Suddenly you think you've got position. You're going to get even with Kane. It's a little late, isn't it, now that he's dead?"

"No, it isn't too late. As long as the deal doesn't collapse, Norman won the ball game. Even dead. If it weren't for your meddling, the whole thing would fall to pieces and Stone would pick them up. You're right, Eddie. I'd enjoy that. My first chance to kick Norman Kane, even in his grave."

"You're kidding yourself. You're not big enough to do it. Somehow we'll get around you. I'm not going to let your lousy four per cent stop me."

"I won't sign." He looked angry now, firm-jawed, stubborn.

"I'll buy you out," I said.

"I won't sell."

"Name your price."

"I won't sell."

"I see. Well, I didn't want to do this, but I see I'll have to. I tried to reason with you, Del, but you wouldn't listen. I don't want to push you around, but I'm going to."

He looked bewildered. "What do you mean? You can't push me around. I tell you, I won't sign and I won't sell." He spoke loudly, but he didn't sound as cocksure as before.

I sighed elaborately. "I'll have to tell Ellie. I tried to keep it a secret, but now I'll have to tell her. Of course, telling Ellie is the same as telling the whole world. She'll start at the club, and pretty soon it will be all over Chicago. You're going to be the laughingstock of this town."

"What are you trying to say? What are you going to tell your wife?"

"About Norman and Tina."

Kincaid smiled uncertainly. "About Kane throwing her in the pool? So what? Besides, he didn't screw her. He just threw her in the water. Kind of a game, right?" Then he became defiant. "Besides, I'm glad it happened. I'm glad I tried to shove Norman off the roof. That sure surprised Tina. Maybe it even scared her a little. But ever since, she's been different. She doesn't taunt me any more. We've been getting along better—much better. Since then, Tina respects me."

I listened incredulously. Then I began to laugh. At first it was involuntary, but when I saw that my laughter was confusing Del, I forced it on.

"What's so funny, Ellison?"

"Respects you, huh? You're getting along better? Del, you're incredible." I began to laugh again.

"I don't get it, Ellison. What's the joke?"

"You. You're such a clown. You think I'm talking about the time Norman threw your wife in the pool. I'm not." I reached for my desk calendar and flipped the pages. "I'm talking about February ninth—the night Kane screwed your wife in the St. Regis Hotel."

Kincaid's jaw dropped. "What the hell are you talking about?"

"Just what I said. Norman called Tina that evening. She flew into New York, and they spent the night frolicking in the St. Regis."

"I don't believe it. You told me he never touched her."

"He didn't—not until then. But then he sure touched her —every goddamn inch of her."

Kincaid was stammering now. "You're lying. You're making it up."

"I'm not lying. I was there. I saw it happen. I didn't plan to watch, Del, but I couldn't look away. I was in the next room, hiding in the shadows, while Norman screwed your wife."

I touched my forehead, as if trying to remember. "Let's see. She had on a black dress with a long strand of pearls. Her underclothes were black, too: a flimsy brassiere, tiny panties, no girdle. Norman almost ripped the clothes off her back. She seemed to enjoy it."

Kincaid was watching me, speechless, his lips drawn back in horror.

"What a body on that dame. Hard, firm breasts. Smooth belly. Norman threw her down on the carpet—"

"Stop it. For Christ's sake stop it." Kincaid was almost screaming.

"It was fascinating, Del. You should have been there. Little Norman humping that gorgeous hunk of woman. I would have liked a piece of that myself."

"Stop. Please stop."

"That's real respect, Del. I'll have to ask Ellie about it. Maybe she ought to poll her friends—ask them whether screwing your husband's partner is a proper way to show respect."

Del had slumped into a chair. He was trembling. His lips were moving but he seemed unable to speak. I waited.

After a long time, he regained some control. "All right," he said. "Tell me what you want."

"I really only wanted you to sign that power of attorney. But now I've changed my mind. I want you out of the deal. I don't want a pitiful creature like you to own even a slice of Kane's deal. I'm going to buy you out. With my own money, Del. It's worth it to be rid of you."

He didn't respond.

"What's your price, Del?"

He shook his head. He couldn't speak.

"Maybe I should take pity on you and give you a profit.

But I don't think I will. I'll just pay you what you paid for the stock. A hundred and sixty grand. Then we're quits."

I did not wait for him to agree. I called in Miss Fritch and dictated the stock transfer papers, while Kincaid sat there steeped in misery, occasionally shaking his head.

When the papers were ready, I brought them to him to sign. He had trouble holding the pen but finally managed to scrawl his signature.

"All right, pal. You'll have my check in a day or two."

He wasn't listening.

"You can go now, Del. Here's your copy of the contract."

He took it, then looked at me beseechingly. His voice was still broken. "Look, we know the same people. We come from the same—the same crowd. You won't say anything, will you?"

"Not a word, Del. Just pull yourself together and get out of here. You're finally finished with Norman Kane. Once and for all."

After Kincaid left, Fritchie came into the room.

"Make me one of your martinis, Miss Fritch. I can use it." Miss Fritch smiled, opened the bar and quickly mixed me a drink.

"Will there be anything else?"

"No, Miss Fritch, there won't. The martini is all I want. No, let me correct that. That isn't all I want. I'd like to take you over to that couch, throw you on your back and really let you have it."

Miss Fritch paled and then turned red. "Please, Mr. Ellison."

"I just want you to know, Miss Fritch, you're a damn desirable woman. Still, I have to turn you down."

Miss Fritch stood primly at attention. "I didn't offer."

"Good, and please don't ever offer again. Just provide the typing, the dictation and the martinis, Miss Fritch. That's all we can share. As far as I'm concerned, that's plenty."

Miss Fritch was obviously crestfallen.

"I guess you think I don't need you. Well, I do. As much as Norman Kane did. You've helped me over the rough spots, Miss Fritch, and I'm grateful. You've been loyal and trusting and a good deal more. But I don't have to play Norman Kane any more. I really wasn't very good at it, was I?"

Miss Fritch began to protest.

"Please, Miss Fritch, don't be kind. I'm not Norman Kane. Not at this desk and not on that couch. Now, that's all I have to say. If you can remain here and help me under these conditions, I'm delighted to have you. If you need more, you'll have to try someone else."

Miss Fritch studied me with a sad expression. "I need to be needed, Mr. Ellison. As long as you need me I'll stick around."

"Is that you, Ellison? What the hell do you want?"

"I want to talk to you, General."

"I haven't got time, Ellison. I told you where I stand on this thing."

"Oh, yes, you told me."

"Well, then, take your problems up with Frank Glover."

"Fuck Frank Glover."

"What did you say?"

"You heard me, General."

"Have you gone mad?"

"Maybe, but I want to talk to you, General, and I want to talk to you alone. If I walk into your office and Glover is there, I'm not going to say a goddamn word."

"Aren't you being a little bold, Ellison?"

"I'm beyond bold. I'm a man with a mission, General. You set the time for me to carry it out."

There was a moment's hesitation at Stone's end of the line. "Why don't you come up this afternoon?"

"What's this all about, Ellison? It better be short and it better be good."

"I don't promise it will be short and I don't promise you'll like it. But I am going to make a speech that I want you to hear from beginning to end."

"Why should I? I'm tired of your sermons, Ellison. I don't plan to make any more contributions to charity this year."

I laughed. "I don't want your money, General. I don't need it. Neither does Lake Shore Plaza. I'm here to tell you just where you stand. No romance, no impassioned pleading, no bullshit. Just the facts."

"I know the facts. All of them. And I know what to do. I don't need any advice from you, free or otherwise."

"All right. If that's how you feel, I'll forget the whole thing. I don't know why I should do you any favors anyway. I don't need you to work this out. I'll shove it through without you." I stood up and began to walk toward the elevator.

"Wait a minute. What the hell are you going to shove through?"

I turned to look at him. "You want to hear this or not? I don't give a damn either way."

The General hesitated. "All right. Go ahead, Ellison. Start talking." He was studying me curiously.

"I'll bring you up to date, General. A lot has happened since the last time we talked. One of the first things I did was to settle our lawsuit with Ernest Barry by hiring him as our leasing agent. You may think I'm nuts or you may think I'm a genius. All I know is that the first week he delivered the lease with Colorado Smelting, and now he's bringing in another fifty thousand feet. So let's not argue about that."

The General said nothing.

"I talked to Hanson. He's not going to jump in and screw up this project. I don't think he'll dance to your tune, either. He's worried about the bank's money, but he's an honorable guy, Vern Hanson, and he won't undermine us."

"Look, Ellison, I don't see the point of—"

"I'm not finished. I instructed Friedrichs and McNeill to prepare estimates of the costs to complete this project. Norman Kane was right. We're going to run exactly twenty million dollars short."

"How do you know?"

"You'll have to take what I say as gospel."

"McNeill say so?"

"Here's his estimate. On his letterhead, signed by him, OK'd by Friedrichs."

"I see."

"As for the dates of completion, you'll find the schedule right there. I expect to keep it. I sat down with Carrelli the other day and knocked four hundred and fifty thousand dollars off his contract, and we'll save some more money by using the cheaper partitions from here on in. Now, don't tell me whether it's a good deal or a bad one. I already signed the papers."

"Where the hell did you get the authority to do all these things?"

"I took it. Nobody else is doing a goddamn thing except waiting for this deal to collapse. Meanwhile I'm trying to save it for everybody. Most important, I talked to Hobbs and Bennett. They worked out a new deal for us on the mortgage —a deal that gets us off the spot."

General Stone was obviously amazed.

"Surprised, huh? Well, here's the deal. They're going to extend the mortgage from a twenty-five- to a thirty-three-year loan. That way our present rental income will cover the operating expenses, the taxes and insurance, and the new lower mortgage payments. And they're going to give us another twenty million dollars."

"That's incredible. How did you do it?"

"It wasn't difficult, General. All I had to do was give them thirty per cent of our equity in the project."

The General was on his feet, sputtering. "Thirty per cent of *my* equity. You had no right to do that. I'll kill your deal in five minutes."

"You're yelling, General. I think you ought to sit down and hear me out."

Slowly Stone sat down in his chair, but he was tremendously angry. "OK, Ellison, I won't yell at you. But you've made a bad mistake. I'm not giving up thirty per cent of my equity. There's nothing in our agreements that would force me to do it."

"Permit me to give you a legal opinion. I don't think you

can stop me. I've studied the development agreement, the articles of incorporation, and every other document that has anything to do with this project. I feel that Kane Enterprises, Incorporated, has every right in the world to make this loan —and the other stockholders are ready to swear that Kane Enterprises has all the powers I say it has. I expect to get a new commitment from Fidelity any hour now. And I expect to have it signed by all of the stockholders, because that's what I promised Hobbs."

"I see. You can't do a thing without me. I'll never sign that commitment."

"That's just talk, General. Kane Enterprises is going to make this mortgage. It's well within the scope of its authority."

"But not *your* authority."

"That's a fine line, General, a very fine line. You may not realize it, but I'm a vice-president of Kane Enterprises, Incorporated. Norman never expected me to make policy decisions, but it doesn't change the fact that I'm an officer. I've been signing documents for years."

The General was on his feet again, pacing up and back. "Go on," he said. "Tell me the rest of your plot."

"Here's where we stand. I'm going to get this commitment from Fidelity Standard. Their loan committee approved it this morning. And I'm going to place it in front of all the investors to sign. Maybe you won't sign, but I think that puts you in a pretty bad position. First off, it makes you *persona non grata* at the Chicago National Bank. Here's a perfectly legitimate way for them to get out of a bad deal, and you turn it down. As big and rich as you are, you're going to have a hell of a lot of trouble doing business in this town."

"Me? Who are you kidding? I can do anything I want."

"I'm not so sure, General. You're not a kid any more. You're worth a ton of money, but you don't have much of a future."

The General was livid with rage again, and he shot an almost unbelievable stream of invective at me.

I cut him off. "Shut up, you son of a bitch. You don't scare me at all. The only mistake I ever made was trying to treat you like a gentleman. Phil Winsley was right. He said you and he came from the same neighborhood. He told me a guy had to act tough with you, because you were used to running a bluff. Well, right now you're running a bluff, and you're not getting away with it. Your position stinks. You try to stop me and you'll have the bank, Fidelity Standard and everybody else lined up against you. You might hold out for a while. But then we'll hit you with so many lawsuits for so many millions that not even you can afford it. You ask Frank Glover about that. Here we are at the end of the deal, and I come up with a way to pay for the shortage—on a basis where you don't have to put up a dime. All the other investors agree, but you try to stop the deal. You can't do it, Stone. You'll never do it. I promise you. I'll see to that."

The General finally sat down again, at some distance from me.

"Think it over, General. You try to find a way to wriggle out. I didn't have any right to go to Fidelity Standard. But I sold them a bill of goods. They went to their loan committee and got a new mortgage commitment. By now it's probably lying on my desk—six copies in black and white. You can't pretend it doesn't exist. Before, you might have stopped me. Now it's too late."

"You son of a bitch. You're sneakier than Norman Kane."

I laughed aloud. "Yes, I suppose I am. I used to think I was an honorable, ethical man. But as you once said, living with Kane I had to learn something. Now you know what Kane taught me. How do you like it, General?"

"You're talking pretty big. You still think I'll go along with this?"

"I think you had better. You're in one hell of a spot. Here's this beautiful commitment. We don't even need your signature to accept it. I don't think Fidelity Standard will insist on it. Remember, you didn't want to be an officer of Lake Shore Plaza. You're just a director. So you vote against it. One out of eight. That makes you a loser, General. Anyway, they all approve it and they all sign it, except you. Then where are you? I'll tell you one thing; Vern Hanson won't let go of that stock. There's going to be one hell of a lawsuit. The stock may be tied up for years. Meanwhile, this whole deal goes down the drain. What then? Tell me, General, what about the millions you've already put in this thing?"

"You really believe I'm barreled."

"There's no doubt about it."

"Where does the thirty per cent come from?"

"Everybody. Right across the board."

"You mean thirty per cent from me, too. Hell, I'm ready to put up my share of the money."

"We don't want your money. The whole twenty million is coming from Fidelity Standard. That's the way I want it. No favors. No special arrangements."

"I still don't believe the deal works out."

"It does. I have all the figures and I can prove it. You'll share in the profits like everybody else. You thought you'd come out on some special basis. But not this time."

The General stared at me for a very long time. "What happened between the last time I saw you and today?"

"A great deal, General."

"A couple of weeks ago you came in here with your hat in your hand and your knees on the floor. Now you act tough. On top of it, you even make sense. When did this happen?"

"I'm not buying your flattery, General. But just for the record, I have to admit you're as responsible as anybody. You made a bad mistake. You let your contempt for me get the best of you. You made me see myself as I really was. And I didn't like the picture. No, I didn't like it one damn bit. I decided I was going to have to change. I couldn't live with myself if I didn't. It wasn't easy. I had to force myself to think like Norman Kane. And that was the answer. A Norman Kane can always handle a General Mervin Lee Stone."

———————

Afterwards, I called Frieda. Somehow I felt the need to tell her what was happening. I did not choose to question my motives. I told myself that she was entitled to know.

I tried to keep my report brief and factual, and apparently I succeeded too well. Frieda's response was vague—almost uninterested. I had no right to feel affronted, but I did. I wondered whether Frieda understood what I was telling her.

I refused to accept her apparent indifference. Perhaps, I thought, my explanations had been inadequate. I decided to tell her some of the details of my meetings with Barry, the boys, and the men from Fidelity Standard. I realized I was simply trying to impress her, but I kept talking. I had told myself that I was calling Frieda for her sake. Now I realized that wasn't true. I desperately needed to have her share this experience with me.

Gradually she became more receptive. She asked a few questions. Good questions. Her voice came alive.

"Then there's still hope," she said.

"Of course. Of course there is. Listen, I believe in this thing. I bought out Del Kincaid with my own money. That's the kind of faith I have in this deal."

"You bought out Kincaid? You didn't have to do that."

"I know I didn't have to. I did it because I wanted to. This is going to be a good deal, Frieda. A great deal."

Then I wondered if I had gone too far. "You must understand, we're not home yet. I can't guarantee anything."

"I know. But it helps a great deal to know that there's still hope, that you have faith in it."

I thought I was satisfied. I had gotten through to her. But now Frieda was too excited to end the conversation. She questioned me about General Stone, the bank, the insurance company. Each new revelation increased her enthusiasm. I became so emboldened, I repeated General Stone's comment about me: "You're even sneakier than Norman Kane."

Frieda laughed. I hadn't heard her laugh in months. I was feeling rather pleased with myself.

"Is it true, Eddie?"

"What?"

"That you're sneakier than Norman?"

"No—Maybe. —I don't know. How can I give a correct answer to that question?"

Her response came smoothly. "The old Eddie Ellison would have been sure of the answer."

"Do you think there's a new one?"

"Without a doubt. A new and rather fascinating Eddie Ellison."

"That's quite a compliment, Frieda."

"It's not a compliment. Just a statement of fact."

"I guess—I guess, Frieda, that's what I've been trying to
prove to you all along."

The shareholders and their lawyers joined me at Norman
Kane's office. Including General Stone.

I told them I had bought out Del Kincaid. They were surprised. They realized my action had some significance. But
their most important questions were as yet unanswered. The
men were silent, waiting to hear what more I had to say.

"Well, we have our commitment, boys. Fidelity Standard
came through. You're all off the hook. They'll put up the
twenty million, and that's the end of it."

There was spontaneous cheering, including some clapping
of hands—except by Stone and Glover. Everyone turned to
them.

"General," I said, "I want you to have the honor of being
the first man to sign."

"I'll wait for the others."

"Have it your own way."

Each of the boys signed the commitment before I put it in
front of General Stone. Up until then, no one had even bothered to read it. Amazing—their fortunes were at stake, and
neither they nor their lawyers dared to read the document.
But General Stone was different. He sat stiffly, holding the
commitment, slowly turning the pages while everyone else
fidgeted.

He looked up. "I thought you said thirty per cent?"

"No, Fidelity finally decided to ask for only twenty."

"But you did say thirty."

"Look, if you're unhappy I'll take the extra ten per cent
myself."

There was jubilation in the room. Only twenty per cent for
the twenty million dollars.

"By God, if that's right," said Phil Winsley, "then a hundred per cent of the equity is worth a hundred million. Boys, we're rich."

While all this back-slapping was going on, I looked at General Stone. He was scribbling his name on the commitment.

"Thanks. That takes care of everything for now. I'll bring a copy over to Vern Hanson. I want him to know we're out of the woods."

"Out of the woods? How do you figure?" It was Winsley talking.

"Now, damn it, Winsley, don't start on me again. I know we still have a hell of a lot to do. The construction must be completed and the space must be leased. But we're over the hump. We're not going to lose the deal. Not to anyone." I could not help looking at General Stone.

Joe Woodward stood up. "You know, men, I think we owe Ellison a vote of confidence. He saved us from disaster."

"Wait," I said, "don't make any speeches. I couldn't take it. I've done my best to straighten this thing out, and if I've accomplished that, I'm happy."

"No, I think you did a great job," Woodward said, "and I feel we would be wise to let you carry this project through from now to completion. You ought to run the whole show."

There were general murmurs of agreement.

"I'm willing to stay on as a consultant, but I'm not going to run this deal. I'm no developer."

Phil Winsley stood up. "You done better than Norman Kane."

"Don't ever say that again, Winsley. Norman Kane was the guy who made this whole damn thing possible. I learned what to do from all the years I spent with him. I didn't have one lousy stinking idea I didn't get from Norman Kane. He may be dead, but don't knock him."

"I didn't mean to knock him. I just think you done a good job."

"I'm not Norman Kane. I'm Eddie Ellison."

"All right, fine. So we thank you, Eddie Ellison."

"OK. That's it. There are still a few things to wind up, but that's it for today."

The boys were on their feet, laughing and talking, shaking my hand, pounding me on the back. They had regained their courage and their good humor. But I had had enough. I led them to the door, accepted their good wishes and eased them out of the office.

Only when the door was shut could I indulge my own sense of exhilaration. I had done it. I was jubilant.

Then I realized that Stone was still in the room. Standing in the middle of the floor. Smiling.

"Congratulations," he said. "You did it."

I did not respond.

"Yeah, you've got those characters eating out of your hand. Of course, if things get rough again, they'll be back yelling and screaming. But I'm sure you know that."

Still I said nothing.

"I got to hand it to you, Ellison. I really do. Not too many guys in this town get the best of Mervin Stone." He stopped smiling. "Some do it once. Nobody's ever done it twice."

"I believe that, General."

"You better. All the same, that was quite a trick you pulled off. I guess I underestimated you."

"That's quite a compliment, coming from you."

The General took a step forward. "But I'm not *over*estimating you either. I heard what you told those guys. You got mad when they said you did better than Kane. I know why you got mad. Because you think the same thing. You think maybe Eddie Ellison is better than Norman Kane after all."

I wanted to protest, but the General hadn't stopped talking.

"You're kidding yourself, Ellison. You're not better than Norman Kane. You're not half as good. You see those buildings out there?" He waved a hand toward the French windows. "You didn't dream up the deal, you didn't design it and you didn't build it."

"Don't you think I know that, General?"

"I'm not sure. Kane carried this deal ninety-seven per cent of the way and you carried it three per cent. Maybe in your mind you're getting the percentages reversed. But I'm not. I know who did what. I want to make sure you do. You're a good actor, Ellison. Real good. But the guy who wrote the script is gone. As long as you stick to the script you'll be all right. Just don't try to write your own material. That could be dangerous—for you and for me. I still own the biggest piece of this deal. I don't want to see anything bad happen to it. You understand?"

I stared at him.

"OK, Ellison. That's my message for today." The General walked to the door, then spun around.

"You're not Norman Kane, Ellison. Don't you ever forget it."